TIN SOLDIERS

M K TURNER

By M K Turner
Meredith & Hodge Series
Misplaced Loyalty
Ill Conceived
Wrong Shoes
Tin Soldiers
One Secret
Mistaken Beliefs

Others
The Cuban Conundrum
Murderous Mishaps
The Recruitment of Lucy James

Acknowledgements

Edited by Sharon Kelly

Cover by ebooks-designs.co.uk

CHAPTER ONE

The child was dead. Her soft flesh was already cool against his hand. He stroked her bruised arm gently. His chest was rising and falling at an alarming rate as panic took hold. He closed his eyes, and forced the memories of when he had first held her into his mind, and slowly regulated his breathing. Control regained, he opened his eyes and looked into the now sightless eyes that had once shown him such trust. He marvelled once more at the thick lashes surrounding them. She had the eyes of someone much older, a woman even.

Placing his thumb and forefinger on her eyelids, he closed her eyes for the last time. His large tanned hand obliterated her face for a moment. He placed a small object in her hand, allowing a tear to fall unhindered as he covered her tiny body.

"I'm sorry," he whispered softly.

He stood looking at the tiny shrouded figure for a few moments longer. Then, with a sudden burst of energy, he drew in a breath and pulled his shoulders back. There was much to do.

Forty-eight hours later he stood in the doorway of the room where she had spent her last moments. Everything had gone. It was as though she had never been there. Closing the door for the last time, he checked the rest of the house, locking doors as he went. Content the house was secure, he was ready to leave. With a bag in each hand, he took the steps leading to the street two at a time.

The time had come to move on.

Noticing his approach, the taxi driver, who had been waiting for ten minutes with the clock running, hurried to relieve him of the bags.

"JFK. International departures," he instructed as the driver loaded his bags.

His hand was on the handle of the rear door when his neighbour called to him.

"You're really going then, Charlie?"

He caught the concern in her voice as she hurried down her steps to catch him.

"I am. I've taken a new job." He cocked his head and smiled. "You used to complain about me to the other neighbours, surely you won't miss me?" His smile revealed he was teasing her. "They told me, you know." Opening the door of the taxi with one hand he squeezed her shoulder with the other. "Take care of yourself, Mrs Winner."

"But I don't understand why. I can't see what England has to offer that you can't find here."

"Everything. I've asked Jim to help you with the garden."

They turned to look at the neat, square patch of lawn in front of the steps that led to her porch. The borders were tidy, and the shrubs carefully trimmed. The flower boxes along the edge of the porch had been cleared a little early, but were ready for replanting next spring.

Mrs Winner pushed the door of the taxi closed as he settled himself on the back seat, and she shrugged acceptance. She had not liked him when he'd first moved in. He was far too distant and secretive for her liking, but after the first six months he'd taken to tending her garden when he did his own. When she'd challenged him, he told her it relieved his stress, and she shouldn't deny him. That was almost five years ago, and her garden had never looked so good. She used to tease him about his stress levels. They'd been worse lately, but despite what she considered to be their friendship, he still chose to keep himself to himself, and not let anyone get too close. Mrs Winner had only ever been in his house once, and he rarely had visitors, so he must have been lonely too. She sighed as she realised she'd be a little lonelier once he'd gone.

"I've not decided what to do with the house yet, so you'll not get any trouble from new occupants. I'm leaving it empty for the time being."

He nodded at the driver, and called goodbye as the taxi pulled away.

July

Lifting the paper to shield his face, the man, who only minutes before had wondered at his chosen path, marvelled at his good luck. He'd parked there when she'd been dropped off at the church hall, hoping to catch a further glimpse of her when she left. But the Brownie troupe was doing some sort of activity in the park, and he could see her talking to a friend standing next to her. He watched as Brown Owl called out instructions to the group of youngsters, clad in brown and yellow, who were lined up in front of her. The windows of his vehicle open, he strained to hear her words as she instructed them to get into pairs, and smiled as the neat lines broke into chaos. There was giggling and shouting as the youngsters found their preferred partner.

To regain control Brown Owl instructed them to sit on the grass. They complied immediately, as they were glad to be out of the stuffy church hall that smelt of damp wood and dust, and they didn't want to go back. From the large wicker basket at her feet, Brown Owl gave each pair a glass jar with a screw-on lid, and explained what they had to do. She held up a badge pinned to a piece of paper. This would be their reward. The pair who found the most interesting insect, and then drew a picture of it, would win a badge each. She lifted her hand and pointed around the perimeter of the small park.

"You may not leave the park area or go into the car park."

She pointed towards him. He remained still, and turned the page of the newspaper he held in front of him, lifting it a little higher.

"You may not play on the swings . . . yet," she added with a smile when the troupe groaned. "You are allowed into the bushes, but not past this line here. We'll be doing something with the pond next week." She put her hands on her hips. "Don't forget, anyone who doesn't follow the rules will lose stars from their chart. Now, if you need any help call me, Mrs Jones, or Mrs Henderson." The two mothers standing behind Brown Owl waved at the children. "Anna and Sammy will also help if you need them." She waved towards the two Girl Guides, who looked up and forced a smile. They hated helping out with the Brownies, it was such a chore. Brown Owl clapped her hands together. "Right, you have twenty minutes, and don't forget to look under the stones." The young Brownies jumped to their feet as she added, "And no running. Those are glass jars."

The pairs dispersed, and began poking around in the shrubs and hedgerows in the park. Brown Owl directed the mothers and the Girl Guides into key positions, ensuring all the youngsters could be monitored. Lowering the newspaper a little, he smiled at their enthusiasm, and raised his eyebrows as one of the more adventurous girls attempted to climb a tree, and clung to the trunk as one of the mothers rushed over to get her down.

His breath caught in his throat as two of the girls who had found nothing of interest in the patch they had been investigating, turned and hurried towards him. It was her! His long, elegant fingers folded the newspaper carefully, and placed it on the seat next to him. Sammy, the Girl Guide, was watching, and she ambled along slowly, yards behind them. His view of the girls disappeared. They had reached the bushes in front of the car park. He could hear them chattering through the open windows of the vehicle. Leaning forward, his eyes searched the foliage, hoping to find a gap through which he could watch them, but he was at the wrong angle, and could only see the odd flash of colour.

Cautiously, he opened the car door. He needed to be closer. As he turned in his seat to climb out, a short blast of music filled the air, and he froze momentarily. Sammy came to an abrupt halt, pulling the phone from her pocket. Turning her back on the girls, she answered the call. He slipped from the seat, and his shoes crunched against the gravel. Walking to the hedge, he dropped onto his haunches and peered into the branches. He couldn't see her face, as she was too busy poking around in dead leaves.

"What are you looking for?" he whispered, and the two girls looked up.

"Insects. Although I want a spider, because I'm not frightened of them, and the others will be," Gemma Lake responded, before continuing her search.

"Great plan. How are you doing?"

"Rubbish. There are only ants and a worm so far." She looked up again. "Why are you whispering?"

"So I don't frighten the insects away," he lied, and smiled as Sammy's voice reached them. She was angry with someone for letting her down the day before. He assumed it was a boyfriend. "I've got beetles in my garden. Great big black ones, they're all shiny. I think there's a nest there. I've got a caterpillar cocoon too."

"What's a cocoon?" the other girl asked.

"It's like a shell. It's what caterpillars live in before they become butterflies," Gemma responded.

He smiled; she was bright.

Gemma stood up and sighed. "There's nothing here. I wish we had a cocoon, we'd win then."

"Would you like me to get it for you?"

They watched as the man altered his position to get a better view of Sammy. Phone clasped to her ear, she was pacing up and down, totally absorbed in her conversation and unaware of his presence.

"Yes!" the other girl answered. "Of course we do." She stood to join her friend. She was a little taller than Gemma, he noticed.

"Will you get us one?" Gemma smiled at him and his heart skipped a beat. She was the one he wanted. "That would be great."

"I will. It's a shame you can't come with me, you could see the beetles too. In fact, you could get both." He sounded excited at the prospect.

"We can come, can't we?" Gemma grabbed her friend's hand. "Ellen, we'll win if we get both."

Ellen shook her head, and turned to look at Brown Owl, worried that even the suggestion would get them into trouble.

"Gemma, you know we're not allowed out of the park. We'll get into to trouble." Ellen looked very serious for a seven year old, and continued to shake her head solemnly.

On the far side of the park, Brown Owl was now kneeling down with two of the others, and attempting to lift a large stone from the bottom of the rockery in front of the swings.

"That's a shame. She's helping them, would it be so bad if I helped you?" He smiled as the two girls agreed with him. "It's only a couple of minutes away. We can be there and back before the twenty minutes is up."

Ellen wasn't convinced. She looked back towards Brown Owl, who had managed to turn the stone over and was getting to her feet. One of the pair she was working with squealed at the insects it had revealed, and climbed to the top of the rockery. Brown Owl straightened up, flexed her back, and looked around the park. She smiled. All seemed calm, and she was glad they'd decided to come out. It had been a long and irritating day at work, and the opportunity to be in the fresh air was much appreciated. Then she caught sight of Sammy. She was on the phone. Again.

"Sammy, come here at once! What have I told you about that phone?" She cupped her hands around her mouth to project her voice. Sammy pretended not to hear. Terminating the call, Sammy slid the phone into her pocket. Brown Owl was not impressed, and bellowed at her, colour rushing to her cheeks. "I said, come here!"

Sammy turned to face her and held out her hands, revealing they were empty, and questioning the order. Brown Owl persisted and, waving her hand frantically, she beckoned Sammy forward. Banging her arms down against her side, Sammy huffed, and walked as slowly as she could towards the agitated woman. All the pairings dotted around the park watched her progress for a while. They loved it when Sammy was there because she always got into trouble.

"They won't know if we're quick," he whispered urgently to their backs as they watched the saga with Sammy unfold. "It looks like Sammy's in trouble."

"She's always in trouble," Ellen spoke without turning. "She never does what she's told."

Ellen drew in a sharp breath as the girl at the top of the rockery lost her footing, and tumbled forward. She landed head first on the stone overturned by Brown Owl. There was silence for a moment, before her piercing scream filled the air, followed by sobbing. Horrified, Brown Owl rushed to help her. Pulling a handkerchief from her pocket Brown Owl held it to the girl's forehead.

"She'll be ages sorting that out. I'll go and get the cocoon for you. Are you sure you don't want to come and get the beetles?" He stood up, careful to keep his head tilted to ensure the peak of his cap hid as much of his face as possible.

"I do," Gemma announced, and she ran to the gap which led to the carpark.

His heart thumped as he scanned the park. The rest of the group had reached, or were making their way towards, the injured girl. All attention was focused on her. He needed to move, and quickly.

"Come on then, we need to hurry or you'll be missed. Are you coming too, Ellen?"

As it happened, he didn't much care if she did, but it would give him vital extra minutes to get away if she wasn't there to raise the alarm.

Gemma increased her pace and entered the carpark. Ellen's mouth fell open. Gemma was going to be in big trouble. Ellen glanced back over her shoulder at the others. They were now huddled in a group around the injured girl, who refused to stop crying. Ellen looked back to the gap and ran.

"Gemma, wait. My dad will kill me. Don't go or you'll be grounded," she called to her friend, as she too entered the carpark.

Gemma was already climbing into the back of the Range Rover. Ellen saw the man smile as he beckoned her forward. She couldn't see his eyes as his cap was too low. She stopped abruptly, knowing she shouldn't get into the car.

"Wow!" Gemma called from inside the car. "Ellen, he's got a telly in here. Oh wow, there are two," she added as she climbed further into the car.

Curiosity got the better of her, and Ellen ran to join her friend. The door closed behind her as she climbed in.

"Put your seatbelts on," he called as he started the engine. "You should always wear your seatbelts."

As he pulled out of the carpark, the screens set into the backs of the front seats came to life, and the girls cooed as the opening titles of *Nemo* filled the small screens. Glancing at them in the rear-view mirror, he tapped his fingers on the steering wheel as the first set of traffic lights turned red, and the car rolled to a stop. The rear windows were tinted, and no one could see the girls properly, but even so, he wanted to be on the move.

"Nearly there," he called as the lights changed colour.

Gemma simply shrugged acceptance, not wanting to miss a minute of the film.

CHAPTER TWO

DCI John Meredith paused at the door to the church hall and collected his thoughts. He had heard the desperation in Rawlings' voice, and had had no words of comfort to offer. He had to keep Rawlings calm and focused. If he was to be of any help in the search for his daughter, he needed to think like a policeman, not a father. Meredith could see the back of a uniformed officer, and beyond him, Dave Rawlings pacing up and down. He focused on Rawlings. He was wearing a bright red and blue striped shirt over a pair of faded jeans. His shirt sleeves were folded back to just below the elbow, and his jeans had frayed a little at the back where they met the floor. As Rawlings ran his fingers through his thinning hair and changed direction, Meredith noted how much younger he looked when not wearing his usual shirt and tie. He had worked with Rawlings for almost ten years, and he felt his pain. Rawlings spotted him and stopped dead. Meredith nodded at him, and, stooping to clear the low door frame, he stepped into the hall.

"They tell me I'm better off here, Gov." Rawlings jerked his thumb towards a doorway to the left of the hall. "But I only waited for you to arrive, I'm best off out there looking for them."

"You're probably right. But before you go charging off, I need to know what's what from someone capable of stringing a sentence together." Meredith looked around the hall. "Where is everyone?"

"Through there." DC Dave Rawlings pointed to a door in the centre of the far wall. "It leads to an adjoining hall. Hutchins is trying to get them organised for questioning. And I know it's got to be done, Gov, but we're wasting valuable time. If they've wandered off, the sooner we find them the better."

There was still the desperation in his voice, and Meredith knew he would have his work cut out trying to control him.

"You sit there." Meredith pointed to a chair against the wall. "I'll go and have a word. When I get back, we'll decide how to move forward."

"I'll come with you." Rawlings stepped towards the door but Meredith put his hand on his shoulder.

"Dave, listen to me. I don't want you in there yet. Someone has cocked up, and you getting angry won't help get the information we need. What?" His eyes narrowed as Rawlings dropped his head. "What?"

"Too late for that, I'm afraid. They know what I think of them."

Meredith shook his head and tutted. "Sit. Trump and Seaton are on their way, wait here for them." Meredith turned to face the uniformed office. "Keep him here. Knock him out if you have to."

"He didn't mean it," Rawlings said, as he turned the chair and straddled it, resting his arms on the back rest.

"Yes, I bloody well did," Meredith called as he entered the corridor.

As he reached the end of the corridor the buzz of voices got louder. Meredith was surprised at the number of people in the room. He spotted Hutchins speaking quietly with another uniform, and called him over. Meredith's eyes scanned the different groups as Hutchins approached.

"In a nutshell, Pa."

Meredith was partial to giving people nick names, and Rob Hutchins had obtained his when becoming a father during the last case.

"Brown Owl, that's her over there." Hutchins pointed to the far corner of the hall, where Brown Owl, still in uniform, was sitting holding the hands of the Girl Guides on either side of her. "She took the Brownies to the park across the road to do something towards their nature badge. There was a bit of a kafuffle when one of the girls fell and injured herself. When they had sorted her out, they noticed that two of them were missing: Ellen Rawlings and Gemma Lake. That's Gemma's parents over there with Dave's wife."

Meredith gave Eve Rawlings a brief smile. She was holding the hand of another woman who looked on the point of collapse. A paramedic was kneeling in front of them, and a man in overalls, hands behind his head, leaned against the wall behind them.

"What happened to her?"

"She had a panic attack. She's calm now, the paramedic gave her something, but she's refusing to go home. Luckily, he was here to make sure the girl who fell was all right." Hutchins tucked his notebook into his breast pocket.

"How long have they been gone?"

"About an hour and a half now. We have a couple of boys out walking the routes to their houses. Both would have known their way home. We also have extra cars covering the area."

"Hmmm. Nobody saw anything according to Rawlings, is that right?"

"Yes, Gov. There were five supervisors, and fourteen Brownies. The last person to see the two girls was . . ." Retrieving his notebook, Hutchins flipped it open. "Sammy Evans, just before the girl fell."

"Which one is Sammy Evans?"

"The Girl Guide to the right of Brown Owl."

Meredith looked at the red-eyed Sammy, and then skimmed the rest of the room. The young Brownies were restless, and a couple of them were crying and being comforted by their parents.

"Right, let's get rid of those who are probably of no use to us."

He walked to the centre of the room and clapped his hands. The low murmur stopped and all eyes looked at him expectantly.

"I'm DCI Meredith, and I'll be heading up the search for Gemma and Ellen. Thank you all for staying here, but rather than keep all of you hanging around, I would ask only those of you who were in the park to remain here, with the exception of the children. Parents, you may take your girls home now, but please make sure you give your details to one of the two officers as you leave. If we need to speak to you or your daughters we'll be in touch. If they should remember anything please call the station, and ask for the incident room. We'll get an officer to come to you."

Those who had been asked to leave did so gratefully. A few said goodbye to Brown Owl, assuring her it wasn't her fault, which only made her surer that it was. A line formed at the entrance to the corridor where Hutchins and the other officer took down contact information.

"I take it we can stay." The man in overalls stepped forward, and his wife whimpered.

"Yes, Mr Lake, for now."

"Can I?" Lake held up a packet of cigarettes.

"In a moment, I'll join you."

When the queue had disappeared, Meredith asked those remaining to wait for an officer to call them. He spoke quietly to the two officers, who then lifted four tables from those stacked at the back of the room, and placed one in each corner with a chair on either side. Meredith beckoned Lake to join him and they went back into the other hall.

Rawlings was no longer sitting on the chair, but was talking quietly to Seaton who was making tea in the kitchen area in the top corner of the hall. Trump was standing in the middle of the room with Jo Adler, and speaking to the uniformed officer. Meredith walked to Rawlings and put his hand on his shoulder. Lake followed him and stood with his hands shoved deep into his overall pockets as Meredith spoke.

"This is what we're going to do. The team will question everyone who was there, and then send them home. If any leads come up we'll follow up on them. You will take Eve home and get a recent picture of Ellen, and Mr Lake will do the same for Gemma. Then we will get them on tonight's news. You'll be the first to hear should anything happen."

"But, Gov, I-" Rawlings was silenced as Meredith raised his hand.

"You have a wife who needs looking after, and you're too close. You know the score, Dave."

Rawlings' shoulders sagged, and he nodded as he stared at the floor.

"Mr Lake here needs a ciggy. I'm going to join him, do you want some air?"

Rawlings nodded, and the three men left the hall. Meredith took a cigarette from the packet Lake passed to him, and then he took the lighter from Lake's trembling hand. He held the lighter in cupped hands up to the cigarette between Lake's lips. After three attempts Lake finally lit the cigarette. The three men stood in silence, backs to the hall, and looked towards the park. They were aware of the handful of uniformed officers moving about in the park, catching the odd burst of light as a torch moved position, but their presence was not acknowledged.

An hour and a half later, Meredith and the rest of the team were back in the incident room. With the exception of Hutchins, who had been invited to join them, the team were in casual clothes. They had found out about the girl's disappearance whilst celebrating Meredith's birthday. They sobered up quickly, and the celebration was long forgotten.

"Hutchins has volunteered to man the incident room with Travers, and given that it's now almost eleven it's unlikely to be that busy. The local news ran the story with the photos, so we may get the odd call but I doubt we'll be run off our feet. The main thrust should come tomorrow morning, after the radio and television news have run the story. All uniforms on duty have been sent to patrol and search the area, and at this stage they're covering a six-mile radius, but we all know if they were taken by car they could be miles away." Meredith sighed. "A female office has been assigned to the Lakes, and Jo went over to be with Eve. Rawlings refuses to stay at home. He and a few of the other fathers, including Lake, are out searching. Not a good idea, but we can't stop him."

Meredith sipped his coffee and walked to a map pinned to the wall.

"If we have no news by first thing, we'll split into three teams and work our way out from the park, along these roads." Meredith ran his finger along the roads in question. "There are quite a few businesses, shops, and garages, and we'll collect any and all CCTV footage from late this afternoon to early this evening."

"What about Blaise Woods, Gov?" Detective Sergeant Tom Seaton stepped forward. He too had worked with Dave Rawlings for many years, and they were close, both in and out of work. Being a little older than Rawlings, he'd mentored him when he joined the department. "It's not far away from the park, and Dave said Ellen loved going there and looking for squirrels. He confirmed she'd probably know the way from the park. They could have gone there and got lost."

"Yes I know, and there are a couple of uniforms walking the main pathways calling out. But not much more we can do until daylight," Meredith looked at his watch, "which will be in less than five hours, so let's get home and I'll see you all back here at six in the morning."

The team dispersed slowly, and Meredith knew that, despite their earlier alcohol intake, none of them would sleep well that night. He stayed with Hutchins for a further hour. They didn't receive a single call, and all updates from the men on the street were negative.

Meredith stood and stretched. "I'll get off. If nothing else I need a shower and a change of clothes. I'll see you before you clock off." Shoving his hands in his pockets he walked to the door. "I'm the first call you make on anything that comes in, and I mean anything."

"Of course. Not much of a birthday, Gov. You'll have to do it all over again once we've found her. I heard you put on quite a show. I'm not a bad singer myself, I might show you how to do it."

Meredith gave a short laugh. "You're on."

Patsy and Amanda jumped up and went to greet Meredith as he opened the door. He smiled but shook his head. His eyes told them all they needed to know.

He accepted Patsy's offer of a drink and hugged his daughter to him. He breathed in her smell, grateful to have her with him.

"I can't imagine what he's going through." He kissed the top of her head. "When I lost you, the pain was incredible, but I knew you were safe. I just can't imagine . . ."

Amanda returned her father's hug. They had only recently been reunited after years of separation, following her mother's death.

"You'll find her, Dad." Amanda pushed him away gently. "Do you want food? There's tons of it in the kitchen. Not much had been eaten when the party broke up."

Taking Meredith's hand, she led him to the kitchen. Plastic boxes and plates covered in foil were stacked on every available surface. Patsy held out his drink. She looked at his eyes, often angry or irritated, but today they simply radiated sadness. He smiled, but there was no amusement. It was a smile which told her he was glad to be with her, and she loved him for it. Deciding to keep things as normal as possible, she continued Amanda's conversation. Tomorrow would be soon enough for him to relive the day's events.

"And the fridge is packed too. I'll help you take it in tomorrow, I'm sure it will get eaten."

"I'll have some of that, that and . . . that." Meredith pointed randomly to three items.

Patsy took a plate from the cupboard and opened the first box.

"You don't even know what you chose." But she took a selection from each of the three boxes anyway. "I'll check it all again in the morning, and bin anything that's no good. How's Eve holding up?"

"Badly. It doesn't help that Dave has rounded up a couple of dads and is out walking the streets. But I can understand that, he needs to do something." Meredith lifted a chicken drumstick from the plate and bit into it. "I need to sit down." Drink in one hand, and drumstick in the other, he turned and walked back down the hall to the sitting room. "Bring food, wenches, I have no strength."

Meredith ate the food, drank two glasses of wine, and fell asleep. Rather than disturb him Patsy left him there while she cleared up.

"I think I might just throw a quilt over him. If I wake him now he might not drop off again."

Amanda smiled at her. "Good idea." She added a card to the small pile on the edge of the table. "It seems wrong to celebrate a birthday, doesn't it?" She tapped the pile of envelopes. "Shall we still give him these in the morning?"

"I doubt you'll see him. He'll be long gone before you're up. Leave them where he can find them, if he's in the mood, of course. Then get to bed. There's nothing else we can do now." Patsy watched as Amanda reorganised the food and balanced the cards in prime position.

"Night, Patsy. See you tomorrow."

Patsy smiled as Amanda waved and left the kitchen. She was still surprised at how close they had become in such a short space of time.

Patsy Hodge had been a police officer, and she had joined Meredith's squad when she transferred to Bristol. She'd left the force and become a private investigator when they had started their relationship. They had had a bumpy ride so far, and had only recently been reconciled following several months' separation. Patsy had been planning to propose to Meredith, but the ring she had bought him as a gift was now carefully buried at the bottom of her underwear drawer. She sighed as she switched off the light and closed the kitchen door.

Meredith stirred as she entered the sitting room

"Come to bed," she whispered, and held out her hand and helped him to his feet.

At five the next morning, and with an inadequate amount of sleep, Meredith pulled a clean shirt from the hanger, lifted out his suit, and tiptoed out of the bedroom. He dressed on the landing and made his way downstairs. Yawning, he opened the kitchen door and stopped dead as he surveyed the kitchen, all thoughts of his party having been forgotten. His eyes flicked to the pile of cards. Deciding his birthday could wait a little longer, and he would get coffee and breakfast at the station, he closed the door, and picked up his keys from the hall table.

The first thing Meredith saw as he entered the incident room was the red and blue striped shirt, worn by Dave Rawlings the night before. It was draped over the back of a chair and was heavily bloodstained. Hutchins looked up from the desk he had been allocated and followed Meredith's gaze.

"He's all right. It looks worse than it was."

"What happened?"

"He had a disagreement with a bloke who caught him in his garden. He thought Dave was a burglar, Dave thought he was a pompous prick. They'll both live."

Meredith rubbed his hands over his face. "I thought you were supposed to phone me?" he snapped. "Where is he, and more to the point, is the other bloke okay?"

"Dave's in the locker room taking a shower. The other bloke was bigger, and once the lads arrived and explained why Dave was there, he offered his apologies. They brought Dave back here as he refused to go home."

"And the rest of Dave's mob?"

"Agreed to go home and get some rest. They knew they would be needed to search Blaise Woods tomorrow, or today as it actually is." Hutchins stood up and stretched. "I'll make the coffee."

"Black with two, and grab some biscuits. I still want to know what happened to my phone call?"

"It was over before it started. I thought you'd need your sleep." Hutchins could see Meredith accepted this, and as he turned away towards the kitchen, he added, "You need it at your age."

Meredith refused to respond and walked to his office. He scooped up the papers left on his desk for his attention, and put them in a tray, which he then placed on the filing cabinet. Whatever they were, they could wait. He looked up as Rawlings entered the incident room.

"My office," he called, and Rawlings changed direction.

Rawlings held his hands up in surrender as he approached. "Before you say anything, I'm sorry. The prick wouldn't listen, but there's no harm done."

Meredith looked at Rawlings swollen nose and nodded to a chair. "Is that the best you could do?" He nodded at the black sweatshirt two sizes too big for Rawlings.

"Yep. Only thing around."

"You know I'm going to send you home, and you are going to stay there and look after Eve, don't you?"

"I guessed as much, but -"

"No buts. You know we'll do what's needed, and so should you. You have to stop being so bloody selfish, and think about Eve. Do I make myself clear?"

"Yep." Rawlings tone revealed he was agreeing because he had no choice, but Meredith ignored this.

Hutchins appeared with the coffee. His eyes scanned Meredith's desk.

"Thank you, Pa. You now have the honour of taking DC Rawlings home. Go and get your things, the pair of you. You can be gone before anyone else arrives and gives him an excuse to linger."

Hutchins placed the tray on Meredith's desk, and the two men made their exit. Meredith picked up the packet of digestives and opened them. He was dunking the first into his coffee when Hutchins put his head around the door.

"We're off now, Gov. Anything else you want? I'll get a couple of hours' kip, and I'll be back in."

"See you later. Make sure he goes in. I want you to see him onto the premises. Jo will do the rest."

"Will do." Hutchins turned to leave.

"And we'll discuss this later." Meredith pointed at the tray of papers, and crumbs fell from the biscuit. Meredith popped the biscuit into his mouth and picked up the telephone. "Now bugger off the pair of you." He waited, finger poised, as they left.

"Thanks, Gov," Hutchins smiled as he held the door open for Rawlings. He didn't think Meredith had seen his application for a transfer to the team, but he should have known better.

Meredith punched in the number of the duty sergeant. "Hello, George, give me a shout when your boys get back in. I want to hear what's what." He glanced at his watch. "Okay, I'll be down in ten." He hung up and took another biscuit.

Meredith looked at the wipe-clean map pinned to the wall at the front of the room. Each of the men had drawn a red line along the streets they had covered during the night. The twelve of them sat on the benches behind him. He turned to face them.

"Nothing at all?"

The men confirmed that all gardens had been checked, bins inspected, locks on sheds tested, and a small area of allotments searched thoroughly. The only event worth a report was Dave Rawlings' punch-up with a disgruntled home owner.

Meredith sighed. "Get home and get some sleep. If nothing breaks in the next couple of hours, you'll be back in." He turned and traced his finger along the boundary of the Blaise Castle estate on the map. "This is a difficult area to search, and it'll be all hands on deck."

The men voiced their agreement, and the room slowly emptied.

Meredith turned to George. "Who's on duty today, and how many bodies have we got?"

"I'm doing a double, ten lads on here, but we can call in from other stations if you get the sign off. I've warned them."

"Thanks, George. I'll get it sorted. In the meantime, I want the next shift down at the park and knocking on doors in the nearby streets. I'll send Seaton down to supervise. Stop anyone in the vicinity, and see if they were there yesterday. The area they were last seen is taped off. They checked it last night, I want it checked again. Someone saw something." He slapped George on the back as he left. "I'll see you later."

When Meredith returned to the incident room, the rest of the team had arrived. DS Louie Trump and DS Tom Seaton were perched on a desk in front of the small television in the corner.

"Morning, sir. Alison called up for you, they've put out a new press release. We're waiting for the local news. Ah here it is now." Trump picked up the remote control and increased the volume.

"The two young Brownies who went missing during an outing to the park early yesterday evening have yet to be found. There has been no word from Ellen Rawlings and Gemma Lake, both aged seven, since their disappearance. A police spokesperson said that a search of the Blaise Castle estate will be undertaken if there is no news in the next few hours. Those willing to join the search should continue to listen to local news bulletins for further updates."

Photographs of the two girls appeared on the screen, and stayed there for the remainder of the bulletin.

"Uniformed officers searched the area immediately surrounding the park during the night, aided by a group of local . . ."

The team perched in front of the screen looked at the faces of the two youngsters, and unbeknown to them, the newsreader was being handed a sheet of paper. Having completed the authorised press release, she added,

"One of the missing girls, Ellen Rawlings, is daughter of Detective Constable David Rawlings, who was involved in an altercation with a member of the public in the early hours of this morning while searching for his daughter. If this is an abduction, the question has to be asked as to whether or not DC Rawlings' position has any connection."

"Bollocks!" Meredith thumped the desk in front of him. "Well if it is, and they didn't know that, they certainly bloody know now." He pointed at the television screen. "Get me the name of whoever's in charge. I'll give them a few bloody questions to ask." Meredith snatched the remote from Trump and switched off the television.

"I'll get on to them immediately, although it is a bit, you know . . . after the horse has bolted."

"Just call them, Trump. Seaton, you'd better get hold of Jo and warn her. What time is she due to be relieved?"

"Not sure, Gov. I don't think we've got that far yet," Seaton shrugged. "We were hoping we'd have found them by now."

"Well, we haven't. Make the phone calls and someone get the kettle on. Briefing in ten minutes."

The television screen went black, and he placed the remote on the work surface. He scratched his forehead, wondering if Ellen's father being a policeman changed things. Reaching the conclusion he could do little about it, he poured orange juice into the glasses on the tray. The girls had still not stirred; he'd leave them sleeping, there was no rush to wake them. He lifted a forkful of scrambled egg to his mouth as the doorbell rang, and he smiled as he replaced the fork. Picking up the padded envelope he walked quietly to the door.

"Mr Smith? I believe you have a parcel for me." The leather-clad motorcyclist lifted the visor of his helmet, and accepted the proffered package. "Thank you. It will be delivered within two hours, guaranteed, or your money back. Have a nice day."

He watched the courier walk back down the path and secure the package in the box behind the seat of his bike. Have a nice day? He hadn't realised the English had started saying that. He closed the door and stilled. Cocking his head, he stood listening for a moment. They were awake. Hurrying back to the kitchen, he sat the pointed hat, complete with face mask, on his head, and picked up the tray.

"Good morning, girls." He kicked the door shut behind him. "Did you sleep well?"

He looked at the two little girls lying side by side in the single bed.

Ellen shrugged. "I can't remember going to bed. Are we in trouble?" Her chin trembled and her eyes filled with tears.

"Why would you be in trouble? I told you I spoke to your parents last night, they knew you were staying. I was going to take you home this morning, but when I phoned your daddy, he said he had something important on at work and would collect you later. It must be exciting to have a policeman for a daddy."

Ellen didn't have time to respond as Gemma sat up and yawned.

"Why are you still dressed like a clown?"

"Because I thought it would be fun. If you're staying a bit longer, we can carry on playing. I'll leave your breakfast here." He placed it on the small table in the centre of the room. "You eat up, and when you've finished, I'll show you where the dressing up things are."

The girls looked at each other and smiled. They loved dressing up. Jumping out of bed they went to the table and inspected their breakfast.

"I don't have juice at home, I have milk." Gemma turned to him and smiled. "I've never had pancakes for breakfast before. I like it here."

"That's good, because I like you being here. I'll go and get you some milk." Punching in the code to release the lock, he left the room.

"Will he take us to school?" asked Ellen.

Ellen watched Gemma rolling up a pancake with her fingers. Gemma shrugged, and lifted the pancake to her mouth.

"We can't go in Brownie uniform, so we can't go to school," Ellen reasoned.

Gemma grinned at her. "Good. I don't want to go to school. We haven't got the cocoon or the beetles yet."

Ellen's hand flew to her mouth and she gasped. "We might not win now. We had twenty minutes, we've been too long."

Listening to their conversation on the monitor in the kitchen, he smiled. They were relaxed and calm. The mild sedative he had given them on arrival had worked as planned. It was good Gemma had some company. It meant he didn't have to worry so much. He glanced at the laptop he had set up on the kitchen table and wondered what the chances were of the package being processed quickly.

"A watched pot never boils," he murmured as he walked to the fridge to get the milk. "It will be on there soon enough."

CHAPTER THREE

Meredith rolled his eyes as the Assistant Chief Constable, Keith Long, concluded the conversation. "I know it goes without saying, Meredith, but the sooner we find these girls the better. Get a decent suit on and sort it out. Oh, and call me if anything happens I should know about."

The click signified he had hung up.

"Idiot." Meredith hung up too and wondered whether coppers lost their grip on reality, as well as their common sense, the higher up the ladder they climbed.

"Trump, any news?" he called out, noticing Trump walking to the incident board.

Trump turned and shook his head. "Sadly, no, not a thing. The team at Blaise has started, although I'm not sure whether I want them to find anything or not."

Meredith looked at his watch, it was a little after midday. He knew once they had passed the twenty-four-hour mark, Rawlings would be lethal. Everyone knew once past that point, the outcome was rarely good. He pulled his mobile from his pocket and called Jo Adler.

"How are they doing?" he asked as she answered.

"As you would expect really. Eve did sleep a little last night, but it was only for a few hours. Dave is on his phone and pacing up and down the back garden. I'm assuming he's checking in with the lads to see what's happening."

"And how are you doing?"

Jo Adler had been held hostage only weeks before by a murderer who wanted Meredith to investigate her sister's death. Jo had dealt with it well, and had come back to work after only a few days' leave, but Meredith was concerned that being so close to this case might not be the best idea.

"I'm fine. I think I slept longer than either of them. When I woke up Eve was in the kitchen making tea. Mind you, I could do without the reporters. Five of them now and a TV van has parked at the bottom of the road. The reporters got the message though – they've only knocked the once."

"Good, let me know if you need any help. The ACC has arranged a press conference for five thirty, to make sure it makes the evening news if we haven't found them by then. They'll want Dave and Eve there."

"Oh boy. I don't know if she'll do it. Do you want me to speak to them?"

"If you would. I've got to go home and change as, apparently, I need my best suit. I'll call into the Lakes on the way."

Meredith hung up and ran his hand over the stubble on his chin. He'd opted not to shave that morning, so now he would have to waste another ten minutes doing so to keep his boss happy. As he left his office his mobile rang; it was Patsy. With no news, the update took seconds. Meredith attempted to terminate the conversation.

"Anyway, I'm off to see the Lakes and then I have to go home to change. Got to go now, but I'll call if anything happens."

"Oh dear, I'd give them a call, but what can you say?" Patsy sighed. "Where do you want me to take all this food? I had to go in to work this morning, but I've loaded it all in the car now." Patsy had received a surprising call at work, and had been hoping to snatch a quiet moment with Meredith.

"There's hardly anyone here. I'd take it up to Blaise Castle. Seaton is running the op there. I'm sure they'll be glad of it. I really do have to go, Patsy."

"Okay, will do. Just one more thing."

"What?"

"Happy birthday."

"Thanks. Catch you later." Meredith hung up, pulled out his note book, and checked he had the Lakes' address. He never enjoyed celebrating his birthday. He had thought this year might be different. It wasn't.

Once in his car, Meredith decided to go home and smarten up before going to see the Lakes. That way he could take them to the station for the conference.

For the second time that day, Meredith ignored the cards on the now empty kitchen table as he picked up his keys.

When he reached the Lakes' street, he parked as close to their home as he could, but the road was particularly busy. He saw the small group of reporters, chatting amongst themselves and leaning on cars opposite the house, waiting for any sign of life. Meredith glanced at the modern semi that was the Lakes' home, and noted the curtains were closed. One of the men spotted him hurrying down the street, and, camera poised, he stepped out onto the road for a clearer shot.

Meredith recognised him instantly, and his nose wrinkled in disgust. Tommy Sealy saluted Meredith with his left hand, which he then used to steady the camera as he took a series of rapid shots.

"Who is it?" asked one of the younger local reporters walking forward, and peering at Meredith.

"DCI Meredith. He'll be heading up the case. Get on over there, he likes the spotlight."

Tommy Sealy traded on people's misery. The nastier the story, the more he liked the challenge. He'd not bothered going to attend when Prince Charles opened a refurbished theatre earlier that month, even though there had been rumours that the ever popular Prince Harry would accompany him. He'd also ignored a tip-off that a TV celebrity had checked into a local hotel under a false name. On questioning his source, he found out the man was alone, and had used a false name as he hadn't wanted any fuss. If they'd told Tommy he was with a woman, or better still a man, he'd have been round there like a shot. As it was, he stayed in to watch the end of the film on television.

Tommy had realised many years before that pain, embarrassment, and anger sold for bigger bucks. He had crossed Meredith's path many times before. The dislike was mutual. Tommy had a sense of humour, though some might consider it warped, and he knew Meredith would chew that lad up and spit him out. There might even be a photograph in it. He kept the lens trained on Meredith as the young man approached him, his handheld recorder pointed towards Meredith.

"DCI Meredith, may I have a word? What's the latest on the abduction of the two young girls?"

"Nope!"

"But you must realise that the public are interested. They may be able to assist you. Have you heard from the abductor?" He had raised his voice and was shouting, as though that would convince Meredith of the validity of his questions.

The other men stepped forward. Two of them had taken their own recorders from their pockets.

"What's your name?" Meredith stopped at the gate of the Lakes' home.

"Bartrum, South West Gazette," Bartrum smiled, hoping it would help. His smile fell away as Meredith held out his hand towards the recorder.

"Okay, give me that, I'll update you."

Bartrum paused, opened-mouthed for a few seconds, before he handed over the recorder. This wasn't usual, but if it meant he could go back with something, who cared? Meredith lifted the recorder to his lips.

"This recording is being made outside the home of parents who have a seven-year-old child missing. Not only does Mr Bartrum think it is acceptable to invade their misery by hanging around outside, he also finds it acceptable to shout at the top of his voice about an abduction, despite there being no foundation for that assumption. It would appear Mr Bartrum is going to go far, in the 'make it up as you go' field of journalism."

Meredith clicked off the recorder and stepped forward. He was a good head taller than Bartrum and he leaned in very close. Bartrum shrank back.

"Go and speak to your paper and find out what the last press release said, and when the next one will be. That way your report will be halfway accurate. If I find you print one word of this story that's not true, I will find you, and I will find a reason to nick you. Now fuck off."

Meredith held out the recorder, but before the startled Bartrum could take it, Meredith allowed it to slip to the ground. Meredith heard the plastic casing crack. Without looking down he stepped over it, and opened the gate to the Lakes' home.

Tommy Sealy smiled. It should be easier than usual to wind Meredith up today; there might be a photo in this for him yet.

"They've been there most of the morning, sir." The door was opened by a family liaison officer. "They were in the garden at one stage, but they got bored. Mr and Mrs Lake are in the kitchen, this way." She walked to the far end of the hall and pushed open the door.

The Lakes were sitting at a small bistro type table in the corner of the compact kitchen. Cold mugs of coffee sat amongst screwed up tissues. They looked up expectantly. Meredith held his hands up.

"I'm sorry." He shook his head, "No news, I'm afraid. What I can tell you is that I have officers looking at CCTV footage of the area surrounding the park, and we are searching the Blaise Castle estate. I've come to run over your statements and speak to you about attending a press conference. It's been . . ."

He stopped speaking as Mrs Lake let out a moan and her hands flew to her mouth.

"That's what you do when they're dead. She's not dead! SHE'S NOT!" Her muffled voice was high-pitched, then, without warning, she stood and slapped Meredith across the face, before she collapsed weeping into his arms. Her husband stood and took her from Meredith. As he did so his eyes penetrated Meredith's own, searching for any sign that that might be the case.

"There is no indication either of the girls have been injured in any way, Mrs Lake. However, as there have been no sightings of them, we have to consider the strong possibility they are with someone. Someone who may respond to an appeal. Let's sit down, and run through a few questions."

He nodded at the liaison officer, and she led the way to the sitting room.

Meredith looked around the Lakes' sitting room. On every surface there was evidence of Gemma. A homemade birthday card for her father on the mantel, a comic book on the arm of the chair, photographs on the wall and windowsill, and one huge spongy slipper made to look like a cat abandoned at the side of the sofa. He cleared his throat.

"Some of these questions will have been asked before, but not by me, and something may come back to you so please be patient."

Meredith established that Gemma did not have a mobile phone. The only time she was not being supervised by either of her parents was when she was at school, Brownies or swimming club. She was not allowed to play out in the street, and only attended organised events, however minor. She did use the internet occasionally, but not for any length of time, and always when her parents were there. She had never run away, or even threatened to do so. She was close friends with a group of four other girls, one of them Ellen Rawlings, and they took it in turns to have sleepovers once a month, which were chaotic. She hadn't been upset recently, she wasn't bullied at school, and she hadn't fallen out with her parents over any restrictions they might have imposed. They had spoken to her about talking to strangers, but they conceded she had never been given a reason not to trust adults. She was a happy, well balanced little girl. She did well at school and was a promising swimmer. There was nothing to suggest she would have disappeared voluntarily, or without coercion.

Meredith was aware that Jo Adler had received an identical response from the Rawlings. He sighed as he mentally ticked off the last question.

"There is no apparent reason either girl would have convinced the other to run away, and if they had simply wandered off, we would have expected a sighting by now. We have to assume they are with someone, and that's why we would like to do the appeal. It does help focus the public's minds on what they may have seen that they didn't realise, and if someone does have them and they're watching, it might convince them to let them come home."

Meredith paused as Mrs Lake whimpered. "You don't have to say anything if you don't want to. I can do the talking. If either of you want to speak, our press officer will help you put a statement together before we go in. It's a horrible thing to have to do, and there will be reporters, photographers and television cameras there. It will be overwhelming, but it is necessary."

"We'll do it," announced Kevin Lake. "I'll speak. I want our little girl home, and if that's what it takes, well, so be it."

"Good. When you're ready, I'll get the car and bring it down to the road outside. There are a few reporters out there, but ignore them and get in the car. Don't be drawn by anything they may say; they are simply fishing for a story. The press conference will be soon enough for you to speak." Meredith glanced at the clock next to the birthday card. "We need to leave in about twenty minutes, so you go and collect your thoughts, and I'll make some phone calls in the garden."

As Meredith walked to the end of the garden, Seaton updated him on the search of the Blaise Castle estate.

"Absolutely nothing. A few bits and bobs brought back, but they've been there for years. We're about three quarters of the way through. I'm not holding my breath, Gov. By the way, happy birthday, Patsy dropped the grub off. It's going down a treat."

"Let's look on the bright side, and assume no news is good news. I'm taking Gemma's parents to the conference in a minute, so my phone will be off in an hour or so. Leave a message if you need me, and I'll get back to you as soon as I'm free. What time do you reckon you'll be finished there?"

"Two or three hours at a guess. More people turned up at lunchtime after the news update, so it's going quicker this afternoon."

"Okay, I'll see you back at the station later." Meredith paused. "Have you spoken to Dave?"

"Briefly. He checked in to see if anything had turned up. I think he's worried we'll keep something from him until we're absolutely sure. You?"

"Not since yesterday." Meredith sighed and turned to face the house. "I don't know what to say to him. I've known the bloke all these years, and I don't know what to say. Pathetic!" Meredith cleared his throat and his tone became business-like. "Have to go. As I say, keep me informed."

Meredith opened the door to the meeting room, and allowed the Lakes to enter. He watched Dave Rawlings turn to look, and Eve Rawlings run to Tina Lake. The two women hugged. Meredith studied them for a moment. They were very different looking women – height, build, hair colour, all different. But they shared the same dazed, frightened and almost vacant expression. Dark circles under their eyes had been disguised with makeup, but still showed through. Neither wore mascara, just in case the tears returned, and their facial muscles seemed to have frozen. The ability to frown or smile taken away.

Swallowing, he looked at Rawlings, and mentally braced himself as Rawlings approached, willing his brain to grasp some offering of comfort. In the event, he took hold of Rawlings' outstretched hand, pulled him into a hug and patted him on the back.

"I know, mate, I know," was all he could manage by way of comfort, and he felt Rawlings nod against his shoulder and knew it was enough. Releasing him, he asked, "Are you speaking?"

"I've got to, Gov. Eve wouldn't cope. I didn't want her to come, but she needed to do something."

Meredith nodded. "I need to sort the Lakes out, so go and get yourself a coffee."

Rawlings shrugged. "I'm all coffeed out. Don't think I'll ever drink the stuff again." He jerked his head towards Alison the PR girl. "Go and get them sorted. Don't worry, I'll keep out of trouble." He attempted a smile but could only manage to lift his cheeks slightly.

Alison Munday worked in the communications department, ensuring that public statements were appropriate, and she fielded calls into Meredith's station from the media, to avoid officers expressing their own opinions. She had the measure of Meredith, and for the best part they got on well. She knew by the look on his face as he approached the Lakes that he was reaching the end of his patience. She was right. Meredith felt his anger rising as he walked briskly towards the group. The fear and pain in the room was palpable. Taking Kevin Lake by the elbow, he directed him towards Alison.

"This way, Mr Lake. Alison will help you write what you want to say."

He deposited Lake with Alison and went to speak to Jo Adler.

"Do you know something? When we catch this bastard I'd happily lose my job just to have ten minutes alone with him."

"I know, Gov. But we have to keep praying they are safe, and he's not hurt them."

"He could send them back wrapped up in a fucking ribbon, he's still caused all this pain. He's still changed their lives for ever. I'll have him, Adler, I swear to God."

Jo didn't respond. The reporters were being allowed into the adjoining room to get ready for the conference, and they made no attempt to do so quietly. To them this was simply another day at work.

Thirty minutes later, and the conference room was full, so much so that a few reporters needed to stand amongst the cameramen at the back of the room. A uniformed police woman opened the door and led the group out to face them. The room fell silent as the door opened, but the silence was soon replaced with a rustling as the reporters readied themselves. The small group took their seats at the table. Alison stood behind them, and to the left of the board which held two large photographs of the missing girls. The sound of cameras taking rapid shots filled the air, their flashes harsh against tired eyes. Meredith drew in a deep breath and pulled his shoulders back. He paused a beat before looking up at the gathered pressmen. He lifted his hand.

"We have called this conference in the hope of securing the safe return of Gemma Lake and Ellen Rawlings. I will make a short statement, followed by the fathers of the girls. We will not be taking questions." A few more flashes caused him to squint. "I would also ask that you refrain from taking any further photos until the statements have been completed. You know what we look like now. This is distressing enough for the parents without being made to feel like they are exhibits."

As he tapped the papers he held on the desk, he noticed a woman wearing a red suit in the front row raise her eyebrows at his statement, and he held her gaze until she looked down at the notebook in her hand. Clearing his throat, he read his statement. He explained where the girls had been when they disappeared, and why they had been there. He gave details about the on-going police operation, and how the search would be widened if they found nothing at the Blaise Castle estate. His eyes looked deep into the lens of the television camera as he asked for anyone who had been in the vicinity the previous evening, from the time the girls arrived to the time they disappeared, to get in touch with the incident room, even if they felt they had no information. Turning to look at Dave Rawlings, Meredith advised them that Ellen's father would make a brief statement. He blinked rapidly as Rawlings nodded confirming he was ready. A lump had formed in Meredith's throat and he coughed to remove it while Rawlings composed himself.

Rawlings looked up and scanned the reporters. He'd been in this room a dozen times. He'd stood to one side watching these people go about their business. On occasion he'd been disgusted with their apparent lack of empathy with the victims. Now he needed them, and he hated them for it. He searched their faces for a glimpse of understanding of his plight. He found it in Ivor Jenson, a middle-aged and tired-looking man sporting a tweed jacket which had seen better days. Ignoring everyone else in the room he spoke as though they were alone.

"Ellen is our pride and joy. I appreciate that is true with most children, and I don't suppose my pain is greater than that of any other parent who has had to deal with this. As a police officer, I have attended more of these things than I should have, but never ever did I expect to be sitting here, on this side of the table, looking at you," he waved his hand towards the audience, never taking his eyes from Ivor's, "and pleading for the safe return of my own baby."

He cleared his throat. "Ellen is seven years old. She is as naive as any seven-year-old should be, but I do not believe she would have gone off with someone willingly." Rawlings ignored the tear that travelled slowly from the corner of his eye, down the contour of his nose, and flicked it away with his tongue as it reached his lip. "She is beautiful, bright, energetic, and a cheeky little madam on occasion. I am her father, I should have protected her, and I should have made sure she was safe. I failed my little girl, and I want a chance to put that right. Please help me find her and her friend. Please get in touch, even if you question your own judgement. If you have them, please give them back. Please do not hurt our babies."

He closed his eyes, not to hold back the tears which had yet to fall, but to hold back the acid that he wanted to spit out. The threats he wanted to make, and the insults he wanted to hurl.

Meredith watched the woman in the red suit raise her hand to her face, and discreetly wipe away the moisture forming there by dabbing the corner of her eyes with her fingertips. Rawlings looked away from Ivor; he dared not say more. Meredith turned to Kevin Lake, who lifted the typed notes with shaking hands.

He opened his mouth several times before he managed to form the words he needed. He held up the two sheets of paper.

"I was going to read this, but Dave has said all that needs to be said. We want our girls back and we'd like you to help us."

Tina Lake lowered her head. It was clear from the jerky movement of her upper body that she was sobbing silently. Her husband put the paper on the table and grasped her hand as he continued.

"We will not survive this if she doesn't come home. She is our world. I know now we should have been more honest with her, and told her about the people out there willing to hurt her. She . . . they, will be frightened and . . ." He gasped for breath as though he were unable to get the required oxygen into his lungs. Slumping forward, he rested the elbow of his free arm on the table and supported his head as though it were too heavy for his neck. "Let my daughter come home, please." He closed his eyes and remained motionless.

Meredith had been staring down at the floor in front of the table, chewing his bottom lip, and he looked up.

"Thank you, ladies and gentlemen, that will be all for now. There will be a further press release at nine thirty this evening."

Standing, he pushed back his chair and held his hand out to Eve.

"Do you blame the Brown Owl for not looking after your children properly?" called the woman in the red suit.

"Have your received any demands from the abductor at all?" shouted a skinny man with greasy hair in the last row.

Camera flashes filled the room as Alison stepped forward, and taking Tina Lake's hand, she led the sorry procession back into the adjoining room. A few more questions were shouted out as Meredith closed the door, having waited for Dave Rawlings, the last in line, to enter. Their eyes met. Rawlings' chin was quivering as though he were shivering with cold.

"I need a pee," he croaked, and walked briskly to the door with the disabled sign in the corner of the room.

Jo Adler held out her arms and hugged Eve, who was still too numb to react. Alison ushered the Lakes to the sofa, and offered them coffee. Meredith waited for Rawlings to reappear. He tapped his hand on the side of his leg with impatience, and a feeling of guilt at his impotence to ease their suffering. He wanted to be anywhere but in this room. He was of no use to them here, and their emotions were seeping in, and weighing him down. He held back a sigh of relief as Rawlings reappeared, the collar of his shirt wet from the water he had splashed on his face. Meredith made his excuses and promised to contact them immediately anything happened. He left quickly, taking the shortest route back to the incident room.

As he reached the door to the street, the reporter in the red suit hurried along the corridor behind him. She called out as he pushed on the handle.

"DCI Meredith, a word if I may?"

Meredith turned around, and shook his head. "Sorry, love, you know the drill, you'll have to wait for the next release."

"I only want to help." Helen Darley had reached him, and stepping forward, her body filled the gap between the Meredith and the door.

"Thank you." Meredith forced his lips into a smile. "We all do, and that means I need to get back. Now, if you'll excuse me." He stepped forward attempting to make her move away. She held her ground and their bodies touched. He stared into her face and she smiled at him.

"Ten minutes, please. There's a good pub on the corner, I'll buy you a drink."

She was a reasonably attractive woman and Meredith guessed she was a little younger than himself. In days gone by, and if he weren't dealing with such a personal case, he might have taken her up on her offer. As it was, he focused on her garish red lipstick and shook his head.

"I have two little girls to find. Do you think I have time to waste?" He looked down as she pressed her body closer. Bemused, he shook his head. "Was that supposed to convince me?"

"It was supposed to convince you it wouldn't be a waste of time," she winked. "The whole time your friend was speaking you were staring at my legs. I got the message."

Meredith looked at her as though she had gone mad. He stepped back and glanced down, as though confirming she did have legs. When he looked up he shook his head.

"I am going to work. I suggest you do the same. I saw you wipe a tear away; I thought you'd been moved enough to help us." He pulled on the handle of the door and stepped forward again.

"I saw you, you were looking." Helen pouted.

His patience at an end, Meredith took her by the shoulders and pushed her backwards until she was against the wall. She smiled as he leaned in.

He whispered in her ear, before catching the door before it closed and hurrying backs towards his car. She looked at him open mouthed. Did he just tell her to fuck off?

Gemma gave a cry, and he picked up the remote and switched off the television. He closed his eyes as an unexpected wave of guilt caused every nerve end to tingle. How could they think he would hurt them? He opened his eyes, realising that's what they would think. Well, he may be causing them a little discomfort, but Gemma would benefit. She'd enjoy being with him, and he'd enjoy being with her. That's what counted. He tapped his head with his fingertips, as though that would help him start thinking logically. First, he would see what was wrong with Gemma, and then he would contact them. He'd let them know it was for the best. Putting on the hat he went to see the girls.

Gemma was sitting on the floor by the bookcase, and Ellen was standing next to her. They looked up, worried expressions on their faces, as he entered the room. He took in the scene. The green tin box was lying open and its contents had spilled across the floor. Gemma was attempting to gather them up.

He smiled. "Have we had an accident here?"

"I'm sorry." Gemma's face cracked and a sob racked her body. "I wanted to know what was in the box. I overbalanced. This one is broken." She gasped out another sob, and tears flowed as she held up a headless soldier. "I want to go home."

"Don't worry about that. I can soon fix it. If you want to go home, then home is where we shall take you. Let's get this lot cleared up, and I'll go and get the phone so we can call your parents. What did you want it for?" He turned the box over and revealed the forty little compartments.

Gemma's tears subsided and she shrugged, "We wanted to look. Didn't we?" She drew Ellen into the conversation.

Ellen nodded and knelt by her friend. "Look, their arms and legs move. Are they yours?" She had picked up one of the tiny soldiers, and demonstrated the movement of the limbs for Gemma.

Gemma leaned forward and picked up another. "They have little faces," she observed, as she placed it in one of the tin's compartments.

"They are mine, yes. They are very old. My great-grandfather made most of them, and when they were old enough, my grandfather, and my dad also helped." He smiled as the two girls continued to fill the compartments. "They were all finished by the time my father was born, but he did help repaint them."

His eyes searched along the now neat rows of soldiers. He chose one, and lifted it from the tin. "This one I helped repaint. You see his rosy cheeks, I did those." Surprised by this memory, he turned it to face the girls, and they inspected it. "If you look closely you'll see they're all different, and they might be tiny, but they're quite strong, so don't worry."

He placed the tin on the floor and the two girls examined the rows.

"There's one missing, did you lose him?" Ellen asked, as she replaced those she had been holding.

"No, it's not lost. It was given to a little girl."

"Was it a present?"

"Yes, I suppose it was, a leaving present."

Wondering if he was doing the right thing, he studied the empty compartment for a while, pondering his actions. The two girls became restless and Gemma stood up.

"I'm starving. Are we having tea here or at home?"

Dragged from his musings, he got to his feet.

"I'll go and get the phone, and we'll check with your parents. We mustn't forget to get the beetles before you go. Get the jars ready. We'll go out and look after I've made the phone call."

Back in the kitchen, he lifted the screen of the laptop and tapped in his password. Sitting heavily on the chair, he logged his code into the website and waited, his fingertips beating out a tattoo on the table. He knew it was a long shot they would have completed the processing yet, but it was worth a try. He smiled as he read that the expected completion time would be in approximately four hours. He checked the time. That would be past ten o'clock, and it would be dark then. He could get rid of Ellen then, if necessary. His hand stretched out and pulled forward the passport. Gemma would stay with him, until he was ready to travel. He tapped the passport, and wondered if he should wait until morning. He pulled down the screen, and lifted the phone from the cradle. He started talking as he returned to the girls.

"No, that's no problem Mr Lake, I would be delighted." He kicked the door shut after him. "Yes, Gemma's here now . . . Hello? Oh good, I thought I'd lost you. Here's Gemma." He held the phone out to Gemma who placed it to her ear.

"Hello, Dad, me and Ellen are going to get some beetles, and then we'll be home. Is Mummy there?" There was no reply to Gemma's question and she shook her head. "He's gone. I bet his battery is dead again. Mum goes mad with him about it."

"My dad never answers his either." Ellen rolled her eyes at her friend. "I think dads are rubbish with mobile phones."

Gemma nodded agreement and handed back the phone.

"He'll call back when he's charged it. But he did say you could eat here. So, what's it to be? I have pizza, spaghetti, beans, meatballs, fries. What do you fancy?"

"Fries like in McDonalds, or chips like from the chip shop?" Gemma was clearly an expert on fried potatoes.

"Fries in a little box that goes in the microwave. Will they do?"

"Yuck! No thank you." Ellen was very sure about that. "They're disgusting, they taste like cardboard. Can I have pizza, please? No mushrooms though, I don't like mushrooms."

"Me too." Gemma didn't really care about the main course. "Is it ice-cream for pudding again?"

"Sure is. We'll also have fizzy orange squash again. I'll put lemonade in instead of water. That makes it magic. I'll remember that. I'll cook while you find the beetles. Get your jars ready."

The walled garden at the rear of the house was about thirty feet square. It had not been tended for some years, but he had made a half-hearted effort to cut the grass and trim back the shrubs. He hadn't been lying and he had noticed lots of beetles, although the chrysalis had hatched a while back. He pushed open the doors to the garden, and turned to face the girls.

"Remember to whisper." He put his finger to his lips. "Insects don't like loud noises."

Stepping to one side he allowed the girls to pass, jars in hand. He hurried back to the kitchen, switched on the oven to heat it up, and pulled open a drawer. He removed a brand new mobile phone, which he slid into his pocket. He then pondered where he should go. He needed to be at least fifteen minutes away, so the girls needed to be occupied or asleep. He decided to be safe, and go for both.

Once the meal was prepared, he carried it to them on a large tray. The tray also contained the drinks to which he had added the sedative. Placing the tray on the small table he pulled a DVD from his back pocket, and waved it at them. They forgot about the insects, including two beetles they had collected, and ran to see what he had.

"I have to make some calls before I take you home, so eat and drink as much as you can. "I think I can trust you to put this on, and have a little lie down to watch it? Can I trust you?"

"YES!" they shouted in unison.

He wondered if he were ever that innocent as he listened to them discussing the merits of *101 Dalmatians*, and tore the sheet from the pad on which he had written the incident room's number. Opening the door which led to the garage, he climbed into the Range Rover. He drove out of the garage, and waited for the door to close behind him, before heading into town.

CHAPTER FOUR

Patsy sniffed, pulled a tissue from the box, and blew her nose. Meredith had looked handsome, very smart, and his plea had been genuine and heartfelt. Patsy hoped the conference would bear fruit for them. The two sets of parents had looked wiped out, and she wondered how they would cope if this went on for much longer. She looked at the clock and sighed. The girls had been gone for almost twenty-four hours.

Having no idea when Meredith would get home, she had already decided it would be frozen pizza with salad for dinner. She had also decided that she wouldn't discuss this morning's call with him; he had enough on his plate, and there was little point in distracting him. Sipping her wine, she wondered whether or not to make the call. In the end curiosity got the better of her, and she picked up her phone.

"Hello, Nicola, it's Patsy Hodge. Sorry I didn't return your call earlier, it's been one of those days."

Nicola was Meredith's former wife. They had been married for a little over seven years. Their marriage had failed due to Nicola being unable to carry a baby to full term, and Meredith's resultant infidelity as Nicola spiralled into depression. When they separated, Nicola was pregnant, and claimed the conception was as a result of a one-night stand. Patsy had heard via mutual friends that Nicola had successfully given birth to a boy several months earlier, and it was clear those same friends had kept Nicola updated on Patsy's change of career.

"Congratulations on the arrival of your son. You must be thrilled. What did you call him?"

"Paul, after my father. Patsy, I've just seen John and Dave Rawlings on the television. How awful, I can't believe it. Do you think it would be okay to give Eve a call? Not that I know what to say, what can you say?"

Patsy advised her as best she could, and the realisation that Nicola had known Eve and Dave for far longer than she had, reminded her how new her relationship with Meredith actually was.

"It's odd, when you think you've got it bad, something awful like this happens, and you're given a sharp slap to remind you to stop feeling sorry for yourself." Nicola sighed. "I suppose you want to know why I need to speak with you."

"I did wonder. The message made it sound quite urgent." Patsy closed her eyes and questioned whether it had been wise to call. Nicola had clearly kept up with her movements, to know that she was a private detective, and Nicola knew Chris Grainger, Patsy's partner, well. "I was surprised you didn't speak to Chris."

There was only a second's pause before Nicola answered. This indicated she had either rehearsed the answer, or her response was genuine.

"Chris and I know each other too well. I think he would either try and give me advice, which I don't want, or get too involved, which I don't want either. When I heard you'd started working with him, you seemed the ideal person. There is a condition though . . ." Nicola paused. "I don't want you to discuss this with John. Not yet. Will it be possible for you to do that, given your involvement with him?"

Patsy was quite taken aback, and hesitated before replying. She would respect Nicola's privacy if necessary, but on what basis did Nicola think she could trust Patsy to do so?

"Of course I will keep it confidential. Let's make an appointment to meet up and we'll take it from there." Patsy looked up and smiled through the open door as Amanda arrived home. Pulling a note pad from her bag, she rummaged for a pen. "What day would be best for you?"

"Tomorrow," Nicola replied assertively. "Tonight would be great if you're free; the sooner you get started the better."

Patsy's curiosity got the better of her. "Okay, where would you like to meet? I can open the office if necessary."

"No, I don't want to put you to that much trouble. Give me five minutes and I'll see if my neighbour can watch Paul for a couple of hours. I'll get back to you."

Patsy hung up and wandered into the kitchen where Amanda was throwing a sandwich together.

"Hi, Patsy, good day? Any news on Ellen? I'm not stopping, I'm meeting a friend. I need fuel first though."

Patsy gave her an update on the press conference and watched her gulp down the cheese and tomato sandwich, which was accompanied by a glass of water. The minute the empty glass touched the table, Amanda jumped up and headed for the stairs.

"Sorry to rush, but we're watching a movie that starts at seven thirty. I have to shower."

With a quick wave she was gone. Patsy smiled as she cleared away the crockery and wiped the crumbs from the table. Any concern she had about sharing a home with Amanda was long gone. She dropped the cloth into the sink, and picked up the promised call from Nicola. They arranged to meet an hour later.

By the time Amanda had vacated the bathroom, Patsy had no time to shower. Instead, she applied fresh makeup, and twisted her hair into a knot on the top of her head. She was pulling on her jacket as Amanda galloped down the stairs.

"Wow. You look amazing Amanda. I'm guessing your *friend* is of the male persuasion." Amanda had on a short linen skirt which showed off the long legs she had inherited from her father, a top which clung to her contours, and she too had scooped her hair away from her face. Her eye makeup was a little heavy, but she looked stunning. Patsy laughed. "I'm glad your father isn't here. I have a feeling he would send you back up to put on something a little less revealing."

"He is. Male I mean, and Dad could try, but he wouldn't get very far." A horn sounded outside. "That's him now. Don't wait up." Amanda opened the door and disappeared up the path.

Patsy didn't bother closing it, but sat on the bottom stair and texted Meredith.

Going to meet a client, will probably be back before you, but if not around 9ish. Assuming no news as I haven't heard from you.

Nicola looked up expectantly as Patsy entered the Cambridge Arms. She smiled and waved acknowledgement as she stood to greet Patsy. Patsy quickly took in her appearance as she approached. There was no sign that Nicola had recently given birth. She was wearing skinny jeans and a fitted V-neck sweater. This surprised Patsy, as the few women she knew who had had children had taken at least six months to get down to that size. Patsy had only met Nicola once before, but something had changed. Nicola had a few more fine lines at the corners of her eyes, and her cheekbones were more prominent than Patsy remembered. Her makeup had been expertly applied and she looked stunning.

"Hi, Nicola, you look great. If I didn't know, I would never have guessed you had recently had a baby." She pointed to the half-full glass on the table. "Can I get you a drink?"

"No, I'm fine, thank you."

Nicola leaned forward unexpectedly and kissed Patsy on the cheek, as though she were an old friend. Patsy smiled awkwardly before making her way to the bar. She drummed her nails while waiting to be served. Now she was here, it didn't seem like such a good idea after all. Fixing a smile, she bought her drink, and returned to the corner table where Nicola sat awaiting her return.

"I hear Amanda is living with you. How is she? I haven't seen her since she was very small."

Patsy's eyes flared a little. Nicola was obviously keeping up with events.

"She's fine, a lovely girl. In fact, a joy to have around if I'm honest."

"Not like John then, he can be so grumpy. He . . ."

Nicola stopped abruptly. There it was. The pretence was shattered. She looked down at her hands.

"Patsy, I'm sorry, perhaps it would be best if we stuck to business. I don't want to embarrass you."

She looked back up, and Patsy thought she looked fearful. Patsy shrugged.

"Nicola, you were married to Meredith for a long time. I'm living with him now, and if I'm going to work for you, it will probably be impossible to avoid the odd mention." She grinned. "But I agree, let's get down to business. That's far more important than Meredith."

As Meredith had been Patsy's boss when they first got together, she had continued to call him Meredith, or even Gov, in the early part of their relationship. So much so, that she now found it impossible to call him John. It simply didn't fit, although she did on occasion call him Johnny, which he hated.

"It's quite simple really. Well, the request is. I'm not sure about the doing of it." Nicola shrugged. "I want you to find Antonio Garcia, and as quickly as possible."

"Okay, may I ask who he is?"

"Hopefully, Paul's father. I've gone back to the bar where I met him, but it was a temporary job and he's moved on. The manager says he has no idea where. It could only have been within the last few months, as I saw him again only a month before Paul was born. I was quite flattered that he remembered me." Nicola looked down, clearly embarrassed and fiddled with the thin silver bracelet on her wrist. When she looked up she smiled, and a flush came to her cheek. "I can see why I was tempted. He was very handsome, and a little younger than me."

Patsy returned the smile, but her mind was racing. Nicola had been so sure that she had fallen pregnant during this liaison, but if she were now using the phrase 'hopefully', could Meredith be the father? Her pulse increased a little as she tried to push the possibility from her mind.

"Did he realise he might be the father?"

Nicola shook her head and gave a laugh. "He had no idea whatsoever. I think he has many one-night stands, and I doubt the dates are etched on his mind." She shrugged. "He was lovely though, patted the bump, and told me I would have a beautiful child, which I did. He even showed me the photographs of his nephews and nieces. How sweet is that, to carry their photos in his wallet?"

"Very. Listen, Nicola, call me cynical, but they could be his own children. Men have been known to lie, and to keep their stories as close to the truth as possible to avoid being exposed."

"I do know, Patsy, yes."

Patsy closed her eyes momentarily. Leaning forward she cupped her hands around her face. Meredith had cheated repeatedly towards the end of his relationship with Nicola. He believed his cheating had led to their child being stillborn. He had no evidence that was the case, only his own guilt at being in another woman's bed, when he should have been with his wife, and she had been left to deal with the death of their child alone.

"I'm sorry, Nicola. Of course you do, I do too. But I am concerned for you. You need to be sure you are not chasing some dream that can never be. You don't know this man. If and when I find him, do you mind me asking what you want from him?"

"I want him to be a father to Paul," Nicola answered simply, as though that were obvious.

Patsy realised her initial reaction that taking this case would be a little too close to home had been correct. She also didn't relish the idea of tracking down yet another missing father. Her last two cases had been similar, and neither had ended happily. She racked her brain for a reason to enable her to let Nicola down gently.

"And how would that work for you? I'm sure you might fancy him, he might even be magic in bed," Patsy allowed herself a smile, "but day to day stuff? He might be a total bastard. It's one thing flirting and being chivalrous to the ladies that pass your way in the evening, but the feet under the table relationship can be a whole different ball game."

Nicola was smiling and nodding as Patsy spoke passionately about the folly of this enterprise.

"I don't want him for me, Patsy, I want him for Paul. I don't want money, or promises, or roses round the door. I simply want my beautiful baby boy to have a father."

Patsy drew in a breath. She knew without a doubt this was not going to end well. But for some reason, she felt some form of responsibility for Nicola, which she knew was ridiculous. But it was there nonetheless.

"Okay, so what do you know about him?" Patsy pulled her pad from her bag.

"Not much. I met him at the Orchid bar on Queens Road. I know I enjoyed his company, and I was ashamed the morning after, especially as I vaguely remembered his name was Toni but couldn't be sure. I went to the Orchid again about a month before I had Paul, and as I was pregnant I stayed sober this time. I found out his full name when he showed me the picture of his nephews and nieces."

She smiled, knowing Patsy's doubts. "I noticed his name on the credit card in his wallet. I've been back to the bar this week, but there's a new manager who only knows of Toni, but not anything about him. He thinks he left about five weeks ago. He didn't want to admit it, but I think Toni was paid cash in hand, so there are no proper records." She shrugged. "I know the street he was living on, but not the house number. I simply can't remember that. I've been back, but it's a long street and nothing rang a bell. That's when I decided to call you. Oh yes, I did steal this from the noticeboard in the office at the bar."

Nicola drew a dog-eared photograph from her bag, and handed it to Patsy. Patsy studied the photograph and looked up at Nicola with a grin.

"Is this him?" The question revealed Patsy's obvious surprise.

The photograph showed a dark-haired man sandwiched between two waitresses. His arms hung casually over their shoulders as he smiled lazily at the camera. He had movie star good looks and, for some reason, naked from the waist up, his sculpted torso revealed he was no stranger to the gym.

Nicola laughed. "No, but I kid you not, Patsy, Toni is from the same school of good looks." She tapped the photo, which Patsy had placed on the table. "This guy was working in the bar on both occasions that I saw Toni. They seemed close, laughing and joking with each other. But I have no idea of his name, or whether he still works there. It's the best I've got."

Patsy nodded. "Then that's what I'll start with. I have a meeting with a client at nine tomorrow morning, I can go to the bar at lunch time to start with enquiries. What street does, or perhaps did, he live on?"

"Pembroke Road. It was near the top, where it meets the Downs, but I'm ashamed to admit I don't even know which side of the road. I was so keen to get out of there and I never thought I'd go back, so it wasn't relevant." She shook her head. "I never thought I'd want to find it again."

Patsy pulled her phone from her pocket. She hadn't missed any calls or texts. Meredith was not home yet. Being early evening, the Orchid bar would be quiet, and it would give an ideal opportunity to speak to some of the staff. Never mind starting tomorrow; if she was going to do this, now would be as good a time as any.

"How long before you have to get home to Paul? I may as well start now, do you want to come?"

Nicola glanced at her watch. "I can't. I have to be back in the next thirty minutes. I'm sorry, Patsy, you'll have to go alone."

"That's not a problem, I'm used to it." Patsy shrugged. "Okay, let's clarify a few things at this stage. If and when I find Toni, what do you want me say to him? Am I to tell him he's a father, or possibly a father, or simply that you want to meet him? You know he will be scared, Nicola. However innocent your needs are. He'll have CSA orders flashing before him, if not boiled bunnies." She flipped her phone into camera mode. "Smile, he might not remember you by name."

Nicola didn't smile, but did allow Patsy to take the photo. Patsy dropped her phone into her bag as Nicola sipped her drink, and considered how much Patsy should tell him.

"Tell him that he has a son. That I am financially independent, but would like his son to know his father, and that he will be rewarded financially."

"What?" Patsy shook her head in disbelief. Toni had been promoted from possibly to definitely the father, and now Nicola was suggesting she would pay him for his involvement. "Rewarded for what? Babysitting? Trips to the park? Really, Nicola, think about what you just said. How is that going to benefit your son in any way?"

"Patsy, I know you think I'm mad, you're not the first," she shrugged, "but I do know what I'm doing. If he was working for cash in hand, then he's probably not got much money. Letting him know that this won't cost him anything may help convince him."

"Oh, I think you're right, of course it will. But what child needs a father who has to be bribed to see him? I'm sorry, Nicola, this isn't right, not in any sense. I'm not sure that I want this job." Patsy pushed her glass forward, and looped the straps of her bag over her shoulder as she stood. "Go home and see your son. Rethink this, please. I'll give you a call in the morning to discuss it."

Patsy's tone was dismissive, and Nicola jumped to her feet, grabbing Patsy's arm.

"Patsy, wait. Tell me how much you charge, I'll pay more."

Patsy's head seemed to gain weight and it dropped heavily as she groaned. When she looked up, Nicola could see the pity in her eyes.

"It's not always about money, Nicola. Sometimes it's simply about doing what's right."

"I don't want your pity, Patsy. I want you to work for me. I want you to find Toni and I'll do the rest. I could have gone to someone else, but I wanted to use someone I could trust. I was wrong about you. I'll find someone new tomorrow." Nicola stepped around the table, and shuffled sideways to pass Patsy. "This isn't wrong, Patsy. This is essential. I don't need to give you my reasons, but you've made your mind up so let's leave it at that."

Nicola turned and made her way towards the door. Patsy followed her, wondering if she should change her mind and take the job. Nicola held the door open for her, and Patsy nodded her thanks as she stepped past.

"Wish John a happy birthday for me. Be happy, Patsy."

Patsy watched Nicola cross the carpark and open the door to her car. Knowing she'd regret it, she called to her, "Okay, I'll do it. I'll drop a contract in tomorrow."

Nicola flew back across the car park and hugged her. Patsy stood rigid, unable to return the hug.

"Thank you, Patsy, I am right. You'll see. I've got to go, but we'll speak tomorrow." She gave Patsy a peck on the cheek, and hugged her again.

Patsy shuddered as she watched Nicola walk back to her car. She wasn't at all sure that allowing Meredith's ex to get so close was wise.

Trump completed the update. Meredith shrugged.

"So, we have a sighting of a black Range Rover in the car park overlooking the area where the girls disappeared, but nothing to back that up on the CCTV cameras. Is the cyclist sure of the time?"

"He's definite. He had ordered a Chinese and was on his way to pick it up. He took a short cut through the park, even though cycling isn't allowed." Trump walked to the map. "If the car took this route," he drew his finger along a suburban street, "the first camera he would come to is here. And that's if he went this way. It's not much but it's more than we had an hour ago. Perhaps in the next press release we can ask for possible sightings."

Meredith screwed his nose up. "There are a lot of black Range Rovers out there. Did he know what model, the number plate, perhaps a description of the driver, anything else at all?"

"He thinks the back widows were tinted so you couldn't see in. He didn't think it was occupied, although he couldn't swear to it. He knew it was a newish shape, but not the model. He doesn't do cars, he cycles."

"Then book the bastard for cycling in a prohibited area, or riding a bike at all, because they're a menace on the roads, or for being so damned unobservant." Meredith turned to walk back to his office, but paused to look at the photos of the girls. "No other calls at all? Even a call from a fruitcake would be welcome. I've never known such a poor response to a televised appeal. Have you spoken to Dave Rawlings?"

"I spoke to him . . . Oh hang on. This is the public number." Trump hit the yellow button flashing on his phone.

The incident room fell silent, all eyes on Trump.

"Incident room, how may I help?" His rounded tones were calm, as Meredith picked up the nearest phone, and he punched in the code which would allow him to listen in on the call.

"I have the girls. I'm calling to let their parents know they're safe."

"That's very good of you, but – and please don't take this the wrong way – how can I be sure you're telling the truth?"

"Fair point. Gemma has a small mole in the crook of her elbow, and Ellen has a scar on her forehead that disappears into her hair. She was hit by a swing when she was younger."

Meredith and Trump exchanged glances. One of the most painful things a police officer had to do in such cases was get a list of any distinguishing marks from the parents. They knew the scar on Ellen's head was accurate, but they didn't know about Gemma's mole. It could be that Gemma's parents didn't consider it relevant. Meredith nodded for Trump to continue and wound his finger in circles in the air, encouraging Seaton to speed up the tracking process, which was, of course, impossible. Seaton nodded anyway, and looked back at the screen in front of him.

"Okay, I'll check that once we've finished our conversation. Assuming it is correct, how do I know they are safe and well."

"I'm phoning for that purpose. I know you're trying to track this call, so why would I bother if I was going to lie? I saw their parents on TV, and I wanted to give them a little peace of mind."

"With all due respect, sir, the peace of mind they need is to have their daughters back safe and well. Will you do that for them?"

There was a pause; it was brief, but he had to choose his words carefully so as not to raise false hopes. He didn't want them angry with him, not yet anyway.

"Ellen should be home tomorrow."

"Only Ellen, what about Gemma?"

"I'm not sure. Look, I promise her parents that whatever happens I will keep her safe and well. That will be my lifetime aim. Goodbye."

There was silence for a moment, before Meredith snapped at Seaton.

"Come on then, where is he?"

"Driving along the Downs, and over Bridge Valley Hill. Pay as you go phone. We have the number so we could try calling back later. The signal's gone now."

"Bastard. There are no cameras around there, not unless he gets caught speeding." Meredith thought for a moment. "Right. Get something down about the car, the location and the time and see if we can find which way he went from the public. You can't turn right there, so he would have had to go under the Clifton Suspension Bridge, and either double back on himself towards the city, or over the flyover and possibly away on the A38. I want to know who if anyone has cameras on those roads."

Seaton was well aware of the numerous routes available, and the chances of finding which one the caller took would be a miracle, but he kept his mouth shut.

"Trump, get me a copy of that call. I want you two in my office with it in ten minutes."

Meredith resisted the urge to slam the door of his office. Dialogue with the man was a positive thing, but someone had to tell Dave Rawlings, and someone had to ask the Lakes about the mole. He knew that should fall to him. Happy bloody birthday. He should warn Patsy it would be a late one. Slumping heavily into his chair, he dialled her number.

"It's me. We've had contact. Just. I have no idea what time I'm going to get back. I thought I should warn you."

"Oh boy. Poor Dave, does he know yet?" Patsy indicated and pulled into a parking bay.

"Nope, I've yet to have that pleasure. Are you driving?"

"No, I've parked now. I guessed you'd be tied up, so I'm doing a little digging on the new case."

"Well, keep an eye out for a suspicious black Range Rover with blacked out windows, and be careful, I've got enough on my plate. I'd ask you about it, but . . ."

"Get on with it Meredith, you can give me the details later. I'll keep the bed warm. Love you." Patsy hung up, relieved that Meredith would be unlikely to show any interest in her work until this case was over.

Patsy turned the corner onto Queens Road and scanned the fascias of the shops and bars along each side of the road. The Orchid bar was sandwiched between a rundown student letting office, and a stationery shop offering back to school kits. A board propped against a lamppost outside told her the bar offered snacks, light bites and tapas. As she had yet to eat dinner, she decided that was a definite bonus.

She smiled at the waitress as she took a table in the window and scanned the room. An older gentleman was hanging wine glasses in the racks suspended above the highly polished bar. A waiter with shocking red hair was delivering tapas to two suited men, and the waitress she had smiled at was taking an order from a couple with two teenage girls, both wearing braces. Having finished delivering the tapas, the waiter sauntered over.

"On your own, madam?" he asked as he waved a sheath of menus at her. She nodded, and he placed a menu in front of her. "Splendid, can I get you a drink while you look? I'm William, and I'll be your waiter for this evening. Oh, I should say the grilled goat's cheese is finished, as is the cheesecake." He leaned forward. "You won't believe how many people get in a strop if they order something that's not available."

"I'll have a small glass of . . ." Patsy flipped the menu over and ran her finger down the list of available wines, "Rioja please."

"Good choice. I'll be two ticks." He turned flamboyantly, before strolling slowly to the bar and calling her order. Patsy had decided on her choice by the time he returned.

"Tomato and basil bruschetta, thank you." She smiled patiently as he pulled his pencil from behind his ear, and recovered his note book from the pocket of his apron.

"Have you worked here long? I don't think I've seen you in here before."

"About a year, but I'm casual. I only work when someone lets them down. Don't get me wrong, I need the money, but I'm a medical student and the workload is incredible. I should be home now, but I've stayed on for a few weeks as they are short-staffed."

Patsy grinned at him. He was a talker, which was what she needed.

"Was the hair some form of experiment?"

"It was, but not of the medical variety. My girlfriend wasn't sure if it would suit her, and one glass of cider too many, I allowed her to test it on me. Needless to say she's not going for it." He threw his head back and laughed. "My mother will kill me when I get home. She thinks medical students should be above partying and pranks." He took back the menu. "Nothing else I can tempt you with?"

Patsy blinked. He'd winked at her, and was now nodding knowingly. She shook her head.

"Did Toni teach you everything you know? If I wasn't so broadminded I'd be offended, William." She laughed as his cheeks flushed red. "But as it happens I'm not. Did you know Toni?"

"Everyone knew Toni. Great bloke, very popular with the . . ." Realising Patsy may have been one of Toni's conquests he finished his response with, "Customers."

"Wasn't he just." Patsy laughed. "Where's he working now, is he still local?"

"I have no idea. Had some sort of family thing to sort out so went home, but was due to come back. He hasn't."

William shrugged and turned to walk away. Patsy reached her hand out and touched his arm. He stopped and turned back, wondering if he had just pulled. He smiled at her, hoping his luck with the ladies had changed. Patsy was far more up market than he was used to.

"Where's home for Toni?" Patsy watched William deflate. "You chaps in here certainly keep coming and going."

"Somewhere in Spain. Madrid, Seville . . . I can't remember. One of the big cities. I should place your order. The boss is watching."

"Yes, so I see." Patsy leaned to one side to get a clear view of the man behind the bar. "He's new. I don't know him. You go away for a couple of weeks . . ." She pulled the photograph Nicola had given her from her bag. "And him, has he gone too?"

"Ah yes. He sold out to him." William kept his head still and forced his eyes towards his manager. "Not been the same since. But the bar down on the waterfront was a good deal apparently."

"And which bar would that be?"

"The Box of Frogs. It's right at the end. Nice though." William turned as his manager coughed behind him. "I'd better go."

Patsy smiled and nodded. Perhaps she was in for a pub crawl tonight.

William tore her order from his pad and handed it across the bar. "Sorry about that, I think she's on the pull. Seems anyone will do. Keep hold of your trousers." He turned away grinning as his manager laughed, and walked to the new customers who were seating themselves at a table. "Good evening, I'm William. What can I get you to drink?"

Patsy pulled her phone from her pocket. There was still no word from Meredith. If she was going to venture further into town, she wanted company. She texted Linda.

Fancy a drink - I'm paying? But next thirty minutes or too late.

She smiled. She'd met Linda when working on her first case in Bristol, before she and Meredith had become romantically involved. When the agency had needed a computer genius, Linda came to the rescue, and was now a permanent fixture at Grainger & Co. Much to everyone's amusement she had fallen into a relationship with DS Louie Trump. Linda was loud, noisy, and colourful, whereas Louie Trump was reserved, calm, and, in Linda's words, spoke as though he were related to the queen. Linda was also indecisive with anything other than her work. It was not unknown for her to change four or five times before settling on an outfit.

Patsy's phone rang as William retuned with her order.

"You've heard then. The chaps will probably be there until the small hours." Linda rarely paused for breath. "Poor old Meredith, I bet Dave will react badly, mind you what other way is -"

"Linda shut up. What's happened?" There was a silence as Linda wondered if she, or more to the point, Louie, had spoken out of turn. "Linda, are you still there?"

"I am. Look you mustn't say anything to Meredith. I don't want Louie getting into trouble." She paused. "I need your promise, PHPI."

Patsy smiled as she heard her nickname. PHPI stood for Patsy Hodge Private Investigator.

Once Patsy had confirmed that her lips were sealed, Linda gave her the few details she had about the call from the abductor. Patsy was no longer surprised at the silence from Meredith. The two women agreed to meet outside the Hippodrome theatre.

Patsy ate half her food and beckoned over the waitress since William was opening another bottle of wine for the two men at the rear of the bar. Patsy asked for the bill. When the waitress returned, she handed her a twenty pound note and told her to keep the change.

"Oh, by the way. Do you know if Toni is still in Madrid?" Patsy pulled on her jacket as she stood up.

"Seville, and no, I haven't heard anything. Sorry." The waitress shrugged as Patsy thanked her and left the restaurant. She had been the third woman asking about Toni in as many weeks. If only he knew; they seemed to get more attractive as the weeks went by.

Patsy decided against moving her car, and with ten minutes before she had to meet Linda, she strolled down past the museum and the university building to Park Street. There were a few more people about now, and a taxi driver and a cyclist were having a heated row halfway down the hill. She was crossing the road when Meredith called.

"Sorry about that, a taxi driver and a cyclist are having a noisy difference of opinion. I'm on Park Street, it's lively. I know something has happened. Linda has invited me for a drink because Louie is otherwise engaged. Are you okay?"

"Yes, of course. We're on our way to tell Rawlings now. Trump's driving."

"Do you think the girls are okay?" Patsy knew she was really asking if he thought the girls were alive, and was relieved when he replied.

"Yes I do. He said Ellen would be back tomorrow. I have no idea how I'm going to explain that to the Lakes. I don't know what time I'll be back, but that bed had better be warm. Don't go painting the town red." A radio crackled in the background. "Got to go, enjoy yourself."

Meredith turned to Trump and nodded at the radio.

"Was that anything?"

"No, the Range Rover involved in the accident near Bristol Airport contained a family ready to embark on a holiday."

Trump turned into Dave Rawlings' street. He pulled onto the pavement and across the drive. Two reporters remained on guard. One of them climbed out of the car, throwing his cigarette into the neighbouring hedge as he did so.

"Any news of Ellen?" the reporter called.

Meredith and Trump ignored him and hurried up the path. Dave Rawlings opened the door before they got there.

"What? What's happened?"

The first flash from the camera caught his distraught face, devoid of colour. The second flash caught Meredith's snarl as he turned around. The third, the grass in Rawlings' front garden, as Meredith bounded towards its operator. Meredith put his hand on the fence and vaulted over. He caught the car door before the reporter could pull it closed.

"If you're here when I come out, this car will be towed away for being unfit to be on the road, and you'll need an ambulance to recover that camera, because I'll shove it where the sun don't shine."

The reporter nodded. "I'll go, but I'm only doing my job, same as you."

"And how exactly will your harassment of these people find those young girls? You've got thirty seconds to pull away."

Without waiting for a further response Meredith turned away. Jo Adler opened the door as he approached. He could hear Trump telling Rawlings to calm down. Jo shut the door and led him into the sitting room. Rawlings was pacing up and down in front of the mantel. An older woman was sitting with her arm around Eve and both were crying. Trump stepped back and let Meredith into the room.

"Sit down, Rawlings, and listen to me. I know this is difficult, but all this pacing isn't helping Eve any."

Rawlings sat on the edge of the chair nearest to him. Elbows on knees, he leaned forward, bouncing his heels up and down to control his impatience. It didn't work.

"Just tell us, Gov. Don't drag it out."

Meredith took him at his word. "We've had a call from a bloke claiming to have the girls. He described the scar on Ellen's forehead, and a mole in the crook of Gemma's elbow. We need to see the Lakes to get confirmation."

"She has." Eve's voice was hoarse, and she coughed. Jo picked up a glass from the coffee table and handed it to her. Everyone looked at Eve as she sipped the water. Handing the glass to the woman next to her, Eve stretched out her arm.

"It's here. Tina got it checked out in case it was cancerous. It wasn't." She placed the index finger of her right finger into the crook of the opposite elbow.

Meredith nodded curtly. "With that confirmed it seems likely he was genuine. He called to assure the parents that the girls were safe. He told us Ellen should be home tomorrow."

"Oh thank God." Eve dissolved into silent sobs, her shoulders rising and falling in the arms of the woman holding her.

Rawlings feet stilled. "Did you believe him?"

"As much as you can, yes. He seemed genuinely sorry for the concern he had caused, but Dave, he said 'should be' home. Not 'will be'. Don't get your hopes up." Meredith blew out a breath and tried to relax. He wanted a cigarette and he could murder a drink.

"What about Gemma? What did he say about Gemma?"

"He didn't really." Meredith jerked his head towards the door. "I need a ciggy. I commandeered a pack from old George, do you want to join me?"

Rawlings shot a glance at Eve, who had missed the unspoken words, and nodded. The four police officers left the room. It was a warm evening but Rawlings felt chilled to the bone, and pulled a sweater off the back of a chair in the kitchen on the way to the garden. As his head appeared through the top, he called to Meredith who was already in the garden.

"What did he say about Gemma?"

Meredith held his hand up, and beckoned Jo forward.

"There were a couple of reporters around. Check they're not still here. If they are, book them for trespass."

He pulled the sleeve of Rawlings' sweater, and took him to the bottom of the garden. Jo waved the all clear, having checked the left-hand boundary, before disappearing down the side of the house towards the front garden.

"You're scaring me now, Gov. What did he say."

Trump gave a shout, and awkwardly cleared the fence near the back door. There was a groan from the other side. Trump's head reappeared.

"I seem to have found a burglar, sir. Attempting to break in next door. I'll take him away if that's all right with you."

"I'm not a burglar! I'm a reporter I work for . . . OW!"

"Sorry, sir, it's quite dark here, was that your ear?"

"No, you bastard, it was my nose, now . . . OW"

"Watch where you're walking, sir, you'll hurt yourself."

Trump led the man away. Meredith turned back to Rawlings.

"He said Ellen should be home tomorrow, but when Trump pushed him about Gemma he got tongue tied. He told Trump to assure the Lakes he would make it his lifelong quest, or something like that, to make sure she was always safe. The inference being they might not see her again, that he was keeping her. I know . . ."

Meredith stopped speaking as Dave Rawlings lurched away from him and threw up in the flower border. He was still retching when Jo Adler came back. Jo paled and her eyes darted from Meredith to Rawlings, as she wondered if something had happened she didn't know about. Meredith walked over and patted Rawlings on the back.

"I know, mate. It's shit. I've got to go now. I have to see the Lakes. I'm not giving them all the detail, so what I've told you remains between us. Don't tell Eve, there's no point in worrying anyone until we have more information."

Rawlings straightened up. "Would you have told me if it was the other way around?"

Meredith considered this for a moment. "No, not yet I wouldn't." He walked back to the house. "Go to bed, Rawlings, get some sleep. Tomorrow could be a long day. Adler, make sure they go to bed. Soon."

He stepped into the kitchen and walked slowly back to the sitting room. Eve Rawlings had calmed and was blowing her nose as he returned. She pushed the tissue into her pocket and jumped to her feet.

"Thank you, John. Thank you." She walked to him, and he hugged her.

"It's early days, Eve, early days. But if Ellen does come home tomorrow, you'll need some energy. I suggest you and Dave get some rest." He smiled as he pushed her away. "Sleep, you hear me."

"That's what Mum said." She sniffed and smiled at the woman on the couch.

"Mums are always right. I've got to go, I'll see you tomorrow." He lifted her hand and kissed it.

Trump was leaning on the gate post.

"What did you do with him?" Meredith asked as he reached him.

"He ran off down the road, sir." Trump nodded at the empty space in front of his car. "They moved the car though. Is Rawlings okay?"

"Not so you'd notice, no. Come on, there's no point in delaying this."

Meredith climbed into Trump's car and slammed the door. As the car turned into the next street, Meredith ordered Trump to stop the car. He pointed across the road.

"They're waiting for us to go before they take their old spot back."

Climbing out of Trump's car he crossed the road. When he reached the reporter's car, he lifted his foot, and rammed his heel into the rear brake light. The plastic casing shattered. The driver jumped out. Meredith pointed down at the road.

"I warned you about this car. Get that mess cleared up and get on your way. I'm calling this in when I get back to the car. I'd hate for you to be towed. Expensive job that."

Lighting a cigarette, he walked slowly back to Trump. Trump pondered whether or not to ask him to put the cigarette out as he got back into the car. Deciding against it, he looked at Meredith.

"Open the window please, sir. There's a good chap."

The Lakes' home was only a few streets away, and Meredith flicked the cigarette out of the window as they approached. Any reporters who were there, remained in their cars. Meredith tapped on the glazed panel in the front door. The liaison officer opened it and nodded at the sitting room door.

The Lakes were sitting hand in hand on the couch. Their eyes followed Meredith as he walked and stood in front of the mantel. The homemade card was still there, and drawing in a breath he turned to face them.

"We've heard from the girls' abductor. It's not much and we were unable to trace the number, but he was moved by the appeal, and assured us it was not his intention to hurt the girls. In fact, he said he would ensure they were not hurt in anyway."

Kevin Lake jumped to his feet and began pacing the small room.

"That's it. That's all he had to say? How do we know they're safe? What help is that to us?" He stopped pacing in front of Meredith and held his hands out. "Did he give any indication of when he would let them come home? Did he say he would let them come home?"

Meredith closed his eyes and sighed. He was going to have to lie, or at least avoid telling the truth. He hated doing it, but to tell them what had been said would only give them further cause for concern.

"I asked of course, but he wasn't specific. He indicated that they may be home soon." He looked down at the floor, unable to meet Lake's eye.

"Indicated? That might be promising. Exactly what did he say? Can I hear it, have you recorded it?"

"We did record it, yes sir." Trump answered the question, and Lake spun to look at him. "But it's being analysed at the moment. It was a short call and we know it was made from the Downs area, but he was in a car, so it didn't help us much."

Meredith chewed his lip. Trump lied well. There was no help an analyst could give them, except perhaps to tell them where the man originated from, but what good would that do? He stepped forward and placed his hand on Lake's shoulder.

"We are going to have to go now. We need to prepare an updated press release in time for tonight's local news bulletin." Meredith applied pressure to Lake's shoulder, encouraging him to sit next to his wife. He did and he took her hand. Meredith gave them a brief smile. "We will be appealing for him to get in touch again. Sometimes these people need to talk." He turned and nodded at Trump, who opened the door. "We'll leave you now, but I promise we'll be in contact if anything else happens."

Meredith strode up the path quickly, eager to be away. He pulled on the door handle of Trump's car before Trump had time to unlock it, and rolled his eyes in irritation.

"How could I tell him?" he asked as he slammed the car door with such force that Trump winced.

"You couldn't. There was no point." Trump sighed as Meredith pulled out his cigarettes. "You really shouldn't, you know. You've only recently recovered from a punctured lung. I thought you'd given up."

To Trump's surprise, Meredith nodded and slid the packet back into his pocket.

"Then feed me. Take me to the nearest fish and chip shop. I need comfort food."

They stopped at Meredith's favourite fish bar, and bought enough food for the team. An hour later the incident room smelled of fish and vinegar, and they watched the phones, waiting for something to happen.

CHAPTER FIVE

Linda linked her arm through Patsy's as they strolled along the waterfront. "So, you're going to work for her then. What does she want you to do?" What do any of them want me to do? Find a man!" Patsy stopped walking and turned to her friend and colleague. "I need you to promise me this conversation goes no further, not even to Louie, who I know is the soul of discretion." She waited for Linda to nod agreement. "I mean it, Linda, this promise is as a friend."

Linda's hands flew to her hips. "Of course. What are you suggesting, that as a work colleague I would blab?" She shook her head, clearly disappointed with the doubt Patsy had cast on her ability to keep a confidence. "Tell me what you have to say before I get offended." She took Patsy's arm and pulled her in the direction of the bar.

"I'm sorry. Work first and then Nicola. I . . . I . . . Oh God, Linda, I think I made the wrong choice when I left the police force. Don't get me wrong, I love working with you lot, and I like the freedom it gives me. But it's not earth shattering, or life changing, is it? Nicola aside for one moment, if I thought that I would spend the rest of my career looking for blokes who had disappeared for one reason or another, I'd pack it in now."

It was Linda's turn to stop walking, but she kept hold of Patsy's arm, making her stop too.

"That statement is so wrong, I don't know where to start." Tutting, she started to walk again, only this time at a quicker pace. "I need a drink now, and I need to look you in the eye when we have this conversation. So shut up until we get there."

The subtle lighting in the bar filtered through dark wood rafters over the sprinkling of customers, and soft music floated around the room through concealed speakers. Linda attempted to remain aloof and calm as they waited for their drinks, refusing to start a conversation until there would be no interruptions.

Patsy held back the smile as she watched Linda rein in her impatience. Linda surveyed their surroundings.

"Nice place. I've not been here before. I hope the service is good, it should be, it's not too busy. But then it is mid-week, so that's to be expected."

"Linda, stop with the small talk. I'm sorry if I threw you, but it's how I felt when Nicola told me what she wanted. If she'd said she'd found she had a sister who was adopted, or an elderly uncle had left her some money but a cousin claimed she wasn't related, I would be fine. But here I go again," Patsy threw an arm into the air. "I want you to find my missing . . . husband, boyfriend, child's father." She sighed, "I don't know, I just have this feeling of being hemmed in." Linda raised her eyebrows as Patsy continued to rant. "I knew I would never get exciting cases, not really, but I need more than this somehow. How do you generate different in this business? As a police officer you dealt with what was thrown at you, and I know it's sort of the same, but . . ." She stopped speaking. "I've made my point, haven't I?" She laughed as Linda rolled her eyes. "Sorry." She slapped her own wrist.

"Not that much, PHPI. I think you're feeling sorry for yourself, but I have no idea why." Pausing, she smiled at the waitress walking towards them, but unable to wait added, "PHPI suits you. If you changed jobs I'd have to find something else."

The waitress placed the drinks on the table. Linda lifted her glass, chinked it against Patsy's and took a sip.

"Can you remember how chuffed you were when the sign writer finished your office door? Patsy Hodge Private Investigator." Linda swept her hand in front of Patsy's face. "The best PI in Bristol, in fact, let's be honest, the South West, if not England! You help people, Patsy. You help people that have nowhere else to turn. If you were a police officer you wouldn't have been able to help Stella Young or Nicola. The police aren't able to stop everything and find missing people in the way you can. I don't know what man Nicola is after, but I'll bet it's not anything the police could help with, is it?" She took another sip. Patsy didn't answer. "Is it?"

Patsy shook her head. "No. I understand what you're saying but -"

"No buts. If you were a police officer at the moment, who would you be looking for? A man. Granted a man that has kidnapped two little girls, but the principle is the same. Actually, I shouldn't have used that as an example. It does make our work pale into insignificance, but you must get my point."

Patsy held her hands up, unconvinced, but eager to change the subject.

"Okay, okay. I provide a vital public service. I accept I was simply having a moment. And as I'm here for work, we should probably concentrate on that."

"Which brings us neatly to Nicola. Which man does she want you to find?"

"The chap she thinks is the father of her son. She says she doesn't want him herself, but wants her son to know his father." Patsy shrugged. "I don't want to do it, but for some reason I couldn't refuse."

"There you go. My point exactly; if you didn't help her, who would? Not the police, they can't. Patsy, you really do provide a vital and necessary service. Unfortunately, at the moment it seems to be men that are disappearing. Next week it could be a grandmother . . . actually that doesn't sound very exciting. Another bad choice as an example." Linda leaned across the table and patted Patsy's hand lightly. "Why is it such a secret? You can't possibly think Meredith would care . . . do you?"

Linda looked concerned, and wondered if she had put her foot in it once more.

"As it happens I think he might, in the protective, need to control, Meredith sort of way." Patsy shook her head. "But as it happens it's because Nicola asked me to. I've already broken that promise, which is why it's important you keep this to yourself."

Patsy's attention was drawn to the bar as two of the staff called out to a man standing in the doorway holding a small bag. She looked at him and smiled: it was the man she'd come to find. Linda followed her gaze as the man thrust his hand into the air.

"I came. I saw. I conquered," he called, grinning. "Fresh mint, the mojitos are back on the menu." The man walked to the bar, smiling and nodding acknowledgement to the customers as he went. His eyes lingered at their table and Linda gave him her best smile.

"Hmmm. Nice. Is that him? Is that Nicola's bloke?" She turned back to Patsy and grinned. "I'm not quite sure how you can complain about this job, you know."

"No, but he's best friends with Toni, the chap I'm after, or so she thinks."

"Well, let's find out. You like mojitos, don't you? You may need a taxi home."

Before Patsy answered, Linda was on her feet and walking to the bar. Patsy watched as Linda swung her hips in a manner Patsy had never noticed before. Patsy's eyes widened a little, as she wondered whether inviting Linda had been a good thing. Linda leaned against the bar, squashing what little cleavage she had forward.

"Did you say mojito?" she demanded. "Listen . . . sorry, what's your name?"

The man grinned and she swooned a little. "Stephen, and yours is?"

"Linda. Listen, Stephen, I had the best mojito ever made on holiday in Cuba. I've not found one to even match it, let alone beat it. If you manage, I'll let you join us."

Stephen laughed. "Oh really, that's too kind of you. Just the one, or are you both wanting to sample my wares?"

Linda threw her head back and laughed. It caused the other staff and several of the customers to turn their heads. She leaned even further across the bar.

"You are a very cheeky and, I hope, talented man. Make it two." She winked and to Patsy's horror repeated the walk on her return to their table.

Linda jerked her head back towards him. "Is he watching me?" she asked in a forced whisper.

"Linda, sit down. Everyone is watching you."

Patsy covered her face in mock horror. Linda sat, and neck stiff to stop her looking, she added, "I don't want everyone else to join us. Did he watch my sexy walk?"

"Sexy?" Unable to control herself, Patsy dissolved into giggles. She was still dabbing her eyes when Stephen arrived with the drinks.

Linda pulled out a free stool and patted it. "Join us for a moment, Stephen. You will need me to sample your offerings before you disappear."

Patsy clamped her bottom lip between her teeth as Linda fluttered her eyelashes, and her eyes filled with tears of mirth again. If nothing else, being with Linda was good for the soul. She smiled a lopsided smile as Stephen straddled the stool. Linda picked up the drink and sipped a little through the colourful straw. She smacked her lips before taking a larger sip. As she drew the liquid up the straw and into her mouth, her eyebrows rose and she gave a nod.

Stephen smiled. "You'll not get better this side of the pond." He leaned forward. "I'm a master at cocktails."

Linda released the straw and, lips still pursed, blew him a kiss. "I think you could be right." She pointed at Patsy's glass. "Patsy, try it. It's to die for."

Patsy lifted the drink as Stephen turned his attention to her. She sipped the cocktail and nodded. "Fabulous. Thank you, Stephen. As Linda says, you are a talented man."

"Oh, there's more to my repertoire than cocktails. I have many skills." He smiled. "I haven't seen you ladies in here before. Are you celebrating or just chilling after a long day at the office?"

"We're here on business, actually. Private investigators. We'd like to ask you a few questions." Linda crossed her legs, and folded her arms onto the table, leaning closer to him.

Stephen's smile dropped away, and he frowned at Linda. "Questions? What about?" His guard was up.

Patsy's eye's narrowed at Linda. She placed her drink down, and held up her arms in mock frustration.

"Excuse Linda's bull-at-a-gate style of introduction." Patsy held out her hand. "Patsy Hodge. I am a private investigator but I'm not investigating you. I'm actually looking for a friend of yours. I have good news to deliver."

Stephen turned to Patsy, his frown remaining. "Who and what news." He held his hands up. "Forgive me, ladies, but it's not often people like you," he waved his finger back and forth, "looking like you, turn up and announce you're investigators." He watched as Patsy pulled a business card from her purse. He took it, and quickly scanned the details before looking back. "Okay, so you're kosher. What can I do for you?"

"I've been hired to find Antonio Garcia. I understand he's a friend of yours, and you worked together at the Orchid. I know he went home to Seville for a while, and during that time you opened The Box of Frogs. I wondered if you knew where he's living, now he's back."

"He's back? I hadn't heard that. I only spoke to him a few days ago. He didn't mention he was coming back." Stephen inclined his head. "You wouldn't be lying to me, would you?"

"No, no. Of course not. I got that information from William at the Orchid." Patsy cursed herself for exaggerating her knowledge. "It didn't sound quite right, I have to admit. He had no details of where and when et cetera. Although, I have no idea why he wouldn't tell the truth." She shrugged as she lifted her drink. "Sorry to have wasted your time. At least we got a decent mojito out of it. Sorry."

"Don't apologise, I got to sit with two beautiful women." Stephen leaned forward, hands on knees. "To the best of my knowledge Toni is still in Seville with his mother. His father died, and he went home to sort things out with her. They are not a wealthy family, and he called from an uncle's house. He didn't want to use his UK mobile, as it would cost too much."

"If you don't mind me asking, why did he call?" Patsy smiled encouragement. "Is he likely to come back to the UK?"

With a little more prompting, Stephen told them all he knew. Antonio was in Bristol studying law. He was due to start his final year in September. He'd done a year's placement with a local solicitor, and while that paid well, he still worked all the hours he could to add to his savings. He had to survive another year as a student, with little or no help from his family. His father had died unexpectedly, and he'd gone home to help his mother. It was his intention to come back at the beginning of September. The purpose of his call to Stephen had been twofold: first to secure himself somewhere to stay when he returned, and second to get work.

"I told him I had a bed for him. It's only a pull-out couch but it'll do. I also promised him some shifts here until he gets something more permanent." Stephen shrugged an apology. "But I don't know his address in Spain. Is it financial, this good news? Is it likely to help him? He's a good bloke, it would be nice to think so."

"I can't say I'm afraid, confidential. Thanks for your help, Stephen. You have my number, please would you ask him to call me when you hear from him."

"Will do. Perhaps we can keep in touch? I . . ." His smile fell away as a man entered the bar. "Oh no, not again." He nodded to one of the other staff as, with a furrowed brow, he watched the man take a seat. "His quest is the same as yours but for different reasons."

Patsy gave the man a casual glance. He was about forty, with thick, dark wavy hair. He was handsome in a conventional way, but had a look of distaste on his face, which made him appear unapproachable. Linda swivelled round to look at him, and turned back eyes wide, tapping the table excitedly with her finger.

"That's whatshisname. Jeremy Carmichael," she exclaimed, none too quietly. The name was vaguely familiar to Patsy, but she couldn't place it.

"Who's Jeremy Carmichael?" She put her finger to her lips in the hope that Linda would lower the volume of her response. In the event, it was Stephen who answered.

"He's a controlling, manipulating bastard, and a second-rate actor." Stephen didn't care that Carmichael knew they were talking about him. When he looked at the man, he did nothing to conceal his dislike. Carmichael grimaced, and made a show of opening a broadsheet newspaper as he snapped his order to the waitress.

"He used to be DI Thingy, in the police series on the television. *Green Street*. He was the one with the psychic wife. He always got her to help him solve the crimes. He lives here in Bristol." Linda attempted to trigger Patsy's memory.

Patsy began nodding. "Oh I know, well I don't, I never saw it, but he's in the new play at the Old Vic, isn't he? Amanda has bought tickets for Meredith for his birthday. She . . ." Patsy stopped speaking as Linda choked on her drink.

"Meredith? The theatre, really? You can't even get him to go to the cinema. Is she mad?"

"I did mention that, but Amanda says it's had good reviews, and some culture would do him good." She turned to Stephen, "But that's a different story. You say he's looking for Antonio Garcia too, why? Do you know?"

"Toni had a brief thing with his PA. He'd go to rehearsals, and she used to come into the Orchid while he was in the theatre. She liked Toni, she came a lot. They saw each other for a while." He shot a glance at Carmichael. "Toni said she had an affair with Carmichael, but it hadn't worked out. When she got involved with Toni, Carmichael didn't like the fact that he wasn't the centre of her world, and he made life very difficult for her. Even came into the bar one night and caused a scene. Toni told her to stand up for herself, and she did." Stephen smiled as he spoke. "It was quite something to watch, but it backfired, and he sacked her in front of a full house."

Linda's hands flew to her mouth. "The bastard. What happened?"

"Toni showed him out quite forcibly, and she stayed with Toni for a few days. It may have been longer. Carmichael bombarded her with calls, and promised her a part in the new play. She was an actress originally, and she took the job as his PA when she had no other work." Stephen shook his head. "I don't know if she was any good, perhaps she couldn't get the break she needed." He shrugged. "Anyway, she broke up with Toni, who I have to confess wasn't heartbroken. It wasn't a big love job, but he was concerned for her. Carmichael was a bully." Stephen sighed. "As I understand it, he didn't make good his promise, told her she was crap, and she went back to running around after him. Then, one night she turns up with a black eye, looking for Toni. He wasn't on that night, and she told me to tell him she was free. She'd told Carmichael what he could do with his job and was going home."

"What happened? Why is he looking for Toni?" Linda stopped sipping her drink, and her eyes darted back and forth between the two men.

"Because she's disappeared, and Carmichael thinks she's with him. He made quite a speech one night. He can't hold his drink though, and he likes to make a scene. That's the actor in him I guess." Stephen rolled his eyes. "It's annoying to the other customers, so I let him sit there until he becomes a pain. It's sad really;

he obviously wants her back, but as he's tied to the job here, he's limited to where he can look. I'm lumbered with him." Stephen stood and smiled down at them. "I'd better get back. Enjoy your drinks. I'll call if I hear from Toni." He leaned towards Patsy. "You never know, I might call anyway."

Patsy put her hand on his arm. "Is there any chance she is with Toni?"

"Don't know. I doubt it. I think he would have mentioned it, but stranger things have happened."

As Stephen walked away, Carmichael raised his hand and clicked his fingers.

"Waiter, I think this beer is off." His theatrical voice boomed around the bar. "Bring me a fresh one."

They watched as Stephen went and had a quiet word, pointing at the door as he spoke. Carmichael didn't get a fresh beer, but went back to reading his newspaper. Linda watched him, giving a running commentary as she finished Patsy's mojito as well as her own. Patsy wanted to drive home. Before they left, Patsy went to the bar to thank Stephen, and remind him to pass the message on.

"No problem, Patsy. How could I forget you?" He smiled and looked at Linda, "Or the lovely Linda. A man could be . . . Shit!"

He flew out from behind the bar as a glass smashed, and Carmichael's chair fell to the floor. Stephen led an unsteady and complaining Carmichael to the door, and saw him out. He watched as Carmichael made his wavering way along the footpath. He held the door for Patsy and Linda.

"With any luck, he'll fall in. Just kidding," he added quickly as Patsy tutted. "Goodnight, and good luck, ladies."

"Thanks, Stephen. What was her name, by the way? His PA. It might come in useful, you never know."

"Beth Durham. I don't think it will help you though. I doubt Toni's with her."

"Perhaps not. Thanks again." Patsy waved as Linda took her arm.

Patsy and Linda followed Carmichael along the river until he had safely reached the city centre. The fresh air must have sobered him somewhat, and after a couple of hundred yards he was far steadier on his feet. Content he wouldn't drown, the two women hurried past, and Patsy drove them home.

Trump's car was parked outside Linda's house.

"Has Louie moved in, Linda? You didn't say."

"No, not yet anyway. But we have this thing, where if he was supposed to see me but couldn't because of work, he has to come when he's finished." She got out of the car and leaned back in smiling. "He needs to relieve the stress, you know."

"And that requires a key to the house?"

"Of course, otherwise I'd have to stay in. Look what I would have missed tonight if he didn't have one. See you tomorrow, PHPI. And remember, that stands for Patsy Hodge, Private Investigator, and not Patsy Hodge, Pretty Irritating." She laughed, slammed the door, and walked away.

Patsy crossed her fingers as she drove away. Hopefully, Meredith would be home too. She smiled when she found he was. Hopefully, he would need some stress relief too. She was greeted by a snore as she let herself into the house. Meredith was lying fully clothed on the sofa, and snoring loudly. A bottle of wine stood next to an almost full glass. He'd fallen asleep before even managing a drink. That was new. As quietly as she could she hung her jacket on the newel post.

"And what time of night do you call this to slink in? Is this how I am to celebrate my birthday? Alone, with only a bottle to keep me company?" he called from the sitting room.

Patsy walked in and leaned over the back of the settee to kiss him. "I thought you'd be tied up all evening, so I thought I'd start this new case off."

"I've not been in long. Grab a glass, I want to catch the local news." Meredith picked up the remote control as Patsy went to the kitchen. "How did you get on anyway? What is this new investigation that takes you out in the evening?" he called as the television came to life.

He swung his legs off the sofa and picked up his glass. The national news reader was discussing the current hike in the property market with an expert, and he lowered the volume.

Patsy returned with her glass and his pile of birthday cards. She handed them to him, and he tapped them on his knee as she filled her glass.

"Happy birthday, Johnny." She raised her glass. "You do have to open them at some stage, you know. Ignoring them doesn't make you a year younger," she nudged him as she sat down, "and you don't have to do cartwheels around the room either. I know now is a really tough time, these might cheer you a little."

She watched as Meredith wrinkled his nose.

"I doubt that very much, but if you insist." He tore open the envelope of the top card. It was from his sister and had a set of golf clubs on the front. He waved it at Patsy. "No imagination. I don't even play golf." Meredith dropped the card onto the table, and opened the next envelope.

He did smile at some of the more amusing cards, and even showed Patsy one or two of them. She had purposely placed the cards from Amanda and herself at the bottom of the pile, and she encouraged him to continue. When he had almost completed the task, and had four or five cards to go, he paused as he scanned the message written in one of them, and re-read it, shaking his head.

"What is it? Is the joke too sophisticated for you?" Patsy held her hand out, and after a second's hesitation Meredith handed it over.

"Bemused, I think the word is. She's clearly still not well." Meredith sighed and opened the next card. Small foil stars fell over his lap, and a mechanical voice called out "Birthday greetings" before bursting into laughter. Meredith smiled and looked at Patsy who was still reading the message from Nicola.

Happy birthday, John. I hope you have a great birthday and that life is being kind to you. I thought I should write to thank you for all you tried to cope with, and let you know I appreciate your efforts now that I have the benefit of hindsight. It's comforting to know that there is someone out there I can always depend on. Have a drink for me. Love Nicola x

"I have no idea why. You know that, don't you? I haven't spoken to the woman for months."

"I didn't say you had, and I'm not sure why you think that would upset me." Patsy added the card to the pile. She wondered whether now was a good time to mention that Nicola had also been in touch with her. She decided against it, and smiled at Meredith. "Finish opening your cards."

Meredith held her gaze. He could see she was troubled about something, and assumed it was the card. Inclining his head, he held out his hand and Patsy gave it a squeeze.

"I don't want any complications, Patsy. Our life together is simple. There's me and there's you. That's it, I swear on . . . Oh yes, and there's Amanda, when she's here. I think you know what I'm saying."

"I do. I've said. Now finish opening your cards."

Sighing, Meredith picked up the final three envelopes, a frown now creasing his brow. The first he opened had a picture of an orangutan showing his teeth to the camera, in what appeared to be a forced smile. The card was from Linda, who said she'd seen it and thought of him. He shook his head and placed it on the pile. As he opened the card from Amanda, an envelope from inside the card fell to the floor. He smiled at her message before bending to retrieve it. Prising open the flap, he withdrew the contents and frowned. There were three tickets for the theatre.

"A play?" he turned to Patsy. "I don't do theatre. Tell me it's not arty." His nose wrinkled, and he looked as though he had a nasty taste in his mouth.

Patsy laughed. "She wanted something you could do together," she shrugged. "I get to come too, and she wanted something different."

"Hmmm. I suppose I'll have to go then." He scrutinised the ticket. This is two days away, I'm not sure I'll be able to go." He tutted. "If this case is still running, I can't be sitting on my hands in a theatre. What's *Dammed If You Do* anyway?"

"Apparently, it's about a man trying to find his place in the world, mostly unsuccessfully. It was described as a light comedy with an underlying message." Patsy laughed at the look of horror on Meredith's face. "And . . . I saw the star of the show tonight. He'd had one too many, but Linda was thrilled."

"Oh God, this sounds worse and worse. How is Loopy? I'm still trying to forget her dancing. Funny, but it should definitely be on the banned list."

"If you thought that was funny, you should have seen her sexy walk tonight." Patsy laughed at the memory. "She has no shame. I don't think she has ever been embarrassed in her whole life. This actor chap apparently played some TV detective. I can't remember what she said the programme was called. I hope he's sober when he performs for you."

"I don't care, I think I might need a few myself." He picked up the last card. "Last one." He gave her a knowing look. "I wonder why this is at the bottom of the pile."

From nowhere Patsy got cold feet. She leaned forward and snatched the card.

"Let's do this later, now I would . . ." The picture on the television caught her eye. "Quick, volume. Here's your news item."

Meredith increased the volume and turned to face the television.

"Police are continuing their search for the two missing school girls, Gemma Lake, and Ellen Rawlings. A spokesperson has confirmed that a man claiming to be their abductor has contacted the incident room. He advised officers that the girls are safe and well. While it is unlikely to be of little comfort to the girls'

parents, he has promised to take care of them. The girls went missing from this park yesterday evening."

The picture changed and a sweeping shot of the park replaced the girls' photographs. The camera then focused on the gap in the hedge leading to the car park, and then a shot of the car park appeared.

"A man cycling through the park at the time of the girls' disappearance claims to have seen a black Range Rover parked in the car park. Police have asked the driver to come forward so he can be eliminated from their enquiries. If you saw a car like this," a still of a modern Range Rover appeared, *"in the vicinity of the park yesterday evening, please contact the police. The number of the incident room is showing on the bottom of the screen. Let's hope they're returned home soon. We will have a further update in our early morning bulletin. In other news."*

Meredith switched off the television and turned to Patsy.

"Take me to bed, Hodge."

Patsy slid the card down the side of the sofa, and placed her glass on the table. Standing she held out her hand and pulled Meredith to his feet. The foils stars and glitter caught in the creases of his trousers fluttered to the floor.

"Leave it. I'll do it tomorrow." She pulled him forward, and switching off the light as they left the room, she led him upstairs.

Satisfied he'd done his best, he didn't wait until the door to the garage had closed before he rushed into the house. He paused in the kitchen to listen to the monitor. It was silent. Tapping the code into the keypad he slowly opened the door so as not to disturb the girls. Despite his care it creaked loudly, and he winced as he scanned the room. As he had hoped the girls were sleeping. They'd eaten half the pizza, all the ice cream, and finished their drinks. They should now sleep until the next morning. He ejected the DVD, switched off the television and tidied the room. Ellen stirred and turned her back on Gemma, whose arm hung over the side of the bed. Carefully he lifted her arm and laid it across her chest. She was still wearing the pink satin princess skirt. He realised she'd get too hot in it, but he had to check if his account had been updated, so he left her uncovered, deciding to undress her later.

Back in the kitchen he left the tray of dishes on the breakfast bar, and crossed the fingers on one hand as he lifted the screen on the laptop with the other. He refreshed the screen. It told him his results would be there in two hours. He shook his head and snarled at the screen, angry that they kept changing the time. That would be far too late for him to do anything this evening. He'd have both the girls for another night.

He went to bed and slept fitfully, but as dawn broke he gave up and climbed out of bed. He checked on the girls, who slept soundly, unaware he was watching them, before going to the kitchen. Drinking straight from a carton of orange juice, he walked to the laptop. As he clicked the mouse, the screen cast a glow across the table. He leaned forward to see if his account had been updated. His breath caught in his throat, and he held it in as he clicked on the green box which announced it had. His shoulders sagged, and he drew in a ragged breath as he read the brief, but negative, message.

That was no good. No good at all.

He would take Gemma home with Ellen, and he'd have to use the people carrier. There was no point in taking chances and using the Range Rover, not if people were on the lookout for it. Now it was a question of timing. He sighed. Now was as good a time as any.

CHAPTER SIX

Peggy Green growled deep in her throat. She didn't want to wake up yet but reluctantly she opened one eye. It was light, and she cursed. She closed the eye and pulled the blanket tighter; a few more minutes would be good. Then she cursed again as she realised what had woken her. She needed to pee. Peggy wondered it if was worth getting up. She could simply do it where she lay, and then go back to sleep. But common sense prevailed. She knew she'd regret it; she had the last time.

Throwing back the blanket she sat up, and grimaced as the pain shot through her back. Grumbling to herself, she stood up and attempted to stretch. The pain returned and she lowered her arms. Kicking an empty bottle out of her way, she hobbled to the corner. The bottle cracked as it hit the wall. Struggling to hold her coat out of the way, whilst she fumbled with the belt securing her oversized tracksuit bottoms, Peggy cursed some more for good measure. She gave up attempting to undo the belt, and simply pulled it up towards her chest. She pulled down the bottoms, before peeling the thermal long johns away from her body. She didn't notice the odour of stale urine and sweat she had released. Bending at the knees, she poked her backside out and released her bladder. The murky yellow urine formed a puddle around her feet. She gave a contented sigh, as she passed wind. There was nothing quite like the first pee of the day.

The coffee shop would open soon, and if Dot was working she'd get yesterday's buns. They called them stale, but they never were. Peggy smiled and shuffled back to get her meagre belongings. As she slung the strap of the hold-all over her shoulder, she paused and inclined her head. Someone was keen to get in. Peggy knew from the light filtering through the gaps in the concrete supports it was still early. Certainly not yet seven o'clock so the car park wasn't open. She shuffled down the ramp leading to the exit. Sure enough, there was the car in front of the barrier to the entrance. She couldn't quite see the driver, but knew that he was reading the sign which some genius had placed on a wall only visible once you had driven up to the barrier. Peggy cackled, as she watched the man reverse back down the ramp. Her stomach rumbled and she smacked her lips together, wondering what she would be given for breakfast. Custard slices were her favourite.

As she reached the exit she had to jump to one side as the car was now reversing up the exit ramp towards her. This jarred her back, and she muttered some swear words.

"And people say I'm mad. Idiot!"

Turning sideways, she shuffled slowly through the gap between the car and the wall. She saw the two girls asleep on the back seat. She'd had one of those once. She screwed up her eyes to get rid of the memory, and thumped the wing of the car.

"Stupid bastard," she yelled. Not wanting to hear the response, she hurried down the ramp, and out onto the street.

The driver's heart rate had increased, and, head bent forward, he let out a sigh of relief. It was only a tramp. Knowing he needed to move quickly, he swung into action. Placing the clown hat and mask on his head, he turned off the engine, and climbed out of the car. He called to the girls as he opened the rear door.

"Wake up, girls. Your parents are waiting." Gemma opened her eyes first and smiled at him. He returned her smile, wishing that she'd been the one. "Quickly now, or we'll be late. Give Ellen a prod."

The two girls held his hands as he led them out onto the main street.

"I'm still tired." Ellen rubbed one eye with the knuckle of her free hand. "Where are we going?"

"Home. That's good, isn't it?" He watched as they nodded in unison. Turning the corner, he saw the lights in the café were on. Perfect timing. He walked a little further with them. "Oh no," he gasped, "I've forgotten to lock the car. I'll have to go back." He knelt down between the two girls. "You see that café there, that's where your parents are coming to pick you up. You go on over, and I'll catch you up."

"Are we having breakfast there?" Gemma asked.

"I expect so. Take these now, in case I forget to give you them later." He pulled a tissue from his pocket. It contained two of the tin soldiers. He polished them with the tissue, and gave one to each of the girls, so now they'd have something of his.

Ellen inspected hers. "This is my favourite one. Thank you, Charlie," she grinned, as she twirled the little figure between her fingers.

Behind his mask, his face had frozen. She'd called him Charlie. He swallowed. "Why did you call me Charlie? That's not my name." There was a desperate quality to his voice.

"Because you're a clown. All clowns are called Charlie or Coco. I don't think you're a Coco."

Relief swept through him, and he released the breath he'd been holding and stood up.

"Hold hands to cross the road. I'll watch from here, and then go and lock the car." He watched Gemma slip the soldier into her pocket and take Ellen's hand. "Bye, girls. Look after the soldiers, and they'll look after you."

Neither girl noticed he had said goodbye. He walked backwards as he watched them skip across the road, only turning away when Ellen put her soldier into her pocket, as she needed both hands free to open the café door. Pulling off the hat, he turned, and hurried back to the car.

Peggy shuffled out of the lane that led to the rear of the café, frowning. "Look after the soldiers?" she mumbled. "That doesn't make sense, they're only small."

Shrugging, she pulled a doughnut from the carrier bag and took a large bite. She ignored the jam that trickled down her chin, gave one chew, and shoved the rest into her mouth. Chomping loudly, with sugar and dough spraying from her lips, she shuffled past the café, and on towards her favourite park bench.

Meredith was gazing at the sleeping Patsy, wondering whether to get back into bed with her, when his phone rang.

"That answers that question," he mumbled as he zipped up his trousers and went to answer it. He glanced at the screen. It was the station. "Meredith." He sat on the edge of the bed, and slipped his feet into his shoes. Patsy opened her eyes and smiled at him. She jumped as he sprang to his feet. "They what? When?" He looked at the clock – it was six minutes to seven. "Who's there? Anyone told Rawlings? Right, get both sets of parents to the station, I'm on my way."

Patsy sat up. "The girls?"

"Yep. Simply walked into a café in Broadmead, and asked what time their parents would get there." Hutchins was on duty when the manager called it in. He's on his way back to the station with them." Meredith walked back to the bed and grabbing Patsy's face, he planted a kiss. "I'm off. I'll catch you later."

As Meredith neared the door at the rear of the station, Rawlings' car screeched into the car park and stopped feet away from him. Abandoning the car, Rawlings sprinted to him, as Eve and the Lakes hurried to catch up.

"Are they all right? Did he hurt them?" Rawlings was already punching the code into the keypad.

"I think they're fine, Dave. I've not been told otherwise." Meredith put a hand on his shoulder. "Take it slowly. Don't frighten them."

Rawlings nodded, and held the door for the others to pass.

"Go straight to the meeting room, Dave, not the incident room. And give me your car keys."

Taking the keys Meredith followed them into the building, and waited until all four had gone into the correct room before he put his head around the door of the incident room. He threw the car keys to Bob Travers.

"Park that somewhere sensible. Where are the girls?"

"Interview three." Travers was grinning like a Cheshire cat. "They're fine, Gov, they seem absolutely fine."

Meredith opened the door slowly. Ellen looked up and smiled.

"Is Daddy here yet?" She looked at Gemma, "That's Daddy's boss. He's bossy."

The two girls collapsed in fits of giggles, and Meredith was tempted to join them.

"Anything?" He looked at Hutchins for an indication of anything that might have been said. Hutchins smiled and shook his head.

"No, Gov. The girls are happy they haven't got to go to school today, and were just telling me the lady in the café let them have cakes for breakfast."

"Where's mine?" Meredith looked at the empty plates, and put his hands on his hips. The girls giggled again. Meredith shook his head and turned back to Hutchins. "Is it all ready?"

"Yes, confirmed when I brought them back in." Hutchins stood up, as Meredith stepped forward and held out his hands.

"Come on then, let's go and find your parents." Taking the girls by the hand, he led them back the way he had come, and paused as they reached the door to the room containing their parents. He gave their hands a little shake, and they looked up at him. "I should warn you, they missed you when you were away, they might make a bit of a fuss. Be kind to them."

The girls exchanged glances as though he were mad, and giggled again. They were still smiling as he opened the door. Gemma's mother turned and, on seeing her daughter, let out a howl and fell to her knees holding her arms out towards her daughter. Gemma looked up at Meredith, and walked forward as he gave her a wink. Ellen simply launched herself at her father. Dave Rawlings swung her around, hugging her close, before taking her to her mother and handing her across. Sobs racked Eve Rawlings' body as her tears fell freely.

Ellen lifted her hands to her mother's face and brushed them away. She told her mother not to cry several times, before turning to her father.

"I think this is your fault," she chastised him. "If you wouldn't let your phone run out of batteries, I could have spoken to you." Ellen looked across to Gemma who was trying to wriggle free of her mother.

Gemma's face had crumpled and she was trying not to join in the tears, but it was hard because her Mummy seemed so sad. She held out her hand to her father and he knelt beside her.

Gemma caught Ellen's gaze, and smiled as Ellen rolled her eyes and looked up at Meredith. "You were right."

Meredith nodded. "I always am, Ellen."

Grinning, he stepped outside leaving the two families to their reunion. Striding quickly to the next room he pushed open the door. Louie Trump looked up and smiled.

"Morning, sir, and what a fine start to the day it's been. Did I see you wiping away a tear a moment ago?"

"Don't be bloody stupid, there's work to do. Have we heard whether it's interview or examination first?" He didn't look at Trump as he spoke, but instead watched the screen and nodded as Gemma's mother gave her first smile.

"We're trying to get hold of the recommended paediatrician now. We could start the interviewing as soon as they've finished saying hello." Trump nodded at the screen. "DC Bird is on her way. She's our local child specialist."

"Yes, I know. Our paths have crossed." Meredith's brow furrowed. That was a liaison which hadn't ended well, but it was a few years back now, hopefully all water under the bridge. "Well, we'd better put some form of game plan together. The sooner this is done, the sooner they can go home."

He gave the families a further fifteen minutes before he went in, and took Dave Rawlings to one side.

"We're setting up for the interview first. We're waiting on the paediatrician, so not sure when they'll be examined, but I think we should crack on. Is that all right with you?"

Rawlings nodded slowly, and stared at his daughter.

"I want to be there." He glanced up at Meredith. "Not in the room, I know that wouldn't be wise. But I want to watch the interview."

"Dave, that's not going to happen." Meredith shook his head. "You know the procedure."

He placed his arm on Rawlings shoulder as he nodded.

"I do, and you know I'll see the tape anyway. So let me watch."

"It could take hours. You need to be with Eve." Meredith shrugged. "I won't hold anything back, I promise you."

"Eve will be fine. She knows what happens; I explained it when we knew he'd called. I'll get her mother down to be with her."

"I said no. I'll go and see if they're ready for us." His eyes flicked up to the clock. "I'll give you another fifteen minutes."

When Meredith stepped outside, DC Bird was waiting for him.

"DC Bird." Meredith nodded and his lips twitched into a brief smile as his eyes flicked over his former lover. She'd put on some weight.

"Sir. The room's ready, needed a bit of a dust. Not been used for a while. Am I okay to go in?" She nodded at the door but her eyes went straight back to Meredith.

He nodded. "You know one of them is a police officer's daughter, don't you?"

"Of course," she snapped. "Quite apart from the fact I'm good at my job, I do watch the news." She nudged him out of the way and opened the door, nodding acknowledgement to Rawlings as she entered.

"Right you lot, we're on the move. The miserable DCI Meredith needs this room for something else, but I've found you a great one with some toys and stuff we can play with." She held out her hand to Ellen. "Do you want to come with me?"

Ellen shrugged. She didn't know why they were at the police station but it was certainly better than going to school

"Okay. I don't think he's miserable, I think he's funny. I like him."

Gemma ran to join her. "And me."

In the next room, Trump tapped the screen. "Your charm works even on children," he observed dryly. "I take it DC Bird was a little more than a business acquaintance?"

"You can take what you like, Trump. It was a long time ago."

They watched Caroline Bird lead the girls from the room while the parents trooped out behind them.

"Seems good at her job, I have to say."

"She was good," Meredith smirked, and left Trump to join the end of the procession.

Trump shook his head as he tapped the keyboard. The screens around him flickered, and a different room from various angles filled the screens. Outside, Jo Adler tapped the door with her foot.

"Da daaa." She held up a small tray containing two bacon sandwiches and fresh coffee. "Your breakfast is served, sir."

"Get in here quick before Meredith gets back. He won't have eaten yet," Louie smiled and glanced as the screen as the sound of talking filled the room. "Here we go, take a seat."

As they settled down with their refreshments, they watched as the parents of the two girls were directed to large comfortable chairs around the perimeter of the room. DC Caroline Bird threw her hand into the air.

"Help yourselves, girls, I need a word with your parents."

The two girls stood for a moment as they scanned the room. They spotted the Lego table, and after a brief discussion settled on that. Meredith watched as they perched on the small stools and began to search for the desired pieces. Caroline Bird spoke quietly to the Lakes who were nodding in agreement. After a few moments, she moved on to the Rawlings. That conversation didn't take quite so long. She walked to Meredith who was leaning on the door frame.

"We're all set. I'll get the girls chatting, and when I think they won't miss their parents, I'll ask them about their holidays. That will be the cue for the adults to leave." She stared at him and shook her head. "You're a total and utter bastard, do you know that?"

Meredith nodded and tried to look appropriately remorseful before turning and leaving the room. He closed the door behind him.

Caroline Bird tutted and went to join the girls. Within twenty minutes, she believed that they were not in any way traumatised by whatever had happened to them, and felt she could begin to question them on the events of the previous thirty-six hours.

"I think your house should have a blue chimney." She pointed at the oblong box Gemma was in the process of constructing. "I stayed in a house with a blue chimney once, when I was on holiday. Are you going on holiday this year?" Her eyes moved across the room and she saw Rawlings encourage the others to their feet. "Oh look, your parents are going to get some drinks. Do you want anything?"

Gemma didn't look up, and Ellen cast but a cursory glance at her parents. They shook their heads and carried on with their constructions.

Meredith hurried along the corridor. He smiled as he reached them.

"Now we don't know how long this is likely to take. We've spoken to the specialist and we're to take the girls to meet her at midday. I'd suggest you go home for an hour or so, but if you want to stay close, there's a canteen downstairs. Dave will show you where. Get something to eat, you must be starving."

He saw Rawlings' mouth open. "Your girls are safe now." He countered any argument or suggestion that might have been coming. "You can relax. I will let you know anything worth knowing, and of course you can come to the hospital with them." Blocking the way to the observation room, he pushed open a door leading to the stairs. "Lead the way, Dave, there's a good chap."

Once the group were on their way, Meredith went back to join Jo Adler and Trump. He wheeled a chair to the back of the room and closed his eyes as he listened to the casual conversation.

"So, where have you two been?" Caroline continued to build her model and didn't look up at the girls.

"Charlie's house," Ellen announced.

"He said his name wasn't Charlie," Gemma corrected her.

Ellen shrugged and bit her lip as she tried to fix a window into the slot she had left for it.

"Who's Charlie? Is he a friend?" Caroline smiled as the two girls nodded. "Is he nice? I don't think I've met Charlie." Again, the two girls nodded. "What's the best thing about being with Charlie?"

The two girls answered at once, and spoke over each other.

"Pancakes," Gemma said.

"Dressing up and the beetles." Ellen stopped work and put her hands to her head dramatically. "We forgot the beetles. We'll never win now." She looked at Gemma. "We'll be in trouble with Brown Owl for the jars."

"We won't, will we?" Gemma looked at Caroline. "He said she knew."

"Yes, she does, it's not a problem. I expect he'll drop them off," Caroline assured her. "Where did you get the beetles?"

Keen to keep the girls talking, and not worrying about their actions, she pressed on.

The girls explained about the garden and the huge number of insects they had found. Ellen remembered Sammy.

"Did Sammy get in trouble for being on the phone?" she asked. "She's always in trouble."

Caroline had read through Brown Owl's statement. She'd been distracted by Sammy only minutes before they found the girls were missing. He must have been in full view of her. Her brow furrowed.

"Well, I think she did. But it's all right now, don't worry. Sammy was more worried about you disappearing. Did Charlie see her on the phone?"

"Yes, of course. That's how we knew we could go and get the beetles. He was watching her through the hole." Gemma went back to her building.

"Oh, I didn't know that. What was his car like?"

To her surprise the two girls stopped what they were doing and started chattering.

"It was massive, and the seats were slidey. It had two TVs, and a radio, and a CD player," Ellen said.

"We watched *Nemo*," Gemma added. "And it had a window in the roof, but he said it didn't work."

"I'll show you some pictures later, and you can tell me which one his car was like. It sounds wonderful." Caroline was pleased with the information she'd received about the car, and changed tack a little. "Was his house massive as well?"

"Don't know. We only went in the playroom and the garden, didn't we?" Ellen looked to Gemma who nodded. "That was big though."

"What, you didn't use the bathroom?"

"There was one in the playroom." Gemma rolled her eyes. "We didn't have a bath though." She giggled. "Mum would go mad if she knew."

"So where did you sleep?" Caroline's eyes flitted from one to the other as she asked the question.

"In our bed, of course. He told us we'd have to share, so we did. Ellen fidgets."

"Well, you make funny noises." Ellen retorted and giggled. She looked up at Caroline. "It was quite comfortable though."

"Good, nothing worse than a lumpy bed." Caroline laughed and waved her finger between them. "I see you're still in uniform, please tell me you didn't sleep in your Brownie uniforms." She threw her hands into the air, as though that would be unthinkable, and the two girls giggled again.

"No, because we dressed up. There was a big box full of dressing up clothes." Gemma frowned and looked down at her clothes, before looking at Ellen. "I thought I was a princess yesterday? When did I get dressed?"

Ellen shrugged. "Charlie probably did it. I was Minnie Mouse."

Caroline's heart sank a little, and she mentally crossed her fingers as she asked the next question.

"Did Charlie dress up too?"

"Only his hat. And his name's not Charlie, that's just Ellen making it up."

Ellen looked at Caroline, her face serious. "I'm not, and he had the mask. But all the clothes were for little girls; he would have looked silly."

Over the next thirty minutes, the girls related the detail of their visit to Caroline. They were totally calm about everything that had happened to them. They seemed to have enjoyed the visit, and were quite fond of Charlie. He always wore a hat with a clown face attached, so they didn't know if he had blue eyes, or a big nose. He was tall, but then most people are to seven-year-old kids. He didn't wear any rings, or a watch, and they were quite sure his hair was brownish blond. There was only one grey area that needed to be covered. Caroline suggested they do some drawing, and they moved to a long table in front of the window. She asked them to draw the best thing they could think of about being with Charlie. She chatted about films with them for a while as they settled into the new activity. Once they were busy and their minds occupied on other things, she stretched her arms up and yawned.

"Phew, I'm tired. I had such a late night last night. Were you two allowed to stay up late at Charlie's?" She watched as they both paused.

Emma shrugged and chose a different colour pencil. Gemma sat back on her chair looking puzzled. "I can't remember going to bed. I didn't clean my teeth." She looked at Ellen. "Did I fall asleep first?" Ellen didn't look up from her drawing.

"I don't know. It was the magic drink, I expect."

Gemma smiled and, nodding, she picked up her pencil, and returned her attention to the picture she was drawing.

"What magic drink?" Caroline leaned a little closer to Ellen to see what she was drawing.

"Orange juice with lemonade. It's lush. Charlie said it was magic." Ellen looked up as someone tapped at the door.

Meredith stepped into the room. "How are you doing, girls? Is Caroline behaving herself?" He walked over and looked at their drawings. Some of the items he couldn't identify, but both had drawn beetles, orange drinks complete with straws, and little blue and red stick men. He pointed to one. "What's that, a doll?"

"It's a soldier." Ellen tutted, "They're special. They keep you safe."

Meredith nodded acceptance. "Well, I've got a favour to ask, but you can come back and see Caroline later." The two little girls looked up at him. Ellen was already getting off the chair. "I've got a doctor friend who needs volunteers to be measured and things like that. It doesn't take long, and I hear you get pizza for lunch afterwards. We have to go to the hospital, but your parents can come too." The two girls nodded, and he pointed to the door. "Go and wait out there for me, I'll be two ticks."

He waited until the two girls were on the other side of the room before turning his attention to Caroline.

"Did you pick up the significance of the magic drink?" she asked, as she glanced at the drawings again.

"I did." Meredith resisted the urge to add that he wasn't stupid. "What else might I have missed?"

"Nothing. The man was nice and kind to them. He gave them nice things to eat, had lots to keep them occupied, and he never got cross. What happened when he got them asleep, perhaps we'll never know." Sad eyes looked at Meredith as she shrugged. "But the examination may reveal more."

Meredith closed his eyes, and pinched the bridge of his nose as he decided not to mention that to Dave Rawlings. When they knew something definite had happened, would be soon enough. He fixed his smile as he went back to the girls.

"Come on then, walk this way."

Meredith stepped in front of the girls. He took two steps forward, and gave a little skip to change the lead foot, and then repeated the move with the other, much to the girls' amusement. He stopped and turned to them.

"I said, walk *this* way." He demonstrated the move again and the girls clung on to each other giggling before giving it a go. After only one false start, Meredith and the girls moved in time along the corridor. Caroline stood watching from the doorway.

"What a wonderfully funny and kind bastard you are. Shame you're not like that with the big girls." She shook her head and closed the door.

As Meredith led the families to the minibus, Dave Rawlings caught his eye. Meredith smiled and shook his head. As the group climbed onto the bus, Dave Rawlings hung back.

"Absolutely nothing, as yet," Meredith kept his voice low. "You can see the tape later."

Satisfied, Rawlings climbed onto the bus in front of Meredith, and sat across the aisle from his daughter. He took her hand. Meredith watched their arms swing back and forth as they made the short journey to the children's hospital. When they arrived, the doctor they needed to see was in the recovery room with a child who had come out of surgery. She'd left instructions with a junior doctor, and they were shown into a brightly coloured family room.

Meredith had been asked to wait in her office. He tapped the door and entered. A man working at the desk glanced up. He looked startled for a moment, before standing and holding out his hand.

"DCI Meredith, please do come in. I'm just running over some notes."

They shook hands as Meredith scanned the pile of medical folders on the desk.

"Have we met?" Meredith glanced at the ID attached to a ribbon around the man's neck. He had a good memory for faces, even if the name came later.

"No, no. I saw you on the news yesterday. I understand you have the girls back safe and sound. That's certainly a relief. Sorry, I'm Graham Charlesworth. I work with Professor Cole."

"Safe anyway," Meredith responded. "Don't you doctors wear white coats anymore?" He looked from the frayed jeans to the faded checked shirt.

"Not often. Seen as too formal, especially with the kids. I can't remember the last time I wore a collar and tie. Ah, here's Rosemary now."

Meredith turned as a short, grey-haired woman with a startlingly large nose bustled into the room. He tried not to look at her nose when he greeted her.

"Right, I'll get out of your way." Graham Charlesworth stepped outside.

"You don't have to go. We'll not be here two minutes." Professor Rosemary Cole placed a large bundle of files on the desk and picked up a leather case containing a note book.

"It's not a problem. I need to check on the ward anyway." He turned and smiled at Meredith. "I hope you catch your man."

"I always have before, and I will this time."

Meredith nodded as he left the room, then he turned to Rosemary Cole. "We don't have much. If he interfered with the girls in any way, they know nothing about it. However, he did make them what he called a magic drink, and they can't remember going to bed on either night. Nor can they remember getting dressed this morning. We're guessing he drugged them."

"Hopefully with something obvious which will still be in their systems. Have they eaten today, do you know?"

"A cake this morning, other than that just water to drink. I've promised them pizza after this though. I take it that's all right, Professor Cole?" Meredith smiled, and realised he was staring at her nose again.

"Take your eyes off my nose. I know it's difficult but you'll go cross-eyed." She punched him on the arm as she left the room. "Come on, let's get this done quickly for them, and call me Rosemary, or Doctor Rosemary. Only people I don't like get to use the title."

For a short woman, she had a quick turn of pace, and Meredith hurried along behind her. Everyone looked up as she entered the room. She looked from one girl to the other.

"I'm Doctor Rosemary. Hands up which of you two is the bravest?" Both girls' hands shot in the air. "Okay, hands up which of you two wants your mummies to come with you?" Past experience had shown that having the mother present was distressing for the child, as the mother was more often than not unable to keep her emotions under control. Both girls dropped their hands. "Okay, hands up who can walk the fastest. We've got nurses waiting to weigh and measure you at the end of the corridor, and it's very, very long." She smiled as both hands went up again. "Let's get going. See you in a minute, mums and dads."

Ellen remained with her hand up, and Professor Cole smiled at her

"Do you have a question, my dear?"

"Can Meredith come too? Because we've nearly got his walk right, and if the corridor's long it will be better."

"No, no, now is . . ." Meredith fell silent as the doctor waved her hand at him.

"I have no idea what you're talking about, but as it seems to have embarrassed Meredith, I think he should come as far as the nurses." She turned to Meredith. "Would you like to lead the way?"

Meredith shook his fist at Ellen who giggled, and he stepped out into the corridor. He walked forward a few paces and stopped. The girls rushed out behind him. Dr Rosemary looked at the parents and smiled.

"This could be entertaining." She bustled after the girls, as she heard Meredith ask if they were ready. Rawlings stood and walked to the door. He called the others over as Meredith and the girls skipped away down the corridor. The girls had perfect timing. About halfway down the corridor Professor Cole joined in.

"I thought you said he was miserable all the time." Eve nudged her husband who shook his head.

"Not *all*, just most. He's having a good day, and he's making our girl laugh. Listen to those two."

Rather than go back to the parents, Meredith waited outside the examination rooms. If there was any indication the girls had been assaulted, he wanted to know before they told the parents. He tapped his feet as the minutes passed. After what seemed like hours, Professor Cole appeared. She opened a door next to Meredith and he followed her into the small office. Closing the door, she smiled at him.

"I'm pleased to say there are no signs of abuse. No fresh bruising on any part of their bodies, no swellings, no anything which isn't perfectly innocent." She shrugged. "I've taken blood and urine samples, which may show the girls were drugged, but they'll take a day or so." She reopened the door. "At the moment, nothing to report. I'll go and get them, they're choosing a sticker."

"Thank you, Dr Rosemary, I could kiss you," Meredith grinned. "I'll go and tell the parents, and put them out of their misery."

Meredith smiled as the girls' parents visibly relaxed. They were now able to put their worst thoughts from their minds.

"You can take the girls home now. I've got some cars coming to pick you up. We may want to speak to the girls again, but I'll give you plenty of warning. If they do happen to mention anything you think may be useful, give me a call."

There was a tap on the door. A nurse showed the girls in, and once more they were totally bemused by their parents' reaction. Meredith excused himself and went outside, hoping to find a quiet spot to call in the results.

Rawlings followed him. "So why did he take them?" he asked as Meredith pushed open the door to the stairwell.

Meredith sighed and turned to face him. "I don't know, Dave. We may never know, let's just be glad they are home. Safe and unharmed," Meredith patted him on the back. "Take your daughter home. Take a few days off, and relax. I didn't want to say, but you look like shit." Meredith's attempt at humour fell on deaf ears.

"But he drugged them. There was a reason for that and you know it."

Meredith closed his eyes. He didn't know who had told Rawlings about the so-called magic drink, but he had a pretty good idea. Now, despite knowing his daughter hadn't been physically abused, Rawlings' mind would probably reach the same conclusion as his own. There was a possibility they had been photographed. He opened his eyes and stared at Rawlings.

"You know we'll catch him. When we do we'll find out if there's anything else we need to know. But as I see it, you have a wife who doesn't need any more worry, and a daughter who needs her daddy to be happy. Let's not worry about things we don't know, and concentrate on catching him. If I . . ." Meredith stopped speaking and pulled the ringing phone from his pocket. He listened for a few moments and hung up. "Right, enough said, I think. The cars are here to take you home."

Rawlings nodded and went to collect his family. Meredith waved to the girls as the two cars pulled away, before climbing into the car that would take him back to the station. When he arrived the mood in the incident room was jubilant. He smiled as he heard the familiar banter being batted back and forth between his officers. Meredith went into his office. He'd give them a few more minutes, before focusing them on the task of catching the man. Sitting at his desk, he signed Hutchins' transfer papers before calling Patsy with the good news.

Patsy hit the ignore button and looked back at Nicola.

"You want me to go to Seville? I have no address, no telephone number, nothing. I'm sorry Nicola, but I think that would be an expensive waste of time."

Nicola's face hardened. "But I think my time, as I will be paying for it. I have the money, Patsy, and I want him found. Unless, of course, you think John wouldn't allow you to go." She gave a brief smile; the challenge had been cast. "I know how protective he can be, but I don't see why not. It's not a dangerous case, simply a missing person."

"That won't work, Nicola. What Meredith does or does not think about the cases I take has absolutely no bearing on how I approach them. I think we should give it a week or so and see if he surfaces. In the meantime, I can try and find some way of getting information from the university. It may be they have his address in Spain on their records. If they do, then I'd be more than happy to jump on a plane."

Patsy pushed her cup to the centre of the table. "I have to go now, but as a by the by, you asked me to keep this confidential and I have. Therefore, Meredith knows nothing about it. Now, do you want me to keep looking here or not?"

Patsy stood and looked down at Nicola, her irritation apparent. Nicola cursed herself silently for attempting to use Meredith as a form of leverage. She should have known better.

"Yes please, of course I do. And I'm sorry if I spoke out of turn, but I am desperate, Patsy. Please forgive my indiscretion." Nicola patted the seat next to her. "Please don't go. This is so important to me, let's start the conversation again."

She blinked rapidly as Patsy shook her head.

"I really do have another appointment, Nicola. It wasn't an excuse. I'll give you a call tomorrow when you've had time to think. It may be that you want to use someone else. I'm sure there are investigators out there who would love a trip to Seville. Not that I wouldn't, but I'm simply trying not to waste your money."

Nicola stood and collected her coat from the back of the chair. Walking forward she placed her hand on Patsy's forearm.

"I don't need you to worry about me in any way, except finding Toni. I am very comfortably off financially, Patsy, so I'm not worried about the cost of a couple of days in Seville. If it wasn't for Paul, I'd go myself." She smiled. "We could have gone together, and you could have shown me how you do what you do." Nicola caught the flash of horror that crossed Patsy's face, and laughed. "You should've seen your face. Can you imagine explaining that one to John?"

Patsy grinned. "It would have been an interesting conversation, that's for sure." She held open the door to the coffee shop, and allowed Nicola to exit. "I'll do a deal with you, Nicola. Give me a week, and if he doesn't show up, I'll go to Seville."

Nicola nodded and smiled broadly as she thanked Patsy. She was about to say something further when Patsy's phone rang again. She watched as Patsy checked the screen before rejecting the call.

"I mustn't keep you. I'm assuming that's work chasing you."

"No, it was Meredith actually. They found the girls this morning, it will be my update." Keeping the phone in her hand, she gave a brief wave. "I really do have to go . . . Oh, he liked the card by the way."

Patsy turned and walked away cursing, asking herself why she'd said that. She seemed to have some odd need to please the woman.

Turning the corner, she returned his call.

"You've been busy, that was my third call." Meredith sounded quite light-hearted.

"I have been with a client. How are the girls?"

"Absolutely fine. You'd think they'd been on holiday. We still have to catch the bastard who took them, but it's easier now we know they're not in danger. I'm putting a work rota together with Trump as we speak." Patsy heard Louie call a greeting from the background. "Hang on a minute," Meredith walked to his office and shut the door. "Please tell me you're not working again tonight."

"No. I only worked last night because you were tied up." Patsy smiled. "Why?"

"Because we are going to celebrate my birthday properly. I want cake, I want presents, and I want you."

"Ha! I can do all but the middle one. You told me you didn't want anything."

"Well, I lied, so now you'll have to surprise me. I'll be home by six thirty, promise."

Patsy hung up and walked slowly back to her car, wondering if she had the courage to go through with it.

Sitting in the middle of the busy restaurant, he was totally oblivious to those around him. He'd checked the local news on his phone. It had confirmed the girls were home safe and well. He'd had a moment of panic when they'd gone into the café on their own. After all, anyone could have been in there. He might have placed them in danger. There was that tramp hanging around, for one thing. He'd have to be more careful in the future.

Sighing, he flipped through to his notes and ran through the list of names. He'd already been to see them all and decided that Dana would be his second choice. Hopefully, she would be the one. He closed the screen as a bell sounded, and a scratchy voice made an announcement over the hubbub of voices. Looking down at his food, he decided he wasn't hungry, and he pushed the plate away. Another hour and he'd be free to go and see her. Shoving his hands into his pockets he ambled out of the restaurant, nodding a greeting at those he recognised from work as he did so.

CHAPTER SEVEN

Amanda walked into the kitchen, and twirled around. "How do I look?" She gave a curtsy as she plucked a tomato from the bowl of salad. Patsy placed down the spoon she had been using to stir the sauce, and turned around.

"Absolutely fabulous. Is that a new top? Do another twirl." Patsy nodded, "Seriously sexy. What's his name? He's going . . ." She looked up at the ceiling and smiled as the sound of Meredith stepping from the bathroom to the bedroom, and singing at the top of his voice, reached them. "As I was saying, whoever it is, and I want a name, is going to be blown away."

"Thanks, Patsy. He's really perked up now the girls are back, which is understandable." Amanda looked heavenward. "I wonder if he'll put his cards up now? I saw they'd been opened. What did he say about the theatre? Was he pleased? I haven't seen him yet. What are you two doing home so early anyway? I thought I'd be gone before you got home."

Patsy attempted to soften Meredith's response. "He was certainly surprised. I think he'll thoroughly enjoy it once we get him there."

"He didn't like it then!" Amanda rolled her eyes, stole another tomato, and popped it into her mouth. "He's got to come out of the Dark Ages." She walked to the hob and, picking up the spoon, dipped it into the gently bubbling sauce. "I can't believe you're having meatballs and I'm going out." She spun round to Patsy. "Damn, I forgot to go to the cash point. I don't suppose you could lend me, say, forty pounds? He'll probably insist on paying again, but I should have some money. I don't want him to think I'm a scrounger."

"Of course, but you'll have to give me a name. I have no idea why you're avoiding telling me." Patsy walked to her bag and lifted it onto the table. She rummaged for her purse. "I really must have a clear out." She lifted a bundle of papers out and put them next to the bag. Finding her purse, she pulled some notes free.

"Patrick. Don't tell Dad but he's . . . ooooh, he's hot. Who's this?" Amanda held up the photograph of Stephen. "Look at that torso." She grinned at Patsy. "Purely from a biological viewpoint, of course. If I wasn't seeing Patrick I'd -"

"Who's hot, and who's Patrick?"

Amanda spun round to face her father. She looked angry.

"Don't creep up on people like that. You scared me half to death."

"Then I apologise, but I wasn't creeping. I don't creep." He winked at her. "And now that's cleared up, answer my questions." He held out a hand, inviting her answer.

"Patsy tried to be nice, but I hear you're not over keen on my birthday gift. You're welcome by the way." Amanda decided that the best form of defence was attack, and she mirrored Meredith's hand gesture.

"I'm delighted. I'm more than happy for you to attempt to bring culture into my sad and uneducated life. Come here." Meredith pulled his daughter into a hug, and kissed her forehead. Trapped in his embrace she closed her eyes and sighed as he added. "Perhaps Patrick can come too, once you've introduced us. Now who's hot, and who's Patrick?"

Patsy had to turn away to hide her smile, as Amanda attempted to wriggle free of her father's arms.

"He's hot. Patsy had a photograph of him in her handbag. I don't know who he is." She grinned as her ploy worked, and Meredith released her to pick up the photograph. He waved it at Patsy who still had her back to them.

"Who's this, the competition?" He peered more closely at the photograph, before looking at his daughter. "This is what constitutes hot these days is it? He's only about four foot two. Those teeth don't look real either."

Patsy burst out laughing and turned back. "That sounds like a little jealousy to me. That's Stephen, a chap who is friends with the man I'm trying to trace. Linda and I met him in the bar on the waterfront. I did mention it."

"You didn't mention he was hot."

"You didn't ask." Patsy laughed. She looked over his shoulder into the hall as the doorbell rang. Amanda glanced up at the clock.

"Shit, I'm late." Amanda fumbled her attempt to pull her bag from the back of the chair.

"How can you be late if he's only just got here?" Meredith grinned and strode into the hall.

"I don't think he was supposed to knock," Patsy called out, and laughed as Amanda chased her father, attempting to overtake him.

Meredith blocked her path, and reached the door first. Patsy watched Amanda brace herself as he pulled open the door theatrically. Trump smiled at him. Meredith blinked.

"I take it you're not here for Amanda?"

Trump frowned. "Why, should I be?" He stepped to one side as a horn sounded, and Amanda pushed past her father. "Oh, I see." Trump smiled as he turned and watched Amanda hurry up the path.

"Idiot. You'd better come in. If you'd not turned up . . . Oh, forget it. What can we do for you on this beautiful summer evening?"

Trump looked at Meredith warily. "Are you feeling okay, sir?"

"Fine. What do you want, Trump?" Meredith turned back to the kitchen leaving Trump standing on the doorstep. "Come in," he called, "and shut the door behind you."

Patsy smiled at Trump as he followed Meredith up the hall.

"Hi, Louie, please tell me this is a social visit." She pointed at the pans on the hob. "Dinner is almost ready."

"Sorry, Patsy, business I'm afraid." He held his hands up as Meredith turned to face him and Patsy's face fell. "But I'm not here to take him away."

"Why are you here? Come on, Trump, I'm starving." Meredith turned his attention back to the food and, taking the pasta from Patsy, gently lowered it into the boiling water.

"Division took a call from the Harbour Master about an hour ago. Someone pottering up the Severn in a small boat got stuck in the mud. They sent out a rescue boat and found an arm stuck there too." He nodded as he acquired Meredith's full attention.

"Just an arm?"

"As far as I know, yes. Oh, it had the hand attached because Frankie Callaghan mentioned he would be able to get fingerprints." Trump stepped forward and looked in at the meatballs. "Patsy, that smells delicious, it's making my stomach rumble."

"I've made plenty and you're very welcome to stay," Patsy smiled.

"No, you're not. How come I don't know about this?" Meredith flapped his hand at Trump, indicating he should back off.

"I've already booked a table, thank you, Patsy." Trump looked back to Meredith. "You'd not long left when the call came in. It was only an arm at that stage, so I went down and met with Frankie. The tide was coming in, and I was assured there was little else we could do before seven thirty in the morning when it will be low enough to search the area. Although the Harbour Master explained that due to the tides the arm could have come from anywhere, at any time. Either this morning, or, because of the mud, months ago. Frankie should be able to tell us more once it's been examined. I left it with him."

"Oh, you did, did you? And at no point during these proceedings you thought it might be appropriate to give me a call?"

"No, sir. Why, would you have done something different?" Trump shrugged. "I thought there would be little point in calling you back in."

"I doubt there was, but I would have appreciated the option. Think a little deeper next time." Meredith couldn't keep it up, and his face cracked into a smile. "Thanks for taking care of it. You should've called, but no harm done."

Trump returned the smile and started to back out of the room. Since Meredith was in a good mood, he'd leave before he really did say something wrong. He waved to Patsy.

"See you soon, enjoy your meal." Reaching the door, he opened it and paused, "I told Frankie to call me if he matched the prints. Do you want him to call you instead?"

"Don't be bloody stupid, Trump, I've got plans." Meredith wiggled his eyebrows up and down. "You can call me if you feel it's necessary."

"Will do, have a good evening sir."

"I intend to."

"I have to say, I thought they'd found another part when I saw Daily outside, he must have been visiting someone. Glad I was wrong. Night, sir." Trump nodded, and stepping over the threshold he pulled the door closed behind him.

Patsy smiled as Meredith returned to the kitchen.

"This is ready, it will take me two minutes to dish up. Take the salad through to the dining room for me please."

"Oh, the dining room tonight? First, we have an extremely early dinner, then we eat in the dining room. What's the occasion?" Meredith winked and took the salad through to the dining room. He smiled at the small iced cake with one candle standing in the middle of the table. He picked up the envelope from the place mat. "I'd forgotten I hadn't opened this. Shall I wait for you, or open it now." He already had his finger inserted in the gap, ready to open it.

"After dinner. Don't touch," Patsy called from the kitchen.

Meredith lifted the flap of the envelope, and slid the card out. He grinned at the picture on the front and opened it. He read the words quickly and frowned, as they made no sense. Glancing at the door he replaced the card, tucked in the flap, and lay it on the table. He shrugged. He had no idea what she had meant to write, but it would provide him with ammunition to tease her with later. He smiled at her, and hurried to hold the door as she entered the room.

Patsy looked at the card and back to Meredith. "What was that look for? What are you up to?" She placed the bowl of spaghetti and meatballs on the table.

"I have no idea what you're on about. I was merely being gentlemanly." He pulled out her chair. "Take a seat."

"We'll see," Patsy commented as he took the seat opposite.

They ate the meal at a leisurely pace, polishing off a bottle of wine as they did so. Meredith repeatedly complimented Patsy both on her appearance and the food.

"You're up to something." She looked at him suspiciously as she cleared away the dishes. "That's the fourth time you've told me it was good."

"It was better than good. I'm allowed to compliment you, aren't I?" He leaned to one side and retrieved the card from the end of the table. "May I?" He waved it at her. "I'm not sure what the delay is about. I'm intrigued to know what you've written."

Patsy's stomach somersaulted, and she forced a smile as she asked herself whether she was ready. Deciding it was now or never, she placed the dirty dishes on the kitchen table and held out her hand.

"Come with me, I'd like to give you your gift first."

Meredith joined her. "Good, I like presents, especially if I have to go upstairs." He followed her up the stairs. They'd not reached the top when the phone rang. Meredith cursed. "Keep going, we're ignoring it."

Patsy's shoulders sagged a little. She knew he wouldn't. His phone continued to ring, and he pulled it from his pocket intending to reject the call. Dave Rawlings' name highlighted the screen.

"It's Rawlings. I'd better take it, but I promise I won't be long."

He sat on the top stair and answered the call. Patsy went and sat on the bed. As she listened to the one-sided conversation she knew he would be going out.

Meredith hung up and peered at Patsy through the bannister.

"From the look on your face I take it you know I have to go out." He held up his hands as she nodded. "But I promise I won't be long. I'll sort it myself so there will be no delays." Using the bannister he pulled himself to his feet. "The bastard gave them presents. Soldiers. Why would anyone give little girls soldiers? Dave's on his own as Eve is dropping her mother home. It'll be quicker if I -"

"Stop explaining yourself. I'll still be here when you get back." Patsy's words and smile were genuine, but she was beginning to wonder if all these interruptions were fate, and it wasn't supposed to happen.

Meredith strode into the bedroom and pulled her into his arms. He kissed her tenderly.

"And that's why I love you, Patsy Hodge. Life is simple with you." He sat her back on the bed. "I'll be back soon."

Patsy listened to him gallop down the stairs, the rattle of his keys as he retrieved them from the hall table, and the slam of the door as he pulled it closed behind him. Once he was out of the house she fell back on the bed and stared at the ceiling. He was right, she mused. Things were good between them. Why change them and risk disaster?

Waving goodbye to his colleagues, he hurried to the car park. He needed to go and see Dana again before he put his plan into action. He wanted to be as sure as he could be before he took her. He climbed into the Range Rover, satisfied that any interest in the vehicle would have diminished now the girls had been returned. He scrolled through the addresses programmed into the navigation system until he found the right one. Checking his mirrors, he indicated before pulling out of his parking space. They might not still be looking for the vehicle, but there was no point in drawing attention to it. He waited for a bus to pass before he joined the traffic.

It was six thirty before he reached Dana's home; the traffic commuting out of the city had been particularly heavy. He parked a few streets away, and walked down the lane that led to the fields behind her house. When he had been checking the girls out, he'd considered getting a dog, so as to look less conspicuous, but had decided he had enough complications in his life without adding another.

He turned left at the end of the lane and spotted a couple on the far side of the field. He walked to the centre of the field, and once there he bellowed at the top of his voice.

"Here boy. Come on, Butch." He whistled as though signalling a dog.

The couple looked over briefly before continuing their walk. Content, he scanned the houses that backed onto the field. Dana lived in the sixth one along. Spotting the top of the net that protected the trampoline poking up above the hedge, he walked diagonally towards it. He crossed his fingers, hoping she would be in the garden. He called his imaginary dog several times as he approached the house.

The hedge was shoulder height and, remaining a respectable distance from it, he walked the length of the garden and peered in for any sign of her. She wasn't there, so he continued walking past the next five gardens, periodically calling the dog. He paused as he heard a child shout. It came from behind him. It could be her. Grinning, he pivoted and retraced his steps, remembering to call the dog. As he approached Dana's garden, he saw a woman standing at the back door, hand up and finger wagging. He continued to walk past.

"You have twenty minutes, young lady, and that's it. I'm fed up with telling you over and over. Your father will have something to say about this when he gets home. Twenty minutes!" The harassed woman sighed, and went back into the house, as the child answered back.

"Daddy loves me. He's not mean like you." Dana sang out in a whining voice, "Twenty minutes, twenty minutes."

When her mother failed to respond, she turned, and walked up the path that separated the lawn and led to the trampoline. He pursed his lips. Dana was a cheeky young thing; she wouldn't be allowed to speak to him like that. The woman was obviously bad at parenting.

He stopped walking away from the property and putting his hands to his mouth called the dog. "Butch. Here boy." He spun quickly and turned to look at the hedge. "Are you in that hedge again?" he called, walking back towards her. "What've you got boy, another fox?"

Dana climbed onto the trampoline and started to bounce up and down. She watched the man approach, and caught him saying something about a fox. Knowing the man was looking at her, and continuing to bounce, she called out, "What are you doing?"

He smiled, and lowering his head to ensure the peak of his cap covered his face, he put a finger to his lips.

"Hush, you'll disturb him."

Without warning the man threw himself down, giving a groan as he landed behind the hedge. Dana watched the hedge, waiting for him to reappear. He didn't. After what seemed like ages to the small girl, her bouncing slowed, and she dropped into a sitting position before she climbed down from the trampoline. She walked quickly to the area of the hedge where she had last seen the man, slowing as his dark shape came into view.

"What are you doing?" she asked, stopping a few feet away from him.

"Well, I was looking for my dog because he escaped from my garden, but I tripped I've hurt my ankle."

"Why did he escape?"

"Because he likes to play with foxes, and he knows they live in this field."

"I know, I've seen them. Where is he?"

The man shrugged as she moved closer. "I think he must be in their den. Last time I saw him he was by this hedge. Have you got a fox den under your hedge?"

"No . . ." Dana hesitated. "I don't think so. Daddy chases the foxes away in case they eat Bella. She's my bunny."

"Well, he's right, foxes and bunnies don't mix. I'd better check the den isn't here, do you want to help?"

"No, they might bite me."

"I wouldn't let them hurt you. You have a look, and I'll check it out," he coaxed as he shuffled closer to the hedge. Dana approached hesitantly and, leaning forward, peered down at the bottom of the hedge. He smiled as he looked at her face, paying particular attention to her eyes. Eyes surrounded by thick dark lashes. "You have beautiful eyes, do you know that? I bet you can help me." He smiled as she knelt down and leaned forward.

"I know. Everyone says that. It gets on my nerves. I can't see a den." Dana squinted at the earth beneath the hedge. Making a pretence of brushing away the debris that covered the ground under the hedge, he moved a little closer and pointed.

"I think you have something living here. Look at this hole. It's not big enough for a fox, but something will live there. I wonder if it's a mouse or a rabbit."

He examined the contours of her face as she held the hedge back with her hands, and pushed her face into the gap she had created, her eyes searching for the hole. Taking his phone from his pocket he told her to smile. She knew she was having her photograph taken, and smiled her best smile. He was delighted, and slipped the phone back into his pocket. A movement behind her caught his attention, and he stiffened as her mother stepped out of the house.

"I have to go now, but I'll come back and see you, then we can take the dog for a walk together. Would you like that?" He grinned as she nodded. "You take this, and we'll play with it next time we meet." Quickly pulling the tissue from his pocket he held out a soldier. "It's a magic soldier. Keep it secret, and keep it safe." As he uttered the words, he wasn't sure Dana was the sort of child able to keep a secret.

Dana had been told on numerous occasions never to accept gifts from strangers, but she hesitated for only a moment before stretching out her hand and snatching the toy. He raised his eyebrows; when she was with him, he'd teach her better than that. He opened his mouth to say goodbye, when Dana's mother called to her.

"Dana, what are you doing now? You'd better not be dirty again."

Dana jumped, her fingers wrapped round the soldier, and she jerked her head out of the hedge. Her hair caught in the twigs, and she gave a shrill scream as she yanked her head free. Her mother called to her.

"I knew I couldn't trust you to be good. Come here now. It's straight to bed for you."

But Dana shook her head. "I don't want to go to bed. I've only just come out. You said twenty minutes," she whined, and her chin trembled. "I'm not coming." She stomped her foot. "I don't like you."

The man was taken aback. That was no way to speak to an adult. Despite knowing he should get away as quickly as possible, he peered through the fence, waiting to see how the woman would respond. His eyes caught on something, and he put his hand into the hedge. Quite a large clump of hair had been torn from Dana's head as she had pulled back from the hedge. Carefully he untangled the strands of hair, and he placed it into the tissue which had held the soldier. As he looked back up, the woman was storming up the path, her face contorted with anger.

"I'm not having it, Dana. This is not acceptable. Get in the house now or you'll be sorry." The woman spat the words out, glancing over her shoulder to ensure the neighbours weren't watching. She saw the curtain twitch in the upstairs room next door, and slowing her pace, she lowered her voice. "Please, Dana, not again tonight. You promised Daddy you would be good."

"It was his fault. Not mine." Dana pointed at the hedge.

The man rolled onto his knees, and on all fours began to crawl back towards the lane.

"Whose fault? What do you mean?"

"The man who was talking to me." Dana pointed at the hedge again. "He's got dogs and foxes."

Dana's mother's eyes scanned the hedge. She saw the movement, and caught the flash of the red on his cap. Her hand flew to her mouth.

"Oh my God, get in the house now." As she ran towards the hedge, the man pushed himself to his feet and took off. He almost overshot the lane, but spotted it just in time as Dana's mother shouted at him.

"I've called the police, you pervert! What do you think you're doing? The police are on the way." She ran her fingers through her hair as he disappeared into the lane. She turned back to her daughter. "What did he say to you?" she demanded.

Dana was confused. Her mother had shouted at a total stranger, a grown up, for nothing. She didn't want to get into any more trouble. She willed the tears to flow.

"Nothing. It's not my fault." To her immense surprise her mother rushed forward, and swept her up into her arms.

"I know, baby, I know. Let's get you a drink and see how long Daddy will be." Clinging on to the tin soldier, Dana's sobs subsided as she allowed herself to be carried into the house.

He was breathless when he reached his car. He'd stopped running once out of Dana's street, but the adrenalin pumped through his veins, and his heart thundered in his chest, as he attempted a casual, if somewhat brisk, walk back to the car. He blew out a breath of relief as he pulled open the door.

"Hello there." A voice called from the other side of the road. Keeping his cap low, he looked up and out through the window of the passenger door. It was the couple from the field.

"Did you find him?" the woman called. A second wave of relief in as many minutes spread through him, and he raised his hand as he called back.

"Afraid not. I'm going to have to drive round the streets now. I'd better get on." He climbed into the car and slammed the door. The couple waved again and walked off.

He drove for a mile before he pulled over at a rank of shops. Taking the tissue from his pocket he gently unfolded the hair. He sat there for some minutes tidying the strands into a neat line across the tissue. Folding it back up, he kissed the tissue, before replacing it in his pocket. He needed to buy some supplies, as he would take Dana as soon as possible. He eyed the rank of shops and decided they were too small. He would be best going to one of the larger supermarkets. Glancing in the mirror he checked the road was clear before pulling out.

Meredith pushed open the door to the morgue and called out to Frankie Callaghan.

"Sherlock, I've got an urgent job for you. Who else is on tonight?"

Frankie Callaghan paused and looked over his shoulder at Meredith. Meredith had nicknamed him Sherlock when he had helped solve a case involving assisted suicide, at which time Frankie had been hoping to become romantically involved with Patsy. Whilst the two men respected each other's expertise, there was always an underlying current of unease, which occasionally boiled to the surface in frustration.

"More important than a severed arm, with no torso claiming it?" Frankie turned back to his work, and ran the scalpel under the nail of the finger he was holding, depositing the material it contained into a small flat dish. "What have you got? I wasn't expecting you tonight. I'm under strict instructions from Trump not to disturb you." He glanced up at the clock. "I'm almost done here, I was hoping to join Sarah for a late supper."

Meredith walked forward, his nose wrinkling in disgust as he looked at the arm. "What do we know?" he asked, taking a step back.

"*We* know it belonged to a female. *We* know she was dead before it was torn off." He looked down at the two evidence bags dangling from Meredith's hand. "What have you got there? I'm not short on fingers." Frankie laid the hand back on the table.

"Tin soldiers," Meredith announced. "Whoever took the girls gave them a parting gift. I want you to test them for fingerprints sharpish. If we have a match we can crack on tonight, if not tomorrow's another day. You did say you'd nearly finished."

"I did. As it's you, I'll do it myself. Let me finish up here, and we'll go across to the lab." Frankie pulled the microphone closer to his mouth. "In conclusion, white female aged between twenty and thirty-five, approximately nine and a half stone in weight, and probably no taller than five feet six inches. X-ray has revealed that the arm was broken, probably in childhood, but apart from the fact it has been torn from the shoulder, very little sign of damage, with the possibility of trauma to the elbow, also caused post-mortem. Estimated to have been submerged for no more than three days. The injury is what one would expect to see in an industrial or car accident, except of course she was dead prior to the event."

Frankie switched off the microphone and lifted the arm into a bag, which he zipped up. "I'll finish cleaning up here, once I've sorted you out." He pulled off his gloves and dropped them into a bin. "I was thoroughly enjoying your birthday party. Are you having a second go at it?"

"No, I don't do birthdays. I don't feel the need to celebrate getting older."

"Now why doesn't that surprise me. Mind you, at your age I expect I'll feel much the same." Frankie smiled as he opened the door. Meredith was only five or six years older than him. "Still, look on the bright side, you have Amanda and Patsy to keep you young."

"I do, Sherlock, I do, and keep them I will," Meredith winked as he walked through the open door, and towards the laboratory. "Come on then, let's get on with it."

Frankie followed him up the corridor. Nothing had ever come of his brief flirtation with Patsy, but Amanda was a medical student, and having been introduced to him, had been in touch several times. Frankie was concerned she had developed a crush on him, but was not about to share that with her father.

He keyed in the code to release the door and flipped the light switches. Walking quickly to the long low table, he took a sheet of paper from the drawer below, and placed it on the desk. He held out his hand.

"Let's check these out then." Frankie allowed the tin soldiers to slide onto the table. He pulled down a microscope and examined them, turning them with the points of the tweezers. He glanced up at Meredith. "There are partial prints on both, and one full print. These toys look very old. Probably late eighteen hundreds, although one of them has been repainted. Have you taken prints from those people we need to eliminate?"

Meredith slapped his forehead. "I knew there was something I forgot." His eyes narrowed, and he put his hand into his jacket and took out two envelopes. "Yes, Sherlock, I have."

Frankie rolled his eyes at the drama, and holding one of the soldiers he dusted it to better reveal the fingerprints. He then photographed them from numerous angles, while Meredith paced up and down, inspecting various jars and papers he came across en route. Having scanned the prints taken by Meredith, and those from the soldiers onto the system, he beckoned Meredith over.

"Here we go. I'm going to cross match them now."

Meredith came to stand behind him and leaned forward as the system searched for a match. Meredith grinned as MATCH was spelt across the screen in large green letters. He tutted as the match from the first soldier was with the prints from Gemma Lake. He didn't hold his breath as Frankie ran the second lot, and shook his head as the second match was with Ellen Rawlings. Frankie swivelled on his chair to face Meredith.

"Not what you'd hoped for. Sorry, Meredith. Let me take some samples from them. I can try and get one of the chaps to date them for you, and check the paintwork out." Frankie stood and faced Meredith. "But it won't be overnight, and it will take a couple of days at least. I don't want you chasing every two minutes."

"Good man, hurry up then. I'll drop them back into the incident room on my way home."

As he drove to the station, Meredith pondered what event might cause a dead body to have an arm torn off. He pulled up outside the front door. It was nine o'clock as he parked, and he promised himself he would be home before ten.

The duty officer was on the telephone as he entered. He was clearly struggling to get his point across.

"I know, sir. Someone will come out and take a statement as soon as they are free." He paused as the man ranted again. "Yes, I do appreciate that two girls were taken earlier in the week, but your daughter is safe now."

Meredith paused as he punched in the code to let himself into the main building. He turned as an old couple shuffled in and stood in front of the counter. The officer on the phone held his finger up and smiled at them.

"We've lost our wallet. Well, he has anyway." The woman nodded at her husband, and the officer put his hand over the mouthpiece.

"Take a seat, madam, I'll be two minutes." He sighed and looked away as the woman pulled her husband by the sleeve and led him to the unwelcoming chairs lined up against the far wall.

Meredith let the door slam behind him, and rather than go straight to the incident room as he intended, he walked to the reception office and tried to read over the officer's shoulder. The officer wrote something down, underlined it, and held the pad towards Meredith. Meredith ran his fingers through his hair.

Third one tonight!!!

"Sir, I can promise you that someone will be there. Yes, I know she's the same age, you said. They will be with you shortly . . . What sort of present? Did you say a soldier? What like Action -"

Meredith snatched the phone from his hand, and elbowed him out of the way.

"DCI Meredith here, Mr . . ." Meredith scanned the notes. "Dwight. Now start at the beginning, and when we're finished I'll come over myself."

Meredith listened to Dana's father give his daughter's version of the encounter in the garden. When he finished he hung up, and tapped the officer on the shoulder, apologising to the old couple who were telling him how they'd left a wallet on the bus.

"Who's supposed to be going there?"

"Hutchins. He's attending a possible break-in. Supermarket alarm going off in Westbury."

"Get hold of him, and tell him to meet me there." Meredith tapped the pad.

"You think it's serious then?" The officer shuffled from one foot to the other, embarrassed.

"I know it is."

Meredith didn't need to say more. The officer heard the unspoken accusation.

Meredith left him to get back to the couple, and took the stairs to the incident room two at a time. Bob Travers looked up as he flew into the room.

"Everything all right, Gov?"

"Nope, he's tried it again." Meredith patted his pocket. "Gave this one a soldier too."

"A what?" Travers stood and followed Meredith to his office. Meredith ran his finger down the list of names in the back of his desk diary, and picking up the phone dialled out. He drummed his fingers on his desk as he waited for his call to be picked up. "Get your coat we're . . . Caroline, it's Meredith."

For a very brief moment, Caroline Bird thought he might be calling for her. She sighed heavily as Meredith told her about Dana Dwight.

"I'm sorry if I'm disturbing your evening, but needs must." He'd heard the sigh and his tone was sarcastic.

"I sighed because it wasn't a one-off, and the fact that it was you. Give me the address."

Dana's father opened the door before Meredith had opened the gate. He stepped out to greet him.

"Thank you for coming. This was a serious attempt, wasn't it? I knew it."

"I don't know, sir. Before we go into this, can we take my officers down to where it happened?"

Dwight led the way to the end of the garden. On the way they passed his wife, pacing up and down, and smoking. She attempted a smile, but turned away as the tears returned. Meredith gave Travers and Hutchins instructions on a basic search and securing the scene, before returning to the house. Caroline Bird arrived.

"This is PC Bird. She specialises in dealing with children who have been traumatised. Rather than go in heavy handed, we'll let her see Dana on her own. I take it she's still awake?"

"Yes, she's not a good sleeper. All this . . . trauma as you call it, has wound her up. She's in here playing."

He pushed open the door to the sitting room. Dana was sitting on the floor surrounded by toys. She looked up and smiled. She was a pretty child.

"This lady has come to speak to you about the man and the foxes. Don't worry you're not in trouble, Daddy will be here."

Meredith caught Dwight's arm as he went to sit down.

"I think we can make the tea, sir, it's better that way."

"Shall we make a little film?" Caroline asked, unfolding the legs of a small tripod. Dana nodded eagerly. "Good then, where do you want to sit? You can be the star, I'll be the camerawoman."

Dwight shook his head and looked at Meredith puzzled.

"Standard these days, sir. We've got to be accurate with what they say, and how they say it. It proves they weren't coerced in anyway. We'd usually do it at the station, but given the hour, it's best we do it here, while she can still remember the details."

They watched as Dana took three dolls and sat with them in an armchair. She arranged the dolls on her lap.

"Ready," she announced confidently.

Caroline smiled at her. She pushed a button and a red light began to flash on top of the camera.

"Hello, Dana, can you tell me about today. About what happened when you were playing in the garden?"

Dana nodded frantically. "Well, first of all Mummy was being horrible to me again. So she let me go out to play after tea."

Meredith closed the door quietly and followed Dwight into the kitchen, where he filled the kettle.

"Her mother wasn't being horrible to her, you know. It's just Dana can be such a handful. We've spoilt her, I know that, but we waited so long for her." He stopped and looked out at his wife, who was lighting another cigarette. "She's adopted. My wife was so desperate for a child that when she got one, she gave in to every demand." He shrugged. "Instead of appreciating it, Dana takes advantage."

"All kids will take advantage, sir, if they can. My daughter used to run circles around me when she was younger. Come to think of it she still does now." Meredith smiled and looked round the neat and tidy kitchen. "Where do you keep the mugs? We'll be better for a cup of tea."

When she had finished, Caroline opened the door and called to Meredith.

"All done. I think Dana is almost ready for bed. She just needs to clear her toys away first."

Dana's mother smiled at how unlikely that would be as she hurried down the hall. She stood in the doorway as Caroline dismantled the camera.

Caroline pointed at the floor. "Come on then, Dana, get this lot packed away."

Dana slid off the chair and scooped a handful of toys to her chest, and walking to the toy box next to the television she dropped them in, before returning for more. Her mother shook her head; if she had suggested that there would have been a tantrum. Meredith pushed her gently into the room.

"Now then, Dana, where's this present? Your Dad said you'd hidden it."

"It's mine. He told me to keep it safe."

"I know, but I can't believe it's a soldier, not a real one." Meredith dropped onto his haunches and winked at her. "Can we do a deal?"

Dana looked suspicious and nodded hesitantly.

"If you let me borrow the soldier, I'll arrange for you to ride in a police car."

Dana turned her nose up. "Why would I want to do that?"

"Because there will be an ice cream at the end of it, and you can have the soldier back." Meredith put his hand to his chest. "I promise."

Without speaking Dana walked to the chair, and knelt down. Shoving her hand under the seat cushion, she fished around until she found the soldier. She took it back to Meredith and dropped it in the bag he held out.

"Why are you putting it in a bag?"

"Because I want to see if there's anything on it, and the bag will protect it."

"There's not." Dana shook her head solemnly. "He's clean, I washed him."

Meredith stood and forced a smile. "Good girl. Straight to bed now, and be a good girl for your mummy, I'm sure I'll see you again."

Once clear of the house Meredith cursed.

"Bollocks. I didn't have much hope, but I had some. How are we doing out back?"

Travers shook his head as he closed the gate. "Nothing that we could see. But it's covered up and there's tape around the wider area, and a cover over the immediate patch. One of the boys will stay on guard. The forensic chaps will come at first light. I doubt they'll find anything, but let's hope they do." He put his hand around his throat, and massaged it. "Do you two fancy a pint? I clocked off an hour ago, and I'm spitting feathers. You make a lousy cup of tea, Gov."

For a moment, Caroline forgot about the boyfriend that she'd left hugging a bottle of wine.

"I might just take you up on that." She smiled at Travers, and then looked to Meredith, who had never been known to turn down a drink after a hard day's work. "What about you, shall we join him?"

"You two go ahead, I'm supposed to be somewhere else."

"You always were, but it didn't bother you before." Caroline nudged him, and missed the face Travers pulled at Meredith, before turning away grinning, and she persisted. "Come on, it will be fun."

"Seriously," Meredith shook his head and stepped away from her. "I can't, someone is waiting for me."

Caroline was about to tell him that someone was waiting for her too, so where was the harm. But she knew where the harm was, and common sense kicked in.

"Off you go then, I'll see you first thing for the debrief. You can buy the doughnuts." Caroline forced the smile to stay put, and turned back to Travers. "I should go too. See you tomorrow."

Meredith walked back to the car smiling. He was glad Patsy would be waiting for him. If she hadn't been, he might have been tempted.

Patsy was in bed, reading, when he got home. He gave her a quick update as he showered. Patsy sat on the toilet, knees hugged to her chest, throwing questions at him. He towelled himself quickly and, still damp, led her back to the bedroom.

"Get in that bed before the phone goes again." He threw back the duvet and Patsy obliged. "I've missed you, Patsy Hodge, come here and let me show you how much." He climbed in and pulled her to him. "I want to sleep, I want my present, but most of all I want you." He kissed her. "This bloody job gets in the way."

"Then let's go on holiday. You had agreed we could before this happened." She drew a line from his forehead to his chin with her fingertip. "You do nee d   a break."

"I know, we will, it's just . . . Shut up, Hodge, we can talk later."

As Patsy obeyed, she crossed the fingers on the hand which pulled him closer, hoping the phone would remain silent. It did.

"Was that my present, or is there more to come?" Meredith asked as he blew some stray strands of hair from her face. He grinned. "I'm happy either way."

"Both. But I've decided I'm not giving you your present until we're on holiday. So it may coincide with your fiftieth and save me buying another." She poked him in the ribs.

"We'll go, I promise. There are a lot of birthdays between now and then, you cheeky madam, but until we catch this bloke, I'm not sure -"

"Meredith, there will always be a bloke who needs catching. If we work on that basis, you will be retired. I think we should just . . ." Patsy tapped his chest. "I might have to go to Seville for a couple of days soon. It's more than likely it will be pointless. You could come." She moved back against his body and took his face in her hands. "You can do two days, three days tops."

"But when, Patsy, if I -"

"Not for a week or so. It's a city break thing, we can easily pick up a flight."

Meredith hated flying, and his head fell forward against hers as he groaned.

"Man up, Meredith. It's that, or you don't get what I've got for you."

"I thought I just had that." Meredith thrust his hips forward, and she laughed.

"Oh, Johnny, you are almost funny sometimes. I'll look at the flights tomorrow, and perhaps we can pencil something in."

The more Patsy thought about it, the more it seemed like a good idea. She could tell Meredith why she needed to go beforehand, and propose to him while they were there. She smiled at the thought of having his undivided attention. She turned over and snuggled back against him.

"Almost funny. I'm always funny, and don't call me Johnny, and then I'll give it my serious consideration."

"Okay. I promise. Night, Meredith."

"Night, Hodge."

Leaning forward, he peered at the close-up shot of Dana on his computer screen. Perfect, he thought, she's just perfect. He ran his finger gently along the strand of hair in front of him and smiled. She might be with him in a couple of days, all being well.

CHAPTER EIGHT

Patsy looked at the woman sitting in front of her, and wondered why she had agreed to meet with her so early in the morning. The woman was clearly teetering on the brink of some sort of breakdown, and Patsy didn't want to be the one to push her over the edge because her mind wasn't yet fully engaged. She blinked at the woman's eager voice.

"When are you going to get started?"

"I can start right away." Patsy held her finger up. "But, having spoken to you, I have to say I'm not convinced you are doing this for the right reasons."

"Ah," the woman smiled serenely, "a non-believer." Her shoulders twitched a dismissive shrug. "I'm used to that. My beliefs won't stop you finding him though?" Doubt crept in. "My reasons for finding him have nothing to do with the basic fact that I want him found, surely?"

"Of course not. My concern, Miss Hawthorne -"

"Call me Freda, please." She almost purred the words, and Patsy nodded as she held back the sigh.

"My concern, Freda, is what happens if I find him, and he doesn't want to have any further contact with you? If you don't mind me saying you seem to be placing an awful lot of weight on things said by a man you've never met, and now a . . . psychic?"

Patsy paused, awaiting some form of reaction. Denial, outrage, anything would have done, but the woman remained silent. She sat, her back straight against the chair, head high, and hands held with fingers linked in her lap.

"I will be fine as long as I know that he is safe. I may never have spoken to him, but his fear was clear enough."

"Yes, I've read through what you've sent me. But he also said he loved you. Your correspondence read as though you were lovers, and yet you'd never met."

"Five years, Ms Hodge." Freda's serenity vanished in the blink of an eye. "When you have no need to hide your insecurities and your failings, it is amazing how liberated you become." Leaning forward, Freda held out her arms like an evangelist preaching to her flock. "To be able to open your heart, and your mind to another individual who accepts your shortcomings, even embraces them without judgement," Freda rapped the table, "that forms a bond which transcends any physical act."

Colour had risen to her cheeks and a few strands of hair escaped the tie-dyed scarf securing it in place. Freda tucked them behind her ears, and drew in a calming breath as she leaned back against the chair. Patsy resisted the urge to smile. This woman was smitten. She was missing the romance of the exchanges with Lyndon Ward, if indeed that was his name. There had been no direct reference to sex in their correspondence, but some of the euphemisms had been quite creative. Freda was an attractive if somewhat flamboyant woman. Patsy guessed she was in her late fifties, and she had no doubt that, provided Lyndon didn't turn out to be a spotty teenager, or pensioner in a wheelchair, they would tear each other's clothes off within an hour of meeting, if of course they ever met, and there was the issue. Despite Lyndon's claims to be working, travelling, poorly, and the less likely in hiding, there was no way he wouldn't have found the time to come and meet the woman sitting in front of her.

Patsy decided to be blunt. "What if he's married with four kids?"

"He won't be."

"But if he is?"

"Then it would be disappointing that he didn't tell me, but it won't change the fact I think he's been kidnapped or is in some sort of danger."

"Why wouldn't his wife have raised the alarm?"

"There is no wife, and if there was, it's because she is keeping quiet to protect him."

"What if he's sitting in front of the fire, ignoring you because he's moved on?"

Patsy saw the flinch, but Freda controlled her voice.

"He won't be, but if he is at least I'll know he's safe." Freda forced a smile.

"Have you ever exchanged photographs?"

"No." Freda clasped her hands a little tighter.

"Why? I can understand Lyndon might have something to hide, but did you not ever think of sending him a photograph?"

"No." Freda pursed her lips, but her chin wobbled.

"Why? In a five-year relationship, all via email or chat room, do you not think that would be a normal course of events?"

Freda held Patsy's eye, but fought to regain control of her quivering chin, and swallowed rapidly to remove the lump in her throat. Patsy lowered her eyes. That had been cruel but she believed it may be best for Freda to allow Lyndon to disappear into the night. She looked up ready to apologise, but having regained control, Freda slowly pushed herself to her feet using the arms of the chair. She faced Patsy.

"I know all these things. I have considered all these things." Freda's body twitched, as though someone had prodded her. "I need him in my life. I was . . . I am, prepared to accept what we had. Now I want to know what's happened, and where he is. I want to know if I should grieve . . ." she lowered her head, "for any reason." Still staring at the ground floor, she added, "I can see you don't want this case. I'll find someone else." She raised her head, her eyes moist, and Patsy gave in.

"Sit down, Freda. I'll take the case. I simply needed to know that you knew what you might be letting yourself in for. I'll get some tea whilst you read this." Patsy smiled as Freda dropped back into the chair, and she pushed the contract across the desk.

Meredith held the three bags up to the incident team, and jerked the thumb of his free hand behind him.

"Here they are." He placed the bags on the desk in front of him. "Our man gives the girls he's targeting a gift. Toy soldiers, of all things. Sherlock is running tests on samples, but we know the only prints are from the girls. They are made of tin. We have no date of manufacture yet, but I want two of you contacting all the specialists and or collectors you can find, and see if we can make out where they came from. I've had a quick scan of the internet; they were not made for the serious, 'I'm going to re-enact battles in the spare bedroom' type." He rolled his eyes, "They are too big. These were for playing with. An early, basic form of Action Man, they bend at the elbows and knees." He stepped back and perched on the table behind him. "So, back to yesterday's attempt. The latest girl, Dana, was hysterical immediately after her encounter, but Caroline thinks that was due to her mother's reaction, rather than her own fear. Caroline, perhaps you'd like to share your thoughts."

Caroline nodded, and swallowed. This was the part of the job she hated, delivering her findings to a group of people, even those she knew. She'd much rather do a written report and let the senior officer deal with it. She drew in a breath and looked down at her notes. She'd already memorised them, but took comfort from seeing the familiar words. She decided not to stand, but pulled her shoulders back and leaned forward against the desk.

"All three of the girls liked this man. He was kind, gentle and, on occasion, funny. He told them what they wanted to hear, of course, and for the best part let them do what they wanted." Caroline inclined her head. "But he reminded them of their manners if they forgot a please or thank you, but in a nice way. None of them were in any way afraid of him, and they were comfortable in his presence. Ellen Rawlings said he was like a kind teacher."

As though a gust of wind had blown in and caused their bodies to move, there was a brief shuffle amongst the team as everyone avoided looking at Dave Rawlings. Caroline smiled at Rawlings, whose face remained impassive. Taking a breath, she ploughed on.

"Dana Dwight is spoilt. She's used to getting her own way and she manipulates her mother. Like the other two she had been told about speaking to strangers, but like the other two had been drawn in by his personality. When her mother appeared she felt guilty, caught her hair in the hedge, and screamed the place down to divert attention. But she wasn't afraid of the man, or alarmed by anything he said or did."

"Are you saying the man is not dangerous?" Rawlings scratched his head. "Because that's what it sounds like."

"Of course not." Caroline looked at Rawlings as though he should know better. "But I think it might be worth getting a profiler to look at what we've got. Given the examination results, my gut instinct is telling me he's not a paedophile, and I hope I'm right."

"That's what I was wondering," Meredith nodded. "But he's after something, so if he's not a nonce, what does he want with these girls? Will he come back for Dana, or perhaps, given the fuss, move on to someone else? I'm not convinced on bringing a profiler in though. Too much mumbo jumbo involved, and I'm not sure we've got enough to make it worth their while, but I'll think on it. Remind us what we have as a description."

Feeling more relaxed Caroline got to her feet, and walked to the board. She lifted the pen and wrote the heading, *Description*.

"We haven't got much really, no facial features at all from any of them, but here it is for what it's worth. Charlie probably has mousy or fair hair. None of them noticed his head, but all agreed he had hairs on his arms and they weren't dark. Height between five feet ten and six foot. Gemma said when he opened the car door, the car was a little taller than him. The average height of a Range Rover, and we're pretty sure that was his car, is six feet two, although they can be adjusted. He wears a silver watch, it was chunky but not bling." Caroline smiled. "Ellen said it was not the stuff of pop stars, but bigger than her dad's watch. Dave wears a Rotary, which is very slim so not much help. He wore different shoes on each day they think, and prefers a slip-on style. Neither girl can remember seeing laces. Dana didn't see his feet. Other than that, he wore dark trousers or jeans, and pale shirts, no tie. He didn't wear any jewellery other than the watch. The cap he wears is black and may or may not have a red logo. They can't agree on that," Caroline jotted down the points as she went, and turned back to face them, "and his phone plays a funny tune. They didn't know what, and couldn't remember enough to sing it to me, but it made them smile and he commented on it. Although again, they can't remember what was said. He didn't answer it when it rang. He used it to take a picture of Dana; it was black, but she can't remember if it was like mine, a Nokia Android, or her father's iPhone."

"What about his voice? Did any of them say anything about his voice? Was it a local accent?"

"This is where the girls give even more conflicting information. Dana said he had a sore throat, but that's probably because he was whispering. Don't forget her mother could, and did, reappear. Ellen said it was normal, and Gemma said he spoke like the men on the telly. Which, if anything, probably tells us he didn't have a local accent." Caroline clipped the lid back on the pen. "That's all I've got I'm afraid. Other than the fact he makes fab pancakes."

"Thanks, Caroline." Meredith nodded, and with that she was dismissed.

She walked back to her seat wishing she could stay on the case.

"A man talking to a girl through a hedge is unlikely to make the news, but *Crimebusters* will run it on their lunchtime 'Did you notice' slot. Seaton, you can get over there as soon as we're done here." He pointed at the photographs of the three girls. "Trump, you work with Adler on how these girls are connected. I don't think they were random. I'm off to see Sherlock in about half an hour. I want the results of whatever they found at the scene. We also have a dismembered arm, don't forget." There were a few murmurs from the team, and he pointed at Trump. "Trump pulled it out of the mud under the Suspension Bridge last night. It wasn't from a jumper though, dead before it got there. Let's hope it was washed there by the tide, I don't fancy piecing her back together bit by bit."

Driving to work with a light heart, he sang along to the radio, and smiled each time Dana's face floated to the surface of his thoughts. There were things he needed to do if Dana was coming, and he was convinced she was. He had to get them done as soon as possible. He was still whistling as he got out of the car. Dana was the one, she had to be. He reminded himself to be patient as he slammed the door. He knew where she was, he knew where she would be. The result would be in before the schools broke up for the holidays, so he could get her before the family went away, if they were going away. It wouldn't be long now. Taking his phone from his pocket, he scrolled through to her photograph and grinned.

"Something's making you happy. Is that a message from a girlfriend?" Sally pouted. "Could you help me with this, please." She held out a cloth shopping bag. It was bursting with papers. He slipped the phone back into his pocket, and took it from her. Lifting out a small battered case, she slammed the boot, and turned back to him. "Is it a girlfriend, a love interest?" She made to nudge him but stumbled as she reached the kerb.

"Sort of . . . not quite. Here let me." He relieved her of the case.

"Thank you." She smiled up at him. "Is it someone here?"

"A gentleman never tells. You should know better," he joked as she held the door open for him. Inside he was sneering. Was she flirting with him? As if he'd be interested in a woman of her age. He shuddered at the thought.

"I know, but at my age there is so little excitement." She sighed. "Put those in my room for me. I need to powder my nose."

He placed the bags in her room and smiled as he looked around. He liked it here. It felt comfortable, like home. But once he had Dana, he wouldn't be able to stay. He'd have her on a plane within hours. Long before they checked. He smiled at the thought, glad he had the passport.

Patsy opened the door of her office, and followed Freda Hawthorne into the main reception area, and towards the exit. As she assured Freda she would be in touch as soon as she had any information, she frowned at Linda. As Patsy's door had opened, Linda had jumped to her feet and hurried to the main door. She now stood next to it, poised to open it and get rid of Patsy's client as quickly as possible. She fidgeted as Freda thanked Patsy for the third time.

Sharon Grainger stopped work and watched Linda. Sharon was the wife of Patsy's partner, Chris Grainger. Very little escaped her attention. She even seemed to know if something had happened when she wasn't in the office. Sharon was very practical, and tended to speak her mind, believing little could be achieved by beating about the bush. As Linda closed the door and made to join Patsy, Sharon held up her hand.

"What's going on?"

"I was about to ask the s -" Patsy was cut off by Linda speaking over her.

"Nothing. Would you like a cuppa?" Linda beamed at Sharon, but couldn't look her in the eye.

"Yes I would, after you've told me what's going on."

Linda walked towards the door that led to the kitchen. "You've been in this business too long, you're very suspicious. Would you like biscuits with your tea?" She put her hand on the door handle.

"STOP," Sharon commanded. "Sit you your arse back on your seat, and tell me what I've missed. It's obviously something to do with the call earlier." She glanced at Patsy. "Everything okay with Meredith?"

Patsy laughed. "Yes, thank you. How are things with you and Chris? Sharon, just because Linda is acting loopy, so no change there, it doesn't mean something is going on with me and Meredith." She shook her head and held her hands up. "I have no secrets." She turned to Linda. "What's got you all excited? Come on, put us out of our misery."

"Nothing has me excited. I'm very calm, look." Linda held out her hands to demonstrate how calm she was.

Sharon stood up, and pointed to Linda's chair. "Sit. Your hands might not be shaking but your face is telling a whole different story. Now sit down and tell us what you are bursting to say, but not to me apparently."

Linda shook her head at Patsy, and her shoulders drooped. The look said 'I told you so'. Patsy grinned at her as she sat down, and held her face in cupped hands.

"Are you sure, Patsy?" Linda asked, now irritated Patsy hadn't protected her from Sharon, which after all would have been for Patsy's own benefit. Patsy looked at her friend and a tiny prickle of fear dashed across the back of her neck. She frowned; there was nothing going on, and she had work to do.

"Get on with it."

Patsy looked at Sharon and shrugged.

"Okay, but don't say I didn't warn you. Are you ready . . . Antonio Garcia called."

Linda looked at her and blinked, and. Patsy cursed inwardly, she should have trusted Linda's instinct. This was a conversation she didn't want to have with Sharon.

She forced a smile. "That's good. Fabulous even, did he leave a number?" It was Patsy's turn to attempt to communicate with facial gestures, and she nodded at Linda, willing her to carry on a normal conversation.

Linda was confused, if not a little miffed. Patsy had obviously told the Graingers that she had taken Nicola's case, but hadn't mentioned it to her. She huffed, because, had she known that, she would have tried to get information from Garcia.

"Can you let me know next time a secret becomes common knowledge? Then I'll not have to mess about. And in answer to the question, no, he said he would call back when I wouldn't give him any information."

"Who is Antonio Garcia, and why would Patsy want him kept a secret?" Sharon winked at Linda. "Which he still was, by the way."

Linda and Patsy exchanged glances, like schoolgirls caught smoking by the teacher.

"I told you," Linda chastised Patsy. "Why did you make me say it?"

"Why did I? You could have just waited, or sent me a text. There really wasn't a need to hop around the office like you were wetting yourself. What was that all about?" Patsy started laughing, glad that Linda was tied to a desk, and for the best part only dealt with things relating to technology. "You are not a good actress." Still laughing, she turned back towards her office.

"Not so fast, lady. You're taking me for a coffee, and you can tell me all about Mr Garcia, and what the big secret is." Sharon glanced at Linda. "Don't worry, we'll bring you something back."

Linda looked incredulous. "Why can't I come? In fact, why can't you stay here?" She was keen to see Sharon's reaction to the news.

"Because, my little flower, Chris is due back, and if madam here has been doing something she wanted to keep from us, then I shall decide whether or not he needs to know." As Sharon spoke she stood, collected her handbag, and, taking Patsy by the elbow, she led her to the door.

Sharon managed to keep quiet during the ten minutes or so it took Patsy to update her. Only the odd twitch of her lips or a slight widening of the eyes indicated she was even remotely interested in what Patsy had to say. When Patsy had finished, Sharon sniffed, cleared her throat, and picked up her coffee, which she sipped slowly whilst looking at Patsy over the brim of her cup.

"Well, say something. You see, nothing to hide. It's not a big deal." Patsy sounded as though she were trying to convince herself. "Why have you gone quiet? That's scary."

Patsy attempted humour, and Sharon replaced the cup, her face uncharacteristically serious.

"Do you want me to be honest, or shall I simply tell you how stupid you are taking a job so close to home?" Sharon clearly wasn't amused, and Patsy's response sounded far more confident than she felt.

"I want you to be honest, of course."

Sharon inspected her finger nails as she considered her words. Patsy knew she was probably attempting to soften a blow, and that made her nervous. Sharon usually hit things head on.

"You think the baby is Meredith's, don't you?" As always, she was blunt, to the point, and now she had started did not intend to pull any punches. "Having considered this, I think he could be too. The question is, what the hell Nicola is up to?"

Patsy's head flew back as though she had been slapped. She hadn't been sure what to expect but it wasn't that. She didn't answer the question.

"Why do you think she's up to anything?" Patsy braced herself, as Sharon first closed her eyes, and then drew in a deep breath.

"I have known Nicola for many years. I went to their wedding. She's a nice enough girl. We weren't particularly close, but I know she was timid, in a general sense, you understand. She would speak to anyone, she wasn't tongue tied or anything like that, unless of course the conversation was likely to be unpleasant. For many years she avoided all confrontations, preferring to come at issues from the side, rather than head on." Sharon raised her finger and pointed at Patsy, "So what I'm asking myself is why choose you?" She withdrew her finger and tapped her lip. "Have you told Meredith? I assume not, which is why this was to be kept secret from us."

"Nicola asked me to keep it confidential. I haven't broken that trust. You don't count, you're work." Patsy attempted a smile. It lasted seconds.

"Which is why I asked what she's up to. Chris and Meredith have been friends for years, and I have never been known for keeping my mouth shut. The woman had three chances, and that's why she came to you." Sharon nodded, satisfied that she had unravelled the mystery.

"Three chances meaning the three of us. But why choose me? Why not go to Chris? It must have taken guts to have that conversation with me." Patsy frowned. "I'm not sure where you're coming from Sharon, the woman seemed quite genuine."

"She probably was. Tell me her exact words again. Why did she say she wanted to trace this man?"

"She said he was *possibly* Paul's father. That's the word she used, possibly, and it's why I took the case." Patsy shrugged. "You were right about that."

"And that being so, you need to brace yourself, as I think what she was really saying was that Meredith is *probably* the father. Rather than confront him with that, she's first eliminating any possibles." Sharon tutted and nodded her head knowingly. "Once that's achieved, she was relying on one of us to point that out to Meredith. He of course would demand to know." She held Patsy's gaze. "I'm sorry, Patsy, that's what I think is happening here. Two birds with one stone, so to speak."

"When I first met Nicola, she was still pregnant. She didn't know I was involved with Meredith, because I wasn't really, and she was adamant that at the time she fell pregnant she and Meredith hadn't had sex for some time. It was why she left him. That's what she said."

Sharon leaned forward and patted Patsy's hand. "Shall I continue being honest?"

Patsy leaned forward and covered her face with her hands, groaning as she did so. "I'm not going to like this, am I?" she asked from behind her hands.

"I doubt it, so shall I proceed?" Sharon smiled as Patsy nodded, her face still hidden.

"Nicola was a nice girl. Nice, in all senses of the word. She was kind, considerate, loving, giving, I'm sure I needn't go on. She didn't mess about either. To my mind, it is remotely possible that she did get drunk, and have a one night stand whilst Meredith was off doing something similar. But I have to be honest, Patsy, it doesn't ring true." Sharon looked down at the table, unsure as to whether to go on.

Patsy peeped out of the gap between her fingers. "Why have you stopped?"

"Isn't that enough?"

"Not really."

"Okay, I shall spell it out. Not that I think you need me to. What if after all the failed pregnancies she experienced before, culminating in the still birth, Nicola found she was pregnant yet again? The difference this time is their marriage is really no more than a sham. Too much water under the bridge. What's the girl to do? Stay with a man that she probably dislikes, despite her love for him."

Sharon saw Patsy flinch, but carried on regardless. "One that sleeps around, one who may make her so miserable she may lose yet another baby? Or would she be sensible? Go and live a nice quiet, simple life. Be healthy, be calm, and think of nothing but the baby. I think there is a distinct possibility it's Meredith's baby. How do you know she hasn't fabricated this other man? This waiter who has conveniently disappeared, and even if he does exist, and you find him, he will deny it. Who wants to be lumbered with a baby after a quick moment of pleasure?" Sharon shook her head. "What if you test him, and it comes back negative, what then?"

Patsy had begun to nod. "Then I would tell Meredith because that's the right thing to do." Patsy pursed her lips.

"And if you're a little bit tardy in getting there, Chris or I would do it for you, because it's the right thing to do."

Patsy shrugged. "Perhaps I'm naïve, Sharon, perhaps my people reading skill is not as good as I think it is, but she seemed genuine. She was insistent I go to Seville to look for him, even though I thought that would be a waste of time and money. She didn't care about the cost." Patsy placed her hand on her chest. "I'm only here now because I persuaded her to wait a week."

Sharon brushed imaginary crumbs from the table to the floor, and positioned the salt and pepper pots to each side of the sugar bowl. She looked up at Patsy.

"I hope I'm wrong, Patsy, truly I do. I hope you get to Spain, drag the man back with you, and they all live happily ever after . . ." She sighed. "But it's not likely, is it? And knowing that, we have to ask why she is doing this?"

"Nicola said she wanted Paul to know his father. She wanted nothing from him, just that he acts as a father to his son. She even said she would reward him financially. You wouldn't say that if you were just playing some sort of game, and a bloody elaborate one according to you." Patsy faltered. "I hope not anyway, I don't want any more complications in our lives."

Sharon became business like once more. She tidied the table, left a tip in the saucer, and picked up her bag.

"Then let's call the man, and get to the bottom of this. As with most things, the truth will out. I hope I'm wrong, unlikely I know, but a tiny possibility nonetheless." Sharon grinned. "In fact, if I'm wrong and I've worried you unnecessarily, I'll . . . I'll do something embarrassing." She slapped her own wrist. "I do that all the time anyway, don't I? I'll tell you what, I'll do anything that you ask me to as a punishment. How does that sound?"

"Unnecessary. Shall we buy a box of buns and get back to the office. I do have work to do, and the boss's wife is a real tyrant on the quiet." Patsy attempted humour, but wanted to get back to start the ball rolling. If Meredith was the father, the sooner they confirmed it, the better.

Meredith slid his phone into his pocket, and walked out into the incident room.

"I'm off to see Sherlock, I'll expect . . ."

He stopped speaking as Trump waved at him. Meredith walked over, and read the notes Trump had jotted down as he finished the call.

Replacing the receiver, Trump looked up at Meredith. "There's good news, and not so good news, sir."

"Get on with it, Trump."

"That was the owner of the café where the girls turned up. It seems one of her regulars, unaware of what was happening with the girls, saw them being dropped off." Trump smiled briefly. "That was the good news. The bad news is, the witness may be unreliable. She likes a drink."

"What, at half past six in the morning? What was she, a clubber on her way home?"

"No, a bag lady. A tramp. Her name's Peggy. She's at the café now."

"Well then, go and get her. I'll wait here."

"What if she doesn't want to come? I don't want to scare her by bringing her to the station. Wouldn't it be better if we went to her?" The café owner had told Trump she hadn't mentioned to Peggy that she was calling the police in case she ran off.

"Trump, you're a policeman. This is a bag lady. Go and get her. You can charm her in, I'm sure you'll have something in common."

Twenty minutes later Trump walked into the café. He glanced around the customers as he approached the counter. There was no bag lady. He pulled his identification from his pocket and smiled at the woman poised to serve him.

"DS Trump, I'm looking for the proprietor."

"That's me. She's out the back. I can't have her in here, she stinks. Sweet old thing though, and sharp as a blade, so be careful." The woman lifted the hatch. "Come on through." She led the way through the kitchen area, along a wide corridor that doubled as a store room and out to the back yard. "All right, Peg? How are you doing?" she called as she approached. Stepping out into the yard, the woman pulled a packet of cigarettes from her pocket and lit one.

"I'll have one of those." Peggy looked up from the plate of food, and smiled. The smile disappeared as she spotted Trump. "Who's that? Have you got a new boyfriend?"

Trump noticed her grab the handle of the holdall by her feet, and saw her eyes flicker to the rear gate. She was considering making a run for it. He looked at her woollen overcoat. It was heavily stained, and large shiny patches glistened in the sun light. He really didn't want to have to apprehend her. It was bad enough to know she was going to sit in his car. He smiled, but take her in he would; he couldn't wait for Meredith to meet her.

"Don't be daft. He's too old for me, Peg, I'm after a toy boy."

Peggy rolled her eyes and stared at Trump who walked forward, hand out.

"What do you want?" Peggy was halfway to her feet.

"I want to do a deal with you."

"Why?"

"Because you have something I want."

Peggy frowned and dropped back into the chair. "What?"

"Ah, that thing most precious to mankind. Knowledge."

"You're terribly posh for a copper."

"So they tell me. You don't sound too common yourself, Peggy. May I call you Peggy?" Trump pulled a rusting chair out from the other side of the table, and perched on as little of it as he could.

Peggy cackled. "But of course, kind sir. That was a long time ago. Let's get down to business. What's in this for me?"

"What would you like?"

"My own yacht." Peggy tutted at what she considered to be a stupid question.

"What budget are we talking about?" Peggy's dark eyes glinted as Trump realised this was going to cost him more than a cup of tea and a bun.

"Well, that rather depends on how good your information is."

"Better than you'll get anywhere else. There was no one else around." Peggy crossed her palm over the table. "We're talking ghost town."

"Well, we'd better get you back to the station and see what my superior will do for you."

"I'm not going to the station." Peggy shook her head. "Here will be as good as anywhere."

"Peggy, be reasonable. We've had two young girls abducted, and we believe the same man tried to take another yesterday evening. The team is flat out on this, so you need to do your duty."

"Twenty pounds and I'll get in the car." Peggy held up a finger, "But that's not part of the deal. Your boss can sort that out." She flipped her hand over and waited for Trump to place a note on it. "Thank you." She grinned as she rolled the note into a tube, and inserted it into her cleavage. This took several minutes as she pulled down the various layers of clothing. Standing, she hauled the handle of the holdall over her shoulder. "Let's go. I'm a busy woman, places to go, and people to see."

"I'm sure you are, Peggy. I'll bring the car round to the gate for you." He smiled as Peggy narrowed her eyes.

"I can help you lot out, but still not allowed to walk through the café, I see. Hurry up then, before I change my mind."

Trump settled Peggy and her holdall into the rear of the car and jumped in. Holding his breath, he pushed the buttons to open the windows and allow an air flow through the car. He hoped the ground floor interview room was free as it had windows that opened. He glanced at Peggy in the rear-view mirror. She grinned at him.

"I know I whiff. It's an acquired taste." She waved her elbows up and down and laughed.

Trump returned her grin. Meredith was going to love this interview.

Having installed Peggy in the interview room with a large mug of tea, Trump went to collect Meredith.

"She's in the interview room downstairs, sir."

"Why? Why didn't you bring her up, is she infirm in some way?"

"Oh no, quite the opposite, in fact, but to be honest she stinks. No nicer way to put it I'm afraid. I think we should hurry. I've left the window open, and she wasn't keen on coming until I told her we'd reward her."

Meredith opened the door to the interview room, and smiled at Peggy as he quickly took in her appearance. He guessed that she was actually half the size she appeared to be, due to the number of layers she had on beneath the heavy gent's overcoat. Both windows were wide open and the breeze was doing its best to lift the strands of grey hair which had escaped the severe pony tail. But coated in grease and grime it needed something stronger than a light breeze. He could see she was assessing him in the same way, and he winked.

"What do you know then, Peggy? I'm Meredith, and I'm going to record this if that's all right with you. It means I don't need to make so many notes." He pushed the button on the recorder and announced the purpose of the recording. Peggy sat quietly watching him. Meredith looked at the empty cup. "Would you like more tea?"

"I thought you'd never ask. Something to eat wouldn't go amiss either." She glanced at Trump, her eyes accusing him of starving her.

"I am sorry, Peggy, old girl. I saw you'd polished off a full English, and assumed you wouldn't be hungry. My mistake, I'll get it right this time." Trump left the room and Peggy looked back at Meredith.

"Get on with it then. Tell me what I get, and I'll tell you what I know."

"Where do you live?"

"Wherever I lay my hat." Peggy touched the top of her head and rolled her eyes. "Oops haven't got one." She grinned as Meredith pursed his lips.

He tried again. "Where do you normally sleep?"

"Ah, same question really. That depends on the weather. What difference does it make?"

"I want to know why you were where you were, what you saw, and if you've seen him before. If you would be able to recognise him again. If you were sober enough to know what you saw, *and* if I can trust any of your answers." He smiled and leaned towards her. "You see Peggy, when people think there's something in it for them, they sometimes make stuff up, you know, just to get the money. Before we agree anything, I have to test you, to see whether or not I can trust you."

Peggy mirrored his stance, and their faces were no more than a foot apart. When she began to speak, Meredith had to use all of his will power not to pull back or look as disgusted as he felt as her stale breath caught him full on. He held his breath as she spoke.

"Look, Merriwinkle, I didn't come all this way to fabricate a story. I may be what these days is called a bag lady, although I personally prefer hobo, or gentlewoman of the road, but it would be folly for you to assume that I lost my conscience somewhere along the way."

She sighed and blew out the breath; Meredith almost passed out. He fell back against his chair and linked his fingers over his midriff in an effort to make the movement seem casual.

"I have information. How useful it would be I don't know, but as you can see I am of limited means, so occasionally I have to barter." She leaned back holding his gaze. "But I promise you this: what I tell you will be the truth, not distorted by drink. I was stone cold sober having had a rather comfortable night, and at least six hours' sleep."

Meredith studied her for a moment, and a smile twitched around his lips. The woman was clearly well educated, her brain wasn't befuddled by alcohol, and she had a sense of humour, hence his new name. He'd play her at her own game.

"Well, I'm certainly glad to hear that. I'll tell you what, Peggy, you tell me what you know, and the better the information, the better your reward. We'll start with, say, a shower and some new clothes, then we'll step up to see if we can get you a room in a hostel." He grinned at her. "Don't worry, I'll buy you a hat. And then I'll see if I can't have a word with the caretaker, and see if I can get you a couple of hours cleaning here. That way, you're presentable, housed, and you'll have some income coming in."

He pursed his lips, and tilted his head as though waiting for her to consider this offer. He saw the horror flit across her expression, and her head began to shake.

"I've been there and done all that, it doesn't suit. People are too nosey. I like to choose who I associate with. No, Merriwinkle, no, you'll have to come up with an alternative."

"Okay, what about breakfast on me, for a week, at that café you like. The one where Trump picked you up." To his surprise, Peggy threw her head back and laughed. It was genuine amusement and tears formed, which she brushed away as she regained control. "What did I say?"

Meredith smiled at her as the door opened and Trump appeared with a tray.

"Oh, Merriwinkle, I haven't had a laugh for over a month." She looked at

Trump and smiled. "You said he picked me up. I was adding two and two, and getting five on the romantic connotation." She lifted a doughnut from the plate as Trump placed the tray on the desk. "It tickled me, that's all." Biting into the doughnut she turned back to Meredith, who was waiting until she'd finished her mouthful. She brushed the sugar from her lips. "Make it the one around the corner, and I think we should agree a fortnight would be better, and you're on."

Meredith nodded. "Done, but why the one around the corner?"

"Because I can still get my hand-outs from Dot. If I've just had a breakfast, she won't be as keen to give me something to take away." Peggy took another bite of the doughnut, and holding her hand in front of her mouth, nodded at the plate. "Have one, they're delicious."

As Meredith did as she suggested, he noted that her manners had not been lost, and wondered what tragedy had befallen her to bring her down so low. Once he'd obtained whatever information she had, perhaps he'd try to find out. He placed his half-eaten doughnut back on the plate.

"Tell me what you know, Peggy. As much detail as possible, then I'll ask you some questions."

Peggy sipped her tea and composed herself. Meredith hoped he wasn't going to get the dramatic version of the story. Peggy was clearly enjoying herself.

"I'd not long woken up, and I was doing what one does when one first wakes up, and I heard the engine."

"Where were you?" Meredith thought he noticed a slight embarrassment before she answered.

"My abode that night was the first floor of the multi-storey carpark at the bottom of The Pithay. They lock the barriers at midnight, and don't open again until seven, so it means you don't get disturbed. I usually go higher up. You occasionally get courting couples in, and it's difficult to sleep when someone is having very uncomfortable sex in the vicinity. Mind you, it doesn't last long." She laughed at Trump's expression. "I didn't go higher that night because my back was hurting, so I stopped. I might not have seen him if I'd gone further up."

"What did you see?"

"I heard him at first, heard him drive up to the barrier. I don't know what genius thought it was wise, but the sign with the opening hours on isn't visible until you get to the barrier, by which time you're committed." She waved her hand at him. "Actually, do you know, looking back I think it was intentional. It costs a fortune to park there, and you can't see the cost until you're at the barrier. Ha! Clever I suppose."

Although she wouldn't admit it, Peggy was enjoying the interaction, and avoiding giving the information.

"Hmm, what happened, Peggy?"

"Sorry, Merriwinkle. I finished what I was doing, picked up my bag, and started down the exit ramp. Dot opens the café at about half past six, and I have to get there before she gets too busy. I heard him reverse back down onto the street, and assumed he would drive away, but he didn't, did he? To my surprise he then reversed up the exit ramp until the car was in the building and up against the barrier. I had to jump out of the way. But I suppose in fairness to him as the carpark was shut, he wasn't expecting anyone to be there." She sipped her tea and nodded at Meredith. "I feel guilty now, I thumped his car."

"What colour was it?"

"A silvery blue colour." Peggy looked from Meredith to Trump as they exchanged a glance. "What was that for?"

"Are you sure?" Trump smiled. "Are you absolutely positive it was a light colour?"

Peggy sighed. "I was sober, Trump. I'm here to help you, why would I lie?" Her eyes narrowed and her irritation was evident.

Trump held his hands up. "I wasn't suggesting you were the worse for wear, Peggy, simply trying to establish that you are thinking of the right car on the right day. You see, we were under the impression the man was driving a black Range Rover." Trump had purposely given the information to her. If she now changed her story, they'd know they were wasting their time.

Peggy looked at Meredith. "Are you his boss, Merriwinkle?" Meredith nodded and allowed a slight smile at her persistence in calling him the wrong name. "Then he needs reprimanding. Is that not leading a witness? Giving them the information you are looking for?" She shook her head and looked at Trump sternly. "Shame on you. It was not a Range Rover, it was a large saloon type car, like a small mini bus, and it was a silvery blue colour, not *black*." She emphasised the colour as she rolled her eyes.

"You're right Peggy, cheap trick. I'll dock his pay. If we showed you some different cars with different paint jobs, do you think you could pick it out?"

Meredith had picked up his pen and sketched a car on his pad.

"I doubt it. I don't do cars, but I know what I saw, and I know it wasn't a Range Rover. I could tell you the basic shape, but I doubt I'd remember enough of the detail to tell one model from another." Peggy pointed at his drawing, "That's worthy of a six-year-old, it won't take long if you're sketching them." She held out her hand. "Give me the pen." Pulling the pad towards her she quickly sketched the outline of a car. "That's the sort of thing, but as I say, not enough detail to do better."

Meredith and Trump looked at the drawing. Peggy was not an accomplished artist, but was certainly better than the average man in the street.

She leaned forward and flicked Trump's tie with the pen. "The colour was similar to the stripe on your tie. But I was looking at them, and not the car, so we should move on from the car." Peggy looked up at the clock behind Meredith.

"Do you have somewhere you need to be?" Meredith asked.

"Not really, but I've been in here long enough, my feet get itchy and my brain stops working if I'm inside too long." Peggy's warning was clear. She smiled at him. "Get a move on, Merriwinkle, I make it a rule never to drink before midday. But today might be an exception."

"Tell me about them." Meredith smiled. "I'll keep it short and sharp, don't worry."

"They were asleep. The little blonde one was sucking her thumb, her head resting on the dark one's shoulder. The dark one's head had fallen forward and was resting on her chest. I remember thinking she would have a neck ache when she woke up." Peggy looked somewhere over Meredith's shoulder. "They were both strapped in," she added eventually.

"What happened then? Did you see the driver?"

"No, not then, I didn't look. I had to squeeze past the car, and I thumped the front of it, as I said. He didn't respond. I was in a hurry to get to the café, and I hurried past and went into the lane."

"What lane?" Meredith frowned.

"I'm not allowed into the café. Some of the other customers don't like my perfume." Peggy dabbed her hands to her neck. "It's quicker to go up the lane than walk all the way round to the back. It's not really a lane, more of a gap between the buildings. Anyway, I went around the back, and Dot gave me a bag of doughnuts. Her boss was coming and she told me not to hang around, and I went back into the lane out of the way. Then I had another call of nature. It was quite urgent, so I had to obey." Peggy's eyes darted between the two men, looking for any sign of disgust. Their faces remained impassive and Meredith nodded acceptance, so she carried on. "I heard him talking to them."

"What did he say? Did you hear what he said?"

"Of course, I'm not deaf either. There was no one about, sound travels you know." She rolled her eyes. "He told them their parents were meeting them in the café, and he'd had forgotten to lock the car. He asked them to go on into the café while he went back to sort it out. Then he said something odd, like the soldiers would look after them." Peggy put her hands on her hips. "What a strange thing to say to a child. What would they know of soldiers?"

"What happened then? Did you see him then?" Meredith smiled as Peggy nodded.

"As I got to the end of the lane, I saw the two girls pass it and saw they were the girls from the car. I peeped around the corner and looked for him. I'd just thumped his car and didn't want any trouble, you see. He had a clown's hat on, with a mask that sort of hung down in front of his face. That's why she called him Charlie, she said. He didn't like that, by the way." Peggy shook her head. "He was careful though. He was walking backwards to make sure they crossed the road safely. I was pleased with that. Then he took the mask off and ran back towards the carpark." She looked at the plate of doughnuts.

Meredith caught her eye. "Tell me what he looks like and you can eat the lot."

"He had fair hair, not blond. He was clean and tidy, shirt but no tie. He was quite good looking, looked like the chap off of *Star Trek*, whatshisname." She tapped the table with her finger. "Kirk, that's it, he looked a bit like Captain Kirk, but with lighter hair. I couldn't see the colour of his eyes or anything like that."

"When was the last time you watched *Star Trek*, Peggy?" Meredith wasn't a fan, but he knew it was a long time since Captain Kirk had been aboard the *Enterprise*.

"Thirty years." Peggy looked down at her hands and blinked. She didn't like to think about that life, and was glad when Meredith spoke again.

"And how old would you say Captain Kirk was the last time you saw him?"

"About your age. Late thirties, maybe early forties. How old are you?" She smiled again.

"Around there, Peggy." Meredith smiled back at her. "Did you see which way he went?"

"No. But he didn't go down past the café, that's the way I went, and he didn't pass me. If I'd known what was going on, I would have said something then. It was only when Dot was telling me about the excitement I realised what I'd seen." She sighed and looked uncomfortable. "He didn't, you know, hurt them, did he?"

"No, Peggy, he didn't." Meredith smiled reassuringly. "Is there anything else you can think of we might want to know?"

"Lots. But none of it has to do with this case." Peggy sighed. "Can I go now?"

"You can. I'll get down to the café and get you sorted for tomorrow morning. A week we said, didn't we?"

"Two, Merriwinkle, I hope you're a man I can trust." Peggy leaned down to the floor and unzipped her holdall. Her head reappeared and she took the plate of doughnuts, "I'd hate to have to chase you." She grinned and emptied the plate into her bag.

"You won't need to. I might join you one morning. Come on, I'll see you out." Meredith turned to Trump. "Go and update the team. They need to check that CCTV again. Moving away from the café, and looking for a people carrier of some description, and driven by Mr Spock."

"I said Captain Kirk." Peggy dug him in the ribs with her elbow as she left the room.

"I know, Peggy, I was just checking he was listening." Meredith grinned at her. "This way."

When they reached the exit, Meredith stepped outside with her. "Thanks, Peggy." He pulled some notes from his pocket. "Get yourself a bed for a couple of nights, not booze, okay."

"I only drink in the winter, really, well, spring and autumn too." Peggy smiled and tucked the notes in with Trump's offering. It had been a very profitable day. "When it's a bit nippy, I drink to keep out the cold for the best part."

"Then go over to the hostel and get a room. That should get you a couple of nights." Meredith nodded towards her chest.

"I might, Merriwinkle, you never know." Peggy winced as she stepped down onto the pavement and the bag swung out, jarring her back.

"Do you need to see a doctor? How bad is that back of yours?"

Peggy began to shuffle away. "Bye, Merriwinkle, don't forget our deal." She didn't turn back, but she did lift her hand and salute. "And don't forget Captain Kirk."

Meredith went back into the station, and pondered what she had told them as he went to join the team in the incident room. He walked to the white board and rapped it with a pen several times to get their attention.

"A couple of things before I go to see Sherlock. First, get on to the e-fit and come up with a Captain Kirk lookalike, but with fairer hair. Get it across to the three girls, with some others naturally, and see if it means anything to any of them. Second," he glanced at his watch, "see if *Crimebusters* have time to update the appeal. The public need to know he may drive either a black Range Rover or silvery blue people carrier." Turning he wrote 'CHARLIE' on the board. Without turning back, he continued speaking as he stared at the name. "Is this his real name? Ellen and Gemma couldn't agree, but Peggy has told us he didn't like being called Charlie. Is it because the girls forgot his real name and he was offended, or because it was too close to home? Check all those offenders registered locally and see if we have a Charlie or a Charles. It's a long shot, but we've not got much else at the moment." He turned back. "That's it, except," he was conscious of Rawlings' presence, "Peggy did say that when he dropped the girls off, he walked backwards to make sure they did go into the café before he left. That tells us he was concerned about them." Meredith shrugged. "Not that I know what that means."

He walked away, the update was over. "Get on with it then."

Hitting the explorer icon on his phone, he waited while it searched out a signal. When it was ready he clicked on favourites then signed in to his account. Results in eight hours. He pursed his lips. He should start making plans; the sooner he took Dana the better. He was careful to sign out before replacing the phone in his breast pocket. Whistling softly, he walked back to the hospital. He'd enjoyed working there, and it was a shame he would have to leave. He gave a little shrug, knowing that Dana was far more important.

CHAPTER NINE

Meredith walked into Frankie Callaghan's office, giving a cursory tap on the door as he spotted Frankie hunched over the desk reading a magazine. "Hope that's not porn you have there, Sherlock." He turned his nose up as Frankie held up the magazine and revealed the cover. It was a scientific publication, the cover showing a diseased pair of lungs. "That looks like an anti-smoking campaign. Well, much as I hate to interrupt you and your scintillating read, I need you to bring me up to speed on the soldiers, the scene from last night, and not forgetting the arm. Did you find anything useful on any of it?"

"You could have called, you know. There wasn't much, certainly not enough to warrant a visit. I rang you but you were already on the way." Frankie pushed the magazine to one side, then stood and walked to a table by the window to collect a pile of slender files.

"Sherlock, if I didn't know better, I'd think you weren't pleased to see me." Meredith pulled out a chair and sat on the opposite side of Frankie's desk. He nodded at the files. "What have you got?"

"Not much, I'm afraid. But it might be useful once you've caught him, even if it doesn't help you catch him."

"That's not what I wanted to hear." Meredith sighed.

"I didn't think it would be. That's why we invented phones. They save wasted journeys."

"I wanted to get out of the office. Here was as good a place as anywhere. Show me what you do have."

Frankie withdrew several photographs, and handed them to Meredith one by one, providing a running commentary as he did so.

"This is from the soldier given to Ellen." Meredith looked at the two flecks on the sheet. "The analysis confirms the paint used is probably from the turn of the century, given the lead content, but this one," he handed Meredith a different shot, "was touched up using paint with no lead content at all, but it had been applied over the older paint."

"So how old is the touch-up paint?"

"Difficult to say, it's a common composition, widely used in modelling. Not as old as the late sixties when they stopped putting lead in paint, but not newer than the eighties. They are still running checks to pin it down closer. These things take time." Sherlock gave a shrug. "The composition of the metal, however," he passed across the last photograph, "is virtually impossible to date. Even taking the age of the paint into account, it could have been painted with paint that was stored. The one given to the girl last night hadn't been touched up. It could have been made with tin from Bristol. Were you aware that there are tin mines weaving their way under our streets?"

"Yep. Anything else of use for me, Sherlock?" He grimaced as Frankie shook his head.

"I've had a quick scan of the history of tin soldiers. I didn't realise they were so popular. Main ones are thirty or forty millimetres tall; these are larger, as you know, but you can get decorative ones up to six feet. I -"

He stopped speaking as Meredith held his hand up. "I know, I've got one of the lads on it. I'm told these were either made for personal use by the original owner, or by special order." He blew out a frustrated breath. "What about forensics from the scene last night?"

"Nothing much. A few fibres from the hedge, maybe from the girl's clothing; that's being tested. But no footprints, cigarette butts, or anything else useful." Frankie scanned the notes in the file. "Ah yes, the girl told our chap she caught her hair in the hedge, but there was nothing there."

"Not what I wanted to hear. I'll phone next time." Meredith sighed. "Okay, let's talk severed limbs, any news on that?"

"That's sorted. I'm sure you'll be pleased to hear I've sent it home." He smiled as Meredith raised his eyebrows. "It's part of a murder victim in Penarth. Victim was thrown into the Bristol Channel from a boat. Her clothes got caught up on a passing vessel and most of her was discovered in the Queen Alexandra dock in Cardiff. She'd lost her arm and foot before reaching there."

"Well, that is good news. That was one I didn't fancy dealing with." Meredith stood up. "I don't suppose I can interest you in brunch, can I?"

Frankie looked stunned. Had Meredith blown him a kiss he couldn't have been less shocked.

"Seriously, Meredith? You are looking to extend the time you have to spend with me? And pay for food? Are you ill?" Frankie managed to keep a straight face, the worry lines around his eyes adding to the effect.

Meredith turned on his heel. "It was a genuine offer, Sherlock. It won't happen again." Meredith strode towards the door. A grin appeared as he heard Frankie scrabble to collect his things.

"Oh, I didn't doubt that, Meredith, my concern was why." Frankie quickly caught up with Meredith. He opened the door, and leaned on it as he put one arm into his jacket. He shrugged in the second as they reached the stairs. "I have no doubt all will be revealed."

As they took the stairs and exited the building into the sunshine, Meredith denied he had ulterior motives. He did, but he wasn't prepared to be drawn until he was sitting comfortably with hot food in front of him.

"I thought we'd walk," Meredith set off at a pace towards town. "Easier than moving the car. Is that okay with you, Sherlock?"

Frankie matched Meredith's stride, and more than a few heads turned as the two handsome men marched in the direction of their destination.

"Oh, so you have somewhere in mind, that's good. Have you been before?"

"No, actually it came by way of recommendation this morning." Meredith looked across to Sherlock.

"I'm sure it will be fine, if it was a . . ." Frankie shook his head as Meredith stopped by the door of a greasy spoon café. "You have to be kidding me."

"Nope." Meredith pushed open the door and waved Frankie in. "After you, Sherlock."

Frankie stepped over the threshold. "They'd better do something healthy." But his mouth was already watering at the smell of frying food. He waved his hand around. "Did sir book, or shall I choose."

Meredith grinned as he took two overlarge menus from the waitress, and joined Frankie at a window table. He handed him a menu.

"It's posher than you think. Look, they even have photographs on their menu. You don't get that often. Sherlock, what'll you have?"

Unable to control himself, Frankie chose a gammon steak, egg, and chips. Meredith joined him.

"Is the governor in?" Meredith asked the waitress as she took the order. He was, and he came to see Meredith immediately, frowning as we made his way between the tables.

"Sir, is something wrong?" The short stocky man eyed Meredith suspiciously, hoping he wasn't an inspector on some health and safety mission.

"How much is your full English?" Meredith smiled.

"Four pounds ninety-nine. It's on the menu." The man's frown deepened, suspecting Meredith was a punter who had been over-charged. "That includes toast, and unlimited tea or coffee, why?"

"How much if I order one every day for the next fortnight?" Meredith smiled at the man.

"Three ninety-nine. That'll be twenty per cent discount."

"I can do the sums, thanks. Right, done." Meredith reached out and shook his hand. "I'll pay in advance when I pick up the bill."

Their food arrived within minutes, and any thought of conversation was forgotten as they tucked in.

Eventually, having eaten over half the food on his plate, Frankie paused and waved his fork at Meredith. "You can tell me now."

"Tell you what?"

"Why I'm here. You have until this is gone if I don't like the subject." Frankie forked a piece of gammon and popped it in his mouth. He watched the changing seasons cross Meredith's eyes, knowing this was either difficult or simply embarrassing for him. He wondered if it was about Patsy. In the end, Meredith made a statement.

"I understand Amanda has been working in your department again, and, not to put too fine a point on it, and present company excepted of course, I think she's too good for it. I think she should work with live patients, not dead ones. More chance of success, and I'm sure a more rounded life." Unable to keep a straight face he looked down at his plate and speared some chips onto his fork. Frankie ignored him, causing him to look up. "I hope I haven't offended you. What I probably meant to say was that there are too few opportunities for her to progress in your field, and that in general medicine she could do better." He shrugged. "Is that better?"

Frankie placed his knife and fork together on his now empty plate and pushed it to the centre of the table.

"I take it Amanda knows we're having this discussion?"

"Don't be stupid, Sherlock, it doesn't suit." Feeling guilty Meredith's appetite failed him, and he pushed his plate to join Frankie's.

"Well, if you bothered to speak to her about it, I think you'll find that I, or more accurately my department, is being used by the lovely Amanda. She has ulterior motives." Frankie chose not to mention the fact that Amanda still seemed to blush or get flustered each time he spoke to her.

"They being?" Meredith didn't like the way the conversation was going. The lines on his forehead deepened.

Frankie smiled. He enjoyed Meredith being uncomfortable. "That she thinks she might want to join the police force. She likes detective work. Working out how someone died is apparently helping in the process." Frankie shook his head. "Really, Meredith, I thought you would have tried to put her off. A medical profession, whatever the field, has to be preferable to joining the police force."

Frankie was enjoying himself, and didn't realise he was about to provide Meredith with his second revelation of the day. "I have tried myself, but you being her father should have more clout . . . not literally. I just hope she's not using poor Patrick to the same end."

Meredith blinked. Patrick. Patrick was obviously a copper. He willed himself not to react. He stood. "Thank you, Sherlock. I shall certainly try. Now I have to pay the bill and get going. It's been . . . educational." Meredith nodded, "Yes, thanks."

He held out his hand. Frankie shook it and took his leave, calling out his thanks. As he turned back towards work, he wondered what he'd said to bring out the civilised Meredith.

Meredith walked to the counter and the owner rushed over.

"Sixty-eight pounds twenty-five pence please, let's call it sixty-five for cash." He beamed at Meredith.

"I haven't got that much on me. Let's call it sixty-five for card." Meredith flipped open the wallet holding his warrant card, and made sure the man saw it. He extracted his card and paid the bill. He turned to leave and slapped his forehead, stopping abruptly. Turning back, he beckoned the man closer.

"This is Peggy," Meredith found the photograph he had taken of Peggy on the steps of the station. "She'll be joining you each morning around sevenish. I'll probably join her on occasion." Seeing the look of horror, he added. "She'll sit outside if it's not raining. She doesn't like it inside, but if it rains, she's in here. Understand?"

Patsy looked up as Linda came into her office and switched on the small TV, which was suspended on the wall above the seating area.

"The update is on now. I've just spoken to Louie. You don't mind if I watch, do you?" Linda perched on the back of a sofa. Patsy shook her head and leaned back in her chair. The *Crimebusters'* theme tune played out. The presenter smiled at the camera briefly before settling on a more serious expression.

"Today, police need your help with yesterday's possible abduction attempt on a young girl in broad daylight." The camera took the journey up Dana's street, past her house, without pausing, and turned into the lane. It then travelled the lane, and panned around the field. "Were you in the vicinity of the field behind St George's Terrace yesterday evening between six thirty and seven thirty? Did you see anything suspicious on or around the area? Do you walk there, perhaps to exercise your dog? If you do, please contact the police on the telephone number shown at the bottom of the screen. Police believe that an attempt was made to abduct a seven-year-old girl while she was playing in a garden backing onto the field. They say it's too early to make a formal connection with the abduction of two other girls earlier in the week, but have not ruled out the possibility. They believe the man may have been driving either a dark four by four vehicle, or a silvery blue people carrier. If you saw anything at all that you think may be of help, please contact the police now. Remember, serious crimes have been solved from the smallest of clues."

The presenter stepped forward and a grin appeared. "Now, we take you over to a bungled robbery. CCTV captured these less than efficient robbers as they attempted to hold up this convenience store. Take a close look, can you put a name to any of these faces?"

Linda watched each face appear, and shook her head at each one. Satisfied she couldn't help, she switched off the TV, and turned to Patsy.

"Why don't they warn parents to keep their children safe?"

"Because they don't really need to, the majority of parents do anyway. Think about the first two; where safer to be than with twenty-odd other people, five of them there specifically to watch you? This chap is good, his actions are well planned. If they did put out a warning, it may cause an overreaction. The girl yesterday was playing in her own back garden. Do you think all kids should be under lock and key?" Patsy shook her head. "They wouldn't do that unless they thought it crucial. It's a tough call." She frowned as Linda came and sat in front of her. "Did we have something pencilled in?"

"No, but you should try Antonio again. You might get him this time."

Patsy picked up the phone and redialled Antonio Garcia. For the third time she listened to the long humming tones that told her this would be an international call. The previous calls had ended when an operator told her to try again later. There was no answer service. She was just about to hang up when the Antonio picked up the call.

"Hello, are you Patsy Hodge?" When she confirmed that she was, Antonio demanded to know why she was bothering him and his friends. "It is not good. Who is it that wants me, and why?"

"I'd rather speak to you face to face. My client has a proposition for you, and I believe it would be to your advantage. Ideally, she would prefer to meet you herself. Is that possible? When are you returning to the UK?"

There was a pause as Antonio considered this. Patsy thought she had lost the connection, or worse, he had hung up. "Hello? Hello?" she said.

"I'm thinking. You are a detective, would you work for me?"

"That all depends on what you want me to do. Before I consider any job you may have to offer, I'd like you to consider my client's proposal. One thing at a time would be wise."

"It may be a trap. I need more time to think."

"I can assure you it's not." Patsy frowned. The man appeared to be in some sort of trouble, and that didn't bode well for Nicola. Her interest secured, she pressed for more information. "What sort of trap."

"One to lure me back into the country. To set me up."

"What? Antonio, I give you my word that's not what this is about." Patsy grimaced at Linda, indicating things were not going well. "Am I to take it you're not returning to conclude your studies?"

"That is for me to know. Something is wrong with this, I know it. I'm going."

With that Antonio hung up. Patsy attempted to call him back but he didn't pick up. She relayed the conversation to Linda.

"Take him on," advised Linda. "Whatever it is he wants you to do, it won't be a conflict of interest, will it? How can whatever he wanted you to do have anything to do with Nicola's baby? Two birds with one stone and what have you."

"Hmm, it is intriguing, but I think he now believes I'm part of whatever it is that he's worried about. We'll have to wait and see if he rings back. In the meantime, see if you can find him on any of the university websites. You never know, we may get lucky and find an email address. Don't forget to check Facebook, although I'm guessing there may be quite a few Antonio Garcias. I'll give Nicola a ring and let her know what's happening."

Patsy dialled Nicola as Linda left her office. The phone rang and rang. Patsy was about to give up when a breathless Nicola answered. The baby was screaming in the background and Patsy flinched. She attempted to explain the gist of her conversation with Antonio, but Nicola was clearly distracted. They arranged to meet an hour later.

As Patsy turned the corner towards the café, she spotted Nicola hurrying from the other direction. As always, she was smartly dressed. She was still an attractive woman, but she looked a little gaunt, and her expression had an almost manic quality. Patsy increased her pace and held open the door for Nicola. Nicola thanked her before she realised it was actually Patsy.

"Oh, it's you. Sorry, Patsy, miles away." Nicola stepped inside and walked to the table in the far corner. Patsy called an order to the waitress and joined her.

"Did you want anything to eat?" She slipped off her jacket as Nicola waved the request away. "Where's Paul? I was expecting you to have him with you. He certainly has a healthy pair of lungs." She smiled as Nicola's expression softened.

"He's with Tina, and yes, he does. That was because his feed was ten minutes off schedule. He certainly runs to the clock."

"Who's Tina, your neighbour?" Patsy lifted her bag off the table as the waitress arrived with their coffee.

"No, she's my au pair, or nanny? Not sure what to call her. She's moved in now. She was at the shops when you called. Now, tell me what Antonio said. I didn't understand."

Patsy's brow furrowed a little as she wondered where Nicola found the money for a nanny since she wasn't working, and also whether Nicola's house wasn't a little too small for the two women. She'd never been upstairs, but was guessing the bedrooms weren't huge, and the third probably no larger than a big cupboard.

"I think he's in some sort of trouble, Nicola. I don't have any details, but he thought that my asking him to meet with you was some sort of trap. It may be why he went home to Spain. I could tell he was genuinely concerned."

Patsy paused and stirred the froth in her coffee. "Look, Nicola, I know you are after a father figure for Paul, and I know nothing about this man, but I think you should maybe think again." She glanced up at Nicola's sigh. "He intimated he might want to employ me himself, but hung up before I could find out why."

"Then take him on. Find out what his problem is and sort it out. Seriously, Patsy, I'm not going to drop this. Call him. Let him know you'll help, go to Seville if necessary, just sort it."

Nicola all but rolled her eyes, and her tone implied Patsy was being slow. Patsy sipped her coffee to avoid snapping out an answer in irritation. Settling her now empty cup back in the saucer, she glanced at her watch.

"I have to go. I will try him, Nicola, but I'm not promising anything. I might not want to take on whatever may be troubling him." Patsy stood, her chair scraping the tiled floor. "I'll call once I've made contact."

Nicola jumped to her feet, knocking the table, and causing her cup to fall to the floor. As the other customers looked round, and the waitress hurried forward, she grabbed Patsy's arm.

"Please," was all she managed, and tears clouded her eyes.

Patsy sighed as she patted her hand. "Leave it with me, I'll do my best." Despite not actually having to go, Patsy wanted to escape the tension. "I have to go now. I'll be in touch."

Although she left the café quickly, Patsy then sauntered back to her car. Nicola was clearly keen to have this man in her life, and Patsy wasn't convinced it was the right thing. She wondered briefly whether it was just company she wanted because she was lonely. After all, au pairs weren't cheap, and to the best of her knowledge Nicola had no regular income coming in, but she dismissed this idea with a shake of the head. If that were the case, Nicola wouldn't be so desperate, particularly as she now knew Antonio may be in some sort of trouble. Patsy sighed as she climbed back into the car, knowing that if it were possible, she would do what Nicola wanted.

Only Chris was in when she arrived back at the office. He was on the phone, and waved as she walked to her office. A bright pink note had been stuck to her laptop. Linda had located an email address for Antonio, and a Facebook account. She had also found four possible candidates for Lyndon Ward. Patsy smiled as she removed the note and opened the laptop.

She sent Antonio a friend request and a brief message asking him to contact her, and a more detailed email. Noting that the email address was connected to the university she wasn't convinced he would pick it up. Sighing, she pulled the file on Freda Hawthorne from her drawer, and read through the notes she had made. Opening an email to Linda, she typed a list of all the contact addresses and names of sites Lyndon Ward had used in his communication with Freda, and instructed Linda to attempt to track him down. She did a cursory search herself, but her heart wasn't in it. More than anything she wanted progress with Antonio Garcia. Frustrated that she was unable to concentrate, she pushed the keyboard away impatiently and banged the desk. Cupping her face in her hands, she stared at the file but was not reading the content. Chris tapped on the door and poked his head in.

"Everything all right? Are you stuck on something?"

"Yes, but nothing you can help with." Patsy smiled at him. "Sorry, did I disturb you?"

"No, I'm awaiting a call. Would talking help?"

Patsy frowned and pursed her lips. "What's she said?"

Chris grimaced. "I'm not sure what you mean?" He pulled out the chair on the other side of the desk and seated himself. "Who, and what, do you think she said?"

"Well, I'm not talking about Linda, so that doesn't leave many options." Patsy allowed herself a smile. "I don't mind. I didn't ask her to not to tell you. It's Meredith that's the problem."

"Isn't he always?" Chris grinned. "If you want my opinion, I think you should hand over the case. The outcome will be what it will be irrespective of who deals with it. It might help you not having to deal with it though."

"Are you suggesting that I might not deal with it professionally?" Patsy leaned back and folded her arms across her chest. "Because if you are -"

"I'm not. Get down off that high horse, it's dangerous." Chris wagged his finger at her. "What I'm saying is that dealing with Nicola can't be easy. Pass it over."

Patsy looked at Chris and shook her head. "I have no issue with Nicola as Nicola, that's not the problem."

"What is?"

"Bloody Meredith of course!" Patsy shook her head. Chris was being particularly annoying today, which was so unlike him.

"But I didn't think he knew anything about it . . . yet." Chris looked genuinely puzzled, and Patsy wondered how he could be so dense.

"What happens when he does?"

"If the child is his, you mean?"

Patsy threw her arms into the air. "Yes, if the bloody child is his. He's not worried about it so far, has he?" She pointed at him. "Are you deliberately being thick today?"

"Patsy, calm down. Meredith loves you. Whatever he had with Nicola was over years ago. She is not a threat." He leaned back as Patsy rolled her eyes and leaned towards him tapping the desk with her finger.

"I know that. I said Nicola wasn't the problem. For God's sake, work with me, would you. Do I have to spell it out?"

"Umm, yes." Chris spoke quietly, and lifted one shoulder as though ready to defend a blow. Genuine concern had narrowed his eyes, and Patsy, deflated, fell back against her chair, groaning.

"What do you think Meredith will do if he finds he has a child he didn't know about? A son."

"He would want to do the right thing." Chris cocked his head. "Does that bother you?"

"Yes . . . No . . . I'm not sure. I think that combined with Nicola, and what he did, how he treated her, he may . . . well, he may do anything, and that's what I'm worried about."

Chris blinked at her. He was being dense, but certainly not deliberately. They had just agreed that Nicola wasn't the problem, but apparently she was. He had no idea how to respond. He smiled and thought about offering coffee in the hope Sharon would return and interrupt. She was a woman, so perhaps she could make some sense out of this contradictory conversation.

"Patsy, I -"

"If Meredith finds out that, despite all his previous failings, he has managed to have the child they always hoped for, perhaps he will want to go back to what should have been."

Patsy stared at her desk unable to meet Chris's eye.

"Don't be ridiculous. There is no going back with something like this. Patsy, where did this come from? Why would you think that?"

"Because he told me. The night he broke his ankle, I stayed to make sure he didn't do any more damage. There was nothing between us then. He told me about Nicola, and how he would give anything to put it right." Patsy raised her eyes. "A son is a pretty strong reason for trying in my book. Meredith would do that." She laughed and shook her head. "The thing is that it might be Nicola who doesn't want to. If she's to be believed, she simply wants the baby to grow up with a father, but not necessarily one under the same roof." She swallowed. "Wouldn't that be a turn up?"

"Patsy, go home. You're not thinking straight. If you think for one moment that Meredith would give you up . . . Do you not know the man? You're off the case. Ridiculous, absolutely bloody ridiculous." Chris stood up and sighed. "Go home. It's been a long day."

"I'll go home, but I'm not dropping this case." Patsy stood to join him. "It's because I know him that we have to sort it out. Quickly. Don't fight me on this, Chris, I know what I'm talking about. He is an honourable man who acted dishonourably."

She waved away Chris's protests. "Whatever his reasons, that's how he sees it. And he will put that right if he can, in his mind at least. Whatever the cost to himself," she shrugged, "or me. I will see this through, and when it's done we'll all know one way or the other."

She bent and retrieved her bag. Walking past Chris, she raised her finger to her lips. "But not a word to anyone until then. Now I must dash. We have tickets for the theatre tonight, I wonder if he'll make it?"

She waved and disappeared through the door before Chris could say anything else.

Meredith drummed his fingers on his desk. His team were doing everything they could with the sparse information they had, and they were no closer to catching him than they had been the first night. Hands in pockets, he wandered out into the incident room. Tom Seaton smiled at him as he replaced the receiver.

"A couple downstairs asking for us, Gov. They were in the field the night Dana had her visit."

"Well get them up here then, and let's keep our fingers crossed that they actually have something useful to say."

He rubbed his hands together in anticipation as Seaton went to collect them. Trump pointed to the printer, which had started chugging away in the corner.

"You might want to take that with you, sir. It's your request on the Captain Kirk lookalike. It may help."

Meredith collected the likeness from the printer and studied it. It looked vaguely familiar, but then again it was a lighter-haired William Shatner lookalike, so that was to be expected. He went to the interview room and placed it face down on the table, and then paced up and down outside the door as he waited for Seaton to arrive with their witnesses.

A smartly dressed couple in their mid-sixties appeared, and he beamed at them as they approached.

Having gone through the formalities he leaned back in his chair. "Tell me everything you can remember. Why don't you do the talking, Mrs Newton, and your husband can add anything you may not have seen or might have forgotten."

Mrs Newton smiled at her husband as she nodded agreement, glad that this rather good-looking policeman thought she would be the better of the two.

"The first time we saw him we were on the other side of the field. We'd done a lap and a half. He was in the centre and bellowing for his dog. Butch."

"Did you see the dog?"

"No, he'd lost it. When we saw him getting into the Range Rover about twenty minutes later, he said he was going to have to drive the streets to look for him." She glanced at her husband. "It happened once to us, didn't it? It was horrible." She shivered at the memory before looking back at Meredith. "We didn't see him with any little girl though, so it might not be him."

"No, you wouldn't have. What was he wearing?" He watched as Mrs Newton shrugged apologetically.

"Well, jeans of course. Everyone wears jeans these days. My dentist was the last time I went." Her husband nudged her and nodded at Meredith. "Oh, sorry. And a dark jacket, it was either brown or sludgy green. We didn't take much notice of him though, did we?" She looked to her husband who shook his head. "We were more worried about Butch."

"That's okay. It might come back to you. Could you describe him?"

"Tall, maybe six foot. White, couldn't see his hair because of the cap. He had nice teeth though. A lovely smile," again she turned to her husband. "Didn't he have a nice smile? That's why I don't think it was him."

Mr Newton rolled his eyes, and Meredith wished he chosen the husband as the spokesperson.

"Mr Newton, anything that your wife has left out?"

"Thinking back now, I don't think he had a dog. No lead. You don't go looking for a dog without something to secure him. The cap was black and had red writing on the peak. I didn't read it though." Mr Newton furrowed his brow. "Don't think I have much more than that."

"What about his voice? Was his accent local?"

"No, I'd say not. We were on the other side of the street, and we only exchanged a few words, but I'd still say no."

His wife was nodding in agreement.

"I'm going to show you an impression of someone seen by another witness. It wasn't at the field and it was on a different day. If it's not him or anything like him, you must say. This is a long shot." Meredith turned over the sheet of paper, and pushed it to the centre of the table. Mr and Mrs Newton leaned forward to look.

"I'm not sure," Mr Newton glanced at Meredith. "Sorry."

Meredith shook his head dismissing the concern.

Mrs Newton pulled it towards her. "Can I touch it?"

"Of course." Meredith frowned, and then realised she was using her hand to cover the likeness where a cap would have been. "Would you like to work with DS Seaton here on a likeness with a cap?" He smiled as the Newtons exchanged a glance which contained more than a little excitement. They both nodded. Meredith stood and opened the door. "Come on then, he needs a computer to do that."

Meredith left Seaton leading the couple to the administration office. Once there he settled them on each side of him, and explained how they could alter the picture. Forty-five minutes later they agreed on the image in front of them. It was startlingly similar to the image they had produced for Peggy. He thanked the Newtons for their help and rushed back to Meredith.

"I think your friend Peggy was right." Seaton placed the two likenesses on Meredith's desk. Meredith nodded slowly. "They both look like Captain Kirk."

"They do indeed. Get some run off, both with and without the cap. Distribute them to the team, and get some off to PR for distribution to the news agencies. You take some round to Rawlings." Meredith paused and looked out into the incident room. "Trump can do the Dwights and I'll go and see Gemma and her parents." He pursed his lips. "He looks familiar to me. Have I seen him, or is it because he looks like whatshisname, Shatner?"

"Don't know, Gov, but if you know him, it will come to you."

"I hope so. How can I expect the public to come up with something if I can't manage it myself?" Meredith looked at his watch. "I'll get straight off home after I've seen them, I've got the theatre tonight." His eyes narrowed as Seaton grinned. "And I'll join Peggy for an early breakfast and see what she thinks of those pictures."

He slammed down the top of his laptop and cursed. Glancing over his shoulder, he was relieved to find that no one appeared to have noticed the unexpected outburst. He massaged his temples with his middle fingers. Dana wasn't the one. He shook his head, unable to believe it. Gemma and Dana had been the most likely two. He screwed his eyes shut, and brought the faces of the other girls to mind; he had to decide which one next. He sighed, unable to believe that his top two choices had failed him. Harriet was the next obvious choice. He decided he would try to get her today. He looked at his watch. He'd leave now. No one would notice if he slipped away early.

Meredith opened the front door, still frowning. Neither Gemma nor her parents recognised the posters Seaton had made, and something niggled at the back of Meredith's mind. It was beginning to frustrate him as he knew it was important. He shrugged out of his jacket. Perhaps a night out with the girls would help relax him, and bring whatever it was to the front of his mind.

In the kitchen, Patsy and Amanda exchanged amazed glances.

Amanda stepped out into the hall. "Dad, you're here, and on time." She pointed up the stairs. "Go and get changed quickly and turn your phone off. Now we can eat together first too."

"Good evening, I'm well thank you. Did you have a nice day too?" Meredith shouldered her out of the way playfully as he walked into the kitchen. "Evening, Hodge, have you got a nicer greeting for me?"

Patsy held her arms out to welcome him as he stepped forward.

"Let's not talk about work. Let's simply go out and have a pleasant evening." She gave him a quick kiss, and hugged him.

Meredith felt the unnecessary pressure of her embrace and hands on her shoulders he held her away from him. "Is everything okay?" His eyes scanned her face for signs of concern, but she smiled and tried to push him away.

"Of course, I'm pleased we get to enjoy Amanda's birthday present to you together. Go, and like the girl said, turn the phone off."

"Come on, Dad, hurry. We can go to the tapas bar around the corner."

Meredith was acutely aware that Patsy was avoiding his gaze, but not wanting to push it and ruin Amanda's evening, he turned to his daughter.

"Tapas? I thought you said we were going to eat, not nibble? I'm a growing man. I need real food, what's wrong with the steak house?"

Amanda pushed him into the hall, telling him he was boring. In the event, the tapas bar was busy, and Meredith got his steak. He would have liked to have sampled something from the sweet trolley, but Amanda insisted they make a move almost immediately the last mouthful was finished. Meredith complained about possible indigestion as she led the way round to the theatre at a brisk pace, only relaxing once she had her father through its main door.

They had good seats in the stalls. The women insisted he sit in the middle of them, and supervised as he switched off his phone. Meredith then complained about the lack of leg room, and fidgeted for a good ten minutes before settling into his seat, his arms folded across his chest.

The curtain went up and the play got underway. It was entertaining, and the first half had some funny one-liners that even Meredith managed to smile at. Jeremy Carmichael proved to be an excellent actor, and after only a few moments the drunk Patsy had seen in The Box of Frogs was forgotten. When the curtain came down for the interval she nudged Meredith.

"You laughed. I said you would enjoy it."

"I didn't laugh. I may have smiled, but I didn't laugh." Meredith winked at her. "Can you get drinks at half time here?"

"If you're quick and you've ordered them. If you haven't ordered, you might not get back on time." Amanda stood and squeezed past her father. "I'm going to the loo. You stay here and I'll get you one."

Amanda arrived back as the house lights dimmed. She handed Meredith and Patsy a small plastic cup, each half-full with red wine.

"What's this?" Meredith tasted it. "Not bad if it wasn't for the taste of plastic." He glanced at his watch as an announcer asked for quiet. The curtains opened and Carmichael was kneeling by the side of a bed, apparently in prayer. "How long have we got to go?" Meredith whispered as Carmichael started to speak. Amanda nudged him in the ribs and put her finger to her lips as the woman behind hushed him. Meredith slid as far down in the seat as he was able, given the limited space, sipped his wine, and resigned himself to watching the rest of the play.

Immediately the final curtain fell, he stood and stretched.

"Well that was good, I shall treat you to a drink," he announced, trying to keep a straight face.

"I'm so glad you enjoyed it, Dad. I knew you would, so much so that I also bought tickets to the new musical that opens next week at the Hippodrome." Amanda laughed as her father's face fell. "I'm kidding, don't panic. You are such a lousy actor."

Meredith and Patsy followed Amanda out of the theatre. It was a slow journey as the rows filed out in front of them. Once outside Amanda led them across the road to a small traditional pub. Meredith ordered their drinks. He drank half his pint quickly, and had it topped up again before joining the girls. They discussed the play which the two women had enjoyed, and Meredith said was all right, but gave a warning that it wasn't something he intended to do regularly. Amanda was relaxed and animated as she related a tale of her own attempts at acting.

Meredith decided now was a good time to find out who Patrick was. As she finished telling her story he tapped her knee.

"I had brunch with Sherlock today." He rolled his eyes as the two women gasped in amazement. "Don't be so surprised, I do socialise sometimes, you know."

"Well, there had to be food involved. But brunch? With Frankie? Are you feeling all right, Johnny?" Patsy laughed as Meredith attempted to push her off her stool by leaning into her.

"Fine and dandy, thank you. Anyway, as I was about to say, we got around to talking, as you do, and he mentioned Patrick." Meredith watched his daughter still. "You didn't tell me he . . . Ow!"

Meredith was rudely interrupted as his daughter kicked his shin.

"Don't look now, but some of the cast have come in. Jeremy Carmichael is here," she hissed in a low voice.

Meredith glanced over his shoulder. "Splendid, you can get his autograph as soon as you've told me where Patrick is based."

"Based?" Patsy looked confused and turned to Amanda as the penny dropped. "Oh no, Amanda, tell me he's not a copper." She shook her head. "You don't want to get mixed up with a police officer, trust me, I know. Unreliable, always late, always thinking about the case rather than the conversation . . ."

She continued to list off all the negative things about her life with Meredith, and his eyes narrowed.

"Is this police officers in general or just me? Because not so long ago you were all those things yourself, and people in glass houses . . ." He winked. "More to the point, don't take us off course. Amanda has to answer me."

There was a shout from the bar, and the cast of *Damned If You Do* raised their glasses, knocked back whatever was in them, and burst out laughing.

Meredith jerked his head towards them. "Dramatic lot, aren't they. I suppose they realise they're not supposed to be the centre of attention now." He turned back to Amanda, "You were saying?"

"He's coming over." Amanda's eyes were wide. She lowered her voice. "He's quite handsome for an older man, don't you think?" She giggled as Patsy nodded, and Meredith began to lean on her again.

Patsy grabbed the table for support as she watched Carmichael approach. He was wearing old jeans with an England rugby shirt. He looked far removed from the drunk she had seen, or indeed the middle-aged, downtrodden father he had just played. His recently washed hair was almost dry and the tousled look suited him. His back straight, and chin up, the handsome man was full of confidence; the only thing marring his persona was the smug arrogance he emitted.

Jeremy Carmichael stopped a little way from their table, and Patsy looked away. The phone in his hand played Yankee Doodle Dandy. He glanced over his shoulder at his colleagues before answering it. He had a brief telephone conversation.

"Of course." He purred his assurances into the phone. "I can't tell you how pleased I am. No, no. Tonight. We're in the pub. Come now, please." His voice lowered in tone and he pleaded huskily. "I can't wait until tomorrow. I can't wait that long. I need you as soon as possible. Ah you minx, you shouldn't tease me. I shall order your drink."

"She gave in then. Who could refuse that?" Patsy whispered to Amanda who giggled, before her face fell. She frowned as Carmichael moved back to the others at the bar.

"What?" hissed Patsy not wanting to turn around. "What did he do?"

Amanda waited until Carmichael was engaged in conversation before leaning in again.

"When he hung up, he looked evil. That's the only way I can describe it: evil. Whoever he was talking to wouldn't bother coming if they'd seen his face. I don't think I like him now."

"Good, because he's old enough to be your father. He's too short, and he makes a living pretending to be someone else. Why are you surprised if he turns it on for the ladies? Now let's get back -" Meredith sighed as Amanda interrupted his planned interrogation once more.

"He's not short, and as to age . . . Good grief, she's here already." Amanda's eyebrows rose. "And she's gorgeous too."

This time both Meredith and Patsy turned to see who had entered the pub. They watched a tall redhead walk over to the bar. Her hair fell in loose curls almost to her waist, and she had the most beautiful brown almond shaped eyes, which searched out Carmichael. She smiled shyly as she spotted him. He walked towards her carrying a glass in each hand.

"You look stunning as always. Thank you for coming back, you won't regret it. Come, let's sit."

Patsy turned away as they walked near them, and nudged Meredith. "Don't be so obvious. You've seen attractive women before."

"I recognise her from somewhere. I can't place her though." He shrugged and grimaced. "That's two of them now. I'll never sleep."

"She's an actress, I expect. You've probably seen her on the TV or something," Amanda suggested. "Who's the other one you can't place? You said 'that's two of them'."

Meredith pulled the folded papers from his pocket, and he lay them on the table and tapped one of them. Patsy and Amanda studied the two images. Patsy shook her head, but Amanda picked one up and inspected it closely.

"He is vaguely familiar, I know what you mean." She handed it back to her father. "I can't put a name or a place to the face though. Who is he?"

"The possible abductor of the girls. Two different witnesses came up with those. I think it's him, and I know I've seen him somewhere but can't bring it to mind. It's driving me round the bend. Now, I'll have her rattling around up there too, distracting me. Like I say, I'll never sleep."

The three glanced over to the couple a few tables away. They were sitting opposite each other, arms resting on the table, and leaning in towards each other. He was holding her gaze and speaking quietly, and she looked spellbound. Carmichael reached across and began to stroke her arm, before tracing his finger across her breasts and up her neck to rest on her lips. She kissed it gently as he nodded approval.

"I think his luck's in," Meredith observed dryly.

"Dad. You've not got a romantic bone in your body, have you? Is that all you can see, a bit of you know what?" Amanda tutted. "Can't you see the love and the tenderness? It's not all about sex, you know."

"What happened to 'she wouldn't come if she'd seen his face'? There's only one thing he's after tonight, trust me." Meredith glanced back over at the couple. The woman was looking down and shaking her head. "Oh, I might have been wrong." He turned back grinning. "That doesn't happen often. So, back to Patrick. Let's talk about Patrick."

Amanda didn't answer, but gasped and nodded at the couple. "Look," she hissed.

Meredith was bored with Carmichael, despite his attractive companion, and rather than turn his head he swivelled in his seat to face them. He was hoping the obvious interest they were creating would encourage them to move to a table further away. He raised his eyebrows as he took in the scene. Carmichael was grasping the woman by the wrist, and had pulled her forward until her forehead rested against his, and her body was forced against the table. The arm he grasped bent at an uncomfortable angle. His words were delivered quietly and through gritted teeth. The look on his face showed they were not kind.

The woman lurched backwards and managed to pull free. She jumped to her feet. "This is why I didn't want to come. I don't want to see your new place. I don't want to jump into bed with you. I want my job back, that's all." She flicked her hand in the air. "Anything else is over. You told me you accepted that."

Carmichael stood to join her. He reached out and stroked her face. She flinched but didn't pull away.

"I'm sorry, forgive me. You are just so beautiful. You can't blame me for loving you." His demeanour had turned full circle, and he looked genuinely remorseful.

Meredith was impressed. This man truly was a good actor. There was no way his anger had dispersed that quickly. He looked at the woman to see if she had been taken in, but she hadn't. Meredith smiled. Good girl.

"You have no idea what the word means, Jeremy. You want me because you can't have me. Accept that, find someone else to play with, and we can get on and work together."

"Princess, you can't mean that. Let's go and get something to eat, we can talk about this." Carmichael's smile fell away as she shook her head.

"No, Jeremy, please. Call me if you want me to work for you." The woman turned. "I'm going now." She made to walk away, but with a growl Carmichael jumped forward.

"Beth! Don't you dare walk away from me."

He swung her back to face him by yanking on her coat. Patsy sat up straight, not believing her luck, and this poor woman's lack of it. This was Beth Durham. This was the woman who had also had a fling with Antonio Garcia.

"Or what? You have no power over me anymore. Let go of my jacket." Beth Durham jerked her shoulder violently, and the coat was pulled from Carmichael's hand.

The bar had fallen silent, and her eyes darted around the faces looking at her. Embarrassed, she felt the heat rise from her neck to her cheeks. Unable to control his temper, Carmichael lunged at her, hand out ready to slap her. Beth stepped back, holding her arms in front of her to shield her from the expected blow.

Meredith jumped up, and grabbed Carmichael's arm as, now off balance, Beth staggered backwards, and ended up sitting on the floor. Amanda got up and helped her to her feet. Meredith frogmarched Carmichael out of the bar. Once outside, he held him against the wall by placing a hand in the centre of his chest and leaning his weight forward.

"Let's just take a moment, shall we? You almost did something stupid then. Not wise to have a row with the ex when you've been drinking."

"Get your hands off me," Carmichael snarled, his chin high, and a look of distaste on his face.

"As the lady said, or what? Listen, pal, you've had one too many and you'll regret this in the morning. Now, let's agree you'll go home and sleep it off." Meredith sighed and released the pressure a little. "If I let you go, you're not going to do anything stupid, are you?"

"Who the hell do you think you are?" Carmichael spat. "I'm not drunk. I've only had one drink. You were there, you stupid man." He hit Meredith's arm away and brushed his hands down his chest as though removing an unseen residue. "Now get off me, and mind your own business."

He turned back towards the entrance to the pub. In one swift movement, Meredith gripped his arm, pulled it roughly up behind his back, and pinned him against the door. Carmichael's face was now pressed up against the diamond shaped window in the heavy wooden door, and he could see Beth sitting with the two women who had helped her up.

"I'm sorry. Passions are running high, now let me go, old chap, and I'll be able to sort things out. As I say, I'm not drunk."

"You're telling me that you hit women when you're sober. I don't think I like that. Now are you going to bugger off home, or do I have to sort you out?"

"What?" Carmichael snorted. "You criticise me for my passion, and then decide to beat me up. Why? Do you fancy your chances with her? She'll probably drop her knickers for you. But I doubt she'll like the thug element. Beth is very sensitive."

"Beat you up?" Meredith leaned closer. "I've got better things to do with my time. You shouldn't judge people by your own standards." Meredith grinned as the man stiffened; he'd hit a sore point. "No, sir, when I said sort you out, I meant arrest you. I can think of several counts that would stick. Now, what's it to be?"

Meredith let go of Carmichael, pulled his ID from his pocket and shoved it in Carmichael's face as he turned around and rubbed the cheek that had been squashed against the door. Carmichael's eyes peered at the ID. Recognition of the possible trouble he was in flickered in his eyes, and his brain worked quickly: being arrested would not be wise. It was bad enough people thought he couldn't hold his drink. He'd sort Beth out tomorrow. He covered his face with his hands.

"I'm sorry. I can't think straight when I'm with her and she's like this. I love her so much." He uncovered his face, and sad eyes found Meredith's. "I'll go, I promise." He stepped away from the building. Glancing back over his shoulder as he walked away, he called to Meredith. "Tell her I'm sorry, and that I love her."

Meredith nodded and Carmichael increased his pace. He cursed silently as he hurried away. Of all the people to have witnessed that scene, for Christ's sake! Then he shrugged. It could have been worse, he supposed. The press might have been there too.

Meredith had no intention of telling anyone anything, and as he walked back into the bar his face fell. Now Carmichael had gone, several of the other actors had come to their table, where Beth still sat with Patsy and Amanda. They were commiserating with Beth.

"I don't know where that temper comes from. He's been in a good mood all day too. Mind you, I've heard he's been drinking a lot lately." A petite blonde woman with too much makeup patted Beth's arm.

Patsy caught Meredith's eye, and she shrugged as the young man who had played Carmichael's illegitimate son squeezed Beth's hand.

"He's always in a bad mood. I was relieved when he got that bug, and James covered for him. It's probably because he was late tonight, got there by the skin of his teeth. Come home with us, love. That bastard doesn't deserve you, you know that."

Meredith walked forward decisively, and placed his hands on Amanda's shoulders. He gave them a squeeze. "Taxi's waiting, let's be off."

Beth seized her opportunity to disappear. She jumped up and took Meredith's arm.

"It's fine, Jamie, really. Jeremy doesn't know where I live, and these very kind people are dropping me off." Much to Meredith' surprise, she linked her arm through his and, waving goodbye, headed towards the door. Amanda and Patsy hurried to join them.

Once outside, Beth released Meredith and turned to them. "I'm so sorry to hijack you. But the thought of spending the night with them . . . well, let's say it wasn't pretty." She scanned the road. "I thought you said you had a taxi." She looked at Meredith.

"I lied. I was trying to escape you lot." Meredith rolled his eyes. "That backfired on me."

A smile twitched as his words registered. Beth threw her head back and laughed.

"Well, I can't say I blame you. I hope our floor show didn't ruin your evening. Jeremy is a brilliant actor, but absolutely crap at everything else." She caught Patsy's eye. "And I mean everything."

A taxi with its light on drove into the street, and Meredith flagged it down. Patsy caught hold of Beth's arm.

"Let us give you a lift. I'd be happier knowing you got home safely." She ignored Meredith's sigh, opened the door, and climbed into the taxi behind Beth. Meredith was pleased to find that Beth only lived a few miles away, and he turned to face Patsy once they had dropped her off.

"She could have lived miles away. That was rash."

"No, it wasn't. She might be useful in helping track down the chap I'm looking for. I wanted to know where she lived." Patsy grinned at him. "You see, there's method in my madness. That might turn out to be a lucky coincidence for me."

"Oh I see, one rule for you, and another for me," Meredith teased her, as he pulled his phone from his pocket, the exchange reminding him he had yet to switch it back on. "I'm not allowed to . . . Bollocks. He's done it again." Meredith nudged the taxi driver and changed the instructions. "Sorry, girls, I have to go to work. The bastard has tried to snatch a girl, from a supermarket of all places."

CHAPTER TEN

Meredith strode into the incident room. Trump and Rawlings were both on the telephone, and nodded acknowledgement. Jo Adler appeared from the kitchen. "Evening, Gov, how was the theatre?"

"Boring. I only picked up your messages a few minutes ago. I had to turn my phone off. I knew there was a reason I didn't want to go. What have we got?" He followed Jo over to the latest entry on the board. A picture of a dark-haired child smiled back at him.

"Harriet Boyles. Seven years old. She was shopping at the supermarket in Thornbury with her mother when he attacked."

"When you say 'attacked', did he assault her, or attempt to take her?"

"Not sure. Her mother left her choosing what fruit she wanted for her packed lunch, and doubled back to get a loaf of bread that she had forgotten. When she came back a man was approaching Harriet, and in the mother's words, 'He didn't look right. It was obvious he was looking at Harry.' She called out, asking the girl if she was all right. He grabbed at the child before running off. Harriet screamed blue murder, as not only was she frightened, but he got hold of the arm she'd injured in a fall a couple of days before. He tore the dressing off in his haste."

"When did this happen?"

"About five this afternoon. The local police took a while before they put two and two together and called us. By the time we'd confirmed it was our man you had turned your phone off."

"CCTV?" Meredith asked, and turned to follow Jo to the TV at the side of the room. Picking up the remote Jo rewound to the beginning of the disc. "This is the one from inside the shop. The camera swivels through one hundred and eighty degrees, and sod's law means it moved just as our man would have revealed his face, so we have nothing, except height and clothing. We've not even got the bit where he grabbed her, although . . . here it is. We have her mother's reaction." Jo stepped forward, and changed discs as Meredith shook his head. Trump came over to join them. "This is outside, and taken from the shop opposite. Unfortunately, it's all we have." Jo pointed at the screen with the remote. "That's him going in."

Meredith watched the grainy black and white recording show a man of about six feet tall, of average build and wearing everyday non-descript clothes, with a baseball cap pulled low over his face, enter the Co-op. It wouldn't be much help identifying the man.

"Anything coming out?"

"Not on him, less than going in, because he runs out. Hang on a minute." Jo fast forwarded to the man leaving; as he did so a group of four girls were going in. One was waving her hands in the air demonstrating a dance move, and totally obliterated the man's face." Meredith cursed her. "Keep watching." Jo instructed. "There." Jo froze the picture. "A black Range Rover, and guess what?"

"We didn't get the registration plate." Meredith pinched the bridge of his nose. "Did we get anything?"

"Yes, more confirmation that your bag lady got it right. One of the store staff and one of those four girls picked out the e-fit. It was definitely our man. I've checked with the newsroom," Trump tutted in irritation, "and they didn't run the e-fit this evening, but the producer has promised to put it on each local news bulletin tomorrow, starting at six in the morning. That's the independent channel. Rawlings is on to BBC Bristol now." He glanced at Rawlings who held his thumb up and nodded. "And it seems he has the same agreement. This should take us a step closer, sir."

"Other than that, we have nothing new. We were going to call it a day, if that's okay with you, Gov. Rawlings is covering tonight." As Jo spoke, Rawlings hung up.

"Right. That's the BBC playing ball now too. I pointed out that if they had played ball earlier it might not have happened. They'll run the footage from the store and the stills."

"Good." Meredith turned back to the photograph of Harriet Boyles and pointed at it. "She lives in Almondsbury. That's a good twelve miles from Dana, and a little more than that from Ellen and Gemma. We can rule out schools and clubs, I'm assuming. So, what's the connection? How is he choosing them? I don't believe it's random." He walked towards the photograph of Harriet. "She might have been, though. It's a tough shout to walk a child out of a supermarket when she's with her mother. Perhaps he thought she was on her own and was going to risk it." He turned back to face them. "Any connections at all?"

The three officers murmured negative comments and Meredith shook his head.

"Well, there is a connection, and once we find it, we'll find him. That's if the wonderful public don't deliver him to us first of course. You two get off. I'll stay here with Rawlings for a while."

Adler and Trump left.

"I'll make the coffee," Meredith announced to Rawlings, "you look at those three little girls, and try and work out what they have in common with your Ellen."

"I've been doing that off and on all evening, Gov. The only thing I can come up with is differences. Ellen is blonde with blue eyes. The others are all dark-haired and brown-eyed. Ellen and Gemma have loads of connections in common, they've known each other since they were toddlers, but they have nothing in common with the others, not that I know of anyway." Rawlings stood and yawned, stretching his arms above his head. "You don't have to hang around for my benefit, Gov. It was my turn to pull the late one."

"I need to think, Rawlings. I do that better in here than anywhere else. I've seen that bastard somewhere," Meredith jabbed his finger at the enlarged e-fit, "but I don't know where. It'll come to me though."

The cap was screwed onto the bottle and it was put away in the cupboard. He'd only drink the one measure. He needed a clear head and a steady hand for tomorrow. But today had been a nightmare, and right now he needed a drink. To remove himself further from temptation he took the glass to his bedroom. Without turning on the light, he placed the glass on the bedside table, and lay fully clothed on the bed. He closed his eyes and, for the first time since he was a child, he prayed. He prayed for forgiveness. He knew the pain he was causing others, and all for his own selfish ends. His mind drifted. It could be Harriet, but what must she think of him. He had totally bungled their encounter. Hopefully, next time they met he would put that right. Reaching for the drink, he emptied it in one gulp. Now, though, he needed to sleep.

Patsy yelped as Meredith pulled her to him. His hands were freezing.

"Well, if I had been asleep, I'm certainly not now. You're freezing." She turned to face him.

"Cold hands, warm heart," Meredith sighed.

"Was it him?" Patsy murmured into his chest.

"Yep. But something's changed. With the others he got them into conversation first, made sure they were alone. With this one, he tried to grab her in a public place. Seems to me like he's becoming desperate, and that worries me."

"But desperate for what? He returned Ellen and her friend unharmed. What is it he wants them for?"

"There is speculation – but obviously not when Rawlings is around – and pornography tops the bill at the moment. Drugs them, poses them, films or photographs them, who knows? But if that is the reason, why would that make him take chances? What happened to make him risk getting caught?" Meredith sighed again. "None of it is making sense. I don't think the choice of victim is in anyway random, but we can't find anything to link them. Not one thing, apart from their age. I find that odd in itself. I don't want another girl to go missing, or worse, because I can't work out what that link is."

"You're not working on your own, you know. You're always so tough on yourself. You have a team for a reason, and I wish you'd realise that part of that reason is that you don't take all failures personally."

"But I've seen him, or a photo of him, or something, and I can't remember where. It's driving me mad not being able to recall where or why."

"Then stop trying. It will come to you. You are clearly not sleepy, so do you want to get up and have a drink or something?"

Patsy laughed as he pulled her closer.

"No, you can tire me out. Come here."

When Patsy awoke the next morning, she slid her hand across the bed to find Meredith. All she found was a cold space where he should have been. Meredith had clearly been gone for a while. Lifting her head, she peered at the clock: it was only six thirty. He'd had barely five hours' sleep.

Unable to get back to sleep, Patsy went to the kitchen. As she sipped her tea, she made a decision. She was going to book them a holiday. She'd take the bull by the horns, and do it. She'd worry about getting him onto a plane at a later date. Collecting her laptop, she refilled the kettle, and braced herself for a few hours of indecision as she searched the internet for the perfect holiday.

As she settled herself with a fresh cup of tea, she remembered she'd been sent an email a few days before from a company advertising last-minute breaks.

Smiling, she opened her email account, knowing that if it were cheap, it would lessen the blow for Meredith.

Patsy never found the email, as the latest communication into her inbox took her attention. She opened the email from Antonio Garcia. It had arrived in the early hours of the morning.

Ms Hodge

I have received your email. I will call you tomorrow morning. I will speak to your client later, but only via telephone. I am not coming back to England yet.

As I have agreed to this, I want you to consider taking me on as a client. My life is being threatened, by two men, possibly three. I have no idea why. At first, I ignored the warnings and they became more violent in their messages. They threatened my family, and now my father is dead. I can't go to the police as I fear for my mother, but I would like to complete my studies. I do have a small amount of information which may assist your search. Will you take my case?

Antonio Garcia

Despite Antonio's situation, Patsy couldn't help but smile. He'd agreed to speak to Nicola, albeit by telephone, and he wanted her to take on a case that didn't involve looking for an errant husband or father. She punched the air at the thought, before typing a quick response agreeing to take the case in principle. She asked Antonio to call between eleven and twelve as she would keep her line clear at that time, and she hit the send button. Within minutes she had a response. Antonio insisted that he would call her at ten. He made it clear that he didn't want her other client to be there as he wanted their conversation to be private. He promised he would speak to her other client later in the day. He didn't give a time.

Patsy wondered if perhaps Antonio thought Nicola was the one threatening him. That would be a logical conclusion for him to reach. At this stage, he didn't know who Nicola was, or why she wanted to speak to him. She would have to try and convince him when they spoke later. Patsy ran her hand across the top of the keyboard. She'd speak to Meredith, and warn him about the holiday before she wasted any money. Closing the laptop, she felt a twinge of guilt. She was using

Meredith as an excuse. She hadn't booked the holiday as it might interfere with her new case.

In his office, Meredith was reading his own emails, or more accurately, the subject line of them, before hitting the delete button. The majority were from various institutions advertising their latest products, or departments within the force offering training or retraining in various fields. It was a long list, and he started with the oldest date. As he deleted the emails he cursed, wondering if it were possible to get his email address off the myriad of lists it clearly occupied. He'd not signed up for any of this. Suddenly, he started and cursed. He had deleted one from Professor Rosemary Cole. He went to the deleted folder and recovered it. Why hadn't the woman picked up the phone if she wanted him? He scanned the brief note. It had been sent from her phone.

Apologies, almost forgot. Negligible trace of a Benzodiazepine in the girls' system. Call me if you need more assistance. Rose

The message had been sent the night before. Meredith decided he would go and visit her later, provided nothing else happened in the meantime. He smiled as Rawlings approached his office. He had been asleep at his desk when Meredith arrived, and Meredith had left him to it, knowing he probably needed it. Rawlings looked sheepish.

"Sorry, Gov, that's not like me. The last thing I remember is looking at the clock at three thirty."

"I'll forgive you just this once." Meredith's stomach rumbled and he stood up. "Do you fancy joining me and Peggy for breakfast? I hear they do a good full English."

Rawlings agreed readily, and Meredith instructed Trump to hold the fort as they passed him on their way out. Trump didn't mind being excluded; with Linda forcing her home baking on him at every given opportunity, his waist line was expanding at an alarming rate. He'd had to go up a notch on his belt this morning.

Peggy waved her fork as they approached her table. "Merriwinkle! What a pleasure." She watched as Meredith scanned the contents of her plate. "Stop coveting my sausages, get your own." She smiled, "I take it you're stopping?"

"We are, and this is Dave." Meredith opened the door to the café and called out, "Two full English please. All the trimmings, we'll be with the lady outside."

Peggy nudged Rawlings. "He's a charmer. How long since I was called a lady, do you reckon?" She balanced a mushroom on top of the bacon on her fork, "A bloody long time I can tell you. He's quite a charmer is Merriwinkle."

"So I'm told," Rawlings smiled warmly. "Personally, I can't see the attraction. It must be reserved for you ladies. What's the grub like?"

"Not bad. The eggs are a bit overcooked, but I'll manage." She dipped a corner of toast in the fried egg to demonstrate. "I like my yolks runny. I'll order more precisely tomorrow."

The door opened and a young man clad all in black with a grubby blue and white stripped apron tied around his waist opened the door. Retrieving the tray, he had balanced on the nearest table, he delivered Meredith's order. His face was sullen.

"Thank you. You don't do service with a smile then?" Meredith rolled his eyes at Peggy, who cackled.

"No, that costs extra at this time of day." His lips twitched as he answered. "Sorry I was miles away. I'll do better next time." He forced a smile and hurried away.

"Bless him." Having finished her breakfast, Peggy opened the little container of marmalade and spread it on the remaining toast. She then dunked it in her tea.

Meredith wrinkled his nose. "I'm all for dunking, Peggy, but not with marmalade on it, surely?"

"I don't criticise you for squirting that brown muck all over your perfectly good breakfast, so you leave me and my dunking alone." Peggy dunked again, and her mouth full, she added, "What do you want anyway, apart from my wonderful repartee?"

"I was hungry, he was hungry," Meredith nodded at Rawlings, who must have been starving as he had almost emptied his plate, "and I thought you might like some company. You don't mind, do you?"

"Not at all. I thought you were checking they'd kept the deal." Peggy nodded into the café. "They didn't give me any trouble." She winked at Meredith. "Thank you, Merriwinkle."

"You're welcome." Meredith smiled as Peggy dabbed at her grubby face with the napkin. She needed a scrubbing brush not a paper tissue. He put his hand in his pocket and pulled out the folded e-fits and passed them to Peggy. "Have a look at these for me."

He continued to eat as Peggy unfolded them. Rawlings lifted her plate up and placed it on his own to provide some space, and she lay them on the table. Rummaging in the side pocket of her bag she produced a pair of glasses.

"You didn't tell me you wore glasses. Did you have them on when you saw the girls?" Meredith was concerned that his one decent witness was going to give an excuse for her evidence to be trashed.

"No, of course not." Peggy perched the glasses on the end of her nose and leaned forward. She tapped the likeness of Charlie without the cap, leaving a grubby fingerprint on the edge of the sheet. "That's him."

"How can you be sure if you didn't have your glasses on?"

"Because I'm long-sighted." Peggy shook her head. "I thought you were a good detective, Merriwinkle. Perhaps I was wrong." She smiled at Rawlings, pretending to ignore Meredith. "That's the man I saw." She looked back at the picture and tilted her head. "Probably a little older though." She lifted her hands and tapped the side of eyes. "More lined here, but other than that not bad. Well done, Merriwinkle."

Rawlings excused himself as his phone rang. Meredith reached across the table and patted Peggy's hand.

"How's your back? Have you seen a doctor?"

"Fine, and not for twenty-odd years. Don't worry about me, Merriwinkle, I'll probably outlive you." Peggy stood up, and Meredith watched her eyes screw up against the pain as she bent to retrieve her bag. "I can't stop and chat. I need to get around the corner to see what they have an offer. Say goodbye to Dave for me."

Meredith watched her shuffle away. Rawlings finished his call and called goodbye. Peggy held up her arm in acknowledgement.

"That was the wife. I didn't think to tell her I'd be late, she thought there'd been a development. I'd better get off. Do you want a lift back to the station?"

"No, I'm going to drop in on Dr Rose whilst I'm down this way. You carry on." Rawlings nodded and walked away. Meredith called to him. "You haven't got any cigarettes on you, have you?"

"Nope, and if I did, you wouldn't get one. You're giving up, remember." Rawlings smirked and continued his journey.

Meredith rolled his eyes, wondering whether to buy a packet. He tapped on the window on the café and wiggled his finger to indicate he wanted the bill. He'd leave the cigarettes until he'd been to the hospital.

At ten minutes to ten, Sharon transferred Antonio Garcia's call to Patsy's office. She then went in and sat opposite Patsy, who hit the speaker button and greeted him, thanking him for calling back. Deciding to take charge of the conversation she began questioning him immediately.

"I should tell you I'm recording this call to ensure I don't miss any details." She didn't wait for any protest. "You say you have received threatening calls. What sort of threats?"

"Initially telling me my life would be in danger if I stayed in Bristol, then when I stayed, they increased in frequency and it was my family who were threatened. I did nothing, and now my father is dead."

"Do you really think whoever was making the calls killed him?"

"I don't know. Possibly. It was . . . I don't know the English word, but acute food poisoning. My mother tells me he ate shell fish the day before, but who knows."

"Why did someone want you out of Bristol?" Patsy ticked off another question from her pad.

There was silence for a while.

"I have no idea, but if I were to guess I would think it was about a woman."

"Any particular woman in mind?" Patsy's tone was slightly condescending, and she heard Antonio give a short laugh.

"No, Patsy. I do not have a particular woman in mind. I have had several relationships since coming to Bristol. I don't even know if that's the cause of this mess. But I have done nothing wrong, not that I am aware of."

"I take it some of these women were married or otherwise spoken for?"

Again, there was a short silence.

"I didn't ask, but I knew a couple of the women were married." As though needing to justify his actions he added, "I didn't go looking, you know, they came to me. I am only flesh and blood, and it's -"

"Yes, I get the picture, I'm sure you were lonely, misunderstood or both." She pulled a face as Sharon stifled a laugh. "Look, Antonio, let's get one thing straight. I deal only in facts. I don't care about why you did or do what you do, I don't judge, I simply -"

"Oh, but you do. I can hear it in your tone. The thing we need to establish is whether you can put your thoughts and prejudice to one side."

Patsy was insulted. She was always professional. She had never let her own personal opinions affect the way she handled a case.

"I can assure you, Antonio, that whatever my thoughts are about you, they will not affect any investigation I may agree to undertake on your behalf. So, back to the matter in hand. You said two maybe three people, did you speak to them?"

"Yes. I answered the first few calls, and the man, probably eastern European, told me to get out of Bristol if I valued my life. I questioned him at first, and thinking it was some kind of prank, I later ignored all unknown calls, only returning them if a message had been left."

"When was this, can you give me dates?"

"I have my telephone records. I can highlight the calls. They came from the same three numbers pretty much. Only one was from a land line."

"Okay, so other than the eastern European, who else called?"

"Two calls about a week apart were from a woman."

"And she threatened you too?"

"No, she told me he meant it. She didn't want me hurt and that I should go."

"But you only left because of your father?"

"Of course. I am not a coward, unlike this man who hides at the end of a call and hurts old men."

"When was the last time you received a call?"

"Two days before my father died. It was not the same man. The last two calls I received were from a local man, local to Bristol, I mean. He had a strong accent. When I think back now, perhaps that was because the other was on his way to kill my father."

"Why would they do that? I don't doubt you've had calls, but if you've done something so bad it would result in the murder of your father, surely you would have some idea what that was?"

"No, nothing. I work hard, at university, my studies, and my placement. I haven't the time to upset anyone . . . or so I thought. That is why I can only think it is to do with a woman. I have had many liaisons. But nothing serious. I am at a loss, Patsy. Truly I am." He sighed. "I should qualify at the end of this academic year. I want to come back to finish that. I'm too ashamed to explain to my mother why I am delaying my return. My parents sacrificed a lot so I could go to university in Bristol. Will you help me, Patsy?"

"I will if I can. You said you had some information, what have you got?"

"I have three telephone numbers – two mobile, one landline – and I have a note. It was left for me at one of the bars where I worked."

"Okay, well, the tracing of the telephones may be straightforward. It depends how clever these people are. I will keep my fee as low as I am able, Antonio, but there will be some costs, you do understand that."

"I do, yes. I have a small amount of savings now, and I am working. If I come back I will also work, so I do have money coming in." He paused. "You also said the person who was looking for me may . . . I can't remember your words, but you indicated there may be money involved."

Patsy looked at Sharon. Antonio sounded quite desperate, and there was a lot at stake with regards to his future career. Given the circumstances, Patsy believed he might agree to become involved with Nicola and the child simply to obtain money. Patsy sighed as she considered this.

"Hello, hello. Are you still there?"

"Yes, sorry, Antonio, I'm here. I was thinking." Drawing in a deep breath Patsy decided honesty was the best policy, and she told Antonio of her concerns. "My other client is quite vulnerable at the moment, and if you are to accept what they want, I need to at least believe you are doing it for the right reasons."

"I don't understand you. What it is they want? Why does this . . . whatever it is, make a difference to you?" Antonio fell quiet; he was concerned by Patsy's words.

"Listen Antonio, I'm not explaining this prop -"

"Give me the name," Antonio demanded aggressively.

"I'm sorry, what -"

Antonio interrupted her again. "Give me the name, and email me a photograph. I will think about this, and if I think this is genuine, I will call at three this afternoon. If not, I will disappear again."

"Nicola Meredith, but Antonio I -"

Antonio hung up. Patsy stopped the recording and turned to Sharon.

"Did I just make a pig's ear of that?"

"Not really," Sharon shrugged and stood up. "If that boy thinks someone will kill his mother, and he's just lost his father, of course he will be suspicious. I think you need to be careful. Nicola needs to be careful. There may be something in what he says." She opened the door to leave. "Of course, he is probably just being paranoid, it's a prank gone wrong and the father wasn't murdered, simply unfortunate. Discuss it with Chris once you get more information. But you need to tread carefully either way."

Patsy called Nicola. She shared the fact that Antonio had called, but not the actual conversation, and arranged for Nicola to be at her office for three o'clock. Nicola was very excited, and Patsy wasted ten minutes trying to warn her of the folly of raised hopes. Eventually she hung up exasperated. Her phone rang again immediately. It was an internal call from Linda.

Ten minutes later, Patsy watched as Linda apparently had an online conversation with the illusive Lyndon Ward. It was a forum on homeopathic remedies, and Lyndon was, according to Linda, using the name Leward. Linda had a split screen in front of her, and while awaiting a response from Leward was scanning the internet for ideas.

"How do you know it's him?" Patsy looked at the avatar. It was Baloo the bear from *Jungle Book*.

"Because I've been tracking what he talked about. The links he shared . . . you know the sort of stuff, Patsy, don't be dim."

"I don't actually. Not everyone spends their life on the internet. But assuming it is him, explain again why you're doing this now." Patsy waved her finger at the screen.

"Because I reckon in the next half an hour or so he will ask me for private contact details, or perhaps give me his."

"And you know this because . . . Oh my God. Linda, you are a witch! How did you know?" Patsy's mouth had fallen open as a new message appeared on screen.

Good point. I can tell you are passionate about this issue. I'd like to discuss this further. Email me your point of reference please. My contact details are in my bio.

Linda smiled at Patsy and shrugged. "Because I am brilliant. I am also, contrary to popular belief, quite good at detective work. I have followed his trail, worked out his MO, and set a couple of traps. This is the second one. I've also noticed that once he's in deep conversation with someone he invites them to take it off-line. They are all women. I think your theory that he was leading her on was spot on." Linda smiled at Patsy. "Shall I reel him in?"

"But of course." Patsy winked at Linda. "Do your stuff."

Meredith stopped at the small reception desk, and he smiled at the nurse who was engaged on a call. She returned his smile. The call took longer than either of them expected, and Meredith began to get impatient. The nurse put her hand over the mouth piece.

"Sorry sir, I won't be long. I have . . ." Her attention was drawn back to the call.

Meredith pulled out his pad and scribbled a note asking where Professor Rosemary Cole could be found. Taking out his warrant card, he lay the note next to it in front of the nurse.

Her eyebrows rose. DCI Meredith was the nicest looking policeman she'd had to deal with for a while. She glanced at his left hand. No wedding ring. She smiled her best smile and nodded. Tucking the phone under her chin, her fingers hit the keyboard. Turning over the sheet Meredith had given her, she began to write. Meredith frowned, it was a long note. Still smiling and holding her shoulders back a little, she handed the note back. A smile danced around Meredith's lips. She had given him Professor Cole's expected location, and her own name and phone number.

He winked, blew her a kiss, and turned to look at the directional signs on the wall behind him. Walking towards Ward G, he heard her saying goodbye to the caller and quickened his pace. Ward G was at the top of a long corridor, beyond which signs, suspended from the ceiling, located various operating theatres, and a children's high dependency unit. He pushed the door to enter the ward. It was locked. He walked to the bell and pushed it. A nurse appeared from a side room and unlocked the door.

"I'm sorry, visiting doesn't start until two this afternoon. The doctors are about to do their rounds, and then we have lunch." She frowned. "You're not a parent, are you?"

Meredith held up his ID. "No, love, not a parent. I'm after Professor Cole. She has some information for me."

"Oh. She's observing at the moment. Come in, I'll buzz her."

The nurse led him into the small office at the end of the ward. Picking up the phone she hit two digits, and Meredith listened as she explained his presence to Professor Cole. The nurse grinned at something that was said and looked him up and down before asking, "Are you squeamish? Dr Rose said if not, you can join her. But if you're likely to faint you need to wait twenty minutes or so."

Meredith wanted to ask what was likely to make him faint as that could affect his answer, but seeing the amusement on the nurse's face, he rolled his eyes.

"In this job? Don't be daft."

The nurse confirmed she would escort Meredith to Professor Cole, and Meredith wondered what he had let himself in for. He followed the nurse back out into the corridor. She turned towards the operating theatres.

"She's not actually operating, is she?" His throat felt a little dry.

"No, of course not." The nurse giggled, and pushed open a door before they arrived at the nearest theatre. "This way." She led him up a small flight of stairs and into a small gallery. Professor Cole was there with a gaggle of medical students. Their noses almost touching the glass, they looked down at the operation taking place below them. Meredith began to look for Amanda, before remembering she was working in the accident and emergency department this week. Professor Cole was explaining what was being done, and why. Even the sound of it made Meredith's nose wrinkle.

"Now he's in, he will search for the hole using air. Much like an inner tube on a bicycle, then stitch or glue it depending on its size." She glanced at the clock. "Doing well for time at the moment, we don't like to keep a child of this age on bypass for too long. Now watch carefully, I will be quizzing you in a moment."

She stepped away from the group and turned to smile at Meredith. The fact he had remained in the doorway didn't escape her. She waved him forward. "Come here, Meredith. Come and see a genius at work."

There was a murmur of agreement.

"No, no. I can see you're busy. I only popped in for the details on the drug used on the girls. I'll call you later."

Professor Cole smiled and stepped towards him. "I can take a few moments. Outside though, this lot need to concentrate."

Meredith held the door open for her, and she pretended not to notice his relief. Once outside, they sat on the top stair, and she explained that the drug used had been a Benzodiazepine.

"They're quite commonly used for sedation purposes, particularly in hospitals and where individuals have suffered a severe trauma of some sort."

"Can you narrow it down to a particular type?"

"Not really, it would be guesswork. There were only minute traces apparently. They might have been missed if they had not been specifically looking for them. How are the girls?" She patted Meredith's knee. "They were a lively pair."

"Absolutely fine. You'd never know anything had happened." He smiled at her. "Am I looking for someone who works in a hospital, do you think?"

"Not necessarily. Although they are prescription drugs, they're used by paramedics, doctors, hospices, the list is quite lengthy. It could also be a member of the public, of course, if they had been involved in helping medicate a loved one." She wagged her finger at Meredith. "I think this hospital has had enough scandal, don't you?"

She was referring to a high-profile case Meredith had previously worked on, and had revealed that two respected and senior practitioners had carried out assisted, or sometimes forced, suicides.

Meredith leaned towards her and nudged her with his shoulder. "I don't plan these things you know, and there was a copper involved too." Meredith sighed at the thought.

"And on that happy note, I must get back to that lot. Graham is a fabulous surgeon, you know. Are you sure you don't want to watch? He's saving a life in there." She held out her hand. "Help me up then."

Meredith laughed and stood to help her to her feet. "No, I'd best get back. Thanks for the offer, and tell Graham I'm sorry I couldn't stick around."

He opened the door for her, and was away before it had closed behind her, silently cursing that another possible clue had evaporated.

Sharon and Chris Grainger had made themselves scarce for Nicola's visit to the office. Linda manned the office whilst Patsy made the call to Seville. Linda nodded a polite acknowledgment to Nicola as she followed Patsy through to her office. Nicola smiled broadly at her and raised her hand in greeting. She was clearly very excited about the call.

Patsy sat Nicola in the chair on the opposite side of her desk. Having established that a glass of water would be sufficient and she was happy to get on with the matter in hand, Patsy hit the speaker button, and dialled Antonio's number.

The long flat notes filled the air for what seemed far too long before, much to both women's relief, Antonio answered the phone.

"I'm here. I'm sorry I was delayed." He sounded tense.

Patsy nodded at Nicola, who had leaned closer to the phone.

"Hello, Toni, thank you for taking this call. How are you? I was sorry to hear about your father." Nicola's voice was full of genuine compassion. "Please accept my sincere condolences." She blinked several times as she awaited his response. When it came, it was short and to the point.

"Thank you. What do you want of me?"

Nicola stammered over her response. "I want . . . that is, I would . . . I'm sorry Toni this is so difficult over the phone. You have a son, I would like you to meet him."

Antonio's short laugh sounded cruel. Patsy swallowed and watched Nicola closely.

"When I saw your photograph, I thought that might be what you were suggesting." Antonio drew in a deep breath. "Señora, I don't think so. I remember you coming to the bar when you were pregnant. But your child is not mine. I don't know why you think he would be."

"Do you not remember the night we spent together? I assure you, that was all it took, Toni. You are an intelligent man, you know these things happen." Nicola frowned. "Or are you perhaps suggesting we didn't have a sexual encounter."

"Ha. I am not suggesting that, I remember our encounter, as you call it. I am saying quite simply I took precautions. I used protection, Nicola. The child is not mine."

Nicola closed her eyes and pressed her fingers to her forehead. It looked to Patsy as though she were trying to remember that particular detail. She caught the wobble of Nicola's chin and braced herself for an emotional outburst. Nicola opened her mouth to speak but Antonio beat her to it.

"What does your husband think? I remember you had a husband. Have you told him the child is mine, is that why he has abandoned you, and so now you feel the need to find a father? You have chosen the wrong man, Nicola." Antonio did not attempt to hide his distaste.

Nicola leaned forward once more. "I left my husband, Toni, I chose to. Falling pregnant with your child did give me the impetus I needed, but I never intended seeing you again." Nicola tapped the desk with her finger nail. "I am not desperate for you, Toni, I do not want a relationship with you, not in that way anyway. I simply want a father for my child."

"How did your husband feel about you leaving him, with what you say is my child in your belly?" Antonio demanded.

Colour dotted Nicola's cheeks, and she stared at the telephone, avoiding Patsy's eye.

"That is irrelevant, and he didn't know about Paul."

"Who is Paul?"

"Your son, I named him after my father." Nicola frowned as Antonio grunted before sighing and softening his tone.

"Nicola, I'm sorry, but the child is not mine. However, do you think your husband thought it was? Is your husband a jealous man? Is he capable of violence, of hurting others?"

Patsy pursed her lips and remained very still. The others had been right: she should never have taken the case. It was simply too weird, sitting as a witness to a very personal conversation, which now seemed to be centred on Meredith.

Nicola raised her eyebrows and shrugged an apology. "Ex, Antonio, he is my ex-husband. He has no interest in me, you, or in the baby. If you don't believe me, you may ask Patsy. She is living with him now. They are happy together."

Antonio fell silent for a while.

"I think you are . . . odd. All of you. But this conversation is over. I hope you find what you are looking for, Nicola, but it is not me. I am not the father of your child. As to your husband, men do strange things, things you may not have thought them capable of, especially if they feel they are threatened or have been disrespected. It may have been him that caused this problem for me." Antonio sighed. "All I know is that I am not, nor will I be, the father of your child."

"But, Antonio, I promise I want nothing from you. I will help you financially, I simply -"

"NO!" Antonio's voice echoed around Patsy's office. "I am not for sale, you mad woman."

Antonio hung up, and Patsy watched Nicola's shoulders sag, and she waited a few seconds before she reached forward and switched off the speaker. Her voice was soft.

"Nicola, even if Antonio is the father, it is clear that he has no intention of becoming involved." Patsy coughed, embarrassed at the question she was about to ask. "He says he used protection, but you clearly didn't remember that. Is it possible you may be mistaken?"

Patsy stiffened as Nicola's head snapped up.

"I am not a whore, Patsy. I did not sleep around. Protection does not always work, as thousands of unplanned babies will testify." Nicola stood abruptly, and lifted her jacket from the back of the chair. "He has to be made to realise that I'm not trying to trap him, Patsy. I want you to find him."

"But that -" Patsy's response was shot down.

"Yes or no, Patsy! I am offering you a job. Do you want it, or shall I find someone that does?"

"Nicola, calm down. Find him and what? Obtain DNA? What if we do that, and even if it's positive, if he still doesn't want to be involved . . . Go home and think this through. Call me tomorrow if you want me to pursue this."

Nicola had reached the door. She pulled it open and turned back to face Patsy. "I'm sorry. I shouldn't have raised my voice. But he has to do this, Patsy. Get on and do whatever happens next. I won't change my mind." She blinked rapidly to hold back the tears. "Just get on with it. I'll be in touch in a couple of days."

She ignored Linda as she strode quickly through the main office. Linda jumped up the minute the door closed behind Nicola. She hurried to Patsy's office and poked her head around the door.

"Well, she's not very happy. I heard him shout at one stage. I take it he's not interested. I'll put the kettle on, shall I?"

She grimaced as Patsy pretended to bang her head against the desk.

"Go on then, although something stronger would be welcome right now."

Thirty minutes later, having updated Linda on the call and eaten a rather large cake, Patsy relaxed back against her seat, as Linda filled her in on the progress she had made in tracing Lyndon Ward.

"In a nutshell, he's local." Patsy rolled her eyes at how many words Linda had used to get there. Linda appeared oblivious to the insult.

"Yes, and I reckon I can convince him to meet me." Linda looked smug. "He's soooo keen, and he's not even seen me. I have him eating out of my hand."

Patsy's eyes narrowed and she shook her head. "No, he's not, Linda. He's agreeing with you, and was pampering your ego. Did you not read the exchanges he had with Freda? That was cyber-sex and he'd never seen her either. Don't get carried away, and don't do anything without running it past me or Sharon."

Linda looked incredulous that Patsy doubted her, but Patsy was worried that the impulsive Linda would put herself in danger if she pushed the man too far. After all, there would be a good reason he didn't want to be found.

"Don't look at me like that, you know exactly . . ." Patsy stopped speaking as her phone rang. She raised her eyebrows. "That's interesting, it's Antonio." She answered the call as Linda pulled her chair closer.

"Patsy, can I assume Nicola is no longer with you."

"Yes, I'm on my own, what can I do for you?"

"I want you to find out who was threatening me. That hasn't changed, has it?" Antonio grunted. "Look, I am so sure I'm not the father I will let you check my DNA, but first I need to know if my mother will be safe if I return to Bristol."

That made life easier. "No, of course nothing has changed. Did you look at our fee structure? I will require a payment up front. Shall we say five hundred pounds?" Patsy could understand why Antonio had responded as he did to Nicola, but even so, he could have softened the blow. If she was going to work for him, he'd pay in advance. There was silence for a moment, before Antonio agreed.

"Okay, but I will expect an itemised bill on a daily basis. I will email you the information I have. Send me your bank details and I will get the money transferred."

Half an hour later, Linda was working on the telephone numbers. She had a result on the landline in less than ten minutes. Frowning, she jotted down the address and took it through to Patsy.

"That was ridiculously easy. I have no idea why Antonio didn't try himself. That number has been in existence for years, it wasn't unlisted. The line is in the name of W Maggs. Whoever was doing this was either really stupid, or very confident that Antonio wouldn't go to the police." She passed the address to Patsy.

Patsy read it and glanced at her watch. "No time like the present. I haven't anything better to do for the next couple of hours. I think I'll do some surveillance whilst I ponder what to do about Nicola. This isn't far from home, so I'll see you tomorrow." She waved her finger at Linda. "And behave yourself. I don't want to come in tomorrow and find that you've got a date with a mad axeman."

As Patsy started the engine of her car, she wondered if she had been firm enough with Linda, or if she had simply given her a bad idea.

CHAPTER ELEVEN

Amanda was exhausted, and she sipped coffee from a plastic cup as she leaned against the wall of the nurses' station. "How many have we had in today?" she asked the triage nurse.

"Only one hundred and ten, that's quiet for us." He smiled. "How long have you got to go?"

Amanda glanced at her watch. "All being well, only another couple of hours. How I ended up with a twelve-hour shift is beyond me. But the weekend is almost here, thank goodness."

"Well, there you go. I'm working all weekend so stop complaining, if you . . ." He stopped speaking and picked up the phone. "There's an ambulance on its way," he told Amanda.

He scribbled notes on the yellow docket in front of him, and tore it from the pad flamboyantly as he hung up. "We have a serious stabbing on the way in. Female victim, in and out of consciousness, has lost a lot of blood. Get yourself ready, grab any nurse who's free to get the trauma room ready, then meet me . . . they're here. Get a move on." He inclined his head as they heard the siren approaching the hospital.

Amanda held open the rubber door as the paramedics rushed forward with the trolley. One was holding a drip, which Amanda took from him as she directed them to the correct cubicle.

"She was out cold when we got there. She was found by a jogger; he scared the attacker off. There was a lot of blood. We found one wound lower left abdomen, but there's another somewhere. We got here before I located it. She keeps coming in and out of consciousness."

Dr Lodge was waiting for them at the entrance to the cubicle. He caught the end of the conversation.

"Get her in here. You two cut the clothes off – all of them. Let's find out what we're dealing with."

The paramedics helped move the woman on to the table, and wheeled the trolley away.

Amanda started on the left trouser leg and the nurse on the right, and within seconds they had removed all but a once pink vest top, and the shoes and socks of the victim. They screwed up their noses at the smell as the layers of clothes were lifted away. A large wad of gauze was taped to the woman's abdomen, and the growing patch of blood on the bed revealed a further wound to the back.

"Roll her over."

Amanda and the nurse did as instructed. The patient groaned. Lodge manipulated the wound with his fingertips.

"That's a deep wound. We'll need a scan to make sure it's not caught a kidney." He stared at the woman and shook his head. "I hear she was mugged. What could they have been after? Get the rest off her, and get it in the incinerator."

As the nurse started to remove the shoes, Amanda cut the restraints on the bra. It didn't move and she had to peel it away from the skin. She found two twenty pound notes sticking to the woman's breast. Amanda glanced at the nurse who had groaned as she removed the first shoe.

"She stinks." The nurse slid the scissors into the top of the sock and began to cut it away. "These haven't been changed for a while." The nurse arched her back and held her head as far from the shoes as possible.

Dr Lodge secured the binding to the second wound. "Come on, come on. Cover her up, let's go."

As they wheeled the bed towards the door, one of the paramedics returned. He held up a large bag.

"Her belongings." He slid it into the room, and held the door open for them to pass.

Lodge nodded at Amanda. "Go through her things. Let's see if we can find out who she is, and get this matched," he handed her a tube which contained a blood sample, "and have blood waiting for us."

Amanda nodded and delivered the blood with the doctor's instructions. She went back to the bag. Before she touched it, she collected the discarded clothes, and dropped them into a waste sack, gingerly checking the few pockets as she went, and grateful that she was wearing gloves. She didn't find anything, and with some difficulty she heaved the bag on to a small trolley at the side of the room. The first thing she found was a paper bag containing two doughnuts. She gave them a squeeze. They were hard, and she added them to the sack.

The next item Amanda found was a heavy, coarse blanket. It was the reason the bag was so heavy. She pulled on it, and allowed it to drop onto the floor. Once a brown and blue plaid, it seemed to have developed a tacky coating, which glimmered in the bright lights of the trauma room. It now had a myriad of stains, the latest apparently a patch of jam. Rolling it up Amanda fetched a fresh sack and squashed it in. Returning to the bag, she found a small cashbox secured with a combination padlock, a pair of fur gloves, two pairs of football socks, and a fleece tracksuit that appeared to be in a worse condition than the one they had cut off. Other than two paperbacks, and some old newspapers, the main body of the bag was now empty.

She unzipped the side pocket and retrieved a pair of glasses. Amanda held them up to the light, and wondered how anyone managed to see through the smeared glass. In addition to the glasses, she found a bottle opener, a couple of stubby pencils, and some loose change.

Amanda sighed as she surveyed the items. It appeared a pitiful collection, no indication as to who their patient was, and absolutely no indication as to her personality.

Amanda gave the cash box a little shake and hoped that the contents held something more personal to the woman. She added the fleece track suit to the sack and knotted the two bags. She placed the remaining items in a clear plastic bag and left it on the table. Social services would need to find the woman some new clothes. She made a note on the blank patient form, and went to join her.

On arrival, she found the patient was being scanned. Dr Lodge beckoned her to view the images appearing on the screens in the adjoining room.

"What do you see, apart from a missing appendix?"

Amanda peered at the screen. "Kidney is intact, but what's that, a tumour?" She circled the dark smudge on the image with her finger.

"My guess is a cyst. At that size, it will be pressing against the kidney; she must have been in agony." Dr Lodge shook his head. "Right, let's get the bleeding sorted, stich her up, and find her a bed. That cyst needs to be removed."

An hour later, alerted by the alarm, Amanda rushed to the cubicle in which her patient waited for a bed. As the nurse drew the curtains back, Peggy waved the alarm pad at them.

"What's all this?" She tapped the drip, which fed blood into her arm, with the alarm. "And why do I feel like I've been hit by a bus?"

"Hello, love, you've woken up again, then?" The nurse tried to grab a wrist to take her pulse.

"Get off me, and don't ask bloody stupid questions." Peggy looked at Amanda. "Are you in charge?" The nurse snorted, and both Amanda and Peggy chose to ignore her.

"No, but I should be able to answer any questions you have until Dr Lodge is free." Amanda smiled at her.

"I was told I was having an x-ray by Dr Lodge. Why am I still here? Is anything broken? When can I leave?"

"You've been stabbed. Two wounds, and one is quite deep. We did scan you to see if any internal damage had been done. But you were lucky on that score. How -"

"Good, I know I was stabbed, I'm not stupid. When can I go?"

Amanda picked the chart up from the side of the bed and smiled at Peggy. "When the doctor discharges you."

"I don't think so. Get this contraption off me, and I'll discharge myself."

"That wouldn't be wise. We couldn't find any ID. What's your name?"

"Peggy, and you'd better have been careful with my stuff. Where is it?" Peggy realised that all she was wearing was a lightweight cotton hospital gown. Her hand flew to her chest.

"Here," Amanda lifted the clear plastic bag from the bedside table, "and your surname please?"

"Peggy. Where's the rest of my stuff?" Peggy saw the two twenty pound notes and relaxed a little.

"Peggy Peggy? I don't think so. Come on, Peggy, help me here, we need to pull your records."

"You'll be lucky. Don't ignore me," Peggy leaned forward and squinted at the ID hanging from Amanda's neck. "I'm not simple. I asked you where the rest of my things were, Amanda Meredith. You're only a bloody student, and think you can call the shots."

"I'm sorry, Peggy, but we had to cut off your clothes to deal with your injuries I'm afraid. Social services will get you some new things for when you leave. Don't worry. Now if you won't give me your surname, what about your date of birth?"

"Thirtieth of June 1952. When will they get here, because I'm going as soon as you get rid of this." Peggy waved the arm with the drip back and forth. Amanda went and took her hand.

"You'll damage yourself. There's something else you need to know, but we should wait for Dr Lodge."

"Go and get him then, I've things I need to do. I can't lie around here waiting on him. Chase whoever is going to get me some clothes too, or I'll be borrowing those trousers." She grinned as Amanda burst out laughing.

"You'll have to fight me for them. There the most comfortable ones I have. I'll go and find Dr Lodge for you."

Amanda returned a few minutes later. "He'll be in as soon as he's finished with the current patient. Now, can I ask the surname question again?"

"You can, but it won't do you any good." Peggy beckoned her forward. "I know your father, and I'd like to speak to him."

"Really?" Amanda looked sceptical. "How do you know him?"

"Given his job, that's a very personal question. I had breakfast with him just this morning, for your information."

Amanda frowned. Peggy clearly knew her father was a policeman, she sighed, realising she really did look a lot like him if a total stranger recognised her as his daughter. Shrugging she fixed a smile; it wasn't Peggy's fault after all.

"Breakfast? Where was that, somewhere nice?"

"Amanda, or are you a Mandy? I'm not dim, and I'm not senile. I have information your father needs, so I need to get out of here to give it to him. Now, are you going to help me or not?"

"Amanda, and of course I'll help." Amanda pulled her phone from her pocket, and Peggy rolled her eyes as Amanda called her father. There was no way Peggy would be leaving the hospital, and she was pretty sure Meredith would deny all knowledge. After the fourth ring Meredith answered the call.

"Amanda what's wrong?"

"Nothing's wrong, but I'm with someone who wants to speak to you."

"To me? Who?"

"A lady called Peggy. She tells me you had breakfast with her this morning."

"Are you working in A and E? Why's Peggy there? Can she speak?"

Amanda frowned at the concern in her father's voice. He clearly knew Peggy, and Amanda fleetingly wondered if perhaps she was related.

"Peggy was mugged. Stabbed, twice, but we've dealt with that. We do need to sort some other things though." Amanda walked to Peggy's side. "Here she is, you speak to her."

Handing Peggy the phone, she stepped back intrigued and looking forward to listening to the conversation.

"Merriwinkle. Peggy here. Come and get me out of this damn place, and I'll tell you where your man is." Peggy nodded at Amanda, in an 'I told you so' manner, and Amanda raised her eyebrows and put her hand over her mouth to stop her laughing out loud at the manner in which the woman was speaking to her father.

"I can't do that, Peggy, not until they say you're safe to go. Where is he?"

"Merriwinkle, don't play games with me. I've been robbed, stabbed and now kidnapped against my will. I'm not playing games. I know where Captain Kirk is, and if you get me out of here, so will you."

"Peggy, I'm in the middle of a child abduction case. Please tell me this isn't a ploy just to get you out of hospital."

"What do you take me for? I'm offended, Merriwinkle. Very offended. Now get your arse down here, and the sooner the better, for all concerned."

"Pass me back to Amanda please." Meredith was resigned to going back to the hospital, but he smiled at Peggy's assertive stance. She couldn't be that bad. Peggy's hand shot out towards Amanda.

"He wants you back."

Amanda's eyes widened. Her father hadn't even argued with the woman, and who the hell was Captain Kirk? She took back the phone, and when her father asked for more details about Peggy's injuries, she pretended they were having a totally different conversation.

"I don't know, I'll go and check." She shrugged at Peggy as though her father were asking something awkward. She stepped out of the cubicle and moved quickly to the end of the hall. "Her wounds will heal, although one was pretty bad, she needs to rest or she will open it up. But she has a growth very near her kidney. Whatever it is needs to be removed. It's huge. It could be cancerous but the doctor on duty believes it's probably a cyst. Our problem is that she won't co-operate with us. She's insisting she's leaving tonight. Naked if necessary, and now she seems to think that she can blackmail you into getting her out. How on earth do you know her, and who's -"

"Okay. I get that. I'm on my way. I'll be there in ten minutes. Seaton, I need a lift." Meredith bellowed as he hung up on his daughter.

Amanda didn't know why she felt surprised as she hung up, but she did. Walking past Peggy's cubicle, she went to ensure Dr Lodge didn't forget to come into see Peggy. He was on the phone at the reception desk.

"Splendid. Thanks for that. Start it running, she's on her way – nearly. I need the space down here." He hung up and punched the air. "Bed number four secured!" He smiled at Amanda. "I'm on a roll, I've just secured your bag lady a bed. Let's go and give her the good news."

"Great news, but you need to give her the bad news first."

"I do indeed. Come on then."

With a spring in his step, and a smile on his face, Dr Lodge made his way back to Peggy. Amanda hurried along behind him wondering how long the smile would last.

"Peggy nice to meet you. I'm Henry Lodge, duty doctor. We need to have a little chat."

He made to sit on the end of the bed.

"That's lovely, you chat away. But get me a bed pan or I'm going to wet the bed."

"Oh right," Lodge opened the cabinet next to the bed, but it was empty. He turned to Amanda. "Would you please?" Amanda disappeared to hunt down a bed pan. He turned back to Peggy whose face was screwed up as though in pain. "Are you hurting? Does it hurt when you pass water? Because -"

"Yes and no. Now stop talking, I have to concentrate. I think it's more than a pee I need." Peggy gasped the words.

"Oh dear, let's see where . . . ahh, here you go, now I'll help you up, and Amanda can get it in position. Arms around my neck, and on three. One, two . . ."

As he lifted her, Peggy farted. It was long and it was noisy. Amanda grinned at Peggy, and the look of relief on her face.

"Sorry, Doctor, false alarm, just a bit of wind." Peggy winked at him. "I still need to pee though, are you going to watch?"

Dr Lodge shook his head and laughed. "Not if the lady would like some privacy, no."

As he opened the curtain to step outside, Peggy spotted Meredith walking past.

"In here, Merriwinkle. Actually, dealing with a call of nature, give me a moment to sort myself out."

Meredith ground to a halt, and he stepped back to join his daughter and the doctor outside the cubicle. He grinned when Peggy called them in.

"All done. Come and take it away. Merriwinkle, you might need to avert your eyes, they've pinched my knickers."

Amanda put her arm on her father's. "Give me two seconds." She appeared moments later with a paper towel draped over the bed pan. Meredith grimaced as she said gaily, "She's all yours, good luck."

Meredith entered the cubicle. He was taken aback by how small Peggy looked without the many layers of clothes.

"Who did this to you then, Peggy? And what for?" He stopped at the end of the bed.

"Don't worry about that until you get me out of here. We've got more important things to sort out. Don't forget Captain Kirk." She looked at the doctor, who had stepped forward, shaking his head. "What? Don't you shake your head at me, Merriwinkle's a policeman, therefore his trumps yours."

Meredith bit his bottom lip, and his eyes twinkled at her. "Listen to the doctor, Peggy. I'm not going anywhere."

"Mrs . . . Peggy. You have a growth very near your kidney, and I know it will have been causing you pain for some considerable time. It's huge." Dr Lodge stopped speaking as Peggy crossed her hands across her chest, and looked unimpressed. "Okay, I can see you need it put very bluntly. Whilst I think there's every likelihood this growth is not cancerous, I believe it to be a cyst, and it will continue to grow if not treated. If it does that you will be in constant pain, your kidney function will become compromised, if it isn't already, and you will become very ill. It will be a slow and painful death, particularly if you continue to live the life you have been living. Is that blunt enough?"

"What if it's cancer?" Peggy's face showed no emotion.

"Then we will need to see what type of cancer it is before we decide on a treatment. But untreated it will, of course, kill you. Again, a painful death if untreated." He patted her leg. "We could do a biopsy and find out before we operate. But as you want to be on your way as soon as possible, I think we should operate," he held her eye, "immediately. I've got you a bed and, subject to a few more tests, we can get you in tomorrow afternoon."

"What happened to the queues?" Peggy enquired.

"What queues?" Doctor Lodge inclined his head as he looked at her. Amanda slipped back into the cubicle, and stood at her father's side.

"The queues to have operations on the National Health." Peggy tutted at his stupidity. "I read the papers. I hear people moaning about it. How come I can roll in here, unannounced, and get an operation at the click of your fingers?"

"Ah, I see. Well, I don't think we have a queue for growths as large as that. You took the lead on arrival."

"Don't try and be -"

"Peggy, love, listen to the man. He works long hours for crap money, much like myself. He wouldn't be standing here arguing with you if he didn't think it was necessary," urged Meredith.

"Ganging up on me won't help. I know they need my consent." Peggy pursed her lips and looked up to the ceiling as though considering the matter. "I'll tell you what, you operate tomorrow and whip out whatever shouldn't be there. If you manage not to kill me, I get discharged the next day." She pointed at Meredith. "I'll take his word for it. Even if it is cancer, I'm off. If I've got to go, I'll go my way, and not lying in a bed with you lot poking things in me." She looked at Meredith. "Is that a deal, Merriwinkle?"

From the corner of his eye, Meredith could see Lodge nodding his head at him encouraging a positive response. He drew in a breath.

"Okay, but you've got to be fit enough to be discharged. I hear what you say about further treatment, but I'm not letting you limp out of here without her say so." He nodded definitively.

"You mean his, not hers. She's only a student. You're losing it, Merriwinkle."

"No, I meant hers. Amanda won't lie to me, or try to blind me with science. Do we have a deal?"

Stillness descended on the little cubicle, as Peggy considered her options.

"Go on then." Peggy nodded. "Now you two get out of here, I need to speak to him alone."

Peggy tried to dismiss the two medical staff.

"I don't think so, Peggy. You've called the shots long enough. I need this bed; there are sick people sitting on chairs out there waiting for the luxury of this. We'll get you up to a ward and then you carry on this conversation." Lodge turned to Meredith. "Sorry, but you'll have to wait."

Meredith shrugged acceptance, and following Amanda's directions went in search of a coffee. He took the opportunity to call Patsy. She seemed distracted and snapped at him when he teased her. Seeing the main entrance, he stepped outside for fresh air, but the smell wafting over from two men smoking caused him to turn back. His need for a cigarette was growing; it wouldn't take much for him to buy a packet. Deciding today was not the day he would give in, he turned on his heel, and following the signs suspended from the ceilings made his way to the ward where Peggy would be treated. He popped into the small shop run by volunteers, and purchased a few items for Peggy, which included a tube of toothpaste and a toothbrush.

As he walked along the final corridor approaching the ward, he could hear Peggy's voice. It was raised, but was disembodied somehow. His pace quickened. He had no idea why, but this woman brought out his protective instincts, despite the fact it was quite clear she could hold her own in most situations. He stopped as everything fell silent. As he pushed the bell for access to the ward Amanda appeared through a side door. Waving to the nurse she pressed the button to allow him access.

"Everything all right?" he queried, as he followed Amanda to a bed at the end of the small ward.

"It is now. Peggy's taking a bath. It was touch and go for a minute, but now she's in, she's gone quiet." Amanda placed the bag she was carrying on the cabinet. "I must get back downstairs, Dad, it's almost time to clock off." She leaned forward and kissed his cheek. "I'll see you later."

Meredith took the bag containing his purchases, and walked around the bed to the cabinet. His eyes took in the items that formed Peggy's worldly goods. Wondering what was in the cashbox, he pulled the newspaper from the bag, and settled into the chair next to the bed. He sat there for the best part of thirty minutes waiting for Peggy's reappearance.

He smiled as she exited the bathroom, shaking the nurse's arm off as she turned to face him. The nurse looked irritated as she followed, wheeling the drip stand behind Peggy. Barefoot, and wrapped in a threadbare off-white dressing gown, complete with several green stamps declaring it to be the property of the hospital, Peggy shuffled towards him. If Meredith had been asked to describe her at that time, the one word that would have sprung to mind was pink, but once again he was struck by her slight build.

Pushing the nurse away, she climbed into bed unaided, complained that Meredith had brought her fruit and not chocolate, and pointing at one of the green stamps announced loudly that even she wasn't desperate enough to want to steal the tatty robe. Once settled, she sat propped up against the pillows, and began eating the grapes one after the other.

"What do you know then, Peggy?" Meredith had convinced himself this was a wild goose chase, but he enjoyed the old girl's company, and went through the motions anyway.

"Captain Kirk was here. I saw him." Peggy popped another grape in her mouth.

"When?" Now interested, he leaned forward, frowning.

"When they took me for a scan."

"But today, you saw him today?"

"No yesterday, I have a scan every day to be sure. Of course today. What's wrong with you Merriwinkle?"

"You didn't think you might mention this when I arrived?" Peggy caught the irritation. "He could be anywhere now. I thought you were going to tell me you saw him in the park, or at the shopping centre." He shook his head. "Where did you see him? Had you told me when I got here, we might have been able to do something."

"Well pardon me for being stabbed and almost dying." Peggy selected another grape and pouted. "You know, Merriwinkle, you've disappointed me. I have already said, when they took me for a scan." Peggy popped the grape into her mouth.

"And what was he doing?"

"Pushing a child in a wheelchair." Peggy circled her hands around her head. "He had one of those cage things on," she raised one eyebrow, "for clarification, Captain Kirk, not the child."

"He's a porter?" Meredith leaned closer.

Peggy was tired, and irritability was not unique to Meredith.

"From my spot on the trolley, I didn't have time to check his attire." Peggy pushed the grapes away, and sunk a little deeper into the pillows. "I was in and out of consciousness, I was ill. Very ill. Yet still I managed to do your job for you." She sighed. "A little bit more appreciation wouldn't go amiss." She turned her head, and looked away from Meredith. A smile came to her lips as she watched a woman in a green overall push a trolley onto the ward. "Oh look, I think I arrived in time for tea."

Meredith stood. "Thank you, Peggy. I'm going to check this out. You stay here, and behave yourself!" He was already ringing Amanda as he strode away.

He watched the motorcycle pull away, and shoving his hands into his pockets, he walked back into the hospital silently cursing himself. He should have found time to have done that before now. It was also a ridiculous risk to take, allowing them to come to the hospital. Still, it had to be Harriet, it had to be. They'd be on a plane and away before too long. He glanced at his watch. There was still time to finish off a few more things before he called it a day. Ever the optimist, he pulled his shoulders back and smiled. Not long now.

Amanda looked again at the e-fit her father had given her.

"Yes, he does look familiar, but no, I don't recognise him exactly. Asking me the same question repeatedly won't change the answer, Dad." She passed it back to Meredith.

"Who took Peggy down for the scan?" Meredith was irritated it had taken him so long to ask Peggy such an important question, and he struggled to maintain his sarcasm.

"Doctor Lodge, and a nurse. The nurse has just gone," Amanda held her hand up. "Yes, I'll find a number. Doctor Lodge is with a patient. If you stay there you'll see him come out of one of those cubicles when he's finished."

"Take these. Someone might recognise him." Meredith shoved the likenesses in her hands. He stood tapping his foot as he eyed the cubicles.

Amanda walked back to the main admin office clutching the e-fits, and although none of the staff there recognised him, she was fortunate in obtaining the nurse's telephone number. Her father rolled his eyes as she shook her head indicating she'd had no luck.

"How could a bag lady be more observant than hospital staff," he murmured, stepping towards the cubicles and calling for Dr Lodge. Lodge appeared a few moments later.

Amanda was apologising before her father had the chance to speak.

"Sorry about that, Doc, I need a few seconds of your time." Passing him the e-fits Meredith explained why he had called him out.

Lodge shook his head. "Vaguely remember the child but not the escort." Lodge turned to Amanda, "Take your father down there and check today's patients. You can find what ward the child was on, and they should know who took him down."

Meredith thanked Lodge as Amanda repeated her apology. Grabbing Meredith by the elbow, she dragged him out into the corridor, complaining about how embarrassing and rude he was as she led him towards the various x-ray locations. It took twenty minutes to find out that the patient they were looking for was Mark Tully, and that he was on Ward G.

"I was there this morning," Meredith told Amanda with a frown.

"Well, it's a children's ward, so I don't know why you would find that surprising. Do you know the way or do you need me to show you?"

"What? You don't want to come with me?"

"Dad, I've been in this building doing my job for almost thirteen hours. I will stay and help with yours if you want me to, but I don't think I can be much further use."

"I thought you wanted to be a copper? Ah well, if you don't, at least it's clear you're not using Patrick. I'll be fine. See you later." Stepping away briskly, he smiled as Amanda opened and shut her mouth, before he waved, turned and hurried away down the corridor.

Patsy sat in her car, and sucked on a mint as she watched the house. She'd been there over an hour and so far, there was no sign of life. She decided to give it another twenty minutes and then head home. Tomorrow she would concoct a story and go and knock on the door. She wondered if the house had been converted into two apartments like many of the others in the street, and how life was full of coincidences. She'd only been on this street the day before. Patsy sat upright. There was movement. The door to the house began to open, and Patsy lifted the small camera from the seat next to her, and switched it on. Resting it on the top of the steering wheel she zoomed in on the front door, and blew out a breath.

"Not such a coincidence then," Patsy muttered as she switched off the camera. Beth Durham slammed the door of the waiting taxi and it pulled away. Patsy started the engine. "I think we need to talk, Ms Durham. I'll be back tomorrow."

Meredith smiled at the pretty nurse who allowed him onto the ward.

"Dr Rose will be here in . . . Oh, here she is now." The nurse quickly opened the door, saving Professor Cole the need to punch in her access code.

"Meredith. Twice in one day, to what do I owe the honour?" She bustled down to a side office and opened the door. "Come on in here. I'll give you ten minutes before I must get on."

Meredith dropped into the chair on one side of the table that took up most of the space in the room. He withdrew the two e-fits and flattened them out on to the table. He didn't mince his words.

"Do you know who this is? A bag lady who was a witness to a crime saw this man here at the hospital. She's being treated here." Meredith tapped the nearest likeness.

Professor Cole pushed her glasses up her nose and leaned forward for a better look.

"Why, what's he done?"

"Is that a yes or a no?" Meredith didn't hide his irritation.

Professor Cole's head snapped up to look at him. "It's a maybe, a possible likeness. Is this something personal, Meredith?"

"No, I just need to find this man. I understand he escorted a young lad, Mark Tully, to the X-ray department earlier." He watched as her eyebrows rose, and she shrugged acceptance.

"In which case that looks like someone I may know. What's your interest in him?" A smile danced around her lips, and Meredith's frown deepened.

"I find it quite disconcerting that you find this amusing in any way." He pinched the bridge of his nose. "Who do you think it . . ." Meredith hit the flat of his palm against his forehead. "Oh course. I bloody knew it. I knew I'd met him." He tapped the e-fit urgently. "What's his name? It escapes me."

"Graham, Graham Charlesworth. He's a senior surgeon here, you saw him in action, or should I say you could have? Very talented, quite brilliant in fact. What is it you think he's done?"

"Where is he? Is he still at work?" Meredith ignored her question, and got to his feet as though he were leaving.

"Probably, he's very dedicated. I'll ask you again, Meredith, and I hope you'll give me the courtesy of a reply this time, what is it you think that he's done?"

"Abducted the young girls you examined, attempted to abduct others, and -" Meredith was silenced as Professor Cole hooted out a laugh.

"Please tell me you are joking. Graham? Don't be silly, Meredith. This likeness is similar but that's it. He's a dedicated professional." She looked at Meredith as though he were a little slow. "I think you need to speak to him. I could give you a quick run through of his work to date, and a glowing reference, but I think a quick word should do it." She picked up the phone and paged Graham Charlesworth. "There, he'll ring in a minute and we can put this madness to bed." She shook her head. "And all on the word of a bag lady?"

Meredith nodded. He could point out that some of the most atrocious criminals in history had been nice people. Dedicated in other fields, but it wasn't worth upsetting the applecart for the moment. Instead, he smiled.

"I'm sure you're right. But this likeness is too close for me to ignore, you must see that." He nodded along with her as she relaxed into her chair. "Let's hope he's still here. That way I'll be out of your hair quicker. What do you lot call him?"

"What do you mean *you lot*? I call him Graham, the nurses call him Dr Charlesworth or Dr Graham. A few of his peers call him Charlie, apparently, it's an old nickname. What an odd question, is there a reason for it?"

Meredith shook his head. "No, I'm trying to get a feel for the man, that's all. Hopefully that will be him."

Professor Cole lifted the ringing handset, and nodded at Meredith as Charlesworth spoke to her.

"Graham, thanks for getting back to me, don't worry, no emergency. I don't suppose you're still at the hospital, are you?" She shook her head at Meredith. "Oh dear, well the police need a word with you. Don't worry, it's just . . . I'll tell you what, I'll pass you over to DCI Meredith, so you can arrange to meet." She handed the phone to Meredith.

"Dr Charlesworth. I'd like to come and see you, where are you?" Meredith got straight to the point. "Shopping? Okay, what time will you be home? I'm assuming I can get your address from the hospital?" Meredith listened to the reply. "Okay, I'll meet you here at eight."

Meredith pursed his lips, and wondered why the man would rather come back to the hospital. Why was he keeping Meredith away from his house? But most importantly, why hadn't he asked why Meredith wanted to see him? Meredith checked the time: he had an hour to kill before the meeting, and that gave him time to check a few details with Professor Cole before the meeting.

Patsy poured a generous helping of bubble bath under the running tap. Amanda was going out and Meredith wouldn't be home for a couple of hours, she would take advantage of that and pamper herself. She had already waxed her legs and applied a face pack. All that was needed now was a glass of wine and some soothing music. Collecting a glass and a bottle from the kitchen she returned to the bathroom. The water was hot, and she skipped from one foot to the other, before finally sitting, and lying out carefully to keep one hand dry. She put in her earphones and switched on the iPod. Closing her eyes, she smiled contentedly as the warm suds lapped around her neck.

Her peace lasted less than fifteen minutes. She opened one eye and confirmed that her phone was indeed ringing. She pulled out her earphones and hit the answer button.

"Linda, this had better be good." She listened for a few minutes. "What? When?" Listening to Linda's explanation she relaxed a little. "So when I told you not to go arranging a meeting, that meant 'do it anyway' I assume?"

"But that's what I'm trying to tell you. He suggested it, not me. I have the evidence, PHPI. Anyway, I'll meet him tomorrow and you can be there, to make sure I'm safe." Linda tutted. "I'll let you get on with your evening. I'd better go now, Louie is waiting."

With that she was gone. Patsy dropped the phone onto the floor, and picked up the glass of wine. Her peace disturbed, she planned the next day. A meeting with Beth Durham was top of the agenda, and then probably a further conversation with Antonio. Patsy had decided not to tell Nicola of his offer to provide DNA for the moment. She'd leave her alone for a couple of days and see how things worked out. Giving a yell, she slopped her drink into the bath water as Meredith came into the bathroom.

"I thought you were going to be a couple more hours? You nearly gave me heart failure! Is everything all right?"

"I had a change of plan. I don't want to see him at work. He's obviously going to deny it. I want to get a feel for his home, see if anything checks out with what the girls described. You see, Ms Hodge, I am more than just a pretty face." He paused and inclined his head. "Unlike you. Green doesn't suit you, it makes your teeth look yellow." He tapped the now cracking face pack. "Get it off, and I'll get in." He began to unbutton his shirt.

Needing no further encouragement, Patsy splashed water on to her face. Leaving his clothes in a pile on the floor he stepped into the bath.

"Ooh that's hot." The water splashed over the rim of the bath as he sat down behind her.

He watched the garage door close before he pulled away. He was so close now he needed to be careful, very careful. With the police apparently stepping up their investigation, it might only be a matter of time. Things may go awry if he didn't tread carefully. He wondered if it was the couple in the field who had put the e-fit together, and as he accelerated he was grateful there was light at the end of the tunnel.

CHAPTER TWELVE

Louie described Meredith as bright-eyed and bushy-tailed as he took the morning briefing. Meredith ignored him, and completed his update of the events at the hospital the day before.

"Now we have to wait until four o'clock today. We could see him at the hospital, and I know that if it's him, he's had a warning. By meeting him at his home we don't need a search warrant, but have enough of a description from the two girls hopefully to be able to check if the property matches the one where they were held." Meredith drained his remaining coffee. "I'll take Seaton with me." He rubbed his hands together. "What else is new?"

There was little progress on other matters. All known offenders with the name Charlie or Charles had been checked, and for one reason or another cleared of any involvement. Rawlings had booked a meeting with Harriet Boyles and her mother for later that morning, but other than that, there was little to report. Despite this, as Meredith walked back to his office he had a definite spring in his step. He was convinced they had their man. Almost.

Patsy sighed and gave in. "Okay today, but make it a late lunch. I want to go and see Beth Durham, if she's in. I have no idea how long I'll be, but not before one o'clock. You really shouldn't have described yourself; if you had described me, I could have gone alone. It's become complicated now."

Linda punched the air. "I would have if you'd said, PHPI, but this will be a good opportunity to show you that I can do this. You can observe me in action."

Linda looked away and began typing her response. Patsy shook her head remembering the hassle the last time she'd seen Linda in action.

"I'll get going now. Text me where and when and I'll make sure I'm there before you."

Having a feeling a fiasco awaited her, Patsy grabbed her jacket and left the office. She drove straight to the property from where the call had been made and where she had seen Beth Durham leaving the day before. She rang the doorbell, and fixed a smile as she heard someone approach the door. A short, grey-haired man wearing an old-fashioned smoking jacket answered the door.

"Good morning." He bobbed his head courteously. "What can I do for you, pray tell?" Despite his diminutive build, his voice was low, and the words floated from his lips.

"I'm looking for Beth, Beth Durham. Is she in?" Patsy gave her warmest smile.

The man eyed Patsy up and down, and without a hint of embarrassment, responded, "Did you not think to ring her to find out?" He purred the words, and his lips twitched, narrowly avoiding a grin.

"I don't have her number or of course I would have." Patsy stepped a little closer. "So, is she in?"

"I have absolutely no idea, I'm not her keeper." The man turned to face the stairs. Patsy was taken aback by the volume of his call, and stepped back. "BETHANY! IS ONE AT HOME?" He inclined his head and listened and turned back to Patsy with a smile. "It would appear she is. Now I would ask you in, but as you are not my guest I must ask you to remain there until Bethany arrives. It would be too embarrassing for the poor girl if she then had to ask you to leave."

He walked away and disappeared behind the first door off the hall.

A few moments later, Patsy saw bare feet appear on the top step, and watched as Beth pulled on a jumper as she made her way to the hall. Beth studied Patsy. She knew her from somewhere but she wasn't sure where. As she pondered whether to admit this, Patsy held out her hand.

"Patsy Hodge. We shared a taxi the other night." She smiled as Beth murmured recognition before asking, "Do I owe you some money? I did offer to pay at the time." She looked a little irritated.

"Not at all, I'm a private investigator, and it truly is a small world as it happens you may be able to help me with a case I'm working on."

Patsy watched as Beth's brow furrowed.

"Look, may I come in, or would you like to go for coffee? I saw a café on the corner."

Beth dithered for a moment before inviting Patsy in.

"Come in." She directed Patsy to a door at the end of the hall. "Let's chat in the kitchen. If we go out I'll have to get dressed properly and, to be honest, I can't be bothered."

Ten minutes later the women were sitting opposite each other at the kitchen table sipping coffee, and Patsy was explaining that she had been attempting to find Antonio Garcia, but ended up working for him.

"Toni is not in trouble in any way, is he? He's a good man."

Patsy pretended she was ignorant of their relationship. "Ah, you knew him well then?" she prompted.

Beth smiled broadly and her eyes twinkled. "I did. For a while. It was never going to be wedding bells, but we had fun at a time I needed it. He looked after me, protected me really." Beth shrugged and shook her head. "If I'd listened to him, even taken half the advice he gave me, I'd be a happier person." She blew out a frustrated breath. "Still, as they say, we are where we are. We just have to get on with it. So how can I help?"

"Did you know Antonio, sorry Toni, left for Spain due to the death of his father?"

"No, I'm sorry to hear that. I've been away. Poor Toni, he idolised his parents. They had worked hard and sacrificed a great deal for him to come here. He truly appreciated that. Is he coming back? He only has one more year and he's done. He'll be able to reap the reward of all their hard work."

"He thinks there is a possibility his father was murdered, and is concerned that if he comes back to Bristol his mother will be the next victim."

"Victim? Why? This sounds very sinister. I'm not quite sure how I can help." Beth looked to Patsy expectantly, awaiting clarification.

"Toni was being threatened. Mainly by two men, but he did have one call from a female." Patsy held her hand up to stop the protest on the tip of Beth's tongue. "No, I don't think it was you. But whoever was making these threats used a series of phones, one of which was a landline. Installed at this address, the account is in the name of -"

"Walter Maggs."

Patsy jumped as the man spoke.

"That is I. I own this house and the phone is therefore registered in my name. But I assure you, Miss, I have never threatened anyone." He glanced heavenward. "Not unless I was on the stage and it was required of me."

Beth rapped the table with her knuckles. "Walter! You've been eavesdropping again!" Beth shook her head at Patsy. "I'm so sorry, Patsy." She held her hand out. "Meet Walter, my landlord. He is nosey, inappropriate, and sometimes damned rude, as you have seen." Her face softened. "But he's a good chap. Like Toni, he tries to steer me in the right direction."

Without an invitation, Walter pulled out a chair and joined the women at the table. "Are you going to tell her who it is, or shall I?"

Patsy looked quickly from one to the other. "You knew about this?"

She watched as they shook their heads in unison.

"No, no, my dear," Walter rolled his eyes, "but it doesn't require Einstein to work it out. As Mr Holmes would say, 'elementary my dear, elementary'." He looked pointedly at Beth. "She knows, and is, as we speak, realising, as I have repeatedly pointed out, the error of her ways."

Placing her elbows on the table, Beth buried her face in her hands and groaned. Patsy leaned back against the chair, and folded her arms.

"Well, I'd like someone to tell me please. You could be protecting a murderer."

Beth snorted, and dropped her hands. "I think not." She stood quickly, her chair scraping the floor. "It's a very long story, and I think we will go out after all. Give me twenty minutes, is that okay?"

"Of course." Patsy waited until she heard Beth's steps on the stairs before she turned to Walter, who was looking very disappointed. "How can you both be so sure who it is?"

Walter leaned in and said quietly, "Because he's a bloody madman. Quite literally, I believe. You'd think it would make him a better actor, but it doesn't. Oops." His hand flew to his mouth. "There, I've already said too much. This is Beth's story, not mine . . . although if you do require a good gossip about him, feel free to call."

He slipped his hand into his jacket pocket and produced a business card. A flamboyant font declared him to be *Walter Maggs – Theatrical Agent*. Patsy put the card into her own pocket.

"Thank you, Walter, I will probably take you up on that." She didn't push for a name. She already knew they were speaking of Jeremy Carmichael. "So, an agent. I would have sworn you were an actor, you have that presence."

"I know, I am. I started my career as an agent, and took several roles myself. Whilst I am stunning in certain roles, my repertoire is limited," he shrugged an apology, "even I knew that, and one has to earn a living. Best of both worlds I suppose." He looked towards the hall. "Here she comes, a beauty," he lowered his voice, "but not a lead, I'm sad to say."

Patsy stood and smiled as Beth entered the kitchen.

Beth looked at Walter suspiciously. "What's he been saying? You must realise he has a vivid imagination, and has been known to make up what he doesn't know."

Beth planted a kiss on Walter's forehead.

"He's been telling me about himself." Patsy smiled.

"Oh lucky you, his favourite subject," Beth joked, and Walter snorted. "Definitely a few exaggerations, I'm sure. I'll see you later, Walter, be good."

Beth led Patsy out of the house, and the women walked slowly to the café.

"What a glorious morning. Shall we grab some drinks and go to the Downs? It seems a shame to stay inside," Beth suggested, as the approached the café. Patsy agreed, and fifteen minutes later they sat on a bench at Ladies Mile watching the Avon River meander its way under the Clifton Suspension Bridge. Beth screwed the top back on her bottle of water and turned to Patsy.

"I think the man who made the call was Jeremy Carmichael, the chap you rescued me from the other night." She paused and smiled. "You don't seem surprised; I suppose you wouldn't be having seen him in action."

She threw her arms into the air helplessly. "I have no idea where to begin, but it is him. Although, like most bullies he is for the best part a coward, and I don't think he could murder anyone. Believe it or not he does have a nice side, and he had an awful start in life. He goes to the hospital several times a week and does a radio slot. Occasionally he will go and give autographs if requested and he has time."

Her face fell as she considered this, but she shook the thoughts away and shrugged. "He has allowed his ego to take over though." She gave a laugh. "Do you know he is actually jealous of so many of those he comes into contact with, it's inexplicable. Why does Toni think his father was murdered?"

"Because the threats he received, which increased in both number and viciousness, said that his family would suffer if he didn't leave Bristol. A week later, the caller changes, and his father is dead. It was food poisoning, but Toni doesn't think it was accidental. His mother ate the same food as his father, and wasn't even poorly."

Beth was shaking her head and Patsy paused.

"He wouldn't have done that. Although I suppose he could have paid someone to do it, but I don't think so. He's done some terrible, terrible things," Beth's face clouded over and her head hung forward, "but I don't think Jeremy would go that far, whatever his motivation."

"Why are you so sure it's him, because there was more than one caller? Is it possible he would have had help? One of the calls was from a woman."

Beth raised her head slightly and looked at Patsy. "Did she have a soft Irish accent?"

"I don't know. Why, do you know who it is?"

"Jeremy's mother. Not in person, she's been dead for years, but he mimics her perfectly. I've heard him use her myself." Beth's nose wrinkled as she remembered. "Until I opened the door I thought there was a woman in his dressing room." She shook her head. "He can be a nasty, horrible man. I suppose he can be evil, and he was doing it to make me jealous. Still, I don't think he's brave enough for murder."

"So you think, what? That he was making the calls to warn Toni off you?"

"Not think. I know! It fits." Beth had raised her voice and glanced around, embarrassed at her outburst. "Sorry, simply thinking about it makes me angry."

Patsy patted her shoulder. "Beth, placing the Toni element of this to one side for a moment, tell me why you met with him the other night. You clearly hate the man."

Beth, her eyes sad, turned to Patsy. "That's irrelevant to this for the best part. Jeremy is a talented actor with a range of accents, and voices. He's good at his job. If Toni was receiving calls from ten different people, I'd put money on them all being Jeremy."

"Yes, I can see that. I'll also go with Toni's father's death being a coincidence, but I still don't understand why? Why go to all that trouble? I don't understand that. Not if he didn't intend to act upon his words in some way. You seem to have made it very clear you weren't interested in being with him."

"Because I'd defied him. First, despite being picked up, and then dropped, for years by Jeremy, I take myself a lover. Toni. At that time, I wasn't *with* Jeremy, but he didn't like it . . . Oh the details are just too painful, but Toni rescued me from him. In more ways than one, at first it was just a mental thing, giving me the courage to do as I wanted, but then it became physical for a while. I actually left him."

Beth held her hands up. "I'm talking about work now. Our romantic involvement . . ." she snorted derisively, "I can't believe I used the word 'romantic'. What I should have said was, our carnal involvement was over and done with, but

I still worked for him. He sacked me, and I accepted that. I went to live with Toni, you see. We had a good time, but it was never going to be a long-term thing. I have far too much baggage. But it was fun. The time came to move on, and I did. Walter gave me a contact in Liverpool, and that's where I went for a while, trying to make some sense of my life."

"Do you think Jeremy made these threats because he wanted you back?"

"I have no idea how long it's been going on, but first it would have been to end our relationship, then it would have been to punish Toni for giving me courage. He plagued Walter, you know. Poor man, what he's had to put up with, and still he let me come back and take my old room. Not that he approves."

She took a long swig of water. Screwing the top back on the now empty bottle, she tapped it restlessly against her leg as she looked out towards the bridge. "Jeremy Carmichael is a man who must have his own way. Absolutely. No compromise, at whatever the cost." She swallowed. "Sometimes, it's a high price that's paid. What he wants, he can't seem to achieve. He wants a big house, a beautiful, talented and dedicated wife. Intelligent beautiful children, one of each sex preferably, and another hit TV show. All the things he dreamed of when he was growing up." Beth laughed. "He keeps choosing the wrong women though. I can't have children." She flushed and looked at her feet. "Bungled termination."

Patsy stayed silent as she watched Beth compose herself. There was a lot more to this story, and Patsy doubted much of it was relevant to Toni. She seemed to have solved that issue, and she was unsure as to whether she should push Beth for more details. In the end, her curiosity got the better of her.

"Beth, why did you come back? You dislike the man, in fact, you think he can be evil. It doesn't make sense." She inclined her head. "Does he have some sort of hold over you? It seems to me that you might be afraid of him for some reason?"

Beth looked away from the bridge and down at her feet again before drawing in a breath, and turning back to Patsy.

"Let's say that it's complicated. I thought it was for the best, at the time . . . well, it's easy to be wise with hindsight." She shrugged hopelessly. "I've made my bed." Forcing a smile, she added, "So Toni can come back and finish his studies. Jeremy won't be brave enough to do it again. He'd be petrified the press would get hold of it."

Patsy placed her arm on Beth's shoulder. "You shouldn't stay here if it's not what you want. You left before, you can do it again. I'll help if I can."

Beth stood, causing Patsy's hand to fall away.

"You can't. Nobody can." She sniffed. "What's done is done, unfortunately. It's time to head back."

The two women walked briskly back to the house. Patsy stopped by her car and thanked Beth for her help, then watched as she walked the remainder of the way up the drive. Patsy knew something was seriously wrong, and she shivered knowing something needed to be done, but what? As she drove back to the office she resolved to call Walter Maggs and see if he could shed more light on it. She allowed herself a smile; at least Antonio Garcia would be able to return to Bristol, and that might just work in Nicola's favour.

"Morning, Sharon, where's Linda?" she asked, as she strode into the office.

"Coffee catastrophe. She's gone home to change. She managed to save the keyboard, but not her trousers." Sharon rolled her eyes. "You look pleased with yourself, productive morning I take it?"

"Yes, not too bad. I need to make some phone calls. I'll update you later."

The first call Patsy made was to Antonio Garcia. She explained Beth's theory about Jeremy Carmichael. Toni cursed in Spanish for several minutes.

"He is an evil man. I shall have to control my urge to kill him when I return. You need not confront him as you suggest. I realise now, it should have been obvious." Toni cursed again.

"So, you are coming back? I'll arrange a refund for you. I wasn't expecting it to be so simple."

"Thank you, and of course I'm coming back. I've worked too hard not to. I know my mother will be safe, and we have decided that she will go and live with her sister, who is also a widow. As you English say, all's well that ends well. Oh, and by the way, I have today posted a sample of my DNA; we should also solve that problem. I won't be back for a few more weeks. I have to sort my mother first."

"Glad to hear you're coming back, and thanks for sending the sample." Patsy was aware that he could have sent anyone's sample, but for some reason she trusted him. "I will email you an invoice. It won't be much, just a couple of hours." She paused momentarily. "Why do you say Carmichael is evil? You are the second person to have used that word. It's a strong word to use about someone, even if they are nasty."

"It's not for me to say. I have promised my silence." It was a statement and he stopped speaking.

"Is Beth in any sort of trouble? Is there any way you think I could help her?" Patsy pushed him.

"I think she needs help, yes. But I have promised, so you must speak to her." There was some background noise, and he added. "I am needed. Is there anything else you want me for?"

"No, you get on. I'll let you know the results of the test in due course. Bye, Toni, good luck."

Patsy hung up and drummed her fingers on the desk. She was now certain that Beth was acting against her own better judgement, and may even be being blackmailed. Despite the fact no one had asked for Patsy's help, and it didn't appear that anyone was in danger, Patsy spent an hour researching Jeremy Carmichael before calling Walter Maggs. She explained why she was calling.

"She's not here, gone to work. Come over now, she'll be a few hours. I'll put the kettle on."

Rawlings pulled onto the drive and followed it around so the car was facing the road again.

"Nice place. I've always wanted an in-out drive."

The two men took in the property as they walked to the front door. It was a substantial house, set in a large plot, and the former home of an Archbishop. The studded wooden door opened as they approached. Harriet peeped out from behind her mother. Meredith winked at her, and held his hand out to her mother. She was older than Meredith had expected given Harriet's age, and dark circles under her eyes revealed she had not been sleeping well.

"Mrs Boyles, thank you for seeing us. We won't keep you long."

They followed her through the house, and onto a terraced area which overlooked the fields behind the property. A jug of homemade lemonade sat on the centre of the table, and they accepted her offer of a glass as they settled themselves.

It was quickly established that Harriet had no connection with the other girls. Harriet fidgeted behind her mother as they spoke, occasionally peeping around her at the men. Eventually her mother pulled her forward and sat her on her lap.

"Say 'hello' to the policemen, Harriet." Harriet mumbled a greeting. "She's always been a shy child, but unfortunately my reaction to his attempt at . . . well you know, has made her more so. She's also having nightmares. It's been a worrying couple of days. Is he likely to try again? Do we know what his motive is?"

Meredith was watching Harriett and he knew she was following the conversation intently. She was a tall girl, and looked awkward balanced on her mother's knee. He chose his words carefully.

"We have some strong leads, and hopefully we'll have him locked up soon. However, it is very, and I can't emphasise that enough, *very* unlikely he will try again. If indeed it was an attempted abduction. I think it was mistaken identity and you'll never see him again." He smiled at Harriet. "Sleep soundly young Harriet, he won't be back."

Something started to niggle at the back of his mind again, but he pushed it to one side as Harriet spoke for the first time.

"He hurt me." She held out her arm, and pulled back her sleeve to reveal a medical dressing. "He pulled my plaster off, and I needed more stitches. He was horrible."

"Did he say anything to you?"

"Not really," Harriet shrugged.

Her mother took hold of her shoulders and turned Harriet to face her.

"What do you mean, not really? You said he didn't speak to you." The agitation in her voice was barely masked. Her daughter didn't meet her eye, but stared into the middle distance, pouting.

"He only said 'sorry'. That's not talking."

Rawlings leaned forward, and spoke before Mrs Boyles could respond.

"He met my daughter Ellen too. He didn't want to hurt her. In fact, he was really kind. Ellen said he was a nice man." Harriet raised her eyebrows. "What did he say then? Just 'sorry' was it?"

Harriet nodded slowly. "Yes, he said 'sorry, Harriet'." Harriet glanced up sharply at her mother's gasp. "What?" Harriet demanded. "That's not talking."

Her mother's eyes darted between Meredith and Rawlings. She wanted them to tell her that this man had not known her daughter. But she saw the knowledge register and she was scared.

Meredith stood and walked out onto the lawn. "I think I'll take a stroll." He turned to Harriet. "Would you like to come?" He smiled when she shook her head. "Perhaps your mum then?" He looked back towards the house as a dog barked. "Have you got a dog? Well, go and get it then," he added as Harriet nodded happily. The minute the child had disappeared he turned to her mother. "It's now clear this wasn't a chance encounter, but I meant what I said: it's unlikely he'll be back, but be vigilant."

"I can't believe it, why? I don't understand his motivation. That poor child. All I want is to protect her, to make her happy." She shook her head sadly. "I'm not doing very well, am I?"

"I think all parents question their abilities at some stage. This isn't your fault, and I'm sure Harriet is happy."

"She's not been the same since her father left. After years of being unable to conceive with me, my husband managed quite nicely after only a few attempts with a neighbour. They now live a little further away, but he didn't keep in touch with her and it hurts. She doesn't understand, poor child. She doesn't know we adopted her, and I'm not sure I'll ever tell her."

Harriet threw a ball across the lawn and a black Labrador came chasing after it. She ran after it shouting and laughing as the dog teased her with it, before dashing away again.

"Is there anything else we can help you with?" Her mother smiled for the first time as her daughter managed to wrestle the ball away from the dog, and Meredith saw the remains of the women she had been.

"No, thank you. We'll leave you in peace now."

Meredith drummed his fingers on his knees as Rawlings pulled out of the drive.

"I could murder a cigarette. This is really getting to me. That bastard has no idea of the damage he is causing."

"They all really get to you. There's a packet of mints in the glove compartment. You don't want a cigarette."

"Yes I do, actually!" Meredith opened the glove compartment and put two mints into his mouth. "It helps me concentrate. I'm getting old, Dave. Something came to me back then, but I filed it away to hear what Harriet had to say, and now I can't remember what it was."

"You will," Rawlins laughed, "it comes to us all in the end. I'll treat you to a late lunch before we go back. There's a nice pub along here, before you hit the main road."

Winding up the cord on the vacuum cleaner, Graham Charlesworth looked around the room satisfied with his efforts. Storing the vacuum in the cupboard under the stairs, he pondered the police presence at the hospital. Chief Inspector Meredith had sent men with e-fits to the hospital that morning. It had been quite unsettling for both staff and patients alike. But he'd remained calm and collected;

after all, if a little thing like that unsettled him, how would he cope with the pressure of doing what he had to do.

He went through to the lounge and sat at his desk. The laptop was already open, and he clicked the mouse to wake it up. Logging in, he drummed his fingers on the keyboard lightly, and hoped the information he wanted would be there. He opened his email account. His eyes opened wide, and his heart sank as he read the message. It told him that, while they were doing their best, there would be a delay. It thanked him for his patience. He slammed the lid down. What good was an apology? He needed to get on with his life! He pondered whether he should forget his plans and move on. He'd managed so far. Charlesworth glanced at his watch. There were things he needed to do, he'd think about it again later. He deleted the email and closed the laptop.

Walter held out a plate of iced fancies.

"Take one. They're to die for. A little lady around the corner makes them, and they're so much better than those one can get at the supermarket. Bite-sized too." He smiled as Patsy selected a pink one, and popped it into her mouth.

"Thanks, Walter, they are fabulous, you're right. And thanks for seeing me."

"You're most welcome, my dear. Beth is a lovely girl, and I'd do anything to help her," he grinned and lifted one shoulder, "and I am, of course, a drama queen, and the most appalling gossip. You could say it's you doing me a favour. Ha! So where would you like to start?"

"At the beginning. I get the feeling Beth would rather be anywhere than near Jeremy Carmichael, yet here she is. Why? What is it she's frightened of, if there is anything? I don't understand why she would consider working for him again. There are a million other jobs she could choose, and yet she comes back to a man she clearly dislikes." Patsy leaned forward. "You talk and I'll have another one of these." She selected another tiny cake.

"The beginning is some time ago, and I didn't know her so well then, but I'll tell it as I know it." Walter raised his eyebrows, and looked mischievous. "You must allow me a little poetic licence though." He topped up his cup from the pot, before settling himself back against the huge cushions that adorned his sofa. "I take it you've heard of Izzy Mansell?"

"The model? Oh yes, I was a teenager once, you know. Didn't she die a few years back?"

"She did, yes." Walter shook his head sadly, and slapped his own wrist. "Right the beginning, you said." He drew in a deep breath. "Izzy was stunningly beautiful as you know, not as bright as some, but very popular because she was the girl next door. Only stunning, and beautiful." He fluttered his hand in the air. "I know, I know, I'll get on with it. She met Jeremy when she was hired to do some cameo role in a television thing. They became an item, the darlings of the tabloids, her on every magazine cover, the handsome Jeremy the lead in the television police drama. But mainly, and behind closed doors, it was a volatile relationship, and the poor innocent was totally overwhelmed by him for the best part. Eventually, she took to drinking, and I'm sure drugs, but I could be making that up, and when she was drunk she stood up to him. Anywhere and everywhere, the press had a field day. The pair were still headline news, but for all the wrong reasons. I'm told his attempts to keep her on the straight and narrow when they were at a function were hilarious. Then he hit her." Walter sighed. "You must remember the backhander; it made the front page of every newspaper, and the television news."

Patsy's hand flew to her mouth. "That's right. I was doing exams at the time, and while I didn't condone him hitting her, I do remember feeling sorry for him. Wasn't she provoking him on purpose or something? Flirting with a previous lover, and making lewd suggestions to other guests? I remember he gave a statement, and spent most of it trying not to cry."

Walter snorted. "Or pretending to. He is an actor, you must remember. People forget that, but yes, she was being a madam. The way I heard it she wasn't drunk though," Walter wagged his head from side to side, "which is why I don't rule out drugs. But she propositioned some poor man who happened to be having a conversation with Carmichael, and when he tried to move away, she told him not to worry, Carmichael was impotent and she had needs. Carmichael went crazy and walloped her. They stayed together a little while longer, but she was seen less and less, then one day she simply disappeared."

Walter popped a cake into his mouth; it lasted seconds. "I did actually feel sorry for him then. He reported her missing after a few days, and the police searched all his houses. Given their history, I think the police believed Jeremy had bumped her off. Then she turns up in America at a *health clinic.*" He used his fingers to emphasise the words.

"I take it you don't believe that?" Patsy encouraged him to tell more.

"I do not. I won't tell you who, but one of my clients was there at the same time; he's got mental issues too. Izzy was a mess. He told me she was skin and bone, incoherent, and had either attempted to . . . you know, or had been self-harming. Apparently, she always wore long sleeves, but you could see the dressings beneath. He left before she did, as she was there a while."

"Now we're discussing it, I can remember snippets of this. But what has any of that got to do with Beth?"

"Ah yes, well, there I blame myself. Well, actually I don't, I simply got the girl a job. How was I to know she'd fall for him?" Walter tutted and rolled his eyes. He smoothed down the lapels on his jacket and smiled at Patsy, "Do you like it? It's new, a gift from a friend who's just returned from the Far East. He said he saw it in the window and thought of me. I can't but help agree with him; a smoking jacket suits me don't you think? I sit at my desk dreaming I'm Noel Coward sometimes." He flapped his hand. "Who am I kidding? A note for the milkman is about my limit." He threw his head back and brayed out a laugh.

Patsy grinned at him. "It's fabulous, Walter, but Beth . . . what exactly wasn't your fault?"

"When Izzy left the clinic, she took up with some plastic surgeon. She moved into his penthouse, they got engaged, and she blossomed. She was a beautiful woman anyway, but a few curves which she'd never been allowed to have transformed her. She went to the Oscar ceremony the following year with him, and our papers were full of it. Even got a few seconds air time on TV-"

"Walter, get to the point." Patsy was losing patience.

"Okay, okay," he huffed dramatically. "I heard Jeremy became even more unbearable that week at work, as some of the crew, who detested him, bought every newspaper and magazine with the pictures in and left them all over the studio. That was the week I sent Beth for her interview. It was a small part, but as the sister of one of the main characters, there was a good chance she'd get repeat work after the main storyline. Two weeks later and Izzy and her man announce their delight at her pregnancy, and *coincidentally* Jeremy falls in love with Beth."

Walter nodded at Patsy's look of amazement. "He's a handsome man, and can be quite charming, in a shallow sort of way. Beth was already smitten. I'm sure it helped that she's a pretty girl, she takes a good photo, and happens to be ten years younger than Izzy. Carmichael wines and dines her in London, Paris, New York, and somehow all the right magazines and newspapers end up with photographs of the happy couple. To be fair they did make a handsome pair. Beth told me it was wonderful to begin with. When Izzy had her baby, Carmichael told Beth she'd never cope, and the poor man would literally be left holding the baby. He told

Beth she would make a far better mother, when the time came. But Izzy coped for quite some time, much to his continued irritation."

Walter sighed and popped another cake into his mouth. "Beth tells me Jeremy couldn't maintain the pretence that he loved her. She was convinced, and rightly so, that he would always love Izzy, and their relationship fizzled to nothing, but not before he had drained Beth of what little confidence she'd had. She stopped applying for acting roles, and I have to confess she wasn't brilliant, but she could have earned a living." He pursed his lips. "Competent, that's what she was: a competent actor. Anyway, Beth stops acting and becomes his skivvy. Personal assistant I believe they called it, but I watched and she was a skivvy."

Patsy glanced at her watch. She had Linda's lunch date to supervise soon.

"Walter, I really am going to have to make a move shortly. Can we -"

"Cut to the chase? Of course, my dear, I did warn you. Eventually, Beth was reasonably happy with the arrangement. She accepted she was never going to realise her dream, but working for Carmichael had its own rewards, and unlike her acting career, she was earning regular money. Then Izzy comes back to England. Jeremy's prediction came true and she abandoned the surgeon and their child. The strange thing was, there was no drama over it. She simply reappeared."

"Really? I didn't know that. Back to Carmichael?" Patsy leaned back against the chair again, Linda momentarily forgotten.

"Indeed. A mystery. Bizarrely, Beth got on well with Izzy, and is fairly guarded in what she says about that time. She's never uttered a bad word about her. Carmichael took her back, delighting in telling her at every opportunity that he knew she'd be back, and would never be able to cope with motherhood."

Walter leaned forward and frowned. "Then something happened. I don't know what, but everything went wrong again and Izzy left. I don't think they'd even managed a year. There was no hue and cry this time, it was old news regurgitated. Three months later Izzy is found dead in a cheap hotel in Bournemouth, having taken an overdose of prescribed medication."

He sighed. "Beth was beside herself with grief. She blamed herself, but mainly she blamed Carmichael and she quit her job. Told me to get her whatever work I could find. He pestered her and she stood firm for about six months the first time. Since then it's been an on-off thing between them." He leaned forward and patted Patsy's knee. "I've tried to work it out, but I gave up long since. It seems to me, Beth copes with him for a while, and then she has to escape, but she always,

always comes back." Walter slapped his hands on his thighs and sunk into his cushions. "But I can't tell you why. Find out why Izzy left him, and I think you'll have the answer, but for the life of me, I can't work it out."

"How odd. What a sad story, Walter." Patsy stood up. "Now I really must go, but I will look into this, I promise."

Walter stood and air-kissed her on each side of her face.

"Good, and you must come back and let me know. It's a mystery that's been running for too long."

Patsy hurried back to her car. Although she had enjoyed Walter's company, and his dramatic story-telling, the whole thing had made her feel melancholy, and she hoped watching Linda in action would cheer her up.

Meredith pulled his jacket on, and took the call from Amanda. As Tom Seaton joined him, he was agreeing to something that he clearly didn't want to.

"Everything all right, Gov?"

"Not so as you'd notice, no. You ask for one simple bloody favour and . . ." Meredith glanced at his watch. "Let's get going, we need to do a detour. I have to visit the hospital."

"I hope it's a quick visit, unless you don't mind keeping Graham Charlesworth waiting."

"Sod it. You're right, I don't want to give him an excuse not to be there. I'll call her back." Meredith hit the call button as Seaton held the door for him. "Amanda, forget what I said, I'll be in later. Tell her she'll get tea, and remind her I'm trying to catch an abductor." He listened for a while before interrupting her. "Tough, you'll cope, it'll be good practice."

Seaton pulled out of the station car park. He looked across to Meredith, who seemed even more irritable than usual.

"You're not going to share then?" He maintained a straight face as Meredith turned to him.

"Share? We're not bloody teenagers, you know. Anyway, you wouldn't believe me if I told you. I'll tell you this though," Meredith tapped the dash with his finger. "Fan as I am of womankind, it is possible to have too many in your life."

Seaton threw back his head and laughed. "Fuck me, Gov. You of all people should have worked that out years ago."

He smirked for the rest of the journey. Meredith agreed with his sergeant's assessment, and remained silent until they reached their destination.

"That'll be it. One of those two on the brow of the hill," Meredith observed as the Seaton slowed down. "Seventy-eight, it's the one on the right."

Graham Charlesworth watched the car pull onto the drive from the landing window. They were early. He sighed as he went down to let them in. This was all very distasteful, but he understood they had a job to do, and better here than at the hospital, or worse, the police station. He opened the door as they reached it.

"Gentlemen, come in." He watched as they wiped their feet on the mat and quickly took in the spacious hall. "I'm not sure how long this will take, do you have time for a drink?" He held his hands up. "Non-alcoholic, of course. I know you wouldn't drink on duty."

"Was that supposed to be a joke?" Meredith snapped. "Because there is nothing about our presence here that is funny, Dr Charlesworth. Coffee, black, two sugars." Uninvited, Meredith walked forward and opened the nearest door. "Are we in here?"

It was a dining room, long, narrow and unlike anything the girls had described.

"Actually, I thought you might be more comfortable in the sitting room, but if you would rather . . ." Charlesworth held his hand forward inviting Meredith to enter.

"No, no. Sitting room will be fine, lead the way."

Meredith and Seaton followed as Charlesworth led them to a door at the other end of the hall. Charlesworth established that a glass of water would suffice for Seaton as they settled themselves on the large leather sofa. He left them to fetch the refreshments.

"Go and check that door," Meredith instructed, nodding at a white panelled door in the opposite wall. "Keep your fingers crossed it's a toilet."

Seaton got to his feet and walked briskly to the door. Pulling it open, he sighed, and stood back to reveal a series of mostly empty shelves. He walked to the very tidy desk in the corner, and opened and shut the drawers after a cursory glance at the contents. He shook his head at Meredith as Charlesworth returned.

Meredith raised his eyebrows. "That was quick. You must have a superb kettle."

"I always have a pot of coffee on the go. This one I put on a little before you arrived so it's fresh."

"Ah yes, the accent, it's not heavy though. You sound like someone on TV, it'll come to me. You Americans love proper coffee." Meredith sipped his and nodded. "That's good."

"Thank you, I'm glad you like it. I'm not American, by the way. My parents were Scottish, but I was actually born in Australia, Melbourne; we were there until I was ten. Then we came to the UK for a few years, although I've yet to visit Scotland, and I studied medicine in America. I like to think I have a universal accent, although I can do all three perfectly as a party piece."

"Very nice too. Where were you at eight o'clock the night before last?"

"Here. I had worked that day, and was absolutely exhausted. I picked up a takeaway on the way home, and was in bed by," Charlesworth shrugged, "nine thirty, latest. Why, where do you think I was?"

"Do you have any witnesses to that?"

"Buying the Chinese meal, I guess so, but being here, no. I live alone."

"No girlfriend? Sorry, that was presumptuous, you could be gay. No partner or significant other then?" Meredith saw Charlesworth's amusement and pulled his lips into a grin. "Glad I'm amusing you."

"Not as such, DCI Meredith, I've just never heard that allowance made before. You are clearly an enlightened man." Seaton cleared his throat, and Charlesworth looked across at him, "Although your colleague doesn't think so. But for the record, I'm not gay, and I do not have a partner at the moment, significant or otherwise."

"What with all those nurses surrounding you every day? What do you do for pleasure?" Meredith pinned him still with his eyes. "What do you do to let off steam?" Meredith made no attempt to hide the look of distaste, and his inference was clear.

"Yes, I date the occasional nurse, female, always over twenty-one, DCI Meredith. I just happen not to be living with someone. I take objection to your insinuation, and would be grateful if you would get on with what you came to do."

Charlesworth was becoming irritated, and Meredith had hardly begun. Seaton tapped his pencil lightly against his pad as the two men stared at each other.

"And where were you at six thirty on Tuesday morning?" Meredith asked without looking away.

"In bed, I expect." Charlesworth held a hand up and looked at Seaton. "For the record, alone, absolutely alone, and if my memory serves me right I wasn't letting off steam." He turned back to face Meredith. "Am I allowed to use that euphemism too?"

"Where were you at seven o'clock on Tuesday evening?" Meredith allowed himself to blink.

Charlesworth frowned and stared at the rug as he recalled his movements. Suddenly he clicked his fingers.

"Shopping." He pointed at Meredith. "Shopping in the large Tesco store on the ring road. Alone, well, apart from the couple of hundred staff and customers. I'm sure someone may have seen me."

"I'm sure they must have. How did you pay?"

"Cash, why? Is it relevant?"

"Of course. Everything is relevant when you are searching for a paedophile. Have you got the receipt?"

"I doubt it." Charlesworth pointed a finger at Meredith. "If you infer, or call me that, one more time, I don't care who you are, I'll knock you out. I am not a paedophile! I work with children, healing them, making them healthy. On occasion helping heal them following their contact with paedophiles, so please let's call it a day before you make me do something which we'll both regret."

Charlesworth drew in a deep breath.

Meredith nodded curtly. "I'm sure you'll manage to control yourself. And that being the case, I am sure you will understand why I am so determined to catch the sick bastard who's doing this, and bring him to justice. If you want this over quickly then I'm sure you will allow us to do a swift search of your home."

Charlesworth held his hand out. "Be my guest. I'd expect no less, I even put the duster over for you."

Meredith and Seaton stood in unison. "Do you want to show us around, or shall we help ourselves?" Meredith was already walking to the door.

"You carry on. I'll take these cups to the kitchen, and catch you up." Charlesworth made no attempt to join them.

Meredith closed the door behind them, and pointed up the stairs. Seaton nodded. The two men took the stairs quickly, and split up to search behind the six doors they found leading off the landing. The first door Meredith opened was the bathroom. Modern, attractive, and the cabinet contained nothing more exciting than toothpaste and mouthwash. In the bedrooms, with the exception of Charlesworth's own room, all the cupboards and drawers were empty. In his bedroom, they found clothes hung neatly in the wardrobe, or folded in the drawers. Meredith did find a packet of condoms in a jacket pocket, but nothing else of interest. The final door revealed an airing cupboard which contained the boiler, and some towels and sheets stored neatly on slatted shelves.

Meredith shrugged. "Nothing up here, let's finish off downstairs. All is not lost."

Seaton placed a hand on his arm. "Take it easy, Gov, you're letting him wind you up."

"I beg to differ. I think that's the other way around."

They checked the dining room, and Charlesworth came out of the kitchen into the hall.

"All very neat and tidy. You have a nice home, if a little on the large side for a single man." Meredith pointed at the door to the only room they had not checked. "Last one. What's in here?"

"A family room, I think the agent called it. It's empty. I haven't used it. Is the size of my home of particular relevance? I had a break-in shortly after I moved in and the officer who attended made a similar comment."

"A break-in, did you lose much?" Meredith asked, turning to face him. "I notice you don't have much of anything."

"Not really." Charlesworth listed off a few of the items which had been taken, but Meredith was only half listening. "I've only been in the country for eight months, so just the basics, as I explained to your colleague at the time."

Meredith nodded, keen to get on, and walked to the door. This could be the one. He pushed the door open, and looked in expectantly. As Charlesworth had promised, it was empty of all furniture, but that could have been moved. He spotted the French doors and strode towards them, a smile playing around his lips. He peered out through the glass and blew out a frustrated breath, as he saw the neatly manicured lawn, the box hedge, and the little mermaid water feature. This was not the garden the girls had described. He turned away.

"Nice garden," he commented as he made his way back to the other two men.

"Thank you. It's very pleasant now it's so warm. Well, if that's all . . ." Charlesworth was trying to dismiss them.

Meredith had other plans. "Just the kitchen and the garage."

"The kitchen . . ." Charlesworth was taken aback, but held his hand towards the open door. "Sure, help yourself."

Seaton avoided Charlesworth's eye as he followed Meredith. He knew as well as Meredith this wasn't the house. Meredith was stringing it out on purpose, although he had no idea why. Charlesworth seemed like a nice enough bloke, and he'd only taken offence where offence had been caused. He rolled his eyes as Meredith smiled at him, and opened the fridge door. Meredith took in the contents. They were sparse and pretty much what one would expect to find: milk, butter, eggs, bacon, a pack of ham, maple syrup, a six pack of beer, and a bag of apples, Meredith shrugged and closed the door then opened the freezer and inspected the contents.

Charlesworth looked over Seaton's shoulder as Meredith closed the freezer door. Meredith smiled at him.

"Just the garage then, through here, is it?" Meredith walked to a door in the corner of the room and pulled it open. He hit the light switch and there, sitting in the middle of the garage, was a motorcycle. He stared at it for a while, before switching off the light. He stepped back into the kitchen and closed the door.

"Why that Tesco?" Meredith asked as he turned the key in the lock.

"I'm sorry?" Charlesworth was thrown.

"Why that Tesco? It's a bit of a detour on your way home. I noticed a couple of convenience stores on the way here that would have been handier."

"Yes, but without the choice," Charlesworth answered easily.

Meredith smiled as he walked past him into the hall. Charlesworth followed him and held the door open as the two men left. He was about to close it when Meredith stepped back into the porch.

"Which Chinese did you buy your takeaway from?"

"The Kowloon Kitchen." Charlesworth started to close the door.

"And what choice were you after?"

"Pardon me?"

"When you went to Tesco's, or was it a big shop?"

"It was average, and it was the overall choice, a bit cheaper too." The irritation had returned to Charlesworth's voice. "Will that be all, DCI Meredith?"

"Not quite. I'll call you if I think of anything else, but the last one for today: how do you do a big shop on a bike?"

"It was average, and you use the back box and a backpack. Goodbye, DCI Meredith."

Meredith nodded and joined Seaton in the car.

"You don't like him, do you?" Seaton observed. "Although, for the life of me, I don't know why. He seems a nice enough chap, does a good job. The house was clean. I don't know where the girls were held, but it wasn't there."

"No, it wasn't."

"What was your problem with him?"

"Methinks he doth protest too much, Seaton. He was nervous when I first met him, when there was no need. Something's wrong, he's up to something. I just can't prove it yet."

"What? How did you get there? Because a bag lady and a couple of pensioners think he looks like Captain Kirk? I'm not convinced."

"And a teenager, and a shop assistant at the supermarket. And he speaks like, and I quote, 'someone off the telly'. He shopped at Tesco, why? Not because of the overall choice, not with the few items he had in that house. Maple syrup."

"Maple syrup?"

"Yep. He went there as the smaller shops don't stock it. What do Yanks have maple syrup with?"

"Pancakes?" Seaton glanced at Meredith to make sure he wasn't winding him up.

"I rest my case. Well probably, we've just got to prove it now. Stop in at that Tesco on the way to the hospital."

CHAPTER THIRTEEN

"Hi, honey, I'm home. But I can't believe you are," Patsy called as she dropped her keys on the hall table. "Wait till I tell you what Linda did today." She walked into the kitchen and Meredith and Amanda smiled at her. "What? What's going on? It's only six thirty and you're home." She smiled at Meredith before swinging round to Amanda. "And you look guilty."

"That's because she is," Meredith responded, and nudged his daughter. "Tell her what you did."

"I didn't do anything!" Amanda rolled her eyes. "Patsy, observe carefully. What you are about to see is the proverbial buck being passed. Dad, why don't you tell Patsy what *you* did?"

Patsy looked from one to the other. It was clear neither of them wanted to admit to whatever had happened, but at the same time it was amusing them, and she couldn't begin to guess what it was. Someone had also made something for dinner. A Mediterranean aroma was emanating from the oven. That definitely spelt guilt. She turned and started to leave the kitchen.

"Well, when you two have decided whose fault it is, or want to tell me, give me a shout. I'm going for a bath."

"No, all joking aside we actually do need your approval." Meredith stood and went to collect her. He sat in her in his vacant chair, and looked at his daughter. "Tell her."

"I'll tell her the truth, or do you want to tell your version so you don't feel -"

Patsy banged her hands on the table. "One of you just spit it out!"

"We're going to have a guest for a few days," Amanda began.

"That's nice, who? And why might I not like them?" Patsy frowned. That wasn't what she expected.

"She's an acquired taste, but I think you'll get on like a house on fire," Meredith assured her.

"She? Who's she? Does this visitor not have a name?"

"Peggy," Amanda said, biting her bottom lip and drawing in a deep breath.

Patsy shrugged. "Peggy? Still none the wiser. Who is . . . oh no! Not the bag lady? How on earth . . . I mean, why?" As though preaching to the small crowd before her, Patsy held her arms aloft. "Why?" she demanded.

"Amanda told her she could." Meredith's mouth twitched. Although he was not best pleased with the situation himself, he could just about see the funny side.

"No I didn't. What I said was it was perhaps a possibility if it stopped her discharging herself, and going to live rough. It will only be a few days, a week tops, and we may be able to convince her to go into a hostel while she's here." It was clear Amanda thought it was the right thing to do, but she didn't want to oversell it, so she shrugged. "But I did emphasise that you two would have to decide."

"But you didn't tell me that. You let me go and see her, unarmed as it were, so -"

"At the end of the day, she needs to go somewhere. That was a pretty major operation. She can't discharge herself to a park bench. Even if she comes here, she may disappear on us, but as I said, it's up -"

"Yes, but still, I do -"

"Shut up the pair of you. You're like a pair of teenagers. I'm sure Peggy will be delightful company. I have no problem with it at all because you two are doing all the work. And if she gets too much, you," she jabbed her finger at Meredith, "will, as they say, have to grow a pair, and get rid of her." Patsy stood up. "Now, I'm going to have a bath. Call me when dinner is ready."

"Ah yes, that's the other thing."

Patsy paused, amazed. Meredith actually looked embarrassed.

"We need to go shopping. It won't take long, a quick canter through M&S should do it."

"What? You hate shopping, as do I. What are we shopping for?" Patsy's hands were on her hips.

"Dinner is in the oven. Amanda has *another* date, but that's a whole different story. We need to get Peggy some clothes, or she comes here in nothing but a hospital gown."

Patsy looked incredulous. "And I have to come because . . ."

"Patsy, please, I know she's a bag lady, but we can't leave it to Dad. Even bag ladies have standards." Amanda laughed. "And as I am going out tonight, I'll use the bathroom first." Amanda stood and side-stepped Patsy. "I'll get going now, and I promise dinner will be on the table by the time you get back."

Tapping the desk for luck, he logged onto the site. He knew there was little chance the results would be in if the previous message had been accurate. But things were not going to schedule, and he wanted to step up a gear with his plans.

"Damn you!" he cursed, and slammed his fist down on the desk in an uncharacteristic display of temper.

Due to unforeseen circumstances, we are experiencing a backlog. Results promised for today should be displayed within the next twenty-four hours.

He read the message out loud, and then yelled at the screen.

"This is becoming farcical. I've kept my end of the bargain, you keep yours, you useless pile of crap!" Knowing there was nothing he could do, no one he could complain to, he picked up his glass and went for a refill.

Linda returned with a full bottle of wine and refreshed Trump's glass.

"And there he was Louie. This . . . how should I describe him? He was nondescript really. A beige man. He was fiftyish, slightly balding, in a well-worn suit, sitting there with half a pint of beer, tearing a beer mat to shreds, and looking guilty. I'll bet my bottom dollar he's married. Anyway, he catches sight of me, and his face lights up. Well, it would I know – but I just saw red." Linda paused for breath.

"Oh dear, that doesn't bode well for the poor chap. What did you do? Please tell me you didn't decorate him with his drink."

"Oh no, better than that." Linda looked a little shamefaced. "I told him what I thought of him. I held out my hand, and he took it. Limp, damp, handshake too, but then to be expected I suppose."

"What did you say?" Trump had not yet become tired with Linda's exuberance. He was one of the few who enjoyed her storytelling.

Linda grinned. "I looked him up and down, and shook my head. 'Oh no,' I said. 'You won't do. You should be ashamed of yourself. No wonder you hide behind a computer screen. You are a predator, sir, yes, a predator, and a sorry one at that. How dare you prey on unsuspecting and vulnerable women, how dare you?'" Linda sipped her wine. "Needless to say, he didn't respond. What could he say? Actually, I think he looked near to tears. I've never had that effect on a man before."

"Oh, I think you have. You just don't notice the devastation you leave in your wake." Trump puckered his lips, and was rewarded with a hand in his face that pushed him away.

"How dare you! I do not. Anyway, I turned on my heel and walked out. I had to keep a straight face, which was difficult as I had to walk past Patsy. I think she looked almost as shocked as he did."

"I'm sure she was. You know, Linda, whilst I appreciate your sentiments, when one is working on such things, one has to control one's personal opinions. What did Patsy have to say?"

Linda flushed and pouted. "I knew you'd take her side." She tutted and ran her hand through her hair, "She wasn't best pleased. She was reasonably nice . . . no, she wasn't actually. She was quite curt, and reminded me that my duties are behind a desk."

"What did he do?"

"What do you mean? He probably sat there and licked his wounds . . . actually he probably made a quick exit, half the bar heard me."

Louie pursed his lips, and looked at her as one would a naughty child. "I thought the purpose of all this was not simply to find him and give him a telling off, but to establish his identity and hopefully an address to pass on to your client."

"Oh yes. That's probably what Patsy was doing. When we spoke she was in the car, and a bit distracted." Linda thumped her hands against her knees. "Oh dear. I need more training, Louie. You're going to have to help me with all this stuff. I . . . What? Why are you laughing?"

Trump was unable to contain himself, which spoke volumes. Linda picked up the remote control and switched the television on.

"Television it is then. I'm sure the spare bed will be comfortable. Patsy had no complaints."

For some reason this also amused Trump, who pulled a tissue from the box on the table, and dabbed at his eyes.

Meredith threw the pillow onto the bed and headed for the door.

"Right, that will do. Stop fussing. You do realise a cardboard box was posh for her before this, don't you? I want to catch *Crimebusters*, they're doing a résumé of all the clues we have. They're adding the tin soldiers in tonight."

"Who's manning the phones?"

"Ha! Old news, we have no one at the studio, they're giving the incident room number out. Rawlings and Jo are covering."

Twenty minutes later Meredith nodded as the item finished.

"It's a long shot, but let's hope something else points us in the direction of Charlesworth."

"You don't really want it to be a doctor, do you? That would really put the cat amongst the pigeons."

"Yes, I know, but to be honest there's an agenda here that we can't see, and if it being Charlesworth means these young girls are safe, then so be it. It'll be over."

"Yes, I suppose so. What time are you picking this Peggy woman up? I've got to try and make contact with that Lyndon Ward chap, apologise for Linda, and then attempt to get him to communicate with my client, but that won't be first thing. I'll wait here for you if you like."

"You're being cooperative, dare I ask why?" Meredith tapped her leg. "And I haven't had my birthday present yet."

"I need you to do me a favour too. As to your birthday present, when this case is over, you get your birthday present. Get your man, and you can have it."

"What's the case got to do with my present?"

"It's a fate thing." Patsy shrugged. "Every time we get within seconds of me giving you it, something horrible happens, so put this one to bed sharpish, DCI Meredith, and you'll get your just deserts."

"Hmm. I'll think about that. If it's not Charlesworth, it could be weeks." He grinned. "I think you'll have to keep me quiet in other ways while I sort this." He inclined his head. "What was the favour?"

Patsy quickly updated him on the calls made by Jeremy Carmichael, and his hold over Beth Durham.

"Toni doesn't want to make it official, and I'm concerned he might confront him, and that certainly wouldn't be a good idea. I thought if you could give him a warning off the record. A caution, that if you find he's done anything else, that sort of thing. I could tell Toni to keep his distance or he too could end up in trouble with the police." Patsy smiled at Meredith's groan. "It won't take long, and you'll enjoy it. He's a nasty man, a bully, and you don't like bullies."

She laughed as Meredith held up his hands in surrender.

"Enough! I'll do it, I can't promise when though. Let me have the details, and when I have a minute, I'll have a word." He nudged Patsy. "What's this Toni bloke like? You seem very keen to help him. After all, from your point of view, case closed."

"No idea, never even seen a photograph. He's still in Spain. But I have my other client to think of, and he's not playing ball yet."

"Oh yes, forgot about that. Remind me . . ."

Patsy froze for a moment, then shook her head, tutting. "I don't think so. We're not talking shop all night. There must be something more interesting we can do. Who knows when we'll next be home alone?"

"Say no more. Get yourself up those stairs."

The next morning, Meredith arrived at the hospital at nine thirty, having briefed the team. He was allowed straight onto the ward, as Peggy had been causing what the nurse described as a commotion. He placed the brightly coloured shopping bag on the end of her bed, and looked at her. Her hair had been arranged in a knot on the top of her head, and it made her look younger. She rolled her eyes at him, and her grip on the butter knife she was clasping relaxed a little.

"What have you been up to? That lot are frightened to come anywhere near you."

"Come closer and I'll tell you."

"What? Peggy, we haven't got time -"

"Are those for me? Give them here." She pointed the knife at the bag.

"They are, put the bloody knife down." Meredith picked up the bag and placed it on her lap, relieving her of the knife as he did so.

"Pull the curtain round, Merriwinkle." Peggy was smiling as she rifled through the bag.

Meredith pulled the curtain. Pushing the bag forward, Peggy swung her legs off the side of the bed, and grunted as her feet touched the floor, and took her weight.

"Do you need help?"

"Nope, I'll be fine, they can keep their distance." Peggy pulled the large pair of knickers from the bag, and stepped into them. Meredith screwed his eyes shut as she pulled them up, and the back of the gown gaped open. "Oh yes, these are nice."

"Peggy, I'll step outside. Give me a shout when you're ready." Meredith kept his eyes shut.

"You've seen a naked woman before. I think you'll control yourself." Peggy cackled at her own humour.

"I've seen many," Meredith responded, "but none that were moving in with me. What would Patsy say?"

"Who's Patsy?" Peggy smiled as she pulled up the soft fleece trousers, the fabric soft and comforting against her skin. Pulling free the tie which held the gown in place, she allowed it to drop to the floor, before grunting her way into a vest that matched the knickers. She winced as she rotated her shoulders to pull it into place. But the smile returned as she picked up a pretty T-shirt; it was quite roomy, and so didn't require quite so much effort.

"She's my significant other. She's waiting at home to meet you. Peggy, I can't stand here with my eyes shut. I'm going to step out."

"Open them then," Peggy cackled again. "I take it you're not married?"

"No, we're not. It's all quite new."

"Oh God, Merriwinkle, you're not going to be drooling over each other, are you? I think I'd throw up." Peggy sat back on the bed, and put the socks on. "Are you going to ask her to marry you?"

"I nearly did, but . . . look it's a long story, and totally irrelevant. How are you doing?" Meredith tapped his foot on the floor. "Shall I call a nurse to help?"

"I should just book it, and do it. That's what we did. No fuss, no bother. I've never seen the point in these big weddings. Never found out who actually enjoys them either. But don't do anything until I've met her. She might not be right for you."

Meredith roared with laughter, and shook his head. "And what would you know about what's right for me? You cheeky bugger, hurry up or I really will open my eyes."

"I'm ready."

Meredith opened his eyes cautiously. Peggy held her arms out. With the pale pink T-shirt, and the soft grey lounge suit, Peggy looked normal. He wondered why he thought she would look any different from any other old lady being discharged from hospital.

"Well, you look a picture." Meredith nodded at her feet. "Sorry about the slippers, we weren't sure of your size. We'll sort you out some shoes once we get you settled."

"I'll not be settling anywhere. As soon as Amanda tells me my wound is okay, I'll be off."

Meredith knew not to push it. "Okay, no problem, you're the boss."

"I am the boss of me, and don't you forget it." Peggy zipped the jacket up. "I'll get my bits, and we can go before he comes back."

"Before who comes back? Is that what the knife was all about?" Meredith perched on the end of the bed, and held up his hand to still her movement.

"It was. Captain Kirk was here. He just stood there looking at me. I pretended to be asleep, but I could see him. Years of practice; you've got to keep your wits about you when you sleep rough."

Meredith jumped to his feet and pulled back the curtain. "You stay there," he told Peggy.

She held her hand up in alarm. "Where are you going? Wait for me."

He returned minutes later with a nurse. "Tell her what you told me," he instructed Peggy.

"Captain Kirk was here, and he was watching me." Peggy eyed the nurse suspiciously.

"When she says 'Captain Kirk', she means a man. Probably this man." Meredith pulled the dog-eared e-fit from his pocket, and handed it to the nurse.

The nurse shook her head. "I'm telling you, DCI Meredith, as I told her. No one has been on the ward. From lights out, until the drinks trolley came first thing, there were just the two of us."

"And you never left the ward at any time?" Meredith took back the e-fit and returned it to his pocket.

"No. Not at the same time." A shrill bleeping noise filled the air, and the nurse spun around. "I have to go. As you can see, we're short-staffed. I haven't got time for this. She was probably dreaming. The doctor has signed the release form, I suggest you take her home. I have to go"

As she walked across the ward, Meredith turned to Peggy. "I'll check it out, don't worry. But she's right. Let's get you home."

Peggy pulled out the final package. It was an oversized toiletry bag still in its wrapping.

"I'll fill this and we'll be off. But that bugger was here. I'm not senile yet, Merriwinkle."

Meredith watched her put the few toiletries she had into the bag, together with a crumpled newspaper, and her glasses. Then from under her pillow she pulled the tin box. As she zipped up the bag, he held out his arm, which at first she ignored, and walked past him towards the exit. But as they made their way down the ward, she reached for him without comment. She linked her arm in his, grateful for his support.

Twenty minutes later, Meredith pulled on to the drive. He'd barely managed introductions, when his phone rang. He walked away leaving Patsy and Peggy making tea in the kitchen.

"It's always like this." Patsy nodded at his back as he paced up and down in the hall. "You get used to it."

"Is that why you're not married?"

Patsy was taken aback. She laughed and turned to face Peggy. "No, there are many reasons. Something always seems to get in the way being the main one. Anyway, he's not asked me." She smiled as Peggy rolled her eyes, "But it's not the job, not really." She glanced up as Meredith cursed and started back towards them. "He'll be gone in less than a minute," she predicted.

"Sorry, ladies, something's come up. I have to go. Peggy be good, and leave the cutlery where it is. Patsy, I'll call you." He raised his eyebrows in an unspoken question, and Patsy nodded her permission for him to abandon her with Peggy. He winked and was gone.

Patsy gave Peggy a tour of the house and then showed her the other clothes they'd bought her, which were in a drawer in her room – the spare room. Peggy said little but nodded her appreciation. Patsy settled her with a pot of tea, and a large packet of biscuits in front of the television, but Peggy didn't like the noise or the content of the numerous channels they tried. Patsy suggested music, and Peggy took seconds to reject many of the CDs available. In the end, she held one up. Patsy smiled; it was her Christmas present to Meredith.

"Do you like Doris Day? I bought that for Meredith, I think it's fair to say 'Que Sera, Sera' is our tune."

"Not particularly, but it's better than the rest of his rubbish." Peggy settled back into the chair.

With the music playing softly in the background, Peggy read her newspaper, while Patsy searched for a home address for Jeremy Carmichael. If all else failed she would ask Beth, but this was the less painful route. It was surprisingly easy as it turned out. He used his own name, and was on the electoral roll. Although she knew he was busy, Patsy sent Meredith the details as a gentle reminder. From the corner of her eye, she saw Peggy's head drop forward. She was nodding off.

Closing her laptop, Patsy spoke quietly. "Peggy, I have to go out and do an errand." She smiled as Peggy's head snapped upright. "Why don't you go up and have a lie down. If you wake up and I'm not back, you know where everything is."

"I've spent days in bed, I'm not tired. But perhaps I'll take a book from the shelf and read lying flat. It eases the pressure on my wound, you know."

Peggy chose her book from the shelves behind the door, and Patsy made sure she was settled before texting both Amanda and Meredith with similar messages. She told them she was going to work, and it would be good if either of them could pop in and check on Peggy. By the time she'd sorted herself out, she could hear gentle snoring coming from Peggy's room. She tiptoed down the stairs.

When Peggy awoke an hour or so later it took a while to remember where she was. She lay there staring at the ceiling wondering how long she would be able to put up with it. She wasn't stupid and she knew she had to be fit when she went back to her usual way of living, and this operation had given her a scare. She may have opted out of what others would call normal society, but for some reason she simply couldn't fathom why she wasn't ready to check out for good. Perhaps she'd give it a couple of days.

She picked up the book and turned to the first page.

"He's actually coming here, is he?" Meredith rubbed his hands together as he strode into the incident room.

"Certainly is, sir. Wouldn't say why, and insisted on talking to you. I hope you managed to settle Peggy in first."

"Settled sweet as a nut, thank you for asking, Trump. She did say that Captain Kirk had been watching her last night at the hospital, so that's something we can touch upon when he gets here."

"He's here, interview three. He must have phoned on his way over." Seaton entered the room behind Meredith.

"Come on then. Let's see what he's got to say for himself."

Trump picked up his pad and hurried to catch Meredith, who picked up a file from his desk, and went straight to the interview room. He nodded a brief acknowledgment to Charlesworth and sat down. Charlesworth opened his mouth to speak, but Meredith held up a finger to silence him whilst he set up the recorder. When ready he hit the button, announced the purpose of the meeting, and finally gave his full attention to Charlesworth.

"Dr Charlesworth, as I understand it, you have what you say is valuable information about the case we are investigating. Before we start I must ask you if you want legal representation."

Charlesworth was unpleasantly surprised and frowned. "No, why would I? Look Meredith, I'm here because -"

"Don't go any further. For clarity, I have offered you the opportunity to have your legal advisor here, and you have said 'no'. Are you quite sure?"

"Yes, I really -"

Meredith held his finger up. "Then we should caution you. Trump."

Meredith watched Charlesworth as Trump read out the caution. He looked totally bemused and shook his head throughout.

"Why are you cautioning me? I came here with information."

"I know, and that information will hopefully be instrumental in securing a successful arrest. That was a precaution. What is it you want to tell us?"

"A precaution? Why, against what? In case you should turn this on its head, and arrest me?" Charlesworth was incredulous.

Meredith smiled at him. "So sir, the information you wanted to share."

"I saw a snippet of last night's crime programme. I don't remember the name. It was on a catch-up thing this morning after the news."

"*Crimebusters*. Yes, they always do a summary the next morning. It helps reach those who missed the programme." Meredith nodded, his eyebrows raised. "This shows that it works. What information?"

"It's the tin soldiers. I'm here about them."

"What about them?"

"They're mine," Charlesworth announced simply.

Meredith and Trump exchanged glances. They hadn't expected that.

"Yours, sir?" Trump leaned forward. "Are you sure?"

"One hundred per cent sure, yes. They were made by my father and grandfather, and started by my great-grandfather."

Again, Meredith and Trump exchanged glances.

"Well, that's very interesting. I'm going to suspend the interview for a few moments if I may, while DS Trump here collects the soldiers." Meredith made the necessary announcement, and Trump hurried back to the evidence box in the incident room.

"I think we've got him." Trump held up crossed fingers, before he pulled the three small plastic bags from the box.

The rest of the team froze momentarily and watched his retreating back. Dave Rawlings stood up and walked towards the door.

"Sit your arse back down, Dave, all will be revealed soon enough," Seaton called, and returned to his own seat only when Rawlings shrugged and walked back.

In the interview room, Trump lay the soldiers in a row along the table as Meredith recommenced the recording.

Charlesworth leaned forward and peered at them. "May I touch them?"

"You can pick them up, but please don't remove them from the bag."

Meredith watched Charlesworth picked one up, nodding repeatedly as he inspected it. He looked at Meredith.

"Yes, they are mine," Charlesworth confirmed. "I knew they would be. What happens now?"

"You are absolutely positive? They couldn't just be similar?"

"No. They're mine." Charlesworth waved one of the bags at Meredith. "I repainted the face on this one myself. I couldn't be more sure. What I don't understand is their relevance to the girls."

Meredith took the bag from him, and pushed all three bags to one side. Opening the file, he lifted out the photographs and placed them one by one on the table.

"Ellen Rawlings, Gemma Lake, Dana Dwight,"

Meredith named the girl in each photo. Charlesworth leaned forward and he scrutinised the photographs. His heart rate increased as he looked at them, and almost stopped when Meredith asked his next question.

"How did these three girls come to have your tin soldiers?"

Charlesworth's head snapped up, before he looked back down at the photographs. "I don't know. That's why I'm here. I'm guessing whoever stole them must be the man you're after." Charlesworth paused, and ran his fingers through his hair, "Although I'm not sure how it will help."

"Ah yes, your break-in. What else was taken? Please remind me."

"As I told you, simply bits and pieces that's all, but nothing of major value. I didn't know these had gone until weeks after. At the time, I was more concerned about getting the security sorted out."

"If I get a copy of the report filed when police attended your house, will these soldiers be on there?" Meredith nodded at the bags.

"No, like I just said," Charlesworth was becoming increasingly irritated, "I didn't realise at the time. He took my watch, but not my laptop, a box of crystal glasses, but not the TV. These were still in a packing crate. I had several, but none of them looked as though they'd been touched, so I didn't look." He fingered the edges of the photographs. "You say he gave them to these girls? Why?"

"Why don't you tell us?"

"What?"

"Graham Charlesworth, I am arresting you for the abduction of Ellen Rawlings and Gemma Lake, and the assault of Dana Dwight and Harriet Boyles. You have already been cautioned, but to be on the safe side," and Meredith repeated the caution.

"You're wrong! You, stupid, stupid man, I didn't do it." Charlesworth banged the table with the palms of his hands. "Why would I have come here? Why would I have admitted that?"

Meredith and Trump ignored him.

"We'll be arranging a line-up. You won't need to be there since we do them with computers now. That may take a while to organise. Is there anything else you'd like to say before we get you booked in?"

"This is madness. I have an operation this afternoon, it's crucial. Stop this madness now!" Charlesworth had started to stand, and Trump leaned forward and pushed him back down. He looked down at the photographs. Staring at them he said without looking up, "I want a lawyer."

"Do you have a solicitor, sir, or would you like us to call the duty solicitor for you?" Trump smiled at him. There was no warmth there.

"I have my own. Not sure he does criminal stuff though. I used him for something quite different. I'll call him." Charlesworth pulled out his phone, and Meredith held out his hand.

"Sorry, Charlesworth, not allowed."

They took Charlesworth to the custody sergeant and booked him in. His solicitor was called, and the team set about finding a series of lookalikes for the identification parade. Meredith told Rawlings he would sack him on the spot for gross misconduct if he went anywhere near the cells, and Rawlings knew he meant it.

Patsy sat in her car watching the house that the man Lynda believed to be Lyndon Ward had entered the day before. Yesterday, he had stayed in there for two hours without re-emerging, and Patsy had decided to leave him there while she pondered how to approach him. But now, rather than doing as she planned, she had been thinking about Meredith and her proposal, or more accurately the lack of it. Noticing the time, she knew she had to make a definitive move, both with Meredith and Lyndon Ward.

Leaning to pick up her bag, she decided now was the time to confront Mr Ward, and then later, as soon as they got a minute to themselves, she would confront Meredith. She smiled at the thought: tonight, DCI Meredith, will definitely be the night! She climbed out of the car and, still smiling, walked across the road to Ward's house. Pulling her shoulders back, she reached up to ring the doorbell. She gave a shout, as from nowhere a hand knocked her own away from the bell, and she felt a pressure in her back.

"Yes, Ms Hodge, it is a gun. Now turn around, walk back up the path, and climb into the vehicle in front of you."

Patsy was still trying to get over the shock, but she glanced up. Parked at the kerb was a long black saloon with tinted windows. The door was open, the engine running, and a man in a suit beckoned her forward. Her heart pounding, Patsy looked to each side, trying to work out which way to run. The solid object in her back pushed harder.

"Don't be silly. There's no need for anyone to get hurt. We simply need a little chat."

Patsy turned quickly and looked down. As she did so, the man raised his hand. Her eyes confirmed it was a gun before it collided forcibly with her temple. The man caught her expertly and, with his hands under her arms, he half dragged, half carried her to the car. She regained full consciousness while still in the vehicle, but remained still, slumped against the door, listening for any clue as to who had attacked her.

Opening her eyes slightly, she found there were three men in the car. The one who had hit her was in the front passenger seat. He was drumming his fingers on his knee. Nobody spoke. After ten minutes or so the car pulled into an underground car park, and maintaining their silence the three men jumped out of the car. Two of them pulled Patsy from the car. She pretended to be disorientated.

"Who are you?" she groaned. "Why did you hit me?"

She stumbled to one side.

"Don't be silly, Ms Hodge, you've been with us a while. If you are going to pretend to be unconscious or asleep, you must work on your breathing patterns. Now stand up straight. It's the door ahead of you."

The well-spoken man in the suit, who had travelled next to her in the car, pushed her forward. Patsy looked at him. She'd not seen him before, and when she looked at the others who were now some way in front of her, neither of them seemed familiar either.

"I asked who you were." Patsy stopped dead, and the man tutted.

"Ms Hodge, please move forward. I think we've established that there's an easy way and a hard way. To be honest, I haven't got the patience for messing about today. I should also warn you, I am not as light handed as my friend. Shall we?"

He held his arm out towards the door. Despite his pleasant tone, Patsy knew he was serious. She walked forward.

Having gone down a series of corridors, they reached a lift. There was the usual panel of buttons, but with no numbers, and Patsy had no idea what floor had been chosen. The doors opened to reveal a huge, open plan office. The blinds at the tall windows had been angled upward so as to let in light, but make it impossible to see the surrounding area. The furnishing was sparse, and Patsy was taken to a circular table midway down the room. Two of the men sat at the table with her, and she was aware that the third loitered somewhere behind, a little out of her eye line. She had hardly had time to draw breath when the questioning started.

"What's your interest in this man?"

A photograph of Lyndon Ward was slapped on the table.

"A client asked me to locate him."

"Why?"

"Because she believes she is in love with him, and that he is in some sort of danger."

A snort. "In love? Please. I'll ask again, why?"

Patsy turned to her questioner and looked at him quizzically. "Why the derision? She was right about him being in some sort of danger by the look of it."

"Very good, Ms Hodge, well done."

"Who is this woman? Was she used to unsettle him?"

A photograph of Linda entering the bar was slapped on the table.

"What? Don't be ridiculous. She's just an IT geek. She got carried away tracking him down, and when she saw him, she responded as she saw fit."

"An IT geek you say?" The two men exchanged glances.

"Yes, spreadsheets, the internet, websites. I don't know, I don't do IT."

"So, Linda Callow may have been working with this woman."

A photograph of Freda Hawthorne was slapped on the table. It was Patsy's turn to snort.

"Now you really are being ridiculous. I don't know who that woman really is, or what your interest in her is, but Linda is not in any way connected with her. In fact, if she's telling the truth, Freda's not connected in any real way to Lyndon Ward."

The men exchanged glances. The younger of the two nodded at the photograph.

"A client, and you don't know who she is. Explain."

"She told me her name was Freda Hawthorne, and that she been having an online relationship, if she is to be believed, with this man. He told her his name was Lyndon -"

"How do you know DCI John Meredith?"

The man that had been behind her walked forward and placed her bag on the table. He held open a small leather wallet containing her credit cards and driving licence. Patsy looked at the photograph of Meredith with an American woman they had met by chance in Paris. The woman was grinning, her arms wrapped around Meredith's midriff.

"He's my partner. Who are you? How do *you* know Meredith?" Patsy wondered if they were police officers working undercover. "Are you on the force?"

"Not quite. Your partner, you say?" The man closed the wallet and pulled a business card from the pocket of her bag. "As I understand it, Meredith is a serving police officer. Does he know what you are up to?"

"What? I'm not up to anything? I am a private investigator and I was asked to find this man," she tapped the photograph, and her nail left a moon shaped indentation as she lifted it away. "I found him. I'm good at my job, and credit where credit's due, Linda is too He's an online collector of women, vulnerable women." She pulled her shoulders back, and looked the man in the eye. "But then you know that. Or you would if you were any good at your job."

The man pulled out a chair and turned it so he had to straddle it to sit. He rested his arms on the back rest and pursed his lips. There was silence for a few moments.

"What is Meredith's involvement in this?" he asked.

"None. He knows nothing about it, well, only the bit about Linda's meeting with Ward . . . if that's his name. It was an amusing story to tell. Now I'm not saying another word until you tell me who you are, and why I'm here."

The man smiled and shrugged. "Let's start from the beginning. What did she say when she came to see you." He nodded at the photograph of Freda Hawthorne.

CHAPTER FOURTEEN

Meredith lifted the laptop from the passenger seat, and walked to his front door. The rest of the team were on their way to the other witnesses to run the identity parade they had created. At Charlesworth's insistence, his solicitor had agreed that for expediency the witnesses need not come to the station. Meredith was going to see Peggy. He didn't have a second, as he knew that her evidence would probably be rubbished in court due to her circumstances, but at the moment every little would help.

He opened the door and called out. "Hello, Peggy, it's me. I hope you've got some clothes on this time." Hearing movement in the kitchen he dropped his keys on the hall table, and walked forward. "Get the kettle on, we've got work to . . ."

He stopped dead as Nicola smiled at him. His eyes moved to Peggy on the other side of the table. She shrugged, and amusement danced across her face.

"Nicola, to what do I owe the pleasure? This is certainly a surprise I wouldn't have second guessed." He gave Peggy an evil look, and she snorted, dismissing it out of hand. Nicola patted her hand.

"Don't blame Peggy. You didn't answer your phone. I called the station. Tom told me you were on your way here. I knocked in case Patsy or Amanda were at home, and found Peggy. She made me tea."

"And why would Tom Seaton be giving you details of my whereabouts?" He pulled out a chair and sat heavily, placing the laptop on the table.

"Because I told him it was an emergency. I needed to speak to you urgently. Would you like a cup of tea, it's not long made?"

"No, I don't want a bloody cup of tea, and I'll remind you that this is no longer your home, so don't get comfortable, Nicola. What's this emergency?"

He heard Peggy's intake of breath at his comments, and from the corner of his eye saw her fold her arms and lean back against the chair. She was clearly expecting some sort of show. He sighed and turned to her. "Peggy, I think this is a private conversation, why don't you go and watch television for a while."

"I'm in the middle of making a chicken pie. I promised Patsy I would." Peggy waved her hand in the direction of a mixing bowl and various other ingredients arranged along the work surface. "Why don't you go somewhere else and I'll get on."

Nicola raised her eyebrows in amusement as Meredith's head jerked towards Peggy, unable to believe his ears. Peggy simply nodded.

"Go on then, get on with it. Are you sure you don't want tea?"

Meredith bit his lip; he'd deal with Peggy later. Standing he pointed towards the dining room door.

"In there. No, I don't want a cup of tea, and neither does she. This won't take long."

Nicola went into the dining room followed by Meredith, who shot Peggy a 'this is not the last of it' look, before closing the door with a bang.

Peggy got up and stretched her back. She smiled; that wasn't as painful as usual, and she had this lovely drama unfolding. She'd get on and make him a nice pie. He'd forgive her anything once he'd tasted her pie. Walking across the kitchen she stared at the ingredients, forcing the recipe back into her mind, before clattering about in a cupboard containing pots and pans, looking for a suitable dish.

Ignoring the noise from the kitchen, Nicola told Meredith why she had come to see him.

Meredith screwed his eyes closed, and held them shut as he replayed the question in his mind. When he opened them, he leaned forward to look more closely at Nicola.

"That wasn't a serious question, was it?" He shook his head as he spoke, hoping she would do the same. He was disappointed.

"Of course. John, what did you think? I would joke about this?" Nicola huffed and slammed her eyes. "Believe me, I've thought about this long and hard. I know it seems odd, but I think it would work. At least agree to think about it."

Nicola had known that this was going to be a difficult situation, and her hand beat out a tattoo on her chest as she chewed on her bottom lip.

"Work?" Meredith shouted, and then blew out a breath in an attempt to calm himself.

In the kitchen Peggy heard the shout, and was now standing on the other side of the door.

"Of course it wouldn't work." Meredith threw his hands into the air, exasperated, but desperate to keep hold of his temper, he gripped the table and drew in a deep breath. "Nicola, let's start this conversation again. I need a drink, but coffee will do for the moment. Do you want one?"

Meredith needed some space to think. Unable to believe what was happening, he had to take a few moments to compose himself. Peggy shuffled away from the door, and turned back as it opened. Unable to pretend she hadn't heard she smiled softly.

"Shall I make the coffee? You go and have a ciggy and calm down."

"I don't have any."

"Second drawer down over there. I found them while I was hunting for the rolling pin."

Meredith pulled a cigarette from the packet, lit it on the hob, and strode down to the bottom of the garden. It was a beautiful summer's day, and yet a shiver ran up his spine. He smoked the cigarette quickly: he wanted Nicola out of the house. He wanted her long gone before Patsy returned. Flicking the butt into the flower bed he hurried to the kitchen. Peggy held up two steaming mugs. He nodded and took them from her.

Peggy shut the door behind him. She didn't return to her pie, but stood there listening to the remainder of the saga.

Nicola twisted the mug around on the coaster. "Did you love me, John?"

"Yes . . . I . . . What the hell has that got to do with anything?" Meredith reached across the table and took hold of Nicola's hand. "I did love you, very much. There is a part of me that will always love you, you know that."

His eyes glistened as he held her gaze, and Nicola was reminded of all she had lost. She swallowed and looked away as he continued.

"I will never forgive myself for what I put you through, and I will help and support you, whatever happens. But you can't be serious about this."

Nicola raised her chin and took back his gaze. "But I am."

Meredith's grasp on her hand tightened. "Even if I wanted to, which I don't, it's ridiculous, and what about Patsy? Does she have a say in this? What if I said 'yes' and she said 'no'? How did you think that would work?"

He watched Nicola draw in a deep breath, the contours of her breasts straining against the fabric of her shirt, and he suddenly wondered if Patsy had already agreed. Perhaps her agreement was subject to his opinion. Irritated, he shook the thought away.

"You always wanted a child with me. You always wanted a son. I'm giving you my son. It really is as simple as that, John."

Meredith dropped her hand, and pinched the bridge of his nose, his eyes screwed shut. The only way he could interpret that was . . . how? That the child was his? Butterflies launched themselves from the pit of his stomach and danced up into his chest. For a moment, it was difficult to breathe. He ran his fingers through his hair, leaving them resting at the back of his head. His phone rang and he switched it to silent, dropping it onto the table.

"Is the child mine?"

"Would that make a difference?"

"Of course it would make a bloody difference, Nicola, come on!" He banged the side of his head in frustration, and indicating she should think. "I know you've had problems in the past, but how can you not see how stupid that question was?"

"A son is a son, John. If this is going to work, you simply have to want a son. Not take on a burden because once, in a drunken stupor, you managed to not only remember your wife, but impregnate her!" Nicola had raised her voice, and she waved her hand as if attempting to waft the noise away. "I'm sorry, I didn't mean to shout."

"You can shout all you like, as long as it makes sense. Is the boy mine?"

"His name is Paul."

Meredith gritted his teeth. "Is Paul mine?"

He attempted to hold her eyes, but she blinked and looked away.

"I'm not playing this game. I came here to ask you as a decent human being to take in MY son. To bring him up, and to love him, to nurture him and guide him into adulthood, and to do so in the way that a proper father would. Is that so difficult to understand?" Nicola's voice had risen again. "I want you to do this because you want to, not because you feel you have to!"

Nicola let out a frustrated sigh, which she gulped back in as Meredith slammed his fists on the table. Their mugs fell over and he ignored the coffee as it dripped to the floor.

"Get a fucking grip woman! Is the boy mine or not?" Resting his elbow in a pool of coffee, he leaned forward, pointing a shaking finger at her. "I want a DNA test, now! I don't know what fucking game you're playing, or even why, but . . . SHIT!"

He jumped up from the table as the spilt coffee trickled onto his crotch and one of the mugs rolled to the floor and smashed.

Nicola stood and calmly walked out to the kitchen. Stepping past Peggy, she went to the sink and picked up a dish cloth. Returning to the dining room she mopped the table as Meredith stood watching, shaking his head. His heart skipped a beat as he heard the front door open. He crossed his fingers it would be Patsy and not Amanda. He walked into the kitchen and looked into the hall.

"Meredith, you have to . . ." Patsy slowed her pace as she took in his appearance, and saw the thunderous expression on his face. "Is everything all right? Well clearly not, what's going -"

"No, it's not fucking all right. Patsy, come here. Come in here and listen to this."

Assuming it was something to do with Peggy, Patsy walked forward.

"Why, what have I missed? But I have to tell you something first, you need to . . ."

Patsy halted as she looked into the dining room. The normally immaculate Meredith was covered in wet patches, there was a broken mug on the floor, and Nicola was attempting to mop up liquid with a tea-towel. Peggy stood resting against the cooker, her eyes darting from one to the other.

Patsy looked at Meredith. "What's going on?"

"I don't know that I have the words, Patsy, I swear to God I don't. I'll let Nicola enlighten you, because she's doing a shit job with me."

Nicola stood up. Hurrying to the kitchen, she rinsed the cloth under the tap, shot Meredith a withering glance, and made to finish the job she'd started. Patsy held her hand up.

"I think we need to sort whatever is going on now." She held out her hand towards the dining room. "Shall we?" Despite her exterior calm, her mind was racing. She couldn't think of a single thing that would make Meredith react in such a way, unless, of course, it was to do with the baby. She wanted to scream, but first there was the other thing that needed to be dealt with.

"Meredith, I will speak to Nicola but first you have to go and speak to someone. They're waiting in a car outside." Patsy gritted her teeth as Meredith looked at her as though she were speaking in a foreign language. "Just do it, Meredith," she added quietly.

"Speak to whom? I'm supposed to be working with her." He jabbed an accusing finger at Peggy. "Who is it, Patsy? Stop playing games, or has everyone gone fucking mad today?"

Patsy walked forwards and pushed him in the chest with the flat of her hands. For the first time since he'd met her, she looked as though she was on the point of meltdown. His eyes flicked to Nicola and back again. Was it him? Did he attract volatile women?

Patsy pushed him again to get his attention. "I have been picked up off the street, knocked out," she held up her hair to reveal the small egg-shaped lump, "and questioned about something I know nothing about, for four hours. FOUR HOURS Meredith, and by men I don't know." She gave a flat laugh. "But they know you. So you get your arse out there, and tell them that whoever they think I am, I'm not." She dropped her hands to her side, and her features softened as she looked into his eyes. "Please. I'll speak to Nicola."

Without a further word, Meredith turned and walked into the hall. As he opened the door he heard Nicola's voice.

"Patsy, come here. You need a hug, you poor thing. I'm sure I'm the last thing you need. Peggy, you'd better get that kettle back on."

Disconcerted, he frowned as he started up the path, his eyes searching for the mysterious men with whom he had to speak. Nicola wanted to hug Patsy? Had the world really gone mad? The rear door of a car opened and, stooping, he peered in. Recognising the occupant, he groaned. The world *had* gone mad. What the hell had Patsy been up to?

"Meredith, nice to see you again. Hop in, we're going for a little drive."

The car pulled away, and inside the house the three women finished clearing up, and took their drinks through to the sitting room. Patsy sat on the sofa next to Peggy, who patted her leg protectively. Unsure whether or not she really wanted to know, she turned to Nicola.

"Nicola, I'd say it was nice to see you, but I'm guessing it's not. I saw I had a missed call from you. Why don't you tell me why you're here?"

Louie Trump walked back into the incident room, his hands shoved deep into his pockets. He looked at Tom Seaton.

"Any word from DCI Meredith? He's not going to be happy. The ACC has been on; Charlesworth has been released on bail. But give the man his due, he says he's going straight to the hospital to perform that operation. I hope he can do that under pressure. A child with a hole in the heart apparently."

"Not a word, but then I'm not surprised. Something's going on. I think wherever he is, he's in deep shit. Patsy's been trying to get hold of him too."

"What do you mean 'too'?" Trump took a doughnut from the bag on Seaton's desk and bit into it, as he stared at the photographs pinned to the board in front of them. He pointed at them with the doughnut. "Meredith's right, you know. There will be a connection. But now Charlesworth has been bailed we can't question him as to what."

Rawlings walked across and also took a doughnut.

"I reckon it's got something to do with their appearance. They're all dark haired, brown eyed, and the same age. He wasn't interested in my Ellen, thank God. He said he was going to release her. Why was that? I reckon it was because she was blonde and blue eyed." He shook his head. "It's like he's looking for a type, don't you think? I almost think we should warn all parents of girls that look like this. Although if it is Charlesworth, he wouldn't be stupid enough to do anything now. We have some breathing space." Rawlings bit into the doughnut. "Who else wanted the Governor" He turned to look at Seaton.

"Nicola. She said it was urgent, and she sounded quite desperate." Seaton shrugged. "I've known her for years, what could I do? I told her he was on his way home."

Rawlings coughed and particles of doughnut flew from his mouth. "I don't want to be in your shoes when he gets . . . hang on."

He pulled the ringing phone from his pocket, and listened to his wife talk excitedly. Eventually he managed to interrupt her.

"We don't know it's him, love, calm down, we've had to let him walk. Nothing's certain yet. I'll call you later." Hanging up, he turned to his colleagues. "Now he really will be unbearable. Eve's just heard we've arrested someone on the local radio. I bet the press are forming a queue as we speak."

"There was no one there when I saw Charlesworth and his brief out," Trump observed, and as if tempting fate the telephone rang. Trump had a brief conversation with the duty sergeant. He sighed as he hung up. "Spoke too soon. The chaps downstairs want to know if there's anyone going to make a statement, so they can get rid of them."

Seaton picked up the handset. "You go and see Alison, I'll try and track down the Gov. Something tells me this is going to be a very long and tedious day."

Rawlings put the remainder of his doughnut in his mouth. "Much like any other then. Nothing changes."

Not wanting to go home until he was sure that Nicola had gone, he asked to be dropped off in the city centre. He needed to walk, and he certainly needed to think. He thanked the driver as he pulled up in a bus lane. His companion in the back called to him as he made to shut the door.

"It was nice seeing you again, Meredith, thanks for your help. I'll wait to hear from Ms Hodge." He gave a knowing smile. "You're a lucky man, but I'm sure you know that. On a totally separate note, we might need your help with something else. Early days yet, but expect a call."

Meredith nodded and slammed the door. The last thing he needed in his now very complicated life was to be working with spooks, although he had to admit they seemed nice blokes, if you ignored what they'd done to Patsy, and it would certainly make a change. He ran his hand over his face. How could he even think about taking something new on? He needed to get Charlesworth banged up first.

He loosened his tie, and then, shoving his hands in his pockets, he walked the circuit of Queen Square, as he considered the many issues he had to solve. Then he walked it again, weaving in and out the trees that lined the grassed area. Eventually his stomach told him to move on, and he went in search of a café. As he walked into King Street, he remembered that the Old Duke pub did a good lunch. He could have a pint while he was at it, and wasted no time in going there and placing his order. Carrying the plate and his drink out into the sunshine, he sat at one of the benches and finished both quickly, vaguely aware of the conversation taking place behind him.

"She said that Jeremy Carmichael comes here sometimes, but it doesn't look like we're going to be in luck today. Mind you, he looks all right, if a bit miserable."

Meredith realised the women were looking at him, and he turned to them. "Jeremy Carmichael is a wanker, and I'm taken. Enjoy your drinks."

He stood and walked back towards the Old Vic. Slowing, he considered the façade. It was a good building, and they'd spent a fortune renovating it. As one of Bristol's claims to fame, being the longest continuously running theatre in the UK, he supposed it was worth it. He blinked, wondering how he knew that fact since he had no interest in the theatre at all. On a whim, he climbed the steps and pulled open the large glass door. He wandered around the foyer aimlessly until a uniformed usher approached him.

"May I help you with anything, sir?" Meredith looked at him blankly for a moment. Did he have a son or not? "Sir?"

The usher peered at Meredith, wondering if he was quite all right. Meredith blinked and put his hand into his pocket and pulled out his ID.

"Is Jeremy Carmichael here? I'd like a word."

The usher looked suitably shocked, and hurried away to find out. A few minutes later Meredith assured the usher he could read as he looked down the long corridor he'd been shown to. The names of each room's occupant was written on inserts on the door. He walked slowly, glancing at the signs as the usher hurried away in the opposite direction. He knew which Carmichael's room was before he reached it. The sound of raised voices caused him to increase his pace. He leaned against the wall outside, listening to the exchange.

"You total bastard!" A woman shouted. "What, to take up my role as your skivvy? To pretend that I could ever take her place? You are deluded. I'm going, Jeremy, and I won't be back!"

"But, Beth darling, I love you, I've always loved you. I simply forget to show you sometimes. The pressures of this job cloud my judgement. Please come back. I'll even marry you, if that's what you want. I never married her."

"*Even* marry me. What, lower yourself to such a thing, how could you? Even if you did, then what? I sit at home while you're out trying to bed every woman who crosses the stage with you. Forget it, Jeremy, let it go, and let go of my arm. You hit me again and I'll call the police. I'll press charges, I swear."

Her voice dropped and she thanked him curtly. He'd obviously let go of her.

"Please," Carmichael's voice was soft.

He pleaded with her, and it sounded to Meredith like he meant every word.

"I love you. I do. We'll marry and have a family, move abroad. I'll turn my back on all this and we'll start again. I have enough money, I don't need to work. I want to settle down, Beth. There is nothing I'd like more than to have a family with you."

"You spiteful bastard!" Beth spat the words. "You know I can't have children, and you know why, and you say that? What's wrong with you? Did you forget, or simply mix me up with another of your lady friends?"

"Of course not." There was a movement from inside. "I'm on one knee, Beth. Perhaps we could adopt, we could make our own family."

Meredith raised his eyebrows as Beth laughed manically on the other side of the door.

"You're too old to adopt! You're not Brad Pitt, Jeremy. Not by a long chalk. I don't know what's going on in your head, but no. No, no, no, no, NO! Making this shit up will not get me back."

Meredith saw the handle move and stepped back. There was a crash as something was knocked over inside, and he stepped forward again. His hand outstretched, reaching for the handle, he stopped as something banged against the door. Had he been on the other side of it, he would have seen Carmichael pinning Beth up against the door, his face contorted with anger.

"You stupid bitch. You have no idea what you're walking away from." He laughed a bitter laugh. "And do you know what? You're right. You will never EVER be as good as her. But you'll be back, you always are. You'd better hope it's not too late, because I will get what I want, and you'll all be sorry."

As Meredith wondered what had happened to Carmichael's description of the sensitive Beth as someone who didn't like thugs, the door opened a little as Carmichael released her. Beth reached behind her to find the handle. Pulling the door open, she stepped into the corridor, still looking in at him. Beth raised her hand and pointed at him, her shaking body causing it to jerk about.

"I will never come back," her voice was hoarse, "and you know what, I might just write my own memoir. But I'll tell you this, and you should listen carefully: if you ever come near me again, I swear I will kill you, and do you know what? I won't be sorry, not for a second."

Reaching forward she grabbed the door handle and shut the door, not willing to look at him for a second longer. Drawing in a deep, shuddering breath, she swallowed, and drew her shoulders back. She turned to walk away, and narrowly missed bumping into Meredith.

"Sorry," she mumbled, and hurried away up the corridor.

Meredith watched her go, hoping she would be true to her word and not go back to Carmichael. Meredith had been in a painful relationship for far too long; those never did anyone any good. His head fell forward as Nicola and her proposal re-entered his brain. Unsure how long he had been standing there, Meredith lifted his head and turned to look at the door. Stepping closer, he reached out his hand and knocked.

"Come," Carmichael's voice boomed out, and Meredith rolled his eyes and walked into the well-appointed room. Carmichael, had calmed himself, but was momentarily taken aback as he recognised Meredith, and he watched as Meredith surveyed the room. When Meredith finally looked at him, he gestured to a chair with the flick of his hand. "Take a seat, and tell me how I can help you?"

"Mainly by behaving yourself."

"I beg your pardon!" Jeremy Carmichael puffed out his chest, and his eyes narrowed. "I know we met in unfortunate circumstances DCI Meredith, but I really don't believe that attitude is necessary."

Meredith sighed. From what he'd heard, he wouldn't like the man if he knew him, but he didn't want any further antagonism today. He simply needed to focus on anything that took his mind away from the fact he might have a son. He stared at the collage of photographs arranged in a large frame. They were all snapshots from Carmichael's life. They were mainly of Carmichael on stage, some with very beautiful women, including Beth. But there was one exception. It was an old black and white shot of the actor James Cagney.

Carmichael watched him frowning, wondering if the man was ever going to speak. He coughed and Meredith blinked, and pointed at the photograph.

"James Cagney, or Jimmy as my grandmother called him. Before my time, but she made me watch *Angels with Dirty Faces* many times." Meredith smiled at the memory of his grandmother, and wondered what she would make of the current predicament in which he found himself.

"Yes, before my time too, but I took the lead in *Yankee Doodle Dandy*, kicked off my career actually, so I studied him for a while. I'd give you my impression of 'you dirty rat', but I think I'll save that for another time."

Meredith continued to stare at the photographs. Unable to contain his pride, and shelving his curiosity for a moment, Carmichael leaned forward and gave a running commentary, pointing to each one as he went. Meredith allowed him to drone on, nodding occasionally.

And this was when I played Fagin to great acclaim. I was far too young for the role but they can do wonders with makeup. That led me to my hit television series, *Green Street*. Here I am with Jane Peterson. We played Charlie and Georgia Benson for over ten years. I still get recognised from it. Finally, the love of my life," he put his fingers to his lips, "but don't tell the ladies. Poor Izzy. Such a loss."

Meredith frowned. He assumed this was the 'she' they had been arguing about. He tutted as he looked at her and another fact escaped him, refusing to surface. Needing space to think, he turned to Carmichael and forced a smile, wanting to wrap this thing up.

"I don't know you, Mr Carmichael, and I was happy to assume our meeting the other night was a one off." Meredith pursed his lips. "But I'm hearing that's not the case. You've been using your skills for quite another purpose." Meredith held Carmichael's eyes, and knew Patsy had been right. The colour had drained from Carmichael's face, and his body twitched as he fought to maintain his composure. Meredith nodded. "I think you know what we're talking about." Meredith leaned back as Carmichael threw his hands into the air theatrically.

"I do not, sir. Perhaps you would like to enlighten me." Carmichael got to his feet and walked to a cabinet on top of which sat a silver tray. The tray contained two crystal brandy bowls and an expensive bottle of brandy. His hand shook as he poured a large measure.

"Thank you, I'll join you." Meredith held out his hand, and a perturbed Carmichael handed him the glass before pouring a second. Meredith knocked it back, and closed his eyes as the liquid slid down his throat.

Handing back the empty glass he got to his feet. "You've been playing silly buggers with Antonio Garcia, I hear. It's clear to me that whatever you had with Beth Durham is over. Done. Finished." Meredith felt the need to emphasise. "You leave them both alone, and I won't be arresting you. But heed my warning, Carmichael, I don't like bullies, and if I hear one word to the contrary I'll call the press to watch while I arrest you."

Meredith walked to the door satisfied. Carmichael relaxed, and regained the ability to both speak and move. He rushed forward and pulled open the door.

"You have my word. I wish you the best of luck with your case, by the way. I heard they've let the doctor go."

Meredith spun round to face him. Carmichael stepped back, a look of fear on his face.

"What did you say?" Meredith demanded. His day was going from bad to worse, and he hoped he could resist the urge to punch Carmichael.

Carmichael pointed at the radio. "It was on the news. They released the man you arrested for abducting the girls, and you were unavailable for comment."

Meredith left Carmichael still pointing at the radio as he ran out of the theatre and jumped into the first available taxi. Once at the station, he barged past people on the stairs, and the door to the incident room banged against the wall as he demanded, "Would someone like to tell me what's been going on?"

Rawlings coughed, and as Meredith passed him on the way to front of the room, he mimicked drinking, indicating that Meredith had been imbibing. Seaton and Trump exchanged glances, and looked at their boss. Meredith looked rough.

His tie was askew, his trousers stained, and his face was a permanent frown. If he was drunk, he was fighting drunk.

Jo appeared from the kitchen carrying a tray of mugs. "Hello, Gov, where have you been? Do you want a coffee?" she asked lightly.

"No, I don't want a coffee. I want someone to tell me what the hell has been happening. I've only been gone a couple of hours . . . Trump, Seaton? Anyone?"

"No one identified him, sir." Trump announced simply. "The ACC got involved, his boss Professor Cole vouched for him, and he was released. Not least because he had an operation booked on a toddler with a hole in his heart." Trump glanced at the clock. "He's probably in theatre as we speak."

"Or on a fucking plane out of the country." Meredith ran his fingers through his hair. Perching on the edge of a desk, he asked. "Who didn't identify him? How can that be?"

"They all pretty much said the same. It looked like the man, but they couldn't swear it was him. What did Peggy say?"

"Let me worry about Peggy. How can they ID the e-fit, but not him? Someone explain please."

That statement told them that whatever else had gone on in his home, running through the mug shots had not been one of them. Seaton looked pointedly at the stain on Meredith's trousers.

"Is everything all right, Gov." His look said more than his words. Meredith gave him a curt nod, and Seaton accepted that. "We don't know how it can be. Look." Seaton walked to the incident board where Charlesworth's photo was pinned next to the e-fit. He pointed at it as he spoke. "Face the same shape, hair the same style, same skin tone, same colour eyes. BUT they say the e-fit is a better likeness. I'm buggered if I can answer you, Gov. We may have this wrong."

"Did you hear the interview? Did you hear what he said? Of course we're not wrong." Meredith stared at the stain on the carpet by his foot, and tried to rub it away. He knew until he'd sorted this thing with Nicola, he'd be useless. He made a decision. "I'm going home. I've got some stuff that needs sorting."

The flurry of head movement as his team looked from one to the other wasn't lost on him. He knew he'd made the right decision. "You lot take his life apart. He's only been here eight months. I want to know where he's been on every day of that eight months." He jabbed his finger in the air. "And check out this burglary. He says most of his stuff was in boxes at the time, as he'd not totally unpacked.

That was only six months ago. Where had he been up to that point?" He stood up and gave a sigh that came from the heart. "I have to go, I'll see you in the morning."

The team remained quiet as he left the room. He heard the talking begin the minute the door closed behind him. Realising he didn't have a car, he turned back and a guilty silence fell.

He grinned briefly: he loved catching them out. "Can someone give me a lift please?"

Patsy was sitting on the end of the stairs, speaking to someone on her mobile when he opened the door. She looked up and smiled a smile that said 'thank God you're here, I wanted you to be here'. His shoulders sagged with relief, and some of the tension left him. He leaned down and kissed her on the forehead tenderly. Patsy concluded her conversation.

"Yes, Meredith has just come home, so I should say no more. Don't let Linda do anything but the accounts, and send that off for me. A couple of days, I'm not sure, I'll call you. Thanks, Sharon, bye."

Meredith held out his arms, and she stood and was pulled into a bear hug.

"You know I love you, don't you?" he whispered into her hair.

"Of course, and you know that's returned tenfold. I've been so worried. Where have you been? Once Nicola had gone I realised how long it had been."

She felt him stiffen at the mention of Nicola. She looked up into his eyes.

"We need to talk."

"No, we need to go to bed, we can talk later. I -"

Meredith stopped as a cough from the kitchen interrupted him.

"Are we still eating now or not? I can dish up and cover yours if you like. What time does Amanda get in?"

Meredith's head fell forward and rested on Patsy's: he'd forgotten about Peggy. Patsy shrugged him off.

"We'll eat with you now, Peggy. There's plenty of time for talking later. As for Amanda, she's due when she arrives." She patted Meredith's shoulder. "Go and have a quick shower, you look like you need it."

Twenty minutes later they were sat around the table eating what Meredith described as a surprisingly scrumptious meal, but the conversation was stilted with so much being unsaid. Eventually, Peggy put her knife and fork down, and looked one to the other.

"Patsy, tell him about the baby, it's no use putting it off, and he'll be here first thing, now that her Nanny's gone."

Meredith literally choked on his wine, and sat coughing violently into his napkin whilst Peggy patted him on the back.

"He'll what?" he managed to ask as he gasped for breath.

Patsy waved her fist at Peggy.

"I'm going to tell you this quickly. Don't interrupt, just listen. If you're good I can answer questions at the end." She attempted humour, but Meredith was clearly not amused.

Patsy twisted the napkin in her hands as she told him that Nicola was about to undergo a major operation. Nicola had a tumour on her brain, and her hurry in trying to find someone to take responsibility for Paul reflected the chances of success. For the operation itself, there was a healthy ninety-five per cent of survival, but with regards to it causing brain damage, the odds were lowered to fifty per cent. Assuming Nicola survived, undamaged, it then had to be established whether it was cancerous. The surgeons already knew they couldn't remove the whole tumour, and therefore if it was cancerous the long-term prognosis was bleak. Nicola had a substantial insurance policy, so Paul would be well looked after in that respect, but with no immediate family to rely on, she was now trying to find someone to act as guardian for the child. Someone she could trust and someone who would love Paul.

Antonio Garcia was a decent man, and very family orientated, she had believed he would do right by Paul. But his refusal, and the fact that time was running out, had caused her to turn to Meredith. Patsy had agreed to take Paul, and to help sort his future out if that became necessary. She'd spoken to Amanda, who had readily agreed, and, she added with a smile, even Peggy had volunteered to help.

Meredith was speechless. He stared at her, his features set. For once, Patsy was unable to second guess his thoughts. She and Peggy watched silently as he poured himself another drink, and emptied the glass. Finally, he sank down in his chair and closed his eyes. He pinched the bridge of his nose as he considered the possible ramifications of Patsy's actions, and willed himself not to consider the possibility of Nicola dying. Eventually his hand dropped to the table, and he opened his eyes, remaining where he was but now staring at the ceiling.

"What happens if she doesn't make it? What happens then?"

"Then we have to do what's best for Paul. We have to believe this will work out for the best though, we have to for his sake." Patsy's voice cracked. "Meredith, I'm going to do this for her, with or without you, but I think we'd be better together. Life is far too short for any more regrets, Meredith."

She watched his pull himself upright.

He turned to face her, and smiled. "If she'd have told me the truth, I would be saying the same to you." His pride in her decision radiated from his gaze. He cleared his throat. "What if he's mine, Patsy? She wouldn't say, she wouldn't give me a straight answer. That may be because she doesn't know, and God knows I can't remember, but it could be because she wanted me to take him for the right reason, not because I felt obligated." He pursed his lips. "There is a chance, you know that, and I will find out, I have to."

Patsy stood and walked to him. Taking his face in her hands she kissed him, before sitting in his lap. His arms wrapped around her, and he hugged her close.

"How the hell are we going to cope with a baby?" he murmured into her hair.

"I don't know, but I've taken a couple of days off. Sharon knows what's going on."

"Well, that's that sorted then."

Then he laughed, and she joined him. It was only when Peggy gave a shuddering sob that they remembered she was in the room. They turned to face her. She wiped the tears away with her fingers, and sniffing loudly, she wiped her nose on the back of her hand. She shook her head at them.

"And this is why you're better off on your own. All this high drama and tension, it's enough to make you sick. When you two have finished canoodling over there, I'll have some pudding." She sniffed again. "And you can clear the table, Merriwinkle. I'm a modern woman, I don't wait on men."

Meredith turned over and looked at Patsy.

"I need you, Hodge."

"I know, Meredith, I noticed." She kissed her finger and placed it on his lips. "I need you too."

"Come here and I'll update you on what else happened today." Patsy turned over and he pulled her to him. "Where shall I start, with the idiot public or the spooks?"

He smiled as Patsy tried to turn to face him, and he held her where she was.

"Spooks? You didn't think to mention them? Is that who they were? What did they want with me, and what have Lyndon and or Freda been up to?" Patsy's hand flew to her mouth. "What about Linda? You did tell them that Linda is an innocent in all this, didn't you?"

"I did, but you'll have to stop her meeting nuclear scientists with a price on their heads."

"What?"

"It's a long story. Years ago, he made some discovery, top secret and all that. But thought he was hard- done by, so he was going to sell out. His wife found out and talked him out of it, but whoever was expecting him to come and work for them weren't best pleased, and put a contract out on him. He's been moved about whilst he works on whatever it is for us. His wife couldn't cope and walked out, so he took to the internet."

"Ah, Freda was right."

"Yes, but Freda was never going to be the one. She was an active anti-nuclear protester in the eighties, lived in one of those camps at Greenham Common. It was them that put the end to their relationship, not him. Linda took a different tack and chatted to him about health foods and the like, then of course she caused her little stir, and the proverbial hit the fan, with him insisting on being moved. Then you turn up. They'd only had time to establish that you were a private investigator working for an anti-nuclear bod. They hadn't sussed that you were sensible and living with a pillar of the community at that point. They send their apologies, by the way."

"So they bloody should. I'm still in pain."

"You don't want to work for them then?"

"Doing what?"

"I don't know, it was a need-to-know thing. I said you'd call if you were interested."

"What?" This time Patsy managed to turn. "Are you being serious?"

"Not really, but sort of," Meredith kissed her. "They are getting in touch with Chris though. They need some stuff sorted and if it goes tits up, it will be better that it's Joe Public getting it wrong. They'll remain untouchable. I told them he'd probably do it, he'll enjoy the drama, although whether he'll be able to keep it a secret from Sharon is doubtful."

"You're telling me, that Her Majesty's Secret Service needs help, that James Bond needs to hire a private eye? You couldn't make this stuff up. What else did they have to say?"

"Not a lot, they're a tight-lipped bunch."

Meredith turned her back over and blew on the back of her neck. He wasn't going to tell her they may also have use for him, as that would simply worry her. There was no point. After all, they had quite enough on their plates at the moment, and if he was going to become a new dad at his age, then he'd probably refuse. Probably. He kissed the back of her head.

"Go to sleep. If there's going to be a baby in the house, we're going to need it."

"Everything will be all right Meredith, you know that, don't you? And if things don't go right, and he's not yours, well, we could adopt him. I don't know why, but I feel responsible in some way. How weird is that?"

"Very, go to sleep." Meredith didn't want to talk.

A cog had fallen into place, and he needed to think it through.

CHAPTER FIFTEEN

Despite his urgent need to be at work, and further explore his thoughts of the night before, Meredith waited for Nicola to arrive. For all he knew, it might be the last time he spoke to her, and despite an overwhelming desire to be standing anywhere but in his hall opening the door to her, he knew he needed to say goodbye. He swallowed as he took the car seat from her and looked at the child who might be his son. The baby gurgled and attempted a smile. He had his mother's eyes, and the shape of his mouth was the same.

"He's a handsome chap, Nicola."

Meredith looked away from Paul, and forced his eyes to reach Nicola's. He was taken aback. Nicola looked beautiful, her makeup subtle, her demeanour almost serene as she smiled agreement and stepped over the threshold.

"I know. Thank you for doing this, John, I can't tell you how . . ."

She stopped when Meredith put his free hand on her arm.

"Nicola don't, just don't. It's unnecessary and will make me feel more of a bastard than I do already." He lowered his voice. "You should have said."

Peggy, who was moving more freely now, came down the hall. "Be that as it may, but let's get this little fellow in, and get the day started. It's like we've all been in limbo here." She rolled her eyes at Nicola.

Nicola smiled and followed Meredith into the kitchen. He deposited Paul on the kitchen table, and turned to her.

"Rest of the stuff in the car, is it? Give me the keys and I'll go and bring it in."

As he hurried away, the knot in his stomach tightening all the while, Patsy came downstairs. She watched him disappear. Walking into the kitchen she smiled as Nicola lifted the child from the chair and held him close.

"Do you want a moment?" she asked softly.

"No." Nicola cleared her throat. "I've done all the goodbyes. We're ready, aren't we poppet?" She kissed the child's cheek, leaving a lipstick imprint behind.

"Thank you, Patsy, I hope dropping me off isn't going to eat into your day. I can always call a taxi."

"Meredith's taking you. He thought it best." Patsy squeezed Nicola's arm. "He needs to do this."

"Oh, right, okay."

Patsy wasn't sure if Nicola was shocked or nervous, and decided probably a bit of both. They both turned when Meredith called from the hall, letting them know that he'd brought everything in.

"Here, take him a moment."

Patsy took Paul and Nicola hurried into the hall. She ignored Meredith, and returned with a brightly coloured baby bag. She pulled a large envelope out of the side pocket.

"All the things for his immediate needs are in here." She patted the bag, and then waved the envelope. "In here are instructions, I suppose, but most of it is common sense. There's also a key to my house. Anything I may have forgotten is there. I've transferred some money to Meredith's account for immediate expenses, and the rest of my papers . . ." she faltered momentarily, "are in the box at the bottom of my wardrobe." She blinked rapidly. "I think that's the lot." Looking up at the clock, she nodded her head. "I'd better get a move on. They wanted me in last night really."

Taking her son's face gently in her hands, she kissed his forehead. Her eyes expressed all the words she couldn't utter and, wrapping her arms around both Patsy and her son, she hugged them tight. Her eyes screwed shut holding back the tears. Peggy sniffed as Meredith drummed his fingers on the hall table and she released them.

"Right I'm off. Good luck."

Nicola turned away and walked quickly towards Meredith. She pointed at a small red case. "That one's mine."

Meredith nodded, picked it up, and followed her to his car. He waited until they were out of the street before he spoke.

"You should have told me, not yesterday, ages ago, when you first knew. I'd have helped. As it is, now I can't find the words." His hand left the steering wheel and he held it out. She took it and gave it a squeeze.

"There aren't enough words in the world for us, John. Who knows why? What I do know now, is that there is nothing, absolutely nothing in this world that is certain."

She squeezed his hand again before taking hers away. "All I can do is deal with a day at a time, quite literally too," her laugh was hollow, "but you, on the other hand, will soon be able to make plans. In a day or so, you'll know what to include."

They made the rest of the journey in silence. Meredith insisted on seeing her up to the ward, and her arrival kicked off a flurry of activity. The first operation on the surgeon's list had been cancelled and she had moved to the top. This time Meredith stood on the other side of the screen as the nurses prepared her. He listened to them checking that she hadn't eaten anything, removing her makeup and putting her in a hospital gown. In minutes the curtain was pulled back and Nicola looked up at Meredith. She looked childlike with no makeup, and her large eyes were filled with fear.

"Goodbye, John, thanks for bringing me in." She forced a smile.

Meredith swallowed and shook his head. "You don't get rid of me that easily." He walked forward, "Shove up."

Nicola shuffled across the bed and Meredith climbed on. Stretching his legs out he crossed them at the ankle, and pushed her forwards so he could put his arm around her. She snuggled into his chest.

"I'll be here until you go in."

They stayed that way until a porter appeared with a nurse at the end of the bed.

"Time to go, Mrs Meredith, your husband can walk down with us."

As they pushed Nicola through the final doors and towards the operating theatre, she raised her hand in a wave. He called goodbye, wondering if it would be the last time.

He was lost in thoughts of the past as he made his way back to the car park. Professor Cole had called his name three times before he heard her. She was breathless from her efforts to catch up.

"I thought you were ignoring me for a moment, Meredith."

"No, not at all, Dr Rose, I was miles away." His smile was gentle. "What can I do for you anyway?"

"It's Graham, I really must try and convince you that's it's not him." She placed her hand on Meredith's arm. "Truly it's not. It's no more him than it is me. How can I make you see that?"

Meredith sighed and patted her hand which still rested on his arm. "By telling me who did it, if it wasn't him. I have no idea what he's up to, but I will find out. I'm sorry, Dr Rose, but the man who gave those tin soldiers to the girls told them their history. When I interviewed Charlesworth, he repeated that."

He shrugged. "I have to say I'm struggling with why he would do that; it is the thing that's pinning this to him, apart from the likeness to the e-fit." He pursed his lips and gave another sigh. "The only thing that I can come up with is that it's a double bluff. Get all the incriminating links ironed out now, and, let's face it, it's working. He's out on bail. That never should have happened, not until the connection was explained. He clearly has friends in high places."

Professor Cole sighed. "What, me? No, Meredith, I'm sorry, I think you are blinkered. What are you going to do now? Because I must implore you not to hound him, it might affect his work . . . Have you got a minute?"

"Afraid not." Meredith shook his head. "I should be working on why these particular girls are being taken. There is a reason, and once I have that, I'll have my man."

"Less than five minutes, please."

Meredith shrugged. She was a dedicated old girl, and today, with everything else he was struggling with, he didn't have the will to resist. "Come on then, hurry up."

Professor Cole led him straight to a children's ward, and walked him up the centre aisle.

"Six beds, Meredith, five of them containing children who wouldn't be here if not for Graham." She stopped at the furthest bed, and a sickly-looking boy, aged no more than eight, smiled at her.

"I ate all my breakfast, Dr Rose." There was an unmistakeable pride in his voice.

"I should think so too, Ben. Well done. How's the pain this morning?"

The boy shrugged. "It's okay, my meds are due soon."

Meredith's eyes widened; it seemed such a grown-up statement to make. Professor Cole pulled some gloves from a box on the cabinet next to the bed and put them on.

"Sit up a little, that's right. Let me take a little peep." She helped the boy sit upright and lifted a large dressing on his back. "Well, that all looks splendid I must say. We'll have you home in no time."

With practised movements, she replaced the dressing, rearranged the pillows, and settled the boy back down. Dropping the gloves in a bin, she said goodbye, and took Meredith's arm.

"Running on one kidney now, and Graham did that. Ben was near death when he arrived." She returned the wave of a girl in the bed nearest the door. "I'm sure you don't want me to tell you what he did for all these patients, but I promise you, without his skill they wouldn't have survived."

"I do understand that, but the evidence has to be explained. I can't work on the basis that just because he does good things during his day job, he couldn't possibly do bad things when he's off duty." Meredith stopped walking and turned to face her. "I really must go. If I do my job properly, then we'll know."

Professor Cole tapped him lightly on the chest. "I can only reiterate that it is not Graham. He lost his own child, and has dedicated his life to saving others. It is not possible it's him. Go and do your job Meredith, and do it well."

As Meredith hurried away to his car, he couldn't help but agree with the logic of that statement, but his experience showed that all too frequently heinous crimes were committed by people who friends, family, and neighbours would never have thought them capable of such acts. He needed to find the link, and he thought he knew where to start.

When he walked into the incident room, everyone to a man glanced at him before continuing with whatever they had been working on. He pursed his lips: something was afoot, and he didn't want to play games today. Seaton was on his feet and walking towards him. He glanced at the clock as he reached him. It was ten thirty.

"Afternoon, Gov, didn't know you would be late today. Has something happened?"

Meredith shook his head. "Very droll. I had some things to sort out, personal things, because contrary to popular belief, I do have a private life."

"Yes, so I hear."

Meredith's eyes narrowed. The grapevine was working particularly effectively today. He looked over Seaton's shoulder. Trump kept his head down.

"Loopy's spreading the news I see, or actually you are. I doubt she's been in to update this lot."

Trump felt heat rise up his neck, as Meredith walked to the front of the room and perched in his usual spot and faced them. He clapped his hands to get their attention from habit. It wasn't necessary – they all wanted to hear the gossip from the horse's mouth.

"First, to put an end to speculation and to ensure you do what you're paid to do and not worry about me, Nicola is having an operation and Patsy has volunteered to look after her baby. He's installed in my house, and I'm likely to lose sleep, so apologies in advance if I appear grouchy over the next week or so."

There were a few snorts, and Rawlings observed, "Think I might book some holiday if you're going to be more grouchy than usual."

Meredith ignored him. "And so to work. With Charlesworth on bail, we need more evidence to enable us to question him further, and we have to find what links these girls. I think, genius that I am, that I'm about to tell you. Once we've established that I'm correct, and that will take minutes, we have to work out why that is of relevance to Charlesworth."

Meredith had their full attention, and turned to the photographs of the girls. He picked up a pen and started with Ellen Rawlings. Beneath her photograph, he wrote 'No Interest'. He moved to Gemma Lake and drew a question mark, then moving to Dana Dwight and Harriet Boyles, he wrote 'Adopted'. There were a couple of murmurs and he nodded.

"That's right. Our man is looking for a specific girl. She won't be blonde," he pointed to Ellen, "but she will be around seven years of age, and she will be adopted, I believe. So, who is he? The father, I'm guessing. Perhaps he's found out his child was given up for adoption, and he wants her back."

Meredith waved the pen at them. "But most importantly, how does he know who to target? Rules on adoption and the secrecy surrounding them are tough. How did he get the names? Trump, I want you to find out where Charlesworth was living seven to eight years ago, and if he visited the UK and if so, where he was. What was he doing then? Seaton and Rawlings, I want you to find out who, if anyone, has been in contact with the adoption agency: if there are private ones, legal or otherwise, and if so who's been asking questions. Jo, I need you to go and visit the Lakes and get confirmation that Gemma was adopted, unless Dave can enlighten us."

Meredith watched Rawlings shake his head.

"Don't know, Gov. I've known Gemma since she was about eighteen months old, but they've never mentioned that she was adopted. I haven't a clue."

"Okay, well, assuming I'm right, and I know I am, the good news is, he was telling the truth: he's not going to hurt them in any way. The bad news, on the other hand, is once he's found who he's looking for, if he can he'll take her, and as sure as eggs is eggs, he'll have a plan to get out of the country. We have to be quick. We have to find out what other girls of that age have been adopted and are living in Bristol. Then we have to warn the parents. Seaton?"

Meredith looked at Seaton who had raised a finger.

"He must have seen the child, or a photograph of her, at some stage? Whoever this was has definitely seen the child. If not, how would he know the hair colour? If he was targeting all adopted girls of that age, I could go with the theory that somehow he found out seven years or so on. But irrespective of the parents' hair colouring, sometimes you get oddities. Take my sister, she's blonde, her husband is mousy and they have a ginger-haired child. Or redhead as she likes to say, but it's ginger, trust me."

There were a few titters and Meredith nodded.

"Perhaps he did know the child up to a certain age? Perhaps she wasn't given up for adoption until she was older. It happens. That's our job to find out, and whatever we find, we have to match it back to Charlesworth."

"What if we can't?"

"Then we'll have to start again. Let's get on with it, speed is of the essence."

There was a murmur and Meredith walked to his office. The briefing was over. Seaton followed him and pushed the door to behind him.

Meredith rolled his eyes. "What?"

"Is everything all right? What I'm trying to say is that this is a bit of a turn up. It must be difficult, you . . . I mean . . ." Seaton gave a grunt of frustration, "What I'm trying to say is if you need to talk, it won't go any further."

He glanced out to the incident room. Meredith considered him for a while. They'd worked together for many years, and Seaton had seen him at his lowest ebb.

"Difficult doesn't come near it, Tom, and I don't know whether I'm on my arse or my elbow to tell the truth, but getting on with this will help. I need a focus, and I've certainly got one."

Seaton looked as though he were about to say something but, changing his mind, turned to leave.

"Spit it out Tom, what were you going to say?"

Seaton drew in a quick breath and shrugged. "I was going to ask if he was yours. Patsy would be an angel if that were the case."

"I don't know, but she is an angel. She's doing this without knowing. I am going to . . ." Meredith thumped the desk, and jumped to his feet. "That's it. That's what he's doing."

"What is?" asked a bemused Seaton.

Alerted by the shout, the team looked up as Meredith hurried back to his previous spot. They looked at him expectantly.

"DNA. He's getting their DNA. Gemma got returned because it didn't match." Meredith swivelled and tapped her photograph. He didn't need to take Dana's because he had her hair." He saw the confused look on Jo Adler's face. "The hair on the hedge, read the notes, woman!"

"And he tore off Harriet's dressing," Rawlings finished for him.

"Exactly. Now we have to find out what labs have been doing paternity testing, and for whom. There are plenty around. I'll give Sherlock a ring and find out where we start." Meredith rubbed his hands together. "We'll have the bastard within a week, you mark my words."

Meredith went back to his office. He sat a while wondering why it hadn't occurred to him before. He was losing his touch. All these things that he knew he knew, but didn't come to him quickly enough. Perhaps he was getting too old. The situation with Nicola didn't help. He pulled the piece of paper with the phone number from his breast pocket, and rang the hospital. He was told Nicola was still in surgery, but the last they'd heard was that things were going according to plan. The nurse promised to call immediately there was any news. He glanced at the clock. She'd been in there for two hours now. He terminated the call and phoned Patsy.

"How is it? Are you coping all right?" He could hear Doris Day playing in the background, and he smiled.

"Everything is fine. He's finished his feed a few moments ago. I have to admit if it wasn't for the nappy changing, I'd be enjoying the experience." Patsy looked at the baby gurgling on the changing mat, totally oblivious to the mayhem surrounding him. He'd only been there a few hours and already the house was in turmoil. She smiled as Peggy began to sing to him. "Peggy certainly knows what she's doing. Any news on Nicola?"

"Still in surgery. I didn't think to ask how long it would take. I've got to call Sherlock now, I'll ask him. I'd better go, and I promise not to be late."

Patsy laughed. "You shouldn't make promises you can't keep. Let me know once you hear about Nicola . . . Oh he's crying. That's a first, speak later. Love you."

Patsy hurried back into the room, and looked down at Paul. His face was red, and his tiny legs kicked out in apparent frustration. Concerned, she bent to pick him up.

"It's only wind. Sit him on your lap and support his chin," Peggy instructed. "That's it, now pat his back." She watched as Patsy struggled for a moment, before securing Paul in a position where he couldn't slip from her knee. "You'll soon get the hang of it. You'll be an expert by the time he goes home."

Patsy looked up while continuing to pat Paul's back. Peggy smiled at her.

"I hope you're right, Peggy. It doesn't bear thinking about, this poor little chap having to survive without his mummy." Looking away she leaned down and gently kissed his head. Paul started to wiggle, grizzling as he did so.

Peggy held her arms out. "Give him here. Let me have a go." Patsy handed her the child. Expertly Peggy sat the child on her knee, put her hand under his chin, and, whilst patting his back she bounced him up and down. He gave a small burp. "That's it, better out than in." She peered at his eyes. "You've still got some in there, you're cock-eyed. Let's get it out."

Placing the hand that had been patting him behind his head, she moved him backwards until he was lying flat against her legs, then sat him up and patted again. This time he gave a burp which came as a low rumble from deep inside, and for good measure he deposited a little blob of posset on the back of her hand. Smiling, she wiped it on his bib.

"There you go, he'll sleep now." She leaned back, and shifted his position until he lay in the crook of her arm, and rocked him gently. He was asleep within seconds. She smiled at Patsy. "Once you know how, you never forget."

Her face clouded. Closing her eyes, she continued to rock the baby.

"Do you want to talk about it, Peggy?" Patsy asked softly.

"Nope." Peggy's eyes remained shut, but her lips formed a thin line.

"Okay, but if you do, I'm ready to listen." Patsy surveyed the mess again. "I'll let you two have a little nap while I clear this lot up."

Peggy nodded, and Patsy left her to it.

"So how confidential are these places?" Meredith tapped the list Frankie Callaghan had given him.

"Very. That's the whole point, Meredith." Frankie sighed. Meredith had the bit between his teeth, and he had someone waiting to see him.

"But not the same confidentiality as a doctor-patient relationship, or a priest for instance."

"No, clearly not. But there will be a contract of sorts, and they'll be worried about breaching that."

"Even better, a list of names. Right, thank you Sherlock . . . Oh one other thing, how long does it take to remove a tumour from the brain? On average, I mean."

"What? Where did that come from? You've asked me some odd questions, Meredith, but that has to be one of the strangest. Where is the tumour? Are they approaching it through the nasal cavity or is part of the skull being removed. How big is this tumour?"

Meredith realised how little he knew and he huffed out a frustrated breath. "I don't know, Sherlock. It's Nicola, my ex. She's in surgery as we speak."

Frankie could hear the concern, and knew, as always, he'd get involved.

"I'll find out what's what, Meredith. Leave it with me. I have someone waiting to see me, should take about twenty minutes, and then I'll make some phone calls."

"Thank you, Sherlock. Much appreciated."

There was none of the usual cavalier attitude, and Frankie realised just how deep the concern was.

Antonio Garcia looked at his mother, and frowned. "Uncle Alberto had no right. That conversation was private. It's not something you should be concerned with."

"But I am, how could I not be? If you have a child, a son, you must sort this out. You cannot turn your back on your own child. Your poor papa would turn in his grave. He's only been gone a few moments." Señora Garcia's voice cracked and she dabbed at her eyes with her apron.

"Mama, please. It is bad enough I have to leave you. This is not real. It's simply not real to us. She is trying to get even with her husband, that's all."

His mother's hands flew to her mouth. "You have taken another man's wife? Is this the man I brought up?"

Her eyes accused him, and despite knowing he'd not done wrong, not really, he felt guilty and looked away.

"You take another man's wife and then walk away when she is in trouble." She cursed a little, and shook her head in disappointment. Her face hardened a little. Her accusing eyes looked at her son and he studied a knot in the wood of the table. "What sort of prostitutas have you been dallying with?" She made the sign of the cross, all the while shaking her head.

"She was not a prostituta." Amused, Antonio laughed. "Mama, don't always look for the worst, it's never there."

His mother jumped to her feet. "Never there? I lose my Pablo, taken before his time, God rest his soul. My son must leave me to complete the studies that will make him rich, and I learn I am to be deprived a grandson, conceived with a prostituta. Tell me Antonio, tell me what good I have in my life."

Antonio joined his mother and took her into his arms. Her head rested on his chest and he rocked her back and forth.

"She was not a prostitute, Mama, calm yourself. She was a nice lady with a bad husband, and we had a little fun. Just the once. The child, Paul, is not mine, he can't be."

His mother gasped and pushed him away. She looked up at him, her eyes wide in amazement. "Paul, you say? It is a sign. She named him after your father. You must find the truth."

It was Antonio's turn to throw his arms into the air. "My mama is loco. It is not a sign, it is a name. No more, no less."

"But you will find out. The scientists can do that, they can tell you with this DNA thing?" She reached up and grasped his face in her hands. "You will do this, in memory of your papa, and for me. You will find out."

Antonio nodded, his face still squashed between her hands.

"When I go back I will have it checked out. I promise."

She let him go and hurried to the dresser on the other side of the kitchen. "No, no, no. You must change these and go now." She waved his air tickets at him. "My heart, if it was not already broken, would break for want of knowing."

Antonio rubbed a weary hand over his eyes. "I will do it tomorrow. But you have to think about this, Mama. What will happen if it is me?"

"Not tomorrow, now." His mother was already leaving the room in search of his laptop. "The sooner the better." Her voice faded as she entered the front salon. She came back hugging the laptop to her chest. "Now sit. I will make your dinner while you sort this." She placed the laptop on the table, and Antonio sat down and opened it, as always unable to refuse her. She ruffled his hair. "Good boy. If I am right, and it is a sign, Mama will come to meet her little Pablo."

Antonio had rarely lied to his mother, but he knew he'd lie about this if the results proved him to be the father. He wondered if the private investigator in England had sent off the swab he'd posted to her.

Amanda sat cuddling the baby. Peggy was in the bath, and Patsy sat on the end of the sofa, Meredith's feet resting in her lap.

"Peggy's third bath in as many days, a miracle. I did some more checking today, and as best I can find out, as not all of her records were scanned in, she lost her daughter when she was fifteen. It was a car accident and her husband was driving. He committed suicide five years later, and Peggy had a nervous breakdown. Well you would, I suppose."

"She's had a tough life then. What happened after that?" Meredith put his arms behind his head to better see his daughter.

"Not a lot. She was discharged, re-admitted a couple of years later, and then nothing. I suppose she opted out. She's not a drunk as you thought though, and other than the cyst she's in remarkably good health, considering her age. Her wound is healing nicely too."

Amanda stirred as the baby started to cry. "That's a lot of noise for one so small. What's the matter? You certainly don't need feeding, and I've changed you." She stood and started to rock the baby. "She'll be well enough to leave soon. In fact, she'd probably have been discharged from hospital today given her remarkable recovery. We're going to have to speak to her, make her see sense. Perhaps we can try and get her some sort of housing."

"I'll have a word with her tomorrow. Much as I like her, I don't think she should get too comfortable, she's certainly not staying," Meredith responded, and frowned as Amanda rocked the baby a little faster.

"No, leave it to me. I'll speak to Peggy when you've gone to work. I don't want you upsetting her." Patsy looked at Amanda. "Do you want me to try?"

"Give him here. It's probably colic." Meredith held his hands up and took Paul from Amanda. Lying Paul face down on his chest Meredith patted his back. The baby squirmed a little and then settled. His hand reached out and curled around Meredith's finger. "Well, if I'm to look after the baby, the least you lot could do is keep me watered. One of you call the hospital, the other get me a drink please. Sherlock said Nicola would probably be kept sedated until tomorrow morning, but we should check."

"I'll do it. Patsy can make the drink. I'm off out later, I need to get ready."

"Again? You're never in." Meredith chose not to push her about her date. He simply didn't have the stomach for any news which might irritate him. He'd find out when everything settled down, if it ever did.

"That's because I work hard and I play hard, much like you when you were young, I'm sure."

Amanda walked out of the room as she called the hospital

"I'm still young, thank you," Meredith called as he lifted his legs and released Patsy.

He lay muttering to Paul about the insults he had to bear as the two women disappeared.

There was no change in Nicola's condition, and Amanda assured Patsy that that was a good thing. They heard Peggy moving about upstairs.

"Right, the bathroom is free. My turn, I'll let you update Dad."

Amanda hurried away, and Patsy carried the drink through to Meredith, only to find both him and Paul sleeping soundly. She placed the drinks on the table, and sat in the chair watching them. They looked perfectly at home with each other. It was a touching and natural tableau under any other circumstances. But it wasn't natural, it was anything but, and Patsy gave silent thanks that Nicola's operation had been a success. Meredith hadn't said anything about having the tests taken, and she hadn't asked, but she wondered if he'd already arranged it. Knowing Meredith, he had, but wouldn't tell her until he knew what the outcome was.

She was right. In Meredith's pocket were two swabs, one for himself, and one he would take from Paul. He was visiting one of the laboratories the next day, and he would deliver them in person.

CHAPTER SIXTEEN

Meredith stormed across the car park with Seaton hurrying behind. "They could have told me that on the phone! Why let us drive all the way down here, and refuse us access. Bloody jumped-up little man. Power crazy. There's no way we'll be refused a warrant, so why bugger us about?"

"Because he can, Gov. Calm down, you need to go back in there."

"I daren't. I might slap him." Meredith slammed the car door. "Come on, hurry up," he called, although his words were lost as Seaton hurried around to the other side.

Once in the car, Seaton turned to him. "You're your own worst enemy. What about your test?"

"It'll wait, another couple of days won't hurt. I wouldn't give them the business now anyway."

"Nose to spite face springs to mind." Seaton looked at Meredith and shook his head. He knew that Meredith would be itching to know. Anyone would. "It will only take a few minutes."

"Drive the car, Seaton, we've got a warrant to obtain."

Seaton fastened his seatbelt, glad that he was driving. The mood Meredith was in, they'd probably end up wrapped around a tree.

Meredith was silent all the way back to the station. Nicola's sedation had been stopped but she hadn't woken up. Amanda had confirmed that the scan had shown no reason for this, and they were going to carry out a series of tests later that day. Irrespective as to who the boy's father was, he needed his mother, and things were looking grim.

Antonio Garcia climbed on the bus and paid his fare, and having stored his suitcase, he took a seat at the rear of the bus. As it pulled out of the airport, he called Patsy at the office. He was told Patsy was on leave, and assuring Linda she couldn't help, he called Patsy's mobile. The messaging service picked up the call.

"Antonio Garcia here, I've just landed in Bristol. I've come back earlier than planned. I wanted to know if my sample has been tested. Please call me, but my battery is almost dead, you will have to leave a message. I am going to The Box of Frogs, I will call you when . . ."

The battery gave up. Sighing, he dropped the phone into his backpack. Stephen would be surprised, but at least he'd have somewhere to stay. He cursed his decision to give up his room when he'd received the news about his father.

"Damn you, Jeremy Carmichael, damn you." He stared out of the window, wondering if he would ever get even with the man.

He scanned the email for the third time. Ranting, he held his hands towards the screen as though it could see and hear him.

"Two more days! How can this be? What sort of second-rate outfit can be floored by a fire? Doesn't everyone have back-ups these days? Isn't everything stored in the cloud? Whatever that is. And you destroyed the original sample? Morons."

His elbows crashed onto the desk and he held his head in his hands, willing himself to keep his temper. If he had to go back and see Harriet, perhaps take her, he needed to be calm. Counting down from ten, he drew in a breath at each new number, and reaching zero he opened his eyes. He had to go shopping. If he had to take her, he needed provisions.

Standing, he closed the screen. Catching sight of himself in the mirror, he took stock of himself. He was a good man, and he would give her a good life. A very good life, so would it matter if she wasn't his? He nodded at his reflection. It would. He had to know.

Peggy turned to Patsy who had received the latest update from Amanda. "I know you won't want to think about it, but you've got to. What are you going to do if she doesn't make it?" "I have no idea." Patsy walked across and watched Peggy rolling out the pastry; today she'd decided to make an apple pie. "I've never seen anyone make pastry as fast as you. It's good too."

"Don't change the subject. You have to face facts, it's not looking good."

"Don't say that, Peggy. It's early days, and at the moment I'd like to deal with the problem IF and when it arises."

"Causes trouble that, take my word for it." Peggy shot her a glance, before expertly picking up the pastry with the rolling pin, and laying it across the top of the pie dish. "In my experience, you should meet these things head on, or the shock . . . well, I think you should make plans, that's all." Lifting up the pie dish she turned it with her fingers and she trimmed the edges. "Would it be easier if Merriwinkle was the father?"

"No one else could get away with calling him Merriwinkle, you know. And I don't know . . . probably. But again, that's a bridge to cross when we get there." She poked her tongue out as Peggy rolled her eyes. "While we're having this heart to heart, can I ask what you intend doing when you leave here? If you're right and Paul is to become a fixture, we're going to have to find you somewhere to live. Your Merriwinkle won't allow you back on the street, you know."

"Humph. Well, he won't have a lot to say about it will he. It's not up to him. *My* Merriwinkle, indeed."

"You haven't answered the question, and I think we should start finding out what your options are."

"I don't need options. I'm fine, thank you."

"Of course you do. If I'm to send you back out on that street, the very least we need to do is buy you one of those posh minimal sleeping bags that fold to nothing. I'll not see you freeze."

Peggy had cleared the scraps of pastry, and with her hands full, she turned to the bin. Patsy blocked her way. Peggy, refusing to meet her eyes, walked into her, forcing her to step backwards.

"Come on, Peggy, this needs to be dealt with."

Peggy pointed to Paul, who was sleeping peacefully in his Moses basket on the table. "And so does he, but I'll take a leaf out of your book; all in good time aye?" Patsy's phone sounded. "Saved by the proverbial." Peggy smirked as Patsy went to collect her phone.

When she returned she had her bag with her. "Something's come up. Are you okay if I disappear for a couple of hours?"

"I thought you'd never go. Carry him through to the sitting room for me, and I'll be just fine. Hurry up, I need some peace."

Twenty minutes later, Patsy walked into The Box of Frogs. A sprinkling of customers sat on the terrace, taking in the sunshine, and watching the boats go up and down the river, but the main bar was empty except for a barmaid, Stephen and Antonio, who were sitting at the bar. Having never met Antonio, Patsy was unsure if it was him or not. Stephen spotted her and jumped from his stool.

"Patsy, how wonderful to see you again. Come, let me get you a drink, what will it be?"

He walked to the other side of the bar, as Antonio turned to Patsy and smiled. Patsy was aware from Nicola's description that he would be good-looking, but not that good-looking. That shouldn't be allowed. She composed herself, and held out her hand.

"Nice to meet you at last."

"You too. Have the tests gone off, when can we expect the results?" Antonio spoke quickly, clearly eager for the information.

Patsy smiled and pointed at the nearest table. "Shall we?"

Stephen served them coffee, and left them to their business. Patsy brought Antonio up to date on the situation with Nicola, and confirmed the results of his DNA test should be back the next day. They were deep in conversation when Jeremy Carmichael walked in. Stephen spotted him and tried to reach him before Antonio noticed him.

"Not today, sir, your custom is not welcome. Go and find another bar." Stephen stood in front of Carmichael.

"I shall not." Carmichael's voice boomed, "You have no good reason to . . ." He smirked as he saw Antonio turn and stand up. "Ah I see, you are a babysitting the young Lothario. Well, you can tell him from me, that should he be interested, the whore is free. Now pour me a drink. I'll take it . . ."

He stopped speaking, as Antonio sprinted forward, pushed Stephen to one side, and grabbing Carmichael's shirt pushed him backwards towards the door at some pace. They tripped and fell to the floor. Antonio landed on top of Carmichael, and placed his forearm across Carmichael's throat. Shifting his weight, he applied a downward pressure. Carmichael attempted to speak but only managed a croak. Antonio leaned down until their noses almost touched.

"If you ever come near me or my friends again, I promise I will hurt you, and hurt you properly, old man. Do you understand?" Carmichael emitted another croak, and Antonio released the pressure a little. "I'm sorry, I didn't hear you."

Carmichael gasped in air. "Yes," he hissed, and Antonio pushed himself up and stepped away.

Carmichael grasped his throat as he struggled to his feet. His eyes showed the hatred he felt, but he knew better than to attempt to voice it. Antonio strode forward aggressively.

"Get out, old man. Get out! Don't forget, I will kill you if you enter my life again. OUT!" Antonio felt no pleasure as Carmichael turned and hurried away. Turning back to Patsy, he shook his head. "I am sorry you had to see that, but never before have I felt such hatred for another man. What could have happened to make him such a person?"

"I don't know, Antonio, but I think he got the message. It's a shame, but it seems to me that for such a talented man he causes discord wherever he goes. Leave him in your past, Antonio, you are about to embark on the first leg of your future." Patsy smiled as Antonio shrugged agreement and checked the time. "I really must get back to Paul, but I'll be in touch as soon as I know anything."

Patsy walked quickly along the dockside, wishing she had more time to enjoy the sunshine. As she neared her car, she became aware of a presence behind her. Pulling her bag in close to her body she turned quickly. Her mouth fell open.

"Not you again! What now? Look . . . whatever your name is, do you have a name? I've told you all I know, and anyway I thought you cleared everything with Meredith."

Ignoring her questions, the man touched her elbow lightly and turned her to face the other direction.

"Hello, Miss Hodge, let me walk you to your car. We can speak as we walk."

"About what?" Patsy walked forward slowly, looking at the stocky man now escorting her.

He pursed his lips for a while. "I don't know, let's talk about you. Are you happy with your choice of career? Do you ever wish you were doing something more useful for Queen and country again?" He smiled a knowing smile, and for one split second Patsy wondered if he'd overheard her conversation with Linda. He couldn't have, could he? She frowned and stopped walking, turning to face him.

"I beg your pardon? I am quite content that I help my . . . Oh shit. Are you trying to recruit me?"

She blinked as the man shrugged, and a slow smile appeared.

"Would you like to be recruited?" He touched her elbow again, encouraging her to continue her journey.

"I can't believe this. You are serious, aren't you? I don't have the qualifications . . ." She paused briefly and looked at him again. "Do I? Dear God, of all the things that I thought could happen." She turned up a side street leading to the carpark. "Talk to me then, I don't go for the strong silent type. You will need to communicate with me."

The man gave a laugh. "Indeed not, I've met DCI Meredith on several occasions."

"Are you trying to recruit him? Who are you anyway?" She entered the carpark as the man laughed again.

"DCI Meredith is far too excitable for our line of work. His sense of fair play is far too well developed."

"You are suggesting that I . . . I'm sorry, I'm rarely lost for words, but this is surreal." Patsy stopped in front of her car and stared at it for a while as though trying to remember why she was there. She ran her fingers through her hair before shaking her head. "I am flabbergasted."

"Most are. We'll be in touch. Have a pleasant evening, Miss Hodge. Think about your options, we'll meet again soon."

Patsy stood opened-mouthed as the man turned, and walked away. Climbing into her car she closed her eyes and replayed the conversation, unable to believe what had just happened. She thought Meredith had headed them off at the pass, and pointed them in Chris Grainger's direction. Did Chris know about this? Starting her engine, she knew that there was only one way to find out. She called Chris and arranged to meet him away from the office. Hanging up, she pulled out of the carpark, and headed to the meeting. Chris seemed to have known he would be needed.

When she got home, she found Peggy sleeping and cradling Paul, a half-finished bottle on the arm of the chair. Careful not to disturb them, she went to the kitchen and called Amanda for an update. Nicola was still in a coma, and her medical team were becoming increasingly concerned. Patsy sat at the kitchen table, and stared into space as she wondered at how one's world could be turned on its head in such a short time. As she willed Nicola to wake up, she went over her conversation with Chris Grainger.

Graham Charlesworth finished his round. It had been a long and frustrating day. He'd picked up a message from DCI Meredith requesting him to volunteer for a DNA test. Damn the man! If they had DNA evidence, why hadn't he mentioned that before? He'd provide DNA if they wanted DNA, but it was probably a ploy to unsettle him. The idiots. Charlesworth was lost in his own thoughts, and was brought back to reality when the duty nurse called to him.

"Dr Charlesworth, you haven't signed these off." She smiled and waved a batch of papers at him.

He closed his eyes and cursed. That would take another twenty minutes or so. He usually preferred to be at the hospital: but with so much to do he had little time to think there. But today he needed space to consider his predicament. His solicitor had assured him that all would be well, and the police only had circumstantial evidence. But now he had this DNA thing to contend with. He needed to think. The smile he gave the pretty nurse was not genuine as he took the papers and sat at her station.

"You're lucky getting out so early today. You're usually here much longer." She smiled at the handsome doctor, hoping the hint she was about to drop wouldn't be too obvious. He didn't look up but nodded agreement and turned to the next prescription. "Is that because you have something on tonight? If not, some of us are going to the new bar that's opened around the corner. You're very welcome to join us, it's usually a laugh. To be honest, I'd be glad if you did, as most of the others are in couples. Not that it makes any difference, but well, it would be nice to . . ."

Charlesworth looked at her as though she were mad. He couldn't concentrate with her constant stream of banality.

"What?" he demanded abruptly, and without waiting for an answer returned his attention to the paperwork.

"I was saying that if you fancy a drink tonight, I'd be glad to -"

He interrupted her. "No. I have plans," he snapped, then realising how rude he'd been, he looked up and smiled. "Sorry, I have a dinner date."

The nurse nodded and walked away, attempting to busy herself with tidying the supply trolley.

Having completed his task, Charlesworth walked to the nurse and tapped her on the shoulder with the pen. She hadn't heard him coming and dropped the bandages she was organising. Bending down to help her retrieve and then restack them, he handed her the pen.

"Sorry about that, earlier, I didn't mean to be rude, my mind's elsewhere." He nodded back to the nurses' station. "I am busy tonight, but perhaps we can get together next week."

She beamed at him and waved as he turned to leave, still grinning at his back as he left the ward. He doubted very much whether that was true – who knew what would happen in the next week – and he had enough on his plate without alienating colleagues. He hadn't lied: he did have a dinner date. He was meeting Professor Cole, and while that would normally have been a pleasure, tonight he wanted to think. He'd had one lot of bad news after the other today, and he doubted he'd be much of a companion.

"Did you know that if you want a DNA paternity test, or a maternity one come to that, you can actually pay for bulk testing?" Meredith shook his head, and adjusted the angle of the bottle he was feeding Paul. "I was seriously shocked, who knew there was such a demand? It's like shopping online: the more you want, the cheaper it becomes. I find it quite unsettling to think there are clearly a lot of people unsure of their origins out there."

He stared at the baby, a typical example, and he stopped speaking. This was another can of worms about to burst open. But when he looked up and Patsy's eyes asked the unspoken question, he nodded and added, "Sherlock's sorting it out."

Peggy rolled her eyes, unable to comprehend why two people so close couldn't talk about the most important things. She'd had a heart to heart with Patsy before Meredith got home, and had probably said far too much about herself, but that hadn't mattered. She'd be gone soon. This was far too cosy a set up for her, despite the high tension that seemed to hang in the air. She opened her mouth to speak, but snapped it shut again as Amanda came flying into the room.

"Nicola is waking up. They have given her a light sedative because when she came to she got quite distressed asking for Paul and M . . ." Stopping at the last moment, she added, "And she's communicating with the doctors. Not many words, but a lot of nodding in the right places." She smiled, "I popped in to check on her before I left." She held out her arms for the baby and cooed at him. "So you, little man, will be back with your mummy before we know it. Perhaps then I'll get a good night's sleep."

Peggy raised her eyebrows at Patsy to confirm that she too knew that Nicola had asked for Meredith. She shuffled restlessly in the chair.

"Are we eating tonight or what? Patsy promised we could eat al fresco, to remind me of better days." She grinned. "Don't worry, Merriwinkle, we don't want you to barbeque or anything complicated. It's all ready, we were just waiting for madam here."

Meredith grinned a broad grin. Nicola was going to be all right, and while there could be no better result for Paul, it also lifted a huge burden from his shoulders.

"Come on then, I thought you'd never ask. I'm famished, so it had better be good."

He held out his hand and helped Peggy to her feet. He noticed she had changed her tee shirt and socks. She had more colour in her cheeks too. He made a note to find a moment to talk to her properly. He wanted more privacy in his home, but he didn't want her back on the street. Peggy picked up a brown leather handbag and placed it on her arm.

"A bag, Peggy? You look like the Queen now. You got your life savings in there? Do I need to act as bodyguard?"

"Stop playing silly buggers. Anyway, if I told you, you wouldn't believe me."

Meredith smiled as he escorted her to the garden.

A few hours later, dinner was done. Paul was asleep, and Patsy and Amanda were busy in the house. Meredith poured himself and Peggy another glass of wine. Folding his arms, he leaned forward on the table. He decided it would be best to start the conversation, tentatively.

"You are looking well, Peggy, a remarkable transformation. I hope you feel as good as you look."

"Well, I never did, are you trying to get in my knickers, Merriwinkle? What a thing to say to a lady of my age." She shook her head, and amusement glistened in her eyes.

"You purposely misconstrued that, but if I was a little older and had enough experience to cope with a woman like you, I probably would be being suggestive." Meredith inclined his head. "How are you? And more importantly, what have you got in the bag?"

"I'm fine. Don't worry, I'll not be troubling you for much longer." She reached down and picked up the bag, placing it on her lap. She drummed her fingers on it. "In here is my life."

"There you go again. I didn't mean that and you know it. Not... -"

Meredith was quite taken aback as Peggy leaned forward and waved an accusing finger at him.

"And that's half your problem, Merriwinkle. You don't make your intentions clear. Not when anything as important as emotions or relationships are involved. I'm a bag lady, a tramp, or as I prefer a lady of the road, but there you sit pussy-footing around, unable to ask a straight question. No wonder that poor girl in there is dithering. I'm not sure she should bother. What happens when you leave work? Where does bull-at-a-gate, straight-talking Merriwinkle go? Because let me tell you, you're an idiot at home."

She folded her arms across her chest. Her body language told Meredith he was a disappointment to her. He blinked, analysing her words.

"Who, Patsy? Dithering with what? What shouldn't she bother doing?"

Peggy ignored him, and as he sat attempting to find the answers to his own questions, she took out her tin and placed it on the table. Her fingers stroked it lightly before she looked back up at him.

"I'm not going to bore you with why I am where I am, but this," she tapped the box, "is all that matters in the world to me, and that's my choice. Like you, I made a good start, an excellent one I presume to think, but things happen. Things go wrong, and you have to make choices. Did I make the right one? I think so, at the time anyway, and now I need to make another choice. Not decided yet on which way I'll jump. But you," she lifted her finger and pointed at him, "you are in a most enviable position, but if you don't buck up this will be your life too." She tapped the tin again, then shrugged with a cheeky grin. "Okay, perhaps yours would be a packing crate, but here," she patted her chest, "we'd be equals, and I wouldn't wish that on anyone."

"What are you talking about? Have you gone senile on us, Peggy?"

Meredith knew full well the meaning of Peggy's cryptic message, but he didn't know why he needed it. His mind raced and, picking up his wine, he leaned back in his chair and pondered this, happy for Peggy to do the same, with one closing comment.

"Nope, not even a little bit, but I can hear what you're not saying, and all I can see is disaster. So think on." Peggy folded her arms.

Meredith wondered if Patsy was on the brink of leaving him. The thought brought an involuntary shiver as he wondered why. Was it because of the situation with Nicola and Paul? That was another conversation he needed to have, and sooner rather than later. Emptying his glass, he picked up the box and gave it a little shake. He heard the rustle of papers, and the clang of something metallic as it bounced from side to side.

"I'm in no hurry to get rid of you, Peggy, and I think you know that. But we have to have a sensible plan first."

"I know. I've discussed it with Patsy, she's not so . . . how did she put it? Ah, yes, not so anal as you. That was it." Peggy rubbed her arms and held out her hand for the box. "Perhaps if you talked to her about more than just work, the land would lie better. Now I'm cold, it gets chilly when the sun goes down. I'll see you in the morning." She held up her hand, "No, don't get up."

Meredith hadn't attempted to move, and he called goodnight missing the sarcasm totally.

Peggy met Patsy in the kitchen. "Thank you, Patsy, for everything. I'm off to bed now, but Merriwinkle is waiting to talk to you."

"Really? What about?" Patsy switched on the dishwasher and turned to face Peggy.

"How would I know? He has that look about him, that's all." Peggy had continued walking and was now in the hall. "Night, Patsy, see you in the morning."

She left Patsy staring at the brooding Meredith in the semi-darkness of the garden. Deciding that head on would be best, Patsy collected some candles from the utility room, found the emergency packet of cigarettes, which somehow only had one left, and went to join him.

"Penny for them." She placed the items on the table and lit the candles.

"Did you call me anal?"

Patsy was glad it was almost dark, and hoped he couldn't see the horror on her face. She composed herself as she wondered exactly what Peggy had said.

"No, I said you appear that way sometimes, and that you were very deep."

"Not how it sounded to me," Meredith grunted and refreshed their glasses. "Why might my life end up in a tin box or packing crate?"

"Oh, did she also tell you about the house?"

"What house?"

Patsy repeated as much of Peggy's disjointed story as she could remember. She told how Peggy lived alone, shut off from the world for six months after her husband's death. Having lost her family, she spiralled downward and, as they knew, was sectioned for a while. She discovered that it was the empty house that was her downfall. While she was living on the street, she got exactly what she expected. Cold damp nights, weak soup from the charity kitchen, stale buns from the café, and spoke only to those people that chose to speak to her. Her way of life became her penance for surviving when those she loved hadn't. She still owned the house, and even paid for someone to keep an eye on it. She had money in the bank, and a twenty–year-old Ford Fiesta sat in the garage with less than ten thousand miles on the clock. Recent events had caused her to re-think her situation and she had asked Patsy to go back and visit the house with her. Something she only did once a year.

"I've agreed to go but I'm torn between trying to convince her to go back, or sell up and start afresh. What do you think would be best?"

Meredith shook his head. "And the old saying stays true: you really never should judge a book by its cover. As to what she should do, what do I know? Apparently, I can't see the wood for the trees, or something like that, and I'm headed for the streets if I don't shape up."

Patsy laughed, relieved that Peggy had had quite a different conversation with Meredith than the one she had feared. Her laugh died as he added, "She also said you were dithering. I'd not noticed but, given all my many failings, I suppose that's not surprising." He reached across and linked his fingers in hers. "She also said she's not sure she'd bother. I want you to bother. Whatever happens with Paul, you have to bother. Nicola is on the mend now, so even if the child is mine, he will be living with his mother."

"Is that all right with you?"

"Of course, Nicola is an excellent mother. What an odd question."

"You won't start chest beating when she finds herself a man. And she will. She's an attractive woman, and, child or not, she will want someone else in her life."

"I coped before, and I'll cope again . . . I have had this experience before, you know." Meredith fell silent for a while. He squeezed Patsy's fingers. "I think she might be right about me. Peggy is a clever old bird. So that's that dealt with, all will be well. What about you?"

"What about me?"

"How will you cope if it's me?"

"If you're a grown up I'll be just fine. We are where we are and we will cope. It's nice watching you with him, being all gentle and soft, instead of grumpy and -"

"Anal?" Meredith interrupted. "And what, pray tell, are you dithering about, if you are as comfortable as you can be with this situation. The way Peggy told it, if you make the wrong decision, or I force you that way, then I'm moving into the cardboard box next to hers." He laughed. "Except she will have moved out, because she's gone home."

Patsy swallowed, and picked up her drink. She sipped it and wondered if she should just go for it. She grinned as she decided she should, but as she opened her mouth, she remembered her meeting with Chris. Until she'd made that decision, it wouldn't be fair.

"I have absolutely no idea. Perhaps the wine got to her?"

Although unable to see her face, Meredith instinctively knew that Patsy was lying. He had no idea what they weren't talking about, but if it meant Patsy was happy to stay with him, that would do for now.

A sharp cry came from inside the house.

"He must have a built-in timer you know. That's every five hours on the button today. I'll go and heat his feed. Would you like me to sleep downstairs, I don't mind. He'll be awake again at four if he keeps to this timetable."

"No, I bloody wouldn't. You're coming to bed with me. You go and feed him and give him an extra ounce, it'll help him sleep longer. I'll clear this lot up."

Later, when they had finally managed to get Paul off, they climbed wearily into bed.

"I'll come with you tomorrow, when you take him into see his mum. Not much we can do until we've got the results of all these tests, and it's not fair you take the full load. You must be itching to get back to work. Out there somewhere is another poor man with your target pinned to his back."

"That would be nice, thank you. But work can wait. I spoke to Chris today, and everything is under control, except Linda of course. Not sure she'll ever be tamed."

"Don't put her into my brain before I drop off. I'll have nightmares. Turn over and come here."

Patsy turned and snuggled into his arms. "Goodnight, Meredith."

"Night, Hodge."

CHAPTER SEVENTEEN

The next morning they were allowed to visit with Nicola for a few minutes. The ward sister was not impressed that they had Paul with them, and warned they would have to leave immediately if he caused a disturbance.

Nicola was very weak, and a little disorientated. She had not regained full use of the left side of her body, but apparently this wasn't unusual and it was thought that this would come back over time. Patsy placed Paul in the crook of Nicola's right arm, and stood next to the bed to ensure he couldn't roll through the bed guard. Nicola murmured sweet nothings to him, and repeatedly thanked them for their support. Meredith looked out of place and very uncomfortable, and was relieved when he saw the nurse coming to ask them to leave.

Until she spoke that was.

"Right, Mr Meredith, kiss your wife goodbye, we need to get on now. Take your beautiful son home and you'll be back in again before you know it."

Meredith froze and looked at Nicola, but she was oblivious to the conversation. Guilty eyes flickered across to Patsy. She had a slight flush of colour on her neck, but smiled and nodded at him, before explaining to Nicola that they had to leave, and that they'd come back that evening. Meredith gave a curt goodbye and was already halfway down the ward, before Patsy had managed to strap Paul into the buggy. She hurried after him; his face was like thunder.

She tutted at him as they entered the lift. "It was an easy mistake, if an uncomfortable one, and you know it wasn't that far from the truth. Calm down, and don't look so miserable."

"Sorry." Meredith was miffed, embarrassed, and felt a guilt he couldn't explain. He needed some air, and space to think, and stifled a groan as Patsy replied.

"Glad to hear it, now you can buy me a posh coffee and cake before you go into work."

The lift door opened, and as they turned into the corridor Patsy bumped the buggy into someone's leg. He smiled kindly and waved her apologies away. His smile disappeared as he saw Meredith standing behind her.

"Are you here to see me? If so, I am on my way to theatre, and you will have to wait."

"No, you carry on. I'll be back when I'm ready."

Graham Charlesworth dashed into the lift before the door closed.

"Is that him? He does look familiar, but not from the e-fit."

"Star Trek then," Meredith observed dryly.

Patsy grinned. "Exactly. Sorry, bit slow today, lack of sleep does that." She looked down at Paul. "Do you mind if we skip the coffee? I've realised that he's going to need another feed, and I have promised to take Peggy to her house. I'd better get back."

"Not at all, I'll drop you off, and you can fill me in later." Meredith smiled. Having seen Charlesworth, he wanted to get back to work and get on with the job in hand.

As the elevator carried him up, Charlesworth simmered. He closed his eyes and attempted to think pleasant thoughts. He'd had nothing but negative thoughts since his dinner with Professor Cole, some that had shocked him, and seeing Meredith had set him off again. He sighed, reminding himself of the plans he had made that were positive, and that he had to calm himself before he operated. He had to stop thinking about what he'd planned. Perhaps there was another way but he doubted it. He opened his eyes as the doors opened, and drew in a deep breath as he stepped into the corridor. In a few hours, he would be able to sort this: he would be able to put his plans in motion.

Lifting his hand, he waved at the nurse from the day before. For good measure, he gave a little wink with his smile. She appreciated the gesture, and watched as he walked towards the operating theatre, not knowing that he was telling himself today would be the first day of the rest of his life, and that she was unlikely to see him again.

Patsy wheeled Paul into the hall, and turned back, her hand held out to support Peggy. She watched as Peggy steeled herself to enter. Her grip was tight as she stepped over the threshold and sniffed.

"Smells musty in here. Get the windows open, it won't do him any good." Peggy nodded at Paul.

Patsy entered each shrouded room quickly, and pulled back the half-closed curtains, opening widows as she went. In the kitchen, she opened the back door and sunshine flooded in. She went back to collect Paul and Peggy followed slowly.

"What do you think, it's a bit tired, isn't it?" Peggy gave a laugh. "Do you know, I can't remember what condition the furniture is in, it's been that long since I looked at it."

"But do you think you could live here again? It's an awful waste, Peggy. It's a lovely house, on a pretty street, and look at that." Patsy pointed to the fields that backed onto the rear garden. "There is nothing wrong that I've seen so far that a coat of paint and a bit of fresh air wouldn't solve. You might want to replace that hall carpet, mind."

She was pleased when Peggy laughed.

"You're not wrong there. Always intended to, but we always seemed to have something else to pay for. I've got plenty now." She tutted and pulled on a sheet that covered the sink and surrounding work tops. It fell to the floor. "Get the kettle on then. Let the tap run though, that water's been stood in the pipes a while. The power's on – she puts the heating on low for me when the weather's bad. Don't want a burst pipe."

Patsy shook her head. The woman heated an empty house, and chose to sleep in a carpark or shop doorway. "You could always sell it and buy something new. This is quite a big property for one. Perhaps a little two-bed would be better, something more manageable."

Peggy struggled to remove the cover from the table and Patsy hurried to assist. She pulled out a chair next to the buggy, and Peggy sat down, giving Paul her finger to hold.

"I don't think so. Not sure I can come back here, but nowhere else would do." Peggy shook her head. "Will you help me get it done up? Freshly painted, maybe a new carpet here and there? I find the bland look that Merriwinkle's gone for quite calming. I'll get rid of all the flowers. Once that's done I'll be able to think about it more clearly. Can't come back here as it is. Go and have a look upstairs, I'll stay with the baby."

Patsy assured her that she would help her as best she could, but warned it was a big job, and not one that they could undertake themselves.

"I know that, I didn't mean literally, I meant to organise." Peggy rolled her eyes. "Your brain is addled with all this dithering. You didn't ask?"

"No, I have to pick my moment. I'll check upstairs." Patsy made a hasty exit.

Peggy extracted her finger from Paul's chubby hand and pulled the tea bags and milk out from under his buggy. She grunted as she straightened up, then smiled, realising that she'd grunted from habit, and not due to any pain. She blew Paul a kiss.

"I'm on the mend, young man, on the mend."

Patsy's phone rang as she came back downstairs. It was Antonio checking in to see if the results had arrived. Patsy felt guilty that she'd not checked.

"I'm sorry, Antonio, not last time I looked. Give me ten minutes and I'll call you back."

"Okay, don't call me Antonio, Toni will be fine. My mother calls me Antonio and you don't remind me of my mother." Patsy's eyes widened wondering if he was flirting with her. "Keep your fingers crossed, Patsy. From Friday I might homeless, what use will I be to a baby then? Stephen has family arriving. He's says it will be okay for me to stay, but it won't be. I'm off to see a room now. It looked horrible, but I can't afford a hotel with what I have."

"They're crossed, Toni, don't worry." Patsy really did cross her fingers as she told the blatant lie. She wanted it to be Toni, because if it wasn't that would mean only one thing. "I'll speak to you later."

Hanging up, she scrolled through to the laboratory and hit the call button. She made her inquiry and sighed as she received the answer. The laboratory had had a major fire, and the computer equipment had been damaged. She was assured that all would be well as data was stored off site. The new hardware was almost ready to go. She asked for a call as soon as the information was to hand. Shrugging at Peggy, she called Antonio back. It went to his answer service and she left the bad news.

"I take it another day of anguish." Peggy lifted the kettle and poured the boiling water. She didn't wait for Patsy's answer, "What will be, will be, Patsy, and there isn't anything you can do about it. Except cope, and you strike me as though you're the type to cope, so stop dithering. Ask him."

"I can't, Peggy, I can't, not yet. Something's come up that I have to sort out first. I'm not sure."

"Not sure you want to ask, or not sure he'll like what's come up?" Peggy lowered herself back onto the chair and smiled at Paul. "You'd better hope you don't get lumbered with her. She may be able to cope, but boy can she dither."

"The latter, as it happens. If this comes off he won't like it. He won't like it at all." Patsy shrugged, "I can't tell him about it, and that being the case I would be asking him without him having all the facts."

"Bigger than 'here's a baby that might be mine, and his mother may die'. Thank the lord the last bit's gone, but that's what you did for him." Peggy shrugged, and left that thought to settle. "Anyway, enough about you, we're here to plan my future, not yours. What do you think?"

Patsy laughed, leaned forward and planted a kiss on Peggy's forehead.

"I'm going to miss you when you go. But as to what I think, let's get a man that can in, get some quotes for the carpet and then we'll worry about it. Is that a big enough plan at the moment?"

"It is, and don't worry, I'll come and visit." The way she said it, it sounded more like a warning, and Patsy laughed again. Peggy got up and poured away the remnants of her drink. "I'd better not drink any more, I can't pee where I want to now. You'd better drop me off at the hospital, I'll get a cab back."

"Don't be silly, I'll wait. Do you even have any money on you?"

Peggy grinned at her. "No, I was going to ask for a loan."

"I'll take Paul up to see his mum while I wait, so two birds with one stone. I'm sure that will cheer her up."

Forty minutes later, Patsy wheeled Paul towards his mother's bed. She was propped up on pillows and looked very frail. There was a small blood stain on the pillow by her head, but her face lit up as she saw Patsy approach. She lifted her right hand and wiggled her fingers at her son. Patsy lifted him out of the buggy and placed him in the same position as she had earlier. Holding onto the guard she smiled at Nicola.

"Well, you look better I must say. How are you feeling?"

"Worse than I look. I feel like I fell off a cliff, only to be hit by a bus." Nicola spoke slowly, and winced as she bent her head forward to kiss Paul. "I've had better days, Patsy, but I'm here, and I'm sane. I wish the painkillers were strong enough to kill this headache though."

Patsy watched the lines deepen at the corner of Nicola's eyes as she bent forward again.

"Can they not give you a stronger dose?"

"No, apparently that would sedate me, and they want me awake to test my reflexes and what have you." Nicola tried to smile. "I suppose it's a small price to pay. I've only got a small bald patch too. If the dressing wasn't there I'd look like a monk. The results should be back tomorrow."

She raised her brows, her eyes showing her concern, and Patsy patted her hand.

"Let's worry about tomorrow when it arrives. Now, is there anything I can get you?"

"No thank you, I . . . I" Nicola screwed her eyes shut. "Oh dear, I came over all dizzy then. You'd better take . . ."

Nicola's head fell back against the pillow, and Patsy quickly lifted Paul into the buggy, calling for the nurse as she did so.

"Don't make a fush." Nicola turned her head towards Patsy, the movement heavy and laboured. "I'm fine, Patshy."

She was slurring, and the left side of her mouth drooped.

The nurse hurried forward and frowned as she measured Nicola's pulse. She picked up her hand.

"Squeeze my finger for me, Nicola, there's a love." She glanced at Patsy as Nicola's fingers only twitched. Grabbing the alarm, the nurse looked at the baby. "I think you should take him up to the family room, it's going to be busy here for a while."

As Patsy wheeled Paul away from his mother, a doctor and a second nurse ran towards the bed. The nurse drew the curtains around as the doctor began his examination. He was shouting instructions, and one of the nurses ran back to the small office and picked up the phone. Patsy closed the door of the little family room. With shaking hands, she too made a call. She closed her eyes as she heard Meredith's answer message.

"Meredith, get to the hospital, quickly, it's Nicola she's . . ." Her voice broke and she cleared her throat. "Just get here please." She was aware of a flurry of activity on the other side of the door, and she turned her back on it.

Meredith was too late. Nicola had died an hour earlier. Patsy found herself stunned. She had been involved in many cases where people had lost their lives at too young an age. But this was the first time it was personal, the first time she had been there, and the first time since she had lost her mother that she felt so afraid of the future. Thanking the nurse, Patsy gave Paul a hug before strapping him in the buggy. She would be the one to tell Meredith. She didn't want to. She didn't want to share that moment, and see the affect it would have on him. She walked slowly to the lift, and watched the lights warn of its imminent arrival, then stepped back to allow the passengers to step out. As she pushed the buggy into the now empty space, someone grabbed her arm. Meredith knew from her lack of awareness of what was happening around her that the news was bad.

"Patsy, I'm sorry I took so long. I was tied up . . ."

He stopped speaking as she blinked and a solitary tear traced the side of her nose. He wiped it away gently.

"Is she dead?"

His voice sounded as though he had smoked a thousand cigarettes, and his eyes dropped to Paul sleeping contentedly in the buggy. Patsy nodded. The lift doors closed and Meredith turned away, repeatedly jabbing his finger at the button to open them. He cursed as the lift jolted and began its journey to the ground floor.

"Bastard thing!" he roared and kicked the door.

Paul gave a wail, and Patsy bent to sooth him, unable to look at Meredith, unable to find the words to comfort him, and wishing that she didn't need to.

Meredith cleared his throat. "I'm sorry, it's just such a shock, that's all. I mean, what happens now, how do we deal with him?"

He fell into silence as the lift stopped. Patsy pushed the buggy out into the busy corridor. Meredith took her arm.

"Let's go home, we should go home."

Patsy turned to face him. "I have to collect Peggy. She's been waiting. For ages." She lifted her eyes to meet his gaze, and her heart rate increased. Meredith looked lost, much like a child in the middle of a busy thoroughfare unable to find his mother. She knew he needed her to comfort him, but she couldn't. He should just look sad, not lost. Not devastated. Forcing a smile, she sniffed back her own fear, and lifted a hand to his face. Her fingers felt the coarse stubble; he'd not shaved again that morning.

"Go and say goodbye, Meredith. Now. You need to let her go."

"But I -"

Patsy put her fingers on his lips, and he kissed them as he searched her face, needing to know what she was thinking. Needing to hug her to him and take the comfort that she would deliver. Needing to be as far away from this place as he could, and needing to be alone.

"I'll go home. You go and say goodbye. I'll be at home when you're ready." Her hand dropped and took hold of the handle of the buggy. Her knuckles were white. "See you later, Meredith."

He stood motionless, watching her walk away. The lift came and went several times before a nurse asked him if he was all right, and he shook her hand away and walked down the corridor.

"I should go. I'll simply be in the way here. I'll sort something out tomorrow." Peggy had grown fond of the little, if unconventional, family that had helped her. But she had her own demons to deal with, and didn't want to inherit anyone else's. It wasn't a case of being selfish, it was survival. Peggy knew she couldn't return to living on the streets, and making plans for the house with Patsy had given her a focus. Sitting in the waiting room at the hospital she'd decided she would take in a lodger, maybe two. Company but not commitment. She could get rid of anyone she didn't like, and if she had trouble she knew Merriwinkle would help her out.

She'd got quite excited once the plan was formulated and was itching to be away to discuss it with Patsy. Then the nurse had told her why Patsy was taking so long. Now it was ten o'clock and they'd been sitting at the table for nearly two hours. Meredith's dinner sat next to the hob, covered in cling film. They had left the hospital four hours ago, and they not seen or heard from him since.

Patsy refused to call him, saying he needed to do whatever it was he needed to do. Patsy had been scrolling through her emails, not really reading them, but attempting to keep her mind occupied. She was reading one from Antonio as Peggy made her announcement. She looked up and shook her head.

"You will not. Don't make this harder than it needs to be, Peggy. I'm going to have my hands full dealing with Meredith and Paul, I don't need you becoming an extra burden." She grimaced. "It'll be all over in a couple of days . . ." She blinked. "Well, the hard bit anyway, and we've made plans that I intend to . . ." She smiled.

Peggy realised it was the first time that she had since they'd arrived home.

Patsy patted Peggy's hand. "I've had an idea. I'm not sure if it will work, but it will certainly give you a start." She lifted her phone from the table and searched her contacts. She winked at Peggy as her call was answered. "Anto . . . Sorry, Toni, I think I may have some work for you, and you can sleep on the job. How familiar are you with a paint brush?"

Peggy grinned at Amanda as she walked into the kitchen.

"Is that Dad? Has he called finally?" she asked.

"No, but Patsy is getting me what she describes as 'a hot Spaniard'." Peggy rubbed her hands together, "I'm going to have someone to boss around."

Amanda pulled out a chair and the two women eavesdropped on Patsy negotiating the deal. They looked at her expectantly as she hung up.

"He said he's not bad. He has experience, but it is limited. However, he will decorate the house as you see fit in return for his lodging. You'll have to pay for the materials, and he goes back to his studies in a month or so. I told him I'd call tomorrow and arrange for you to meet with him at the house."

"Yes, I heard that, I'm not deaf, woman." Peggy shrugged happily. "No offence, but it's good to get going, so to speak."

"Don't thank me yet, Peggy, he might be rubbish, but there, what harm will it do?"

"I don't care if he's useless. All the better, I can knock him into shape. I wonder how he'll take to my cooking? I haven't got a great knowledge of Spanish cooking. All that tapas! I ask you, a growing man will need a substantial meal. I'll educate him on that too."

Peggy closed her eyes and rubbed her forehead. She opened them and pointed at Amanda. "Do you know, I think I have a cookbook there somewhere. One of those Christmas presents you get but don't use. *European Cookery Made Easy*, that was it. It must be thirty-odd years old, but food's food. I'll borrow a pen and paper if I may, I have plans to make."

Patsy smiled. "Your take on food is identical to Meredith's: large substantial portions and not too much messing about." She jumped to her feet. Meredith was back in the conversation, and that wouldn't do. "I'll go and get you a note pad. I have one in my bag."

She hurried from the room.

Peggy looked at Amanda. "Your father needs a talking to. He's an insensitive bastard, if not a little selfish."

Amanda nodded in agreement. "But he loves her."

"That's as maybe. He should know that, for an intelligent man, he can be quite stupid."

Helen Darley sighed as she walked across the carpark. She knew her job was at risk if she didn't get something soon. Her editor was growing tired of cooking competitions, missing cats, and generous citizens. She had to get something meaty. If that meant chatting up a load of boozy coppers, hoping one would be indiscreet, so be it. She'd done it many times before, but the trouble was the internet. News spread so fast these days it was hard to get your foot in the door before it was common knowledge. She knew the team working the abduction case drank in the Dirty Duck. Perhaps she'd pick up a snippet on that for tomorrow's evening paper.

The bar was quite lively. It had been a warm day, and the smell of bodies and beer greeted her as she pushed open the door. She walked to the bar and climbed onto a stool, surveying the occupants as she did so. Ordering her drink her heart fell. There was no one she recognised, a lot of couples, and a noisy group of lads. She glanced at her watch: it was nine thirty. As she paid for her drink, a man stumbled down the step leading to the bar from the corridor. He steadied himself, and checked that his fly was fastened. He had a glazed look in his eyes, and he mounted the stool and picked up his pint. Helen looked at the empty shot glass next to it and smiled.

DCI John Meredith, and he was drunk. There was a God. Lifting her drink, and dragging her stool behind her, she went to join him. Meredith glanced at her legs as she made a pretence of pulling down her skirt and settled on the stool. He went back to his pint.

"Hello, DCI Meredith, I wasn't expecting to see you in here." She leaned forward allowing her top to fall away from her body, but hoped it wasn't too obvious. Meredith stared at her ample cleavage before looking back at her face.

"Why, who were you expecting?" He looked around quickly to see whoever it was. He turned back slowly, his head swimming. "Do I know you?" He frowned. "You look familiar." He closed his eyes, trying to place her, and swayed a little. He opened his eyes and they narrowed. "You're press."

"Not tonight I'm not. I'm looking for a bit of fun and relaxation. It's been a bitch of a week so far, and I'm going to have a drink to forget it for a little while."

Meredith nodded solemnly before emptying his glass. He beckoned the barman and grinned at her. "I'll drink to that, but first we need alcohol. What are you drinking?"

They sat companionably for the next thirty minutes or so, passing the occasional comment on the silent news footage on the screen in the corner of the room. Beginning to feel a little tipsy herself, Helen excused herself and went to the ladies. She washed her hands and allowed the cold water to run over her wrists, then dabbing the excess moisture from her nose, she reapplied her lipstick and went back to find Meredith. He might be drunk, but he was a copper, and handsome. She smiled as she returned, aware that he was watching her approach.

"You have legs. That's how I know you." He leaned back as she climbed onto the stool. "You were at the conference." He pointed an accusing finger at her. Helen's heart sank. She needed to recover her position and fast.

"I was, and if it helps I'm thoroughly ashamed of myself. But you were looking at my legs – I get lots of compliments on them – I just made a mistake in your intentions." She shook her head. "I'm sorry. How's the case going" Helen inclined her head and tried to look humbled.

Meredith leaned forward and patted her thigh. "Don't be sorry, just timing. You do, as it happens, have nice legs."

His hand remained on her thigh. She shifted forwards causing his finger tips to disappear beneath the hem of her skirt. He looked up and raised his eyebrows. She smiled and leaned in towards him.

"Thank you, you're a generous man, DCI Meredith. I wish I had a boss like you, I wouldn't mind getting up in the morning then."

"Is that so? I think you over estimate me Ms . . ." He squeezed her leg. "I feel I should know your name."

"Helen." She gave a laugh and rested her forehead on his. "Are we worried about names, DCI Meredith?" She pouted. "I know I'm not."

Meredith shrugged, his eyes struggling to focus. He had a niggle in his groin he wasn't sure he could deal with. He opened his mouth to speak, but gave a shout as Helen Darley flew backwards off her stool. She landed unceremoniously on her backside. Blinking, he looked down at her. Well, that answered that question: she was wearing knickers. He looked up to see Patsy, arms akimbo, face pale but calm.

She shook her head at him, composing herself before she allowed herself to speak. Helen was livid. She pushed herself to her knees ready to give Patsy a piece of her mind, and then she saw the look on her face, and decided to stay where she was. Patsy, aware of the silence that had fallen over the bar, glanced down at the now kneeling woman.

"Sorry, but you were easier to shift than he would have been." She looked back at Meredith. "Two choices, Meredith: either pick your lady friend up, it's embarrassing, and then you can finish your drink with her, or pick your lady friend up and get your arse into the car sharpish."

Meredith blinked at her, the heat from the fear he felt enveloping his body. He opened his mouth but didn't know what words to choose, so he closed it again. He jumped as Patsy clapped her hands in his face.

"Instant decision needed here!" She felt the tremor in her chin, and then stepped back as Meredith slid from the stool and walked quickly towards the door. Patsy watched it close, and then held out her hand and helped Helen to her feet. "He's not known for his manners, but he is taken." She pulled a five pound note from her purse and placed it on the bar. "Get yourself a drink."

When she entered the car park Meredith was vomiting violently into a tub of flowers. She went to sit in the car, and watched as he emptied the contents of his stomach. Meredith retched until he felt dizzy with the effort, eventually standing and wiping his mouth on his forearm. Knowing he was being watched by both Patsy and the people in the bar, he walked carefully to the car and got in.

They drove home in silence. As Patsy stepped into the hall Amanda rushed out of the sitting room.

"You found him then." She looked at her father standing dishevelled on the doorstep, and sighed with relief.

"I did. He'll be sleeping on the sofa. Get him a blanket, a bucket, and a glass of water. I'm going to bed."

Meredith opened his eyes, and stared at the sitting room ceiling as his thought processes woke up. The house was silent, and he groaned at the pain that turning his head caused. He lay still, staring at the cup of now cold black coffee, and focused on his name, written on the folded sheet of paper propped up against it. Once he'd maintained the focus for a few minutes he closed his eyes, then opened them quickly, drawing in a sharp breath as the image of Helen Darley, sitting on the floor of the bar with her pink lacy knickers revealed in all their glory for anyone to see, sprang into his mind. He tried to stop it wandering as far as Patsy.

"Oh fuck me, what have I done?" he groaned as he pulled himself to a sitting position.

His mind worked its way backward from that moment, and then he remembered. He fell back heavily and covered his face with his hands. His stomach convulsed several times as the sob escaped his throat, and rolling over he spewed what little he had left in his stomach into the bucket. When he was done, he sat up and drank the cold coffee, wincing at the throbbing in his head. Undeterred, he ignored the note and carried the bucket out of the room. Taking double the recommended dose of painkiller, he drank two pints of water, before splashing some on his face. It was still dripping from him as he answered his phone.

"Sorry to bother you, Gov. Patsy called. I'm sorry, and I wouldn't bother you now, except the results are back. We've found which lab tested the girls and -"

"Come and pick me up. I'll jump in the shower now, and I'll be ready in twenty minutes."

"But, Gov, that's not necessary, all I wanted to -"

"Twenty minutes, Tom. I'll be waiting."

Meredith took a cold shower, and despite the warmth outside, shivered as he pulled his clothes on. Having washed the bucket out and taken a further two painkillers, he walked into the sitting room. He picked up the note and flipped it open.

Amanda had to go to work. I'm taking Peggy to her house. I'll go into Nicola's and make sure everything is OK, and find out if she's left instructions. She'd indicated she had. Text me and let me know your movements, I'll see you later.

P x

PS. I do NOT want to talk about it.

Meredith replaced the note, collected his phone, and went outside to await his lift. His face warned Seaton that he wasn't going to talk about it. Seaton said nothing at all, knowing Meredith would be struggling, and there was no point in antagonising him.

"Tell me now why you phoned," Meredith said eventually and opened the window, hoping the fresh air would dispel the feeling of nausea. He loosened his tie. "It's bloody warm, isn't it?"

"They reckon it'll hit thirty degrees and more this afternoon. The DNA matches for the girls have been found, as has the paternal DNA. It wasn't Charlesworth." Meredith's head snapped towards Seaton, and he had to close his eyes to stop his senses swimming around. He opened his eyes. "Not Charlesworth?"

"Nope, and no, they didn't have a name, only a number and an email address. Funnily enough the email address wasn't Mr Guilty, just a series of jumbled numbers and letters. We have people working on it. Apparently, it shouldn't take long."

"But not Charlesworth?"

"Nope."

"Then who the fuck was it?"

"We'll get him, Gov. It's only a matter of time now. As they say, the net is . . ."

Seaton stopped speaking as his phone rang. He hit the button on the steering wheel and picked up the call.

Louie Trump's voice filled the car. "Hello, Tom, have you got Meredith yet?"

"He has," Meredith answered.

"Good. Then you want to change direction. We have a murder on our hands, and Frankie Callaghan has asked for you. I didn't like to mention the circumstances, so -"

"There are no circumstances Trump, life goes on. Stop being such a bloody old woman and get to the point. Who's been murdered and where?"

"Jeremy Carmichael was found dead in his dressing room this morning by a cleaner. You need to get to the Old Vic."

Seaton had already indicated, and was swinging the car in a U turn. Meredith grabbed hold of the dash and the door handle to steady himself.

"Tell Sherlock we're on our way. Why did he want me in particular? Flattering, but not usual."

"Because he had a tin soldier."

"What?"

"I know, sir, hence the call. Shall I meet you there?"

"Nope, find out who the bastard is that's been taking these girls. And draft in Loopy if our boys are taking too long. I hear it's one of the things she does well."

"One of the few, yes, sir. I'll call you later."

Meredith stared at the body of Jeremy Carmichael. He had been bound to his chair with what appeared to be a dressing gown belt and a length of gold cord. His head was resting against the back of the chair and he faced the ceiling. Rivulets of blood travelled down his face, and had stained the shoulders of his pale blue shirt. That had been torn part way open, to reveal a very hair chest. Meredith leaned closer to look at the tiny wounds on Carmichael's face, glad he hadn't anything left to throw up. Finally, he looked at Sherlock.

"Well, those wounds didn't kill him, Sherlock. Not nice but not lethal. Not enough blood. Judging by the state of this room, he's been tortured to get into that safe." Meredith pointed at the small-hotel style safe which sat with its door open on the shelf above the shoe rack. "Heart attack, do you think?"

"Don't know? It's possible. As always, Meredith, as soon as I know et cetera." Frankie nodded at the clear plastic evidence bag. "That struck me as odd though . . ."

Meredith lifted the bag and looked at the tin soldier.

"Definitely part of the set. It was in his hand. That's when I called, then one of the chaps found these."

Frankie lifted a small plastic crate from the floor and placed it on the table in front of the mirror. Meredith stepped forward and peered inside. Frankie handed him gloves, and he pulled them on before opening the lid of the green tin. He stared at the rows of soldiers looking up at him. There were six empty compartments.

"Well, there's a turn up. You'd better get a match on his DNA pronto. He might be our man. What?" Meredith frowned as Frankie shook his head.

"He's our man, I'm convinced of it." Frankie reached into the crate and pulled out a large evidence bag. Meredith squinted at it.

"Is that a wig?"

"It is Meredith, and this," Frankie gently pulled some flesh-coloured rubber from the bag, and, splaying his fingers, eased the mask open, "this is Captain Kirk, unless I'm very much mistaken."

Meredith closed his eyes and rubbed his forehead. "I was only here a few days ago. There's something here to tell us why, I know it." He opened his eyes and looked around the room. "Have you finished here?"

"Almost. Ten minutes and it's all yours."

Frankie called to his assistant and together they started to untie the body of Jeremy Carmichael. Meredith walked out, issuing instructions to Seaton as he did so.

"I'm going to buy cigarettes. You get Adler and Trump down here, and you and Rawlings can find out where he lives and get around there. I want every piece of paper, every photograph, anything that might tell us who the biological mother was of his daughter, and hopefully who did this."

"You don't think it was a theft gone wrong then?" Seaton held his phone, poised to call out.

"Don't know, but I want too. I need a smoke, I'll meet you outside in a moment." Meredith walked away, head down, hands deep in his pockets as he tried to remember what he knew.

When Meredith arrived home that evening, the women in the kitchen had not heard him enter, and he stood in the hall listening to their conversation. Peggy was buzzing about her house, and what she called her Spaniard. She was telling the others that he had convinced her to have laminate flooring in the hall and kitchen, and if the car started the next day, he was going to drive her to a DIY store to show her.

Meredith smiled at the new lease of life she had found. He threw his jacket over the banister and pulled off his tie as he sat on the stairs.

"What's the latest from Dad, Patsy? No doubt he still has his tail between his legs, and rightly so. I can't believe how much you've achieved today, and with the baby too. I'm off tomorrow so you can have a break."

"That's very kind of you," Meredith caught the slight sarcasm in Patsy's tone, "I have to go into work. Being a working mum was not part of the plan. With regards to Meredith, he said he'd be in time for dinner. But with this murder, who knows. That reminds me, I should give Beth Durham a ring. It's all over the news."

Patsy turned to Peggy. "Toni won't be shedding any tears, that's for sure. I'll drop you off on the way in. I'm glad you like Toni, he's a bit of hunk, isn't he?"

"Well, I have to say I was quite taken aback. I thought some modern movie star had walked in." Peggy chortled. "It will be better than watching someone working with a beer gut and a builder's bum, that's for sure." She caught hold of Amanda's hand as she made to leave the kitchen. "Not so fast, madam. What did you decide about Patrick?"

Meredith sighed. This woman, this bag lady, had been in their lives but a couple of days, and yet she knew more about what was happening with his family than he did.

"I cancelled. It's not serious. I just thought that if Dad met him, he'd stop going on." She gave a laugh, "I think he was relieved. The thought of meeting Dad at home scared him to death." Walking to Patsy, Amanda put her arm around her shoulders. "It'll be okay, Patsy, one way or the other."

Patsy wasn't so sure. She shrugged. "We'll see. But for now, let's keep busy; that usually works while things sort themselves out. Now, get in that shower – you still smell of antiseptic. Dinner will be twenty minutes."

Amanda agreed and, walking out of the kitchen, she gave a scream as she bumped into Meredith unexpectedly.

"Dad, you could have called out. I nearly . . ." She stopped herself, and snuggling into Meredith's outstretched arms, she hugged him close. "I'm sorry," she whispered.

"I know," he whispered back as he kissed her head. "Go and shower, there's a queue now."

Peggy saw Patsy stiffen as she realised Meredith was back, and she stood to face him as he entered the room. He smiled at her.

"Don't you smile at me, Merriwinkle. So, some actor got himself killed. You have men that could have dealt with it. There were things for you to do. Things that other people shouldn't have had to deal with." She jerked her head at Patsy who lowered her eyes as he looked at her. Peggy stepped forward and poked him in the chest. "I thought you were made a stronger stuff, Merriwinkle, don't let me down again. Now, I'm going to make myself look beautiful. I'll await the call to dinner, but if necessary a tray on my lap will do."

As she left the kitchen she closed the door behind her.

Patsy remained where she was, looking down at the salad she was fussing with.

Meredith stepped forward. "Are we speaking?"

"Of course, why wouldn't we be?"

He caught the hint of sarcasm in her tone.

"Because I was a stupid bastard, a drunken one, but stupid nonetheless, and Peggy clearly thinks I messed up today too. That seems to be enough to be going on with." He held his hands up helplessly, "Nothing happened, Patsy, and quite apart from anything else, I wasn't capable."

He ducked as Patsy hit the salad bowl with the flat of her hands and it flew through the air. The salad spread itself around him before the bowl hit the floor and clattered to a standstill. Patsy marched towards him, and with the flat of her hands hit them repeatedly against his chest, causing him to walk backwards until the kitchen door blocked his path. He didn't resist her.

"Oh well that's all right then, isn't it! All I have to do now is hope that every time you go out, you get pissed, just in case any female with a pulse comes within groping distance. Or is it the other way around, Meredith? Should I hope that you don't have a drink, so your brain doesn't get fuddled and you forget that you have someone waiting at home for you?"

Her fists were clenched against his chest, and she had an overwhelming urge to punch him in his beautiful, lopsided and, at this moment, shocked face. Instead, she went for a shot below the belt. "How that poor woman ever put up with you is beyond me. You didn't deserve her, and you don't deserve me."

Patsy dissolved into tears and sunk to her knees, cursing her weakness.

Meredith remained pinned by an unseen force. He wondered how he'd allowed himself to hurt her so much that she spoke those words out loud. He had no doubt it wasn't the first time she'd thought them, but to hear them, and know they were true, had stunned him.

Eventually, he looked down at her. Knelt before him, head bowed, she looked as though she were worshiping him in some way. His back slid down the door until he sat on the back of his heels.

"Patsy, I'm sorry. That's not enough I know, and I know I don't deserve you. Please look at me."

Patsy raised her eyes. Pinching the end of her nose to stop it running, she wiped the residue along her thigh.

"Fuck off, Meredith," she said quietly, as she brushed her cheeks with the flat of her hand. "Go and change for dinner, or not, just leave me be. I don't want to talk to you."

Meredith nodded and pushed himself up. He helped her to her feet before leaving the kitchen, closing the door quietly behind him. He hadn't gone far before Peggy pushed herself off the stair on which she was perched, and came hurrying towards him. Once more, she jabbed him in the chest with her finger. Meredith snarled. He liked the woman, but there was a limit.

"Don't you look at me like that," Peggy hissed. "Get back in there and sort it out. I think the modern expression is 'strap a pair on'!"

"She wanted me to leave her, Peggy, so keep out of it."

With a dramatic flourish, Peggy threw her arms into the air. "And suddenly you know about women. Well, let me tell you lad, you know shit from sixpence. Get in there and ask her."

"Ask her what?" He grabbed at his hair in frustration, wondering what had possessed him to allow this interfering woman into his home.

"I rest my case. Think about it, you stupid man. Really, Merriwinkle you disappoint me. I thought you might be the son I never had, now I know I'm glad I didn't." She rolled her eyes.

"You and the rest of the world." He looked her in the eye, and she turned her nose up.

"Don't look at me with those eyes. I'm too old, it doesn't work." She turned, not as quickly as she would have liked, and walked to the stairs. "I'm getting hungry, so whatever you're going to do, do it quickly"

Meredith stood looking from the kitchen door to the slowly ascending Peggy. He flinched as the kitchen door opened. Patsy sniffed as she walked past him.

"I might be mad, but I am certainly not deaf."

Meredith grabbed her arm as she put her foot on the first stair. "Is she right? Because I swear from the bottom of my heart, I hope she is."

Patsy's lips twitched and she looked away. "Don't be so ridiculous. You've missed your place in the queue, by the way. I'll use the bathroom while you make a new salad."

She bit her bottom lip as Peggy leaned over the banister and looked down on them.

"Sorry, Merriwinkle. Lucky I'm not your mother or that would have been embarrassing." She shrugged at Patsy and went to her room.

Dinner was a stilted and interrupted affair. Amanda had missed the drama, and couldn't understand why everyone was so stiff and formal, but was headed off each time she made to enquire. Paul decided he wouldn't sleep after his feed, and got passed around the table as everyone attempted to eat.

During the meal, Meredith discovered that Patsy had taken Paul to his former home, and found that, as Nicola had indicated, she had left all her affairs in order. Her funeral had been planned and paid for, her solicitor had her will, and there was a letter asking Meredith to at least look out for her son, to act as a form of guardian, even if he couldn't live with him. Patsy had spoken to the hospital, and collected the death certificate. She had been to the undertaker, and the funeral was booked and was to be held in four days' time. Not knowing Nicola well, she had no idea who to contact, but had found an address book for Meredith to go through. All Nicola's money and assets had been left to Paul, and she had appointed Meredith executor of the estate until Paul reached eighteen. If Paul was with his natural father then they were to have a stipulated monthly allowance, and any additional money they requested that was deemed to be beneficial to Paul's welfare. When Paul reached eighteen, Meredith could stop paying any allowances to others, and pay Paul an allowance instead. At the age of twenty-one, the balance of the estate could be transferred in full. If Meredith declined this position he was to appoint someone suitable in his place.

At this point Patsy had quipped, "Which won't be me, thank you." Thus indicating that she didn't think Meredith would step up to the plate.

Amanda asked how much money there was, as that seemed to cover an awful lot, for a very long time. Patsy had no idea, and they both looked to Meredith. He shrugged and his eyes sought Patsy's but she avoided his gaze.

Paul eventually settled down, and Patsy took him up to bed, stating that she was having an early night too. She lay for an hour, staring into space, listening to the occasional murmur from the baby, which she found oddly comforting. Eventually, her eyes began to close, and Meredith's head appeared around the door.

"I take it I'm on the couch again."

"Are you drunk and liable to throw up?"

"Of course not." Meredith smiled and closed his eyes in relief. "I'll go and make sure we're all locked up then."

"That would be sensible, yes."

She listened as he ran back downstairs. He returned minutes later, undressing in the dark so as not to wake the baby and his clothes fell where they landed. He climbed into bed, and without any preamble he pulled her to him.

"I love you."

"I know, but is that enough? Goodnight, Meredith."

"Night, Hodge."

Meredith had no idea whether she meant enough for her, or enough for him, but he wasn't brave enough to ask.

CHAPTER EIGHTEEN

The next day both Meredith and Antonio Garcia received the results of their DNA tests. Their reactions were not dissimilar. Meredith had bowed his head as though in prayer, and then with a gentle smile he'd called Patsy. She already knew, of course, as she had shared the news with Antonio. The young Spaniard had walked out of Peggy's kitchen and, head bowed, strolled slowly to the bottom of the garden. When he returned, he stood looking at the sleeping baby, a gentle smile on his face, and then he had phoned his mother. Patsy and Peggy exchanged startled glances as she screamed in excitement, before bursting into tears. At that point Toni grinned.

"I have a son." He lifted Peggy's hands and shook them excitedly. "I have a son, Senora Peggy. A son. Me. I didn't think it true, but I am a father."

Peggy nodded slowly, agreeing with each statement, the look on her face indicating she thought he was a little slow.

"Then let us get on. I have plans to make." He lifted the large tin of paint from the table and headed for the hall, then without warning he rushed back. "You will be able to care for him, until I have a plan, a proper plan?" Patsy nodded, and he bent and kissed the baby on his forehead, before heading off again grinning.

"Well, that's good." Peggy looked at Patsy, "That makes life far more straightforward. Everything is out in the open. You can all get on with previous plans, don't you think? Everything can get back to normal for you."

"Who knows what normal is, Peggy, because I'm sure I don't." She pulled her phone from her bag. "It's Meredith."

She walked away from Peggy and stepped out into the garden.

"It's not me. It must be the Spaniard. I thought I should let you know."

"I know, and his name's Antonio Garcia, or Toni. I received his results earlier. I think it's still sinking in, but he seems pleased."

"And you never thought to call me? Not even a text to put me out of my misery?" Meredith fumed, unable to believe he hadn't been her first call. "I thought . . . well, it doesn't matter what I think, does it." Meredith hung up.

Patsy could have told him the results came through while she was with Antonio Garcia, but she didn't. She wondered why as she slid the phone back into her pocket, and didn't have the answer.

Trump found Meredith on the fire escape lighting his second cigarette.

"May I have a word, or are you better left alone?" Trump asked through the gap of the open door.

He smiled and Meredith waved him to come out.

"I'm thinking of becoming a monk, Trump, a silent, celibate monk. Halfway up a mountain, where you get snowed in for six months of the year, and women are not allowed to set foot anywhere near. Couple of good books and I'd be fine." He took a long drag on the cigarette, and tilting his head, he blew the smoke up towards the cloudless sky.

Trump smiled ruefully. "What about the praying and being nice to everyone, whatever the provocation? Don't get me wrong, sir, I know you would help weave the baskets and repair the latrines, but you have to do so with a song in your heart, and quite frankly . . . well, enough said." Trump laughed as Meredith shook his head. "Can we talk business now?"

"Get on with it."

"Frankie called. They think they had a minimum of ten different people leaving finger prints in that dressing room. Most match with people who can be eliminated, except three: two we haven't got a match on, and Beth Durham. Her prints are everywhere, but she has no one to confirm her whereabouts at the time of the murder."

"Bring her in. Get Adler to go and get her. You can also ask Antonio Garcia to volunteer his prints, and get his alibi while you're there. Call, Patsy, she'll give you the address."

Trump knew from Linda that Garcia was possibly the baby's father, but knew nothing of his relationship with Beth, or his showdown with Carmichael, and he frowned.

"Is that necessary sir? Is it wise?"

Meredith turned around in a circle, looking over his shoulder as he did so. "Are you questioning me? Because that's what it sounded like, and I'm sure you're not that stupid. The man threatened to kill Carmichael, in public, so yes, it is fucking wise. Now get on with it!"

Meredith lit his third cigarette as a sheepish Trump apologised, and hurried back to the incident room. His throat began to object to the chain smoking, and glancing at his watch, Meredith flicked the cigarette away. Without reference to his team, he took the fire escape to the car park, and went to see Frankie Callaghan.

"Sherlock, have you got time for brunch? I want to run over some of the evidence, and I paid for a fortnight's worth of breakfasts, and Peggy only had a couple before she got mugged. I want my money's worth."

Frankie glanced at Meredith and could see something was amiss, but it wasn't with him, which made a change. And breakfast had been good the last time. He nodded.

"Give me five minutes to finish this lot, and I'll be with you."

Frankie finished his mouthful and looked at Meredith. "To summarise, they have yet to finish the post-mortem examination. But it looks like it was an embolism. Now that could have been waiting to happen, or it could have been brought on by the stress of the situation. We may never know. That being the case, if you find who did it, it may be difficult to make a murder charge stick, and manslaughter may be the way to go."

"Okay, so what else did you find?" Meredith rolled a sausage from one side of the plate to the other. Frankie had already given the team this information, but Meredith was clearly agitated and he decided not to mention it.

"The Kirk mask had been used by Carmichael. It's a perfect fit, and while we have to await the results on the skin and hair found inside both the mask and the wig, it appears, upon basic examination, the hair at least, is Carmichael's. The prints have all been cleared except -"

"Yes, I know that bit. Anything else." Meredith finally speared the sausage and examined it before biting into it.

Frankie chewed his bottom lip. He rarely found Meredith good company, and today he was particularly irritating. He sighed.

"We couldn't find any fingerprints, footprints, other than the cleaner's, on a tiny spot of blood, on or around the body. It's almost as though Carmichael had been placed there after the event," Frankie held his finger up, "which he wasn't. There weren't many cupboards or drawers, although there was a safe. All had been ransacked. No obvious traces of the person that did it were found. He was killed between eleven thirty at night and one thirty in the morning, and not found until eight the next morning when the cleaner arrived. Whoever did this turned the lights off and locked up. Probably took Carmichael's key. *Again*, as you know, the room had been checked and found locked at twelve thirty when security gave it the once over before securing the building as a whole. They didn't go in, they simply checked that it was locked. Unless our chap was hiding in there and managed to get out without setting off the alarm system, it narrows the time of death to between eleven thirty and twelve thirty. I understand from Trump that the last person to see him was his understudy at eleven fifteen. So that also fits."

Frankie placed his knife and fork on the side of his plate. "I'm going to check the post-mortem results later this afternoon. But I doubt there is anything else. If you don't mind me saying, Meredith, you seem agitated. Was there another reason for meeting with me?"

"Not really, Sherlock. I just wanted something to eat, and to get out of the station." Meredith jerked his head towards the kitchen. "This lot also owe me. I like value for money and thought I'd treat you. Again."

Frankie took in the half-finished meal on Meredith's plate, and glanced back up at Meredith who looked what could only be described as rough.

"Well, if you don't mind me stating what is commonly known as the bleeding obvious, only eating half of what you pay for isn't good value. Look, Meredith, if you have something to say, spit it out. The suspense is killing me."

Meredith shook his head, as though Frankie was mistaken in his understanding of their meeting.

"Nothing to spit, Sherlock. How long until we can confirm that the DNA used for matching to the girls was Carmichael's?"

"Twenty-four hours tops. They know it's urgent, so maybe within twelve." Frankie picked up his mug and took a sip.

"Do you think I should ask Patsy to marry me?"

Frankie coughed and spluttered, and then coughed some more. "What? Is this a joke, a test of some sort?"

"Nope. I know you have a soft spot for her, I know you don't like me, but I know you're the type of man that usually gives a straight and honest answer." Meredith linked his fingers behind his head and leaned back in the chair. "Do you know, Sherlock, I've probably had more women than you've had dates." He shrugged. "I'm not bragging, it's how it is, how I am . . . was. But I'm buggered if all that has given me any useful knowledge with regards to how their brains work. I'm all right with the rest of their anatomy," he ignored Frankie, who shook his head, "but their thought processes floor me every time."

Closing his eyes as if in pain he blew out a laboured breath. "With Nicola, I thought it was due to her problems, the breakdown. But it seems I was wrong. I can't fathom Patsy at the moment, and I know it's been a rollercoaster of a week, but even so . . ." He opened his eyes and looked at Frankie. "I feel like I'm balanced on a knife edge: one false move and everything we had will be cut free. I don't want to lose her." He sniffed, released his head, and sat upright. "I ask again, do you think I should propose?"

"Do you want her to be your wife, absolutely forsaking all the other bits of skirt you chase . . . sorry, chased. Will she be allowed to be as important to you as you are? Will you accept that you are absolutely not always right, and allow her the freedom to remain her? To still be Patsy Hodge, the girl you fell in love with?"

"Bloody hell, Sherlock, a yes or a no would have done, but as you asked, yes of course."

"Then it seems to me that you should ask her. After all, nothing ventured nothing gained. What's the worst that could happen? She might say no. That doesn't mean you will lose her, simply that she's not ready, or perhaps," Frankie allowed himself a little smile, "not sure." Frankie finished his coffee. "Now is there anything else, because quite frankly I'm feeling more than a little uncomfortable."

"Yes, me too. Let's make a move." Meredith stood abruptly, and waved to the waitress. "Tell the boss, I'll be back."

His phone rang as the stepped outside, and he was glad he didn't have to walk back with Frankie. He mumbled his thanks and saluted him as Frankie made his excuses, and set off in the direction of the hospital.

Meredith listened to an excited Seaton. "Text me the address, I'll call Rawlings."

Meredith hurried up the path of the ancient cottage. Seaton was standing on the step waiting for him. He led Meredith into the room opposite the entrance. Meredith walked in and looked around. He opened the door on one side of the room and nodded. Then, walking to the French doors, he stepped out into the garden and nodded again.

"That's not all, Gov, come and see this."

Meredith noted the key pad for the lock on the door as they exited the room, and followed Seaton through the kitchen. Seaton opened the door leading to the garage. Meredith looked at the silvery blue people carrier and nodded again.

"Peggy was right. What about the Range Rover?"

"Hired. In a company name, but Carmichael was sole director of the company. We've not found it yet." A noise in the hall caught their attention, "That'll be Dave."

They walked back through the hall and opened the door to Dave and Ellen Rawlings.

"Hello, Meredith, hello Uncle Tom." Ellen wiped her feet carefully and entered the house.

Meredith bent down and took her hand. "Right, young lady, I've got a job for you. Without touching anything, I want you to tell me what you know about this house."

"Why?"

"Because it will help us."

"Why?"

"Because we're not as clever as you, and Uncle Tom thinks this is the house Charlie lived in, but I'm not sure. Do you think you'll remember?"

"Yes." Ellen looked at her father and rolled her eyes. Meredith pushed open the door opposite and, still holding her hand, walked in with her. "Yes, this is it. That was our bed. The dressing up is in that box, and the . . . Oh, the box with the soldiers is gone." Pulling free from Meredith she ran to the fireplace. "Look, there are our jars. Up there on the shelf."

Seaton pulled some gloves from his pocket and lifted one of the jars from the shelf in the alcove.

Ellen put her hands on her hips and huffed. "It's dead, isn't it? That's not nice. Brown Owl will go mad. She said we had to let them go afterwards." Her face dropped and she turned to Meredith. "Will we be in trouble?"

"No, Charlie will, he was supposed to do it." Meredith pulled his phone from his pocket, and hitting the call button he held the phone in his hand rather than put it to his ear. The phone, secured in an evidence bag, and tucked in Seaton's inside pocket played out its ring tone.

"That's Charlie's phone." Ellen looked up at Seaton. "Uncle Tom, have you got Charlie's phone?"

Meredith hung up, and smiled as Seaton nodded confirmation. He held out his hand and led her back into the hall.

"Time to go, young lady. Thanks for all your help." He ruffled her hair, and, standing next to Seaton, he waved goodbye to Ellen as Rawlings took her back to the car.

"Right, get forensics out here. I've got an apology to make."

"Charlesworth?" Seaton asked as he followed Meredith to his car.

"The very same."

Chris Grainger walked Patsy to her car. "Are you sure about this?" he asked as he opened her door for her.

"Almost. I'll think some more, but I'm ninety-nine per cent there. That's why I needed your help, and you've been great. Thanks, for everything." She pecked him on the cheek.

He grabbed her arm as she sat in the car. "Think and then think again. I'll see you on Thursday. I hope Meredith knows how lucky he is."

Patsy shrugged. "Perhaps, we'll see. Now I must dash, Amanda's been on her own with the baby for hours."

"It'll be tough if you lie to him. Because once you take that route, there's no going back, not without fallout. With Meredith, it could be catastrophic."

"Don't I know. I really must go now. Thanks, Chris, now get back in there, or Sharon really will be suspicious."

Chris laughed. "She was born suspicious. Give me a call if you need to talk." He closed her door for her and sighed as she pulled away.

Meredith smiled as Professor Cole hurried towards him. As she got closer he could have sworn her nose had grown bigger still.

"Hello, Dr Rose, I'm here cap in hand. Wasn't sure how to track down Dr Charlesworth, but knew you'd point me in the right direction."

"Have you got your man?" Professor Cole beamed and wagged her finger. "I told you it wasn't Graham. Here, hold these." She shoved a pile of files into his arms and unlocked her office door. "Stop looking at my nose, Meredith, you really will go cross-eyed. I'm sorry to say you'll have to catch him at home. He's taken a few days' leave. Probably due to the stress of putting up with you."

She relieved him of the files and waved him into a seat. Sitting at her desk she brandished a sheet of paper at him.

"What's that?"

"It should be a holiday request form. What it actually is, is a note saying all his patients are on the mend. No ops scheduled until next week, so he was taking a few days. My own fault, it's what I told him to do. I wasn't expecting it so soon though. Luckily, we found a locum available for ward cover."

Smiling, she leaned forward, her arms folded on the desk in front. "Jolly decent of you to come in, I have to say. Graham will be more delighted than anyone that you have your man, and not because it clears him."

"Let's just leave it that someone got him. I saw the notice up outside about your fundraiser. Give me some forms and I'll get the lads to pass them round the station."

"Will do, and Meredith, the nose, stop. Please." Professor Cole shook her head. "Do you know, when Graham first arrived I toyed with the idea of asking him to fix it. I have no problem with it at all, but it seems the rest of the world are fascinated."

"Charlesworth? Why him in particular? And I'm sorry, it does draw the eye."

"That's what he used to specialise in. He was a plastic surgeon, the best. Specialised in reconstruction on burn damage, but being based in America he dabbled in making people look more attractive. When his daughter fell ill, he swapped to paediatrics, so much more rewarding." Her face fell. "But you can't win them all. He lost his own daughter, you know. That's why he came here. Fresh start and all that. Ah, here you go." She held out the sponsor forms Meredith had requested.

"I'm sorry to hear that. He probably thinks I'm an insensitive bastard." Taking the forms Meredith stood up. "I'll leave you to it."

Meredith knew he had little choice but to go back to the station. He had hoped for an excuse to keep busy elsewhere, but something was niggling him, apart from his problems at home, and his brain seemed to function better while he was on the move.

As he reached the top of the stairs, Trump was leading Beth Durham past the incident room. He nodded acknowledgement. She looked pale and frightened.

"I know you heard what I said, but it was an empty threat, one of those things you say in the heat of the moment . . ." She faltered and her eyes welled up. "It wasn't me. I didn't like him, but I still loved him."

"Well, if that's the case you'll soon be out of here." His phone rang and he answered the call from Frankie, walking away from Beth Durham as he did so. "What does that mean? Maybe nothing, but still you thought something enough to tell me? Yes, yes, I'm sorry, it will probably be very useful eventually."

Trump had settled Beth Durham in the interview room, and was walking back to fetch the requested glass of water.

"Nothing useful then?" Meredith asked, having overheard the end of the conversation. "Do you want to sit in with me?"

"No, Sherlock has checked Carmichael's post-mortem. There were two minute markings on him. One in the crook of the elbow, the other on his neck. Probably nothing, but they're testing the bloods for drugs now. I will sit in with you. Let's get on with it."

Beth Durham looked up and blinked back tears as they set up the recorder and read her her rights.

"I didn't do it," she repeated.

"Okay, Beth, I'll accept that, but it seems to me you were closer to him than anyone else, and you didn't like him very much. Tell me, who might have disliked him enough to torture him."

Beth's hands flew to her mouth. She clearly had no idea Carmichael had been tortured.

"No one. Who would do that?" She pushed her hair from her forehead. "He wasn't always like that. He used to be as sweet as he was handsome. Then he met Izzy."

"Izzy Mansell. I remember her, quite a looker. What happened?"

Beth told them as much about the volatile relationship as she knew. When she reached the part about Carmichael hitting her in public, Meredith began to nod.

"Yes, I knew I had some knowledge of her. What happened then?"

"Everything collapsed for him for a while, and she went off to America. His ring had left her with a small scar above the eyebrow, and she fell for the plastic surgeon. They'd met before when he'd done a similar job for her."

Beth now had Meredith's full attention and he leaned forward as she continued.

"But as always with Izzy she messed that up too, and left him with their child. She came back to Jeremy, said she loved him, and always would, that they had to be together. Then they found out she was pregnant. Jeremy was over the moon at first, even went with her for the scan, but that backfired."

Trump frowned. "How can a scan backfire?"

"She was too far gone. Possibly only by weeks, but it cast doubt over whether or not it was Jeremy's. They rowed about that too. Constantly, but somehow they kept it from the press. Izzy couldn't model, Jeremy was not doing anything too high profile, and it arrived early too."

"Meaning it cast yet more doubt." Meredith suggested and Beth nodded.

"What happened to the child?" Meredith already knew the answer, but he needed confirmation.

"She was adopted. She was a sweet little thing, great big eyes with long lashes." Meredith and Trump exchanged glances. "I arranged it. It's my fault Izzy's dead. I found a private adoption agency, and she went to a lovely couple. I took her to them with the case worker. But Izzy couldn't handle it. She went . . . mad. It's the only way I can describe it. Then she disappeared and a couple of months later turned up dead. Suicide."

"Did Carmichael still think the child was not his?"

Beth nodded. "I tried to do the right thing, really I did. I contacted her ex. I told him that she'd had a child that was being rejected, and would probably be adopted. We had a brief exchange, but he thought it was Izzy playing games and changed his email address. He told me not to contact him anymore. I couldn't risk Jeremy finding out so I dropped it."

"Do you remember the name of the ex?" Meredith was already preparing to leave, and he collected his phone and pen from the desk.

"Charlesworth."

Meredith leaned forward as Trump murmured in surprise. "Interview terminated at three fifteen. Miss Durham is free to go." He hit the button and got to his feet.

"That's it?" Beth looked from one to the other.

"It is. This way."

Meredith was impatient to get on. As he stepped into the corridor, Rawlings appeared with Antonio Garcia.

Beth rushed into his arms. "Toni, am I pleased to see you! Why are you here?"

Antonio lifted her face and kissed her gently. "I don't know. Someone has killed Carmichael, perhaps they think it is me."

"No we don't, you can go." Meredith looked the man described as the hot Spaniard up and down, and begrudgingly admitted he might have a certain charm. "Excuse me. You two, briefing now."

Beth and Antonio stood bemused for a second before Rawlings insisted they could go. He dashed back to the incident room having seen them out.

"Jeremy Carmichael put Graham Charlesworth's child up for adoption out of jealousy. Then for reasons we have yet to discover, he decided that she might actually be his, and began his search. He abducted Ellen and Gemma, but settled for DNA on the other two. None of them were his. But here's the strange thing: although he seemed keen to prove she was his daughter, he also tried to set Charlesworth up as the abductor. Why? Who knows?" Meredith shrugged. "But it nearly worked. We were on to Charlesworth, all circumstantial, but nothing he could explain away. Carmichael may have found his daughter and left Charlesworth to carry the can. If we hadn't found out, we would have assumed Charlesworth had murdered her."

"So how did Charlesworth find out?"

"We told him. Whoever did this, knew all about Charlesworth, knew that the soldiers could be traced back to him. Perhaps Charlesworth worked out who that was. I think Charlesworth killed Carmichael, and conveniently has just taken leave from work. Seaton and Travers, get over there now. Kick the door in, if necessary. I'll deal with the fallout if I'm wrong."

"But how did Carmichael track down the girls?" Jo Adler held her hand up.

"He knew which agency had been used, so perhaps he bribed someone, perhaps he broke in. But he only got a list of names because he didn't know which child was his." Meredith shrugged. "So he went on their looks . . ."

Meredith stopped speaking and pinched the bridge of his nose. "The girls may still be in danger of abduction." He turned and tapped the board. "What if one of these is Charlesworth's daughter? If he tortured Carmichael before he killed him, he may have found out that he'd drawn a blank, but why had he made it look like a burglary? To put us off the scent or to find something else that had been stolen." Meredith clapped his hands. "And it is murder, I'll guarantee it. Two needle marks found on the body, one in the crook of the arm, one in the neck. He killed him."

"Should we call the parents, Gov? If they are at risk, the parents need to know." Rawlings had his hand on the telephone.

"Yes, get onto it now, Dave. If any of the girls are not in sight of their parents, get a car over to them, and find them. We may need to consider putting someone in the house with them. He's killed now, and who knows how desperate he is."

CHAPTER NINETEEN

In an effort to get somewhere near normality, and once they were on their own, Meredith updated Patsy on the latest news on the case. She nodded in the right places and asked the right questions, but her mind seemed to be elsewhere. He didn't voice this observation.

"So how was your day?"

"Busy. Introduced Toni Garcia to his son and Peggy, ordered flowers for Nicola, and went into work for a while. Not to mention dealing with Paul, although to be honest he's very little trouble."

"Thanks for sorting the flowers. How did the introductions go?" Meredith was relieved the baby wasn't his, but frowned at the stirring of jealousy the mention of Antonio and Paul caused.

"He's delighted, if a little shell shocked. His mother, on the other hand, is overjoyed, and was arranging to come over to meet him. I don't know how it will all work out, but at least he has family now. Perhaps he'll be brought up in Spain." Patsy gave a shrug as she turned to face Meredith. "Did you have a chance to go through Nicola's address book? A long shot I know, but if not I think you should do it tonight."

"Give me a hug and I'll do it now." He held out his arms and Patsy walked into his embrace. He whispered into hair. "It will always be enough. Always."

They stood in the centre of the kitchen, not talking, simply hugging for several minutes, and only pulled apart when they heard Paul begin to stir. Amanda called out to say she'd deal with him.

"I think she's disappointed he's not related," Meredith observed as they heard her cooing to Paul.

"Yes, I think you are a little too, if you're honest." Patsy searched his face for evidence of this.

"No, Patsy, I'm delighted not to have another issue, albeit as cute as that baby, getting in the way of us. We already have enough distractions with the work we do. Bringing up a baby as things stand at the moment, and in these circumstances, is not welcome."

"I'm glad, because Toni is coming around to see him later, and he has flooring samples for Peggy to look at. I don't want you to make him feel uncomfortable. This is as difficult for him as it is for you." Patsy's eyes betrayed her concern.

"Why would I do that? I want nothing but the best for the boy." Meredith spoke the truth, but the feeling he had lost something remained, and he shrugged and attempted to inject a little humour. "That said, as his guardian or executor or whatever my title is to be, the Garcia bloke had better get it right."

A sigh escaped from deep inside as Patsy smiled. "You're going to do it? I'm pleased. It's the right thing, Meredith. Well done."

She gave a little scream as Meredith pulled her into his arms. He kissed her forehead, then her nose, and then her mouth. His passion increased as he felt her respond.

"Is it too early to go to bed?" His voice was husky as he kissed her again.

"Merriwinkle, I need your advice about . . . Oh, am I interrupting something? Put her down a moment. I need to get the car on the road, I have to sort out an MOT. Toni will need a car."

Unabashed, Peggy stood, arms akimbo, looking at them. Meredith didn't move: he knew his response to Peggy would be obvious. Patsy grinned.

"Give us a minute, Peggy. Bob Travers' brother runs a garage; they helped me out when my car was vandalised. I'll get you the number."

"Good, well, don't be long, I've got lots to sort out." Peggy turned to leave. "I might move out tomorrow. Toni is doing my bedroom first, and I'll be on hand to make sure he does a good job. Unless you want me to stay until after the funeral?" Her face saddened and she added, "I'm not sure I can go yet, we'll have to see."

Lost in her own memories, memories she'd buried long ago, she left them without waiting for a response.

"One down, one to go. If we can get rid of Amanda, we can get back to normal. I'm pleased for old Peggy though. Sort of riches to rags and back again."

He smiled as Patsy snorted.

"What has ever been normal about us? I like having Amanda here, if anything she reminds me what normal really is!" Patsy pulled away from him and looked down. "You're safe to move now." She failed in her attempt not to laugh and, delighted, Meredith pulled her back.

"I've not finished with you yet. I'm glad you're back. I have my Patsy back." He rolled his eyes as the doorbell rang. "Dear God, what's a man got to do to get some peace around here?"

He released her and went to answer the door. Patsy was glad of the distraction. She'd not been anywhere, he'd just forgotten where to look, and he might lose her again if he knew. She closed her eyes and drew in a deep breath, pushing the thought to the back of her mind. She'd given herself until after the funeral to decide, and that would be soon enough to start worrying about it.

She greeted Antonio as Meredith showed him through to the sitting room where the baby was sleeping. Offering him a drink, she left the two men alone.

"What are your plans?" Once more the jealousy stirred as Meredith watched the baby respond to Antonio Garcia's voice.

"At the moment, I have no idea. My mother arrives on Thursday, we will discuss it then." Lifting the baby into his arms, and snuggling him into his neck, Antonio looked at Meredith. "You are a very lucky man. To be surrounded by these women who support you. If it were not for Patsy I would not know my son." Watching closely for Meredith's reaction, he added, "If I am unable to take him at the moment, what are your intentions? What will you do?"

"I'll look after him." Meredith shook his head as though it were a stupid question, and was taken aback as Garcia gave him a broad smile.

"Then you will be godfather? That is wonderful news. Patsy explained what Nicola wanted . . ." His face fell, and he looked at his son. "I am sorry for your loss." Sighing, he looked back up. "Patsy told me you were a good man and you would do it. But I have to confess I thought it a little odd, but Nicola was clearly correct."

"Godfather? You mean guardian, I think."

Paul stirred and gave a little whimper, Meredith held out his arms. "Here, I'll take him."

"No, no. I must practice. It is a long time for me. My brother lived with us for a while with his family, so I know what to do, I do have to remember though." He sat on the sofa and lay the baby on his lap. Clucking and cooing, he checked Paul's nappy and his nose turned up. "I think I have found the problem."

Meredith grinned, grateful the baby hadn't been surrendered. He pointed to a bag by the coffee table. "Be my guest. It's all in there. I'll watch you remember."

After a false start, Antonio removed the baby's clothes, and the offending nappy. He smiled as the baby gurgled and kicked, free of the restraint. He had just finished cleaning him when Amanda entered the room.

"Patsy said to bring these through . . . Oh right." She cleared her throat. "You must be Antonio, I'm Amanda. I would shake your hand but you seem to have them full at the moment." She gave a little giggle, and then flushed as her father looked at her as though she'd lost her mind. "Here." Placing the cups on the table, she handed Antonio a clean nappy.

"Thank you, Amanda, you are most kind."

Antonio held her gaze and Meredith stiffened.

"Are you two flirting in front of me? I don't think that's appropriate with . . ." lost for words he pointed at the baby, "him watching." He looked at his daughter and shook his head.

"No, Dad, we were being polite. It's what civilised people do," Amanda answered, her voice firm, but her colour had deepened. She turned back to Antonio. "I'm sorry, Antonio, my father is prehistoric when it suits. I'll see you later, good luck."

Slamming her eyes at her father she left the room.

"Please call me Toni," Antonio called as he watched her depart.

Meredith's nose wrinkled. Antonio looked down and smiled at the baby. He rattled something off in Spanish which Meredith didn't understand. Had he been able to translate he would have heard Antonio observe, "Possessive fathers, my son, they are always an obstacle to avoid."

Antonio completed his task, and placed the soiled nappy and wipes in a small, sweet-smelling bag.

"About this godfather thing. You understand that guardian and godfather are not the same thing now, don't you?"

"I am training to be a solicitor, sir. I am almost there. I know the difference, but that is not good enough. I have booked his christening for Sunday at St Peter's. You will be his godfather." Antonio lifted the baby and stood smiling at Meredith. "I know it is right."

"A christening? Already?" Meredith was incredulous. "Godfather, me?" He held his arms out. "When did all this happen?"

"My mother is coming here. I don't know how long she will stay, a few weeks at least, but it is our tradition. The baby must be accepted by God. It is right."

"Give me that, I'll be back in a moment." Meredith held his hand out and took the nappy sack from Antonio. "Have a seat, drink your drink."

Giving an awkward smile he set off for the kitchen.

"Patsy, I nearly passed out. He is gorgeous. Now I know what they mean by breath being taken away. Wow." Amanda pulled out a chair and sat down. "How long will he be here?" she asked a laughing Patsy.

"Not bloody long enough for you to get involved. I thought you had a bloke, not that we've met him." Meredith marched into the kitchen. "Gorgeous? A man isn't gorgeous." Meredith stopped in the middle of the kitchen and looked at Patsy. "Did you know he'd organised a christening and wants me to be godfather?"

"Yes, he wants me and Peggy to be godmothers. It's just what Peggy needs. He asked me not to mention it, as he wanted to meet you and ask himself." Patsy smiled at the look on Meredith's face.

"What, check me out? The cheek of it!" Meredith allowed himself a smile. "I obviously passed. I'd better go and sort out the details." He swung the bag towards her. "A gift for you." Patsy smiled as he strode back to the sitting room, and turned to Amanda.

"He likes it when he's appreciated. I don't think it happens often."

Graham Charlesworth lay on the bed in the small family-run hotel he'd found on the outskirts of Bristol. He stared at the pattern on the wallpaper as he considered his actions since he'd arrived in England. Why had he gone to see Jeremy Carmichael? Why didn't he leave well alone? It had seemed too good an opportunity to miss when he knew Carmichael worked in the hospital. Now it seemed he was right, and there was nothing he could do about it. His fists clenched as he replayed the first conversation with Jeremy Carmichael.

"Charlesworth, an unexpected and, if I may be so bold, unwelcome meeting. What do you want?" Carmichael removed his earphones which hung from his neck, and handing them to the next presenter, he had done nothing to hide his displeasure. But Graham had assumed he could still get the information from him. He just needed to find a way to get Carmichael talking. At the time, he thought he was being clever as he followed Carmichael into the reception area.

"I'm sorry you feel that way. I simply wanted to clear my conscience. You know, put the past to rest." Graham had then started to lay the bait. "I assume you know Izzy and I had a daughter, Jilly. She died, and it's a pain I can't describe, so when I realised you were working here, I knew I had to say something. I wanted you to know the joy of having a daughter, even if it needs to be from afar." He'd turned to walk away. "If you want to hear what I have to say, this is my address." He pulled the paper from his pocket; he'd prepared ready for this moment. "Call me. I'll cook you dinner, if you like. I know about the other child."

Scene set, he'd walked away and waited. It took Jeremy Carmichael three days to make the call. When Graham had opened the door, it was like another man had arrived. Carmichael had suggested dinner was too intimate, so it took minutes for the niceties to be out of the way, and, drinks poured, they got down to business

"What do you know about Izzy's other child?" Carmichael sighed, and helplessly held up his hands, as though the memory still hurt. "It was a very painful time, and now I can only imagine what it was like losing your daughter as you did."

"I had an email. It was anonymous. It told me Izzy had had a daughter, who was probably mine, and she was putting her up for adoption. It warned I only had weeks to act before it was signed and sealed. I asked the date of birth, which was provided, and I knew the child wasn't mine. Although Izzy and I were still technically together, she'd gone into her own little world when Jilly was diagnosed. Towards the end she didn't even live in the same house, she stayed at our holiday home. Whoever the father was, it wasn't me."

"So why call this meeting? Why come and see me?"

"Because I believe it was Izzy emailing me. I have no idea why. I assumed you didn't want the child, hence the adoption, and she'd actually found some maternal instinct and was grasping at straws in an attempt to keep the child." Graham shrugged. "She liked the playing and the dressing up, but couldn't bring herself to change a messy nappy, let alone get up in the middle of the night to give a feed. Anyway, rather than contact you, I left it. I simply said I wasn't interested." Sad eyes looked at Carmichael. "You have to understand, I had Jilly and her illness to deal with."

"Lazy and spoilt." Carmichael nodded and his nose wrinkled. "Yes, Izzy was a princess about most things. But that doesn't explain why you're here now."

Graham pointed to two of the boxes he had yet to unpack.

"In that box is a set of tin soldiers, made by my great-grandfather, my grandfather, and my father over a period of thirty odd years. As a boy I played with them constantly. Even helped repair and repaint them when they became damaged. They are my most precious possession, the only thing left of my family. My reminder of happier days."

Graham went to collect the green tin. Opening the lid, he passed it to Carmichael, who managed a cursory glance before it was placed on the table. "When Jilly died I placed one in her hand to see her through her final journey. It was the last gift I gave her, if you like. As I closed her fingers I wondered about her sister, or half-sister as it is. I loved Izzy very much at one time, and I adored my daughter, and I wondered about the other member of their little family. As I was coming to England, I thought I should make sure you knew she was yours, or probably yours anyway. I also wanted to see her. To give her one of those little soldiers and tell her about her sister if possible, although I know some adoptive parents wouldn't like that. I suppose it was curiosity, and ensuring you knew."

"But now? All these years later, what good is that to me even if I were the father?" Carmichael was genuinely confused and, unbeknown to Graham, he was more than happy to receive this news. Now he wanted information.

"I know Izzy could be spiteful, and even if there was nothing you could do to reverse things, I . . . well, I'd want to know." Graham topped up their glasses. "Do you know who adopted her, or the name of the agency? I will, of course, go through the proper channels. Even if you don't investigate further, I'd like to meet Jilly's half-sister."

Carmichael threw back his drink and stood up. "I don't, I'm afraid, not a clue. Izzy sorted it all with our assistant at the time. The child was not mine, and I can't help you. I'm sorry, but this has been a total waste of time. I'll be off." He held out his hand, "I'm sorry I can't be of help to you. But we have little in common, except perhaps once loving the same damaged woman. I doubt we'll meet again."

Closing his eyes against the memory, Graham Charlesworth clenched his fists and pushed them into his forehead. They had met again. Blinking back tears of frustration, he asked himself why he'd gone there. Why had he gone prepared to kill the man? Why had he not gone to the police? Why? Why?

"WHY?" he roared. Sitting upright, he swigged from the bottle beside his bed. He knew why. He'd started to plan it the minute Meredith showed him the soldiers, and professor Rose had said about the abductor knowing their history. No one but Carmichael knew he'd given Jilly that soldier. No one knew he'd painted some of them, only Jilly. Carmichael had either broken in to his home himself or paid someone to do it. But his main sin was to take Jilly's passport.

He gave a shuddering sigh as he remembered pushing the scalpel into Carmichael's cheek the second time. It was then Carmichael had started talking.

He confessed that he'd had thought Graham was right, that the child had been his. Something he hadn't believed at the time. He'd insisted on the adoption, even found the agency, and made sure everything went smoothly. Carmichael had told Izzy she'd failed as a mother once, and she was sure to fail again. After the meeting with Charlesworth he knew he had to find her, and take her back. He was getting on, and he wanted a family. He wanted someone that would always be his. Carmichael admitted to Graham that if he found his daughter, he was planning to use Jilly's passport to take her out of the country. There was the few years' age difference, but that wouldn't have mattered. Carmichael had been relieved Graham had got her a British passport, less likely to draw attention to them.

Graham rubbed his hands over his eyes as the memory of drawing air into the syringe filled his vision. Graham had injected Carmichael in the neck first, hoping that using that artery the bubble of air would travel to his heart quickly, but Carmichael hadn't died, so in a panic he gave the second injection. Graham already had what he wanted by then: there was no need to kill. But he had to. Carmichael's plan had become his own. He'd failed, and failed again with the agency he'd employed to track her down. Carmichael's investigators had been paid handsomely to steal the records, and the problem had arisen when it was found they were incomplete. They had stolen only where the girls were now, not where they had come from. As he'd sucked the air into the syringe, he'd thought that with Carmichael dead, there was a still a chance to get away with it. He'd convinced himself of that until he'd left the building. It was then he knew without a doubt, that he had days at best before they made the full connection. So here he was. Holed up in a second-rate hotel, wanting a glimpse of his daughter in the flesh before they caught up with him.

Graham had recognised Dana Dwight as his daughter as soon as Meredith had shown him the photograph. She was the double of Jilly. They both had his nose. They both had their mother's eyes, but his nose. Carmichael had inadvertently found his daughter for him. Graham now knew where she lived, what school she went to, and the time and location of her swimming lessons. She had a swimming lesson every Thursday.

On the afternoon before the funeral, Señora Garcia arrived in Bristol. Peggy's old Ford Fiesta had been made fit and legal for the road, and Peggy went with Antonio to pick her up. She'd now admitted to herself that she was enjoying easing herself back into normal society. Señora Garcia was beside herself with excitement. Her other two grandchildren now lived in America and she only saw them twice a year, if she was lucky. Antonio watched, amazed, as she with her broken English, and Peggy with a few tourist phrases, discussed baby Paul, or Pablo as Señora Garcia insisted. Antonio had completed Peggy's room at the house, but she gave it up for his mother, insisting she could stay at Meredith's until another room was ready, or Señora Garcia went home.

When Patsy arrived with Paul, his grandmother had cried for an hour non-stop. Not bawling or wailing, but a constant flow of tears as she gabled away to her grandson, telling him about his wonderful namesake. Antonio had watched Peggy's reaction as his mother told the baby she would pack up her house in Spain and come and live in this house with him. It wasn't right he should be separated from his father, and it wasn't right she was separated from either of them. She was needed here. Peggy's grasp of Spanish wasn't adequate enough to understand the detail, and she smiled as she passed yet another tissue. Having no idea of his long-term plans, or how he was going to sort out their lives going forward, Antonio had not passed comment.

The day of the funeral arrived. Patsy was glad. Too much was being left unsaid, and too many things seemed to hang in the air waiting to explode into their lives. But first they had to say goodbye to Nicola. It was a small gathering: the Garcias had arrived with Paul, and Peggy had steeled herself to cope with emotions she may not want. Searching through her old clothes, she'd revived a bright floral dress and unable to cope with formal shoes, she'd borrowed a pair of flip flops from Amanda, and had also painted her toenails. Several of Meredith's team also attended with their partners. Meredith had managed to contact a few of Nicola's friends, and a distant aunt and cousin turned up.

Nicola had opted to be cremated. She had chosen two short poems to be read by the appointed minister, which were touching and poignant given her young age, and her favourite hymn from her school days, 'Jerusalem'. Peggy belted it out at the top of her voice.

Finally, a letter from Nicola to Paul was read out. It expressed her love, her hopes, and a little bit of advice on how he should treat others. Before the minister was halfway through, the majority of the small congregation were wiping away tears. Meredith held his until the final sentence.

"And finally, never be afraid to ask for advice. Do not wander blindly through problems that can be shared. Your guardian, John Meredith, is a good man. Let him help guide you when necessary. Trust him. Finally, please know that I loved you with all my heart, and will be watching over you. Mummy."

Amanda glanced up at her father as the coffin slid through the maroon velvet curtains. He made no attempt to halt the tears he shed and he put his arm around his daughter and squeezed Patsy's hand tighter as the curtains closed.

Once outside, they walked through the garden of remembrance and Meredith blew his nose noisily on the tissue Amanda pressed into his hand. They reached the small display of wreaths and floral arrangements for Nicola, and Meredith sighed.

"Not much to celebrate, a life, is it?"

As he spoke Paul let out a sharp cry and his grandmother began to comfort him, singing softly in Spanish.

"But he is. I think I'll miss him."

Patsy turned and waved to Antonio, who was walking behind his mother, Peggy on his arm.

"You're right, as always," Meredith smiled at his daughter. "Just as when my time comes, however big a balls-up I've made, I also made Amanda. Comforting thought." He glanced across to the entrance. "The men need to get away. I'll go and thank them, and then give Trump a quick call." Meredith fingered the silent phone in his pocket. "I won't go back in unless it's necessary."

Meredith had his phone to his ear before he reached Rawlings, Seaton, and Travers. Patsy watched him pause his journey as he listened to Trump. She watched him gesture the men forward, and then glance over his shoulder at her. She knew he would be going back into work, and she knew what her answer would be when she called them the next day. She linked her arm in Amanda's and completed the circuit of the small garden.

"Your father is about to disappear. The Garcias will want to get home with the baby, and as they've adopted Peggy that leaves just the two of us. What say we go and find a bar? It's almost five, and I don't think that's too early to have a drink. We could . . ."

She stopped speaking as Meredith hurried back.

"You know what I just said -"

"Go, Meredith."

"I'm sorry, but Charlesworth has been caught, and -"

"I said 'go', Meredith, I'll see you later. Call me when you can. I'm taking your daughter out to dinner." She stepped forward and pecked him on the cheek.

"Bit early for dinner, isn't it?" Meredith hugged her close. "Have fun, and if you do get home before me, wait up!"

"Go, Dad, now." Amanda punched his arm. He turned to smile at her and winked. She noticed how much older he looked today. A few more lines had appeared at the corner of his eyes, he had no colour in his cheeks, and his red eyes reflected his sadness. Smiling, she returned his wink. "Don't be late. You look awful, you need a good night's sleep."

"Thank you. And on that happy note . . ." Meredith returned her smile.

Jo Adler had been with the Dwights, providing them with contact numbers and checking their security, when Graham Charlesworth was spotted by a beat bobby in the centre of town. He called it in, and waited for other officers to join him in his search. The sighting had been deliberate. Once he'd confirmed the officer had recognised him, Graham Charlesworth had dashed up an alley, in through the front, and out of a rear entrance of a multi-story car park. Stopping short of the exit, where he was sure no cameras were watching, he pulled on his leathers and jumped on his bike. He would see his daughter swim today.

Jo explained what had happened to Dana's parents.

"We can stay here if you like, or I'll come to the pool with you. Which would you prefer?"

"We'll carry on as normal, after all if . . ." Mr Dwight glanced over his shoulder to ensure Dana wasn't in earshot, "if the man is her father, he won't hurt her. The town centre is quite a way, the pool is not that far. With them on the door," he nodded at the two officers pacing the front garden, "I'm sure it will be okay. She's been practising for this badge for so long she'll know something is amiss if we don't go."

"If that's what you want." Jo smiled at him. "I hope you don't mind me asking, but will you tell her she's adopted?"

"We already have. We've told her she was special and we chose her. A bit more than that of course and we mention it occasionally. Don't thinks she understands properly now, but she will. Can you imagine the shock when she understands fully who her parents were though?" He sighed. "But that's a problem for another day." He glanced at the clock. "Let's get going."

Graham, now complete with darker brown hair and eyebrows, was already sitting on the back row of the spectators' seating area when the two officers arrived. He was now wearing a wildly patterned Hawaiian shirt, and sat head bent forward as though engrossed in the magazine he had picked up on his way in. The two officers gave him a cursory glance before leaving. One of them remained stationed at the door. Graham relaxed. Whatever happened now, he would see her. The seats in front of him began to fill up a little, but it wasn't many. Just a few parents staying to watch their child achieve their next badge. The humming of low conversation filled the air, and he looked up as the first gaggle of children burst out from the changing room door. Their teacher blew a whistle, and the shrill noise bounced from wall to wall. Even the spectators fell silent for a while. Dana was not amongst the first group.

He watched as the first group completed the exercises to gain their bronze swimming award. He hadn't been aware that this was happening, and was glad to be witness to at least one important moment in his child's life. He smiled as the excited children lined up to take a bow, and their rightful applause, when they had completed their tasks successfully.

He held his breath as they filed out and watched the next group enter. He spotted her immediately, and goose bumps covered his arms. He eyed the woman in the crisp white shirt standing against the wall near the door, and knew she was a police officer. Ignoring Jo Adler, he returned his attention to Dana. Dressed in pyjamas, on their teacher's command she and her companions lined up, spaced evenly along the two sides of the pool. He saw her wave to a couple in the front row, who smiled proudly, and returned her wave. They looked like decent people. He was glad. The whistle blew and the children launched themselves into the pool. Using doggy paddle to stay afloat, they gasped in air as they pulled off the pyjama bottoms. He grinned as she tied the knot in the first leg, her smile triumphant as she grabbed the other leg.

Graham was so intent on watching Dana, he didn't notice the girl who had drifted to the centre of the pool begin to struggle, having entangled herself in her clothing. It wasn't until the lifeguard hurried down the side of the pool, discarding his flip-flops as he went, that Graham had an inkling anything was wrong. Graham frowned and surveyed the rest of the pool. One of the children was under the water. She didn't surface. He stood and stepped into the aisle, taking the first step down to the pool. His gasp joined the rally of others as the lifeguard slipped and hit the floor with a thud. It was clear he'd damaged his leg, as he limped to the edge of the pool and dived in. On the other side of the pool, the teacher was calling the other children in the pool to come to the side. The lifeguard lifted the girl clear of the water and made his way to the side of the pool in front of Graham. Two parents lifted her onto the side as the lifeguard heaved himself out. Lying next to the girl, he winced as he tried to position himself.

Graham completed his journey to the poolside.

"Move out the way, I'm a doctor," he announced quietly, but with a confidence that convinced the lifeguard. Kneeling down next to the girl, Graham helped her vomit the water she had swallowed and soothed her as she lay shivering in the recovery position. Her mother stood watching, calling for a blanket. When it arrived, Graham wrapped it round her and picked her up. The mother was thanking him. Taking him by the elbow, they followed the teacher through to the changing room. Jo Adler returned her attention to Dana immediately it was clear the girl had been resuscitated. She walked forward, giving Dana a wave of support as the girl was taken through the door she had been guarding. The girl was a friend of Dana, and Dana looked very worried.

Having examined and spoken to the girl, Graham explained to her mother that she would be perfectly well once she had recovered from the shock. She'd swallowed a little water, but all her vital signs were perfectly healthy. The teacher had left them alone in the staff dressing room, and went to collect the others. As she led them back through to the main changing room, Dana broke rank and ran in to see her friend. She called as she disappeared, "I'm going to make sure Lisa is all right."

Jo was at the end of the queue and she smiled. When she reached the door and looked in, she saw the mother wiping drips from her daughter's face. The man who had resuscitated the child was kneeling down, his face at the same level as Dana's. He had his back towards Jo and was speaking quietly, Dana frowned at something he said, and he took her face in his hands. Jo saw Lisa's mother turn to look and a lump of concrete hit the bottom of her stomach. She strode into the room purposefully calling out as she did, "Charlesworth, I know that's you. Move away from the child."

Charlesworth froze, and what was only seconds felt like minutes to Jo before he turned to face her. She saw his tears, and his eyes pleaded with her.

"One minute please. Don't alarm the girls."

Jo stopped feet away from him, and from the corner of her eye saw Lisa pulled closer into her mother's arms. The silence hung heavily around them. Graham turned back to Dana. Reaching in his pocket he pulled out a tin soldier.

"I have to go now. One day, when you're older, perhaps we'll meet again. In the meantime, keep this little man." He lifted his hand and placed the soldier gently onto her palm. As he folded her fingers around it, his tears flowed more freely as he remembered Jilly. "You can send this back to me when you understand, if you don't want to keep it. But if I don't get it back, I'll know you do." Giving a short laugh he wiped his face with the back of his hand, aware his tears were frightening Dana. "You are a very special girl. You look after your mummy and daddy, and the soldier will look after you." He tapped her hand.

Grabbing her suddenly he pulled her into his embrace and hugged her. Jo placed a hand on his shoulder. He released Dana and stood up. "I have to go now. Whatever else happens, Dana, know that I'll be waiting." He waved down at her, and the stunned Dana gave a small flick of her wrist. The other two men were now standing in the doorway.

Hutchins beckoned him forward. "It's time to go, Dr Charlesworth."

Graham took one last look at his daughter before he was led away.

"Well, I am breathless. What a kind man, saving Lisa while knowing it might get him caught. I hope they think about that, you know, when they sentence him." Lisa's mother turned to Dana. "Are you okay?" Dana shrugged and nodded, bemused by the whole situation.

Jo Adler nodded at the woman. She didn't pass comment. In her book murder was murder. There had been no need to kill Jeremy Carmichael. That had been planned and carefully executed. Charlesworth should get his just deserts, but a little part of her hoped that Dana would keep the soldier, and not send it back to him.

She smiled as Dana's mother came rushing in. "No panic, it's all over."

As she left she heard Lisa's mother repeating what a wonderful man she thought he was. Jo pulled her phone from her pocket and called Meredith.

By the time Graham Charlesworth's solicitor had arrived, and the hotel where he had been staying had been searched, it was almost midnight before Meredith got home. He climbed into bed hoping he'd not woken Patsy. He knew she'd worked flat out for the last week or so, dealing with the funeral, and sorting Peggy and the Garcias out. She snuggled into him as he pulled the duvet up.

"You don't have to be so quiet, the baby isn't here anymore."

"I was thinking about you actually." Meredith sounded weary.

"How did it go? Did he confess?"

"Couldn't shut him up once he got going. His solicitor tried many times, but he wanted to get it off his chest." Meredith hugged Patsy closer. "It's a bloody waste. He'd planned it, but he didn't think he would do it. He thought common sense, or someone else being there, would stop him. He can't even claim manslaughter because he went with the equipment to do the job. It's at times like these that you realise how little it takes to push a person over the edge."

Meredith fell silent, thinking about the kind and talented man who would spend the best part of the rest of his life in jail.

"I hope they go for an insanity plea. God knows having a man, especially a man like Carmichael set you up, is enough to push anyone over the edge."

"Did Carmichael have the mask made especially? Was it planned?"

"No. Charlesworth asked him that. Carmichael told him he'd had it made by a makeup artist years before for a fancy dress. Everyone thought he looked fabulous, except Izzy. She'd called him Graham by mistake. That's why he hit her at the party. Not because she was chatting someone else up. The likeness was so close to Graham Charlesworth that she forgot herself, and called him by the wrong name, and he gave her a backhander. She wasn't even involved with him then. He'd done a discreet procedure to remove a scar from her chin. Once Carmichael had the list of names he knew he'd need a disguise. Carmichael told Charlesworth that if he were seen, he was happy to throw suspicion his way, and furthered the plan with breaking in and stealing the soldiers. His ultimate aim was to get his daughter, get out of the country, and leave a trail that led to Charlesworth. He admitted that he hoped they'd think Charlesworth had murdered her and dumped the body."

"Wow. How much must you hate someone to do that? It's not like Charlesworth ever did him any harm." Patsy shivered involuntarily. "He really was an evil man."

Meredith laughed a hollow laugh. "Carmichael hated Charlesworth totally, utterly, and completely. In a desperate attempted to save his life, he tried to butter Charlesworth up. He told him Izzy had made it clear, when he forced her to have the child adopted, that he was not a fraction of the man she loved, and would always love Graham Charlesworth." Meredith fell silent and Patsy listened to the sound of his breathing wondering if he'd fallen asleep. She gave a start when he added. "That's what I want to be to you. The only man you'll ever love again."

"You are."

Meredith fell silent. "But as you asked yourself, is it enough?"

"It is for me. Go to sleep, you've had a long day. Goodnight, Meredith."

"Night, Hodge."

CHAPTER TWENTY

Meredith blew out a breath of relief as he walked up the aisle with Patsy. It had been a long service, with four children being baptised. He was now officially the godfather of Pablo Antonio John Garcia, and not all the infants had been as well behaved as his godson. He knew he'd never call the boy Pablo. Now, for some reason he couldn't work out, Patsy had invited them all back to their house for tea. His one consolation was that it was a lovely warm day so at least they would be sitting outside, and as he wasn't driving he could have a beer. He'd also heard a rumour that Amanda's friend would be in attendance. He allowed himself a small smile. That would be fun.

For the next few hours, he watched Patsy tend to their guests, play with the baby, and endure a sing song with Peggy in her now favourite floral dress, when she'd had one too many. Señora Garcia insisted on helping Patsy at every turn. Patsy accepted her help graciously, even though the communication of what was needed was at times painful.

As a sign of his goodwill, he'd even been relatively polite to Patrick Daily. He watched as Daily fell into easy conversation with Antonio Garcia. He didn't consider Daily to be a bad bloke, but he wasn't good enough for his girl. He wondered if anyone would be. He shivered at the thought of having to walk her down the aisle to a man he didn't like. Thinking of weddings, he looked across at Patsy, who was having a discussion with Peggy about the size of the measure she had been poured. He wondered if today should be the day. His musings were interrupted rudely by Linda.

"Yoohoooo," she called from the side of the house, "can we come in?"

Meredith's eyes widened. That the girl was slightly skewed was a given, but today's ensemble was even more outlandish than usual. Linda was wearing a floor-length print skirt in various shades of pink, beneath which poked out the highest-heeled shoes he had ever seen. On top of the skirt she wore a red halter-neck silk waistcoat so sheer it left little to the imagination. To crown it all, a long, striped chiffon wrap trailed from one of her shoulders. He couldn't hold back the shout of amusement as she teetered onto the grass and immediately halted when the heels of her shoes impaled themselves into the ground. The gift bag swinging from one hand, and a bottle of champagne clasped to her body, she waited for Louie Trump to come to her assistance. Dropping to his knee, and aware they now had everyone's attention, he unbuckled her shoes. Stepping out of them, Linda thanked him by blowing him a kiss, and leaving the shoes stuck where they were, she hurried to the baby.

Peggy nudged Patsy. "I thought I had bad taste. I feel quite superior. Now don't worry about topping me up, I'm sure that young lady intends to share the champagne . . . Oh, she's given it to Toni. Ah well, more of that'll do nicely."

Patsy poured a quick splash into Peggy's glass, and smiled at her. She'd not seen Peggy at her worst, but with the bright dots of colour in her cheeks, a tan appearing on her newly exposed arms, and the flower Meredith had popped behind her ear, she looked like a different woman to the one who had shuffled into the house only a week or so earlier.

Patsy turned to look at Meredith. He and Amanda were so kind-hearted to take this woman in. Patsy knew she'd done her part, but that was only after the arrangements had been made. Her breath caught in her throat, and her stomach somersaulted, as Meredith caught her eye. His eyes told so many stories, and right now she was glad it was only she that could interpret this one. Grinning, she knew very soon he would be attempting to get rid of their guests.

With a small hand gesture, he beckoned her forward. Never taking her eyes from his, she walked across to him. She burst out laughing as he spoke.

"How long is this going on for? I have plans." He looked hurt. "What did I say that was so funny?"

"Nothing, I simply knew what you were going to say." She yelped as he pulled her on to his lap, and whispered in her ear. "I can assure you, you didn't. I had to temper it in case anyone was listening, and you wouldn't have laughed, you'd be blushing as you made your way upstairs. Guests or no guests. Oh God, I can't wait to get back to normal."

He turned away to look at Linda who was now calling Patsy. "Hello, Loopy, you look wonderful as always." He winced as Patsy elbowed his ribs. "New frock?" he continued undeterred.

"No, actually I found it at the back of the wardrobe. I wanted something chic but cool. It's boiling today, isn't it?"

Meredith buried his laughter in Patsy's body, and he hugged her a little tighter.

Patsy grinned at her friend, hoping she hadn't noticed. "You look lovely. Louie looks rather handsome too. I hope you find enough food left in there to eat." Patsy waved at Trump as he left the house carrying a plate.

"He'll be fine, this will be a snack. We're going to visit his mother this evening."

"Dressed like that?" Meredith spluttered.

"Why, I thought you liked it?" Linda looked down towards her feet. "What's wrong with it?"

Patsy rescued Meredith, "I think he meant the bare shoulder, no bra thing. But you look fabulous, you look like you." Digging her elbow into Meredith's ribs she pushed herself to her feet. "Did you want me?"

Linda shook away thoughts of her meeting with Mrs Trump, and grabbed Patsy's elbow. She walked her to the bottom of the garden before she spoke.

"Something's going on in work." Her face now deadly serious. She pulled Patsy closer and pointed out across the neighbouring garden.

"What do you mean, and what are you pointing at?"

"I'm trying to make it look as though we are having a normal conversation." Linda rolled her eyes. "I'm seriously concerned, Patsy. I think Chris is up to something?"

"What does that mean?" Patsy turned to face Linda. "Explain."

Linda pulled her back round to face the garden.

"I left my new shoes in the office. The ones now impaled in your lawn, so I popped in this morning to collect them. Chris was in your office." Linda nodded a knowing expression on her face. "He wasn't alone."

"Who was he with?" Patsy's eyes widened. "Not a woman, surely."

"Of course not." Linda slapped Patsy's arm lightly. "With Sharon for a wife, who'd be brave enough? Not Chris, that's for sure. No, it was a man."

Patsy laughed. "Well, it was probably business then." Linda was already shaking her head, and Patsy saw the genuine concern on her face. "Linda, tell me. I have guests to get rid of if I listen to Meredith."

Linda cleared her throat. "I thought it was a client at first too. I remembered an email I hadn't responded to on the way in, so fired up my PC. It didn't open properly. Someone has messed about with the set up. I didn't have time to look, but there's something added I couldn't find. I did what I set out to do, thinking I'd leave it until tomorrow, and went to ask Chris and his guest if they needed anything before I left. I knocked and entered. The man was working on a laptop at your desk. It was plugged into our system. I wouldn't have noticed if Chris hadn't jumped three feet into the air when I went in."

Linda rubbed her hands together, clearly anxious about what she believed she had walked in on.

"Linda, calm down. You are probably reading too much into it."

"I most certainly am not! Chris couldn't get me out of there fast enough. The other chap was cool as a cucumber though."

"And what exactly do you think is going on?"

"I have no idea, but I'll find out what they've done to the system, you know that. It was the other two that clinched it."

"What other two?"

"When Chris shoved me out of the front door, there were two men standing in the shade of the porch. Sharp suits, expensive shoes, and drinking, well, I suppose it was water. They turned their backs to me as I glanced at them."

Patsy closed her eyes visualising the scene and smiled. "Do you mean 'peered at' or 'examined' rather than glanced?"

She gave Linda a hug as she shrugged an admission.

"Quite possibly, but one had my Lion King glass, and the other had that horrible thing with the swirly pattern. They'd been in our kitchen, and here's the thing that makes them suspicious." Linda clasped her hands together. "Chris ignored them. He would never do that. He didn't want me to know he knew them."

Patsy pursed her lips in thought. "What did the guy inside look like?"

"Stocky, big shoulders like a rugby player, brown hair, cut very short but not shaved." It was Linda's turn to close her eyes. "Oh yes, he wore a big watch. You know, like a diver's watch. Average looking though, nothing outstanding to comment on. Do you know him?"

Patsy took a small step back. One plus one had just totalled ten. She knew the man with the watch. Not his name, yet, but she knew him. Linda's skills of detection were improving. She was right: there was something going on. The question she needed answered was what Chris Grainger was up to? She tried to play it down.

"You are so funny. Good description though, you'll make a detective yet. If it helps I'll have a word with Chris later and update you in the morning. Now, go and rescue Louie from Peggy, I need the loo."

Once in the bathroom, Patsy called Chris Grainger. Sitting on the edge of the bath she whispered harshly at his answer service.

"Chris, I don't know what happened today, but Linda knows something's going on. She knows they've tampered with her system, and she knows you were hoping to keep the meeting, or whatever that was for, secret. She will find whatever it is they've done, you must know that. And while we're on the subject, what have they done? I've not said 'yes' yet, for God's sake. I don't know how to contact them, so make sure they contact me. Although, not for a while, I've have guests, but. . . Look I have to go, someone is calling me."

Getting up she walked to the toilet and flushed it. She then ran the tap for a couple of seconds. "I'm coming," she called as she unlocked the door.

Amanda stood at the bottom of the stairs looking up at her. "The Garcias are going and they're taking Peggy with them. I'm going to disappear now too. Dad has been far too nice to Patrick, it can't last." Laughing, she turned away.

Patsy went to say goodbye to her guests. Meredith put his arm around her waist as he gave a short salute to Patrick as he walked up the garden path.

"Just Loopy and Trump to go, then I will have my way with you." He squeezed her hand, and led her back round the side of the house.

Louie was pulling the shoes from the lawn. "I'm told we have to go home and change." He rolled his eyes. "Linda thinks something more demure is appropriate. We're bound to be late." He glanced over his shoulder at Linda. She was collecting glasses to help Patsy clear up. "I think she looks perfectly fine. Still, women aye? No offence, Patsy."

"None taken, Louie, and I agree with you."

Meredith had opened his mouth to speak, and she squeezed his hand to warn him to be tactful. He glanced sideways at her, grinning, before looking back at Louie Trump, who now held the spectacular shoes.

"You should marry that girl. You're a pair well-matched." He looked Louie up and down; he was immaculately presented as always. Then he glanced over at Linda in her mismatched ensemble, and he shook his head. Perhaps Trump only did blokes clothes, he thought, as Linda hurried towards Patsy jerking her head.

"Patsy, come and show me what you want done with these." She lifted the glasses, and Patsy collected some herself and led the way to the kitchen.

"Well, that was a pleasant end to an unpleasant week." Patsy opened the dishwasher and began to load the glasses. "I hope all goes well with Mr and Mrs Trump this evening."

"Right at this moment I don't care. You called him, I know you did. What did he say?"

"Linda, I didn't. We'll sort it all out tomorrow. Go and get Louie. If you're going to change, you'd better hurry. You don't want to keep his mother waiting."

Meredith was walking back to the kitchen. Through the window, he saw the look on Linda's face, and he slowed his pace.

Linda frowned at Patsy. "You did call him, and you're up to something. But you're right, I have to go. I'll see you in the morning, when I shall expect a full confession." Linda almost bumped into Meredith on her way out. "Sorry, Meredith, in a rush. It's been fab." Grabbing his shoulders, she stood on tiptoe and planted a kiss on his cheek. "Come on, Louie, look sharp, your mother's waiting."

Releasing Meredith, she grabbed Trump's arm and led him away.

Meredith put down the glasses he was carrying. "What's wrong with Loopy? She looked a little odd then, something on her mind?" Coming up behind Patsy, he put his hands around her waist. "Tell me quickly because there's something more pressing on mine." He wondered if he imagined the momentary stillness in Patsy's body.

"Well, let's deal with your mind first. Linda is having a moment about Chris, that's all. She's seeing shadows where there are none."

Patsy was glad Meredith couldn't see her face as she loaded the last of the dirty crockery.

Meredith released Patsy, and locked the back door. He held his finger up. "Listen to that . . . Silence. Home alone. I need a shower. You may join me, Hodge, in fact I have to insist upon it."

He returned Patsy's smile as she turned to face him. She nodded and took a few steps towards the hall.

"Come on then, race you."

She skipped out into the hall, and to appease her Meredith pretended to hurry. Like Linda, he knew she wasn't telling the truth, but he'd find out more later. Now he had other things on his mind. Patsy went into the bedroom, and stripped off her clothes. She heard Meredith go straight to the bathroom, and shortly after, the sound of running water. He was singing 'Que Sera, Sera'. She hated what was technically lying to him, but she would tell him. Eventually. She sighed, knowing she had to pick the right moment or there would be hell to pay.

Meredith called to her. Her frown dropped away, and she smiled; it wouldn't be tonight. Tonight she would do it. She would ask him. She'd decided on that much at least.

Lying back against the pillows, Meredith smiled as Patsy hunted through her underwear drawer.

"It's too late for sexy undies, Hodge, I'm spent. I'll need nourishment first. What are you looking for?"

Patsy turned around, hiding something behind her back. "Look under your pillow." She instructed.

She watched as Meredith slid the birthday card out. He flipped open the envelope. He knew what the card said, just not what it meant. He read it aloud.

"'Wherever, and whenever, big or small, but honesty will certainly be the best policy. I love you, Hodge.' I like the kisses forming the heart." He stared at the card, before raising his eyes which locked hers. "What does it mean?"

Patsy walked to the end of the bed, suddenly nervous. "I have something to ask you, and I need you to be totally honest with me."

"I'm always honest with you."

She caught the flicker of amazement in Meredith's eyes, and she knew he knew. He smiled, and her heart thumped loud in her chest.

"The answer is yes, I don't care, and small."

He laughed as she launched herself onto the bed, squealing in delight. Her hand shook as she knelt at his side, and held out the box on the flat of her palm. He put his finger to her lips as she opened them to speak.

"One moment, Hodge."

Rolling onto his side he opened the drawer in his cabinet. Cursing, he rummaged around, until he too produced a similar shaped box. One he'd bought way back in December when he first knew she'd be his wife one day. Rolling back, his eyes found hers, and they both froze for a moment, naked on their bed, looking at each other. Meredith had never been more certain of anything in his life, but he had to make sure she was. "You are sure, aren't you?"

"Yes."

"Because there's no going back once it's done, you know."

"Yes." There was a little impatience in her voice.

Meredith curled his fingers around the box in his hand.

"Because, once you say 'yes', you will be saying yes for all time. I won't let you go. Ever. So, are you sure you're sure?"

"Meredith, give me the bloody ring before I explode." She laughed, and threw herself across him as she tried to grab the box. He held it out of her reach, and clamped her body to his.

"I mean it, Hodge. When we say 'till death do us part', it will mean it. If you ever try to leave, I won't allow it."

"What, you'll kill me? Meredith, I won't ever leave you."

"I might consider it." He kissed her. "I'm lying, of course, but I mean escaping won't be easy. You have to be sure."

"Can I say something that isn't a lie anyway? I'm being deadly serious now." Patsy stared up into his eyes, and knew she was about to lie. She held back the smile. Meredith nodded permission. "If you are going to be this irritating ever again, I've changed my mind. The answer's 'no'. You're a royal pain in the arse, and death would separate us sooner rather than later, because I'd be obliged to kill you. Now give me the ring!"

Meredith laughed. "Okay, okay. Should I do this properly and get down on one knee?"

"No. Not unless you're going to get dressed, it wouldn't be dignified. Give me the ring."

"I should at least sit up, surely?"

Patsy pulled away from him, and returning to her kneeling position, she placed her box on his chest.

"You go first."

Meredith was done messing. She noticed the slight tremor as he opened the box. He closed his eyes, and swallowed. When he opened them, she knew his emotions were running high, and she accepted the nod of approval as she also accepted the little box he offered. Her reaction was the exact opposite of his. She squealed in delight, and bounced up and down.

"Meredith, it's beautiful. I couldn't have chosen better myself." She slid the ring onto her finger and waved it in front of his face. "Look, it fits perfectly. It is perfect. I love it." A sob escaped. "And now you've made me cry. While I compose myself, try yours. Do you like it?"

Meredith slid the ring on his finger. He flexed his hand as he looked at it. It felt odd. It felt right. "I love it. I loved Paris, and I love you." He pulled her back down. "I might have lied about needing nourishment first."

Patsy left Meredith watching the television, and went to fetch a drink. As she removed the clean glasses from the dishwasher, a smile played around her lips as she admired the ring yet again. Meredith had agreed that he didn't mind where they got married, or when, but it would be a small ceremony with just the closest of friends and family, and that suited her too. She reminded herself that she should call her father with the news. She was still smiling as she un-corked the bottle, and her telephone rang. She glanced at the flashing screen. The number had been withheld. Patsy usually ignored those calls, but something made her pick up. Her smile fell away as she recognised the voice.

"Hello, Patsy, Chris tells me we have a problem. We should meet as soon as possible, and before you go into the office. Where, and when?"

"Yes, we should." Patsy's whispered. "Meet me where you found me the first time at eight thirty tomorrow morning. I don't know if anything will be open, but it hardly matters. I have to go, goodbye."

Not wanting to ruin what had been a perfect evening, Patsy hung up and dropped the phone into her bag. She gave a small gasp as she turned back to the wine to find Meredith standing in the doorway.

"Did I hear a phone ring? I don't believe I'm saying this, but I don't know where mine is?"

"It was mine, one of those withheld numbers, asking if I'd had an accident recently. I shouldn't have answered."

Again, she lied, but she would tell him soon, she told herself.

Meredith raised his eyebrows. "Really, on a Sunday? You'd think they'd know better. Give mine a ring, I should track it down."

Patsy retrieved her phone, and called his. They looked at the ceiling as the phone first vibrated and then rang. Meredith went to the bathroom to collect it. He had no missed calls or messages. He went back down to join Patsy on the sofa in the sitting room. Sitting next to her, he put an arm around her shoulder.

"I'm not wanted. I'm yours for the rest of the night, fingers crossed." He lifted his glass and took a sip.

"You're mine forever, you made that point quite forcibly." Patsy snuggled closer.

"Hmm, so I did," he murmured looking at the television screen, but ignoring the programme.

Meredith knew the street Patsy had driven into was a dead end. He pulled in around the corner and got out of his car. He waited until he caught sight of her at the end of the road, before starting to follow her. Stepping behind a large display advertising a restaurant's latest menu, he watched them meet. He pursed his lips as he recognised her companion. They took a seat at a table outside. Meredith shook his head. They really should have gone inside. Unable to hear the conversation he watched their body language. Patsy had looked stiff and awkward at first, but after ten minutes, she became engrossed in the conversation, and leaned forward, elbows on table, hands supporting her chin. The sun occasionally caught the ring on her finger when she moved her hand, making Meredith a little angrier each time it did so. A boy on a skateboard rattled past Meredith from behind, he turned to look as the noise became louder. He didn't look back for a few moments in case the boy had also attracted their attention. He doubted it as they were engrossed. When he turned back, the man was paying the bill. It was time to go. He walked away swiftly.

"Thank you, Patsy, I'll leave it to you to discuss with Chris, and I'll see you tomorrow." He grinned, "Don't look so worried. We're going to have fun you and I, I promise you that."

"I don't think that's what I'd call it, but it will certainly be a challenge. It's nice to finally have a name for the man who's been following me. I'm glad training will start immediately. I'm certainly looking forward to that."

James Benson grinned at her, as he waved the waiter carrying his change away.

"Why are you grinning like that? I take it that indicates that you think I need it?" Patsy stood up and lifted her bag from the adjacent seat.

"I do. I'm not the only man following you, although you do know the name of the other. You haven't been as secretive as you thought, and Meredith is clearly a jealous man. Have you given him reason to doubt you?"

Patsy spun around. Her stomach turned liquid, and seemed to bubble up through her body. She swallowed it back down.

"Please tell me he wasn't watching."

"He most certainly was. I won't walk you to your car, he may be waiting. I don't do jealous husbands: they get hurt. I'll see you tomorrow." Grinning, he put his hands in his pocket, and slowly walked away in the opposite direction.

Patsy's heart was beating fast as she hurried back to her car. It wasn't like she'd done anything wrong, she told herself. It was business, and Meredith should trust her, not be following her around like some lovesick child. She stopped walking and looked down at the pavement. She'd done the same to him, and she had been proved wrong. He'd been meeting Amanda. Well, this was similar. In fact, in her opinion, not as huge a thing as a daughter. Patsy nodded to herself, and lifting her chin, she took a step forward, but stopped as she spotted Meredith leaning against the side of her car. Drawing in a breath, she walked towards him smiling.

"Hello, what are you doing here? Have you got five minutes? I have something to tell you." Patsy would not tell him that she knew he'd followed her.

"Don't do it." Meredith wasn't going to mince words.

"What? How do you know what . . . Why?"

"Because it's not you. It won't work, with us."

"I think you should listen to what I have to say before jumping to conclusions. Meredith, I have -"

"I said, don't do it." Meredith remained perched against Patsy's car. Hands in pockets, and shoulders hunched as though he were cold. His face was set, revealing his anger, but his eyes were sad. This threw Patsy. Plain anger she could deal with, but mixed emotions from Meredith were a whole new ball game.

She stepped closer and put a hand against his cheek. He turned his face to kiss her palm.

"Meredith, this changes nothing. You've not even let me -"

Again, he interrupted her. "I said, don't do it. Perhaps I should ask. Patsy, don't do this, please." He pushed himself away from the car as she shook her head. Leaning on the car with one hand, he lifted the other and tapped his finger on her nose. "I think this was too big not to mention last night before we made commitments." He pursed his lips and turned away. "Don't do it, Patsy, it changes everything."

He ambled slowly away wondering if he'd done enough to stop her.

Patsy watched him walk away, wondering why he wouldn't let her explain? Why it mattered so much? Sighing, she stepped forward to open the car door, and her hand flew to her mouth in disbelief.

Sitting on the roof of the car was the ring. It appeared that their engagement had lasted less than twelve hours. Patsy snatched it from the roof.

"You stupid, selfish bastard!" she shouted at a now empty street. Fighting back tears of anger, disappointment, and frustration, Patsy climbed into the car.

She sat staring at the ring, wondering if she should go after him. Perhaps he was right: she should have discussed it with him first, but this was something she wanted to do. She thumped the steering wheel, and would have screamed, except the passenger door opened, and she blew out a frustrated breath. Expecting to see Meredith, she attempted to calm herself. Her mouth fell open as one of her possible new colleagues climbed in.

"What?" Patsy shook her head, still irritable, and, ready to eject him, she pointed at him. "If we're about to have a conversation I want a name."

"Call meeee . . ." He looked at Patsy and raised his left eyebrow, "Burt. I've never been Burt before." He smiled, "Now, Patsy, I want you to follow Meredith, and agree to his demands."

"I beg your pardon?"

"I think you heard me, but for clarity, go and tell Meredith that he is more important than work, and you won't take the assignment."

"You heard that conversation? How? And no, I won't lie to him." Patsy turned in her seat to face him. "I made my terms clear. I didn't want to live some sort of double life, so, no I won't do it."

"That was before Meredith decided to go all macho and demanding though." Burt shrugged. "Maybe you're right. Perhaps you are too weak to work with us."

Patsy laughed. "What was that supposed to be? Some sort of reverse psychology. Come on, Burt, you can do better than that surely."

"Patsy, it was a reminder that you are your own person, and should be able to choose what you do, and don't do. We already know the answer to what would Meredith do if roles were reversed. The real question is why you put up with inequality." He opened the door and climbed out of the car. Leaning back in, he added. "Go and tell Meredith you agree. You'll be based at Grainger's so he need not know. Chris certainly won't tell him."

He slammed the door and walked away towards the dockside.

Patsy thought about Chris. Meredith had no idea that Chris had previously worked for SIS, still did on occasion, and Sharon certainly didn't have a clue. Would it be so bad for her to do the same? Shaking her head, she dropped the ring into her bag, and started the engine.

The Doris Day CD began to play 'Que Sera, Sera'. Patsy rolled her eyes as she pulled out of her parking space.

"It certainly will be, Doris," Patsy murmured as she merged into the traffic.

AUTHOR'S NOTE

Thank you for reading Misplaced Loyalty. I hope you enjoyed reading this story as much as I enjoyed writing it. If you did, I'd be grateful if you would be kind enough to leave a review, or contact me with your thoughts and any comments. Constructive reviews are invaluable to authors. If you would rather contact me personally the details are below.

If you would like to read more of my work, then I would be happy to gift you a FREE e-book from my website: http://mkturnerbooks.co.uk/ Please click contact, and leave your request in the comment section.

ABOUT THE AUTHOR

Having worked in the property industry for most of my adult life, latterly at a senior level, I finally escaped in 2010. I now work as a consultant for several independent agencies, but I dedicate the bulk of my time to writing and, of course, reading, although there are still not enough hours in the day.

I began writing quite by chance when a friend commented, "They wouldn't believe it if you wrote it down!" So I did. I enjoyed the plotting and scheming, creating the characters, and watching them develop with the story. I kept on writing, and Meredith and Hodge arrived. I should confess at this point that although I have the basic outline when I start a new story, it never develops the way I expect, and I rarely know 'who did it' myself until I've nearly finished.

I am married with two children, two German Shepherds and a Bichon Frise, and we live in Bristol, UK. I can be contacted here, and would love to hear from you:

Website: http://mkturnerbooks.co.uk/
Twitter: @MarciaKimTurner
Facebook: M K Turner

36121522R00193

Printed in Great Britain
by Amazon